Praise f

SPIN THE SKY

"*Spin the Sky* takes a poignant look at what happens when the line between chasing big dreams and escaping a tough past starts to blur. Magnolia's passion and fire leap off the page in this heartfelt and hopeful debut."

—Kathryn Holmes, author of *How it Feels to Fly*

"In *Spin the Sky*, Mags trades the unforgiving focus of a small town for the glaring lens of the nation in her own version of *So You Think You Can Escape Your Past?* Confronting other dance contestants equally dedicated to their art shatters not only Mag's stereotypes but the reader's. Everyone needs a win. Everyone has a past. Every life is complicated. Populated with dimensional characters, this book urges you to see both friends and enemies through new eyes."

—Liz Coley, author of *Pretty Girl–13*

"Jill MacKenzie's lyrical prose dances across the page and leaps into your heart. Magnolia is funny, flawed, driven, and every bit as real as a young adult heroine should be. *Spin the Sky* made me want to get up and dance, but I couldn't bring myself to put it down! A truly inspiring debut about personal identity and overcoming your past by taking a blind leap into your future."

—Beth Neal, author of *My Last Kiss*

"A gripping novel about friendship, family, prejudice, redemption, and the bright and dark sides of fame and reality TV. From beginning to end I could not put this down. A stunning debut from Jill MacKenzie."

—Cara Chow, author of *Bitter Melon*

"Magnolia's (and MacKenzie's) infectious passion for dance radiates from every page as she discovers truth in the unlikeliest of places—a reality show!"

—Liz Czukas, author of *Ask Again Later*

"Mackenzie deftly explores the idea that each person experiences pain, often deeply hidden from the world, as well as the maturity that comes from that understanding."

—*School Library Journal*

"A lively and absorbing story with all the drama of teen life."

—*Kirkus Reviews*

SPIN
THE
SKY

SPIN

THE

SKY

SPIN
THE
SKY

Jill MacKenzie

Sky Pony Press
New York

Sky Pony Press books may be purchased in bulk at special discounts for sales promotion, corporate gifts, fund-raising, or educational purposes. Special editions can also be created to specifications. For details, contact the Special Sales Department, Sky Pony Press, 307 West 36th Street, 11th Floor, New York, NY 10018 or info@skyhorsepublishing.com.

Sky Pony® is a registered trademark of Skyhorse Publishing, Inc.®, a Delaware corporation.

Visit our website at www.skyponypress.com.

10 9 8 7 6 5 4 3 2 1

Library of Congress Cataloging-in-Publication Data is available on file.

Cover design by Kate Gartner
Cover photo credit iStockphoto
Interior design by Joshua Barnaby

Print ISBN: 978-1-5107-4242-0
Ebook ISBN: 978-1-5107-0687-3

Printed in the United States of America

For my girls. For showing me that in order to tell you to follow your dreams, I had to first follow my own.

SPIN

THE

SKY

SPIN

THE

SKY

ONE

My hands reach up to move stars, rearrange space.

I pivot on my left foot and in one perfect circle, I turn, turn, facing all four walls of this studio. Here, I am alone. Here, I can be anyone.

My leg extends. It is one fluid wave. Drawing in, drawing out. Governed by tide.

The music releases its breath, and with it, mine.

My leg comes down, torso folding, until I'm on the ground. Stomach down. Face down. Pulled flat by wicked earth.

My hands rise, taking my heart, legs, soul with them. I run, twist, turn. Fly. *Fly.* Beat my chest with open hands. Crush my skeletons with my feet, inches from the floor.

I sink. Back rounded. Sink. A semicircle. Sink. A crescent moon.

The tempo speeds. Drums beat fast, fueling my limbs and blood.

In the air, my body coils, never landing. But the gravity betrays me, as always, so I leap again. Fly. Soar. Dance again.

I am invisible. I am invincible.

If only for a second.

George bursts through the studio door like his ass is on fire.

His face is all flushed and his hands are clutching this flyer that is, I guess, the source of his wide, wild eyes. My stomach gets this tight, wobbly feeling. Because I've seen this look on him before.

I scurry over to the side of the room and slap the OFF button on the stereo before he has the chance to grill me on what, exactly, I'm doing here in Katina's studio. A whopping thirty minutes before class. Without him. I'll never tell him that I often come alone. Never, when I know he'd never understand.

He waves the flyer in my face—so close I can't even read it—and pumps his fist in the air like he's some kind of rock star. "They're coming to Portland, Mags. We've got to be there."

"Who's coming where?"

"See for yourself. Read it and weep, suckers."

He hurls the page at me, releasing it inches above my face. It sails down in a back-and-forth motion, so I scramble to catch it. George's mouth breaks into a smile that's as wide as our Wick Beach. "It's fate. You know it is."

I read the last line of the flyer out loud: "If you can dance, don't miss this *dancertunity* of a lifetime!" I look up at him. "Seriously?"

"We're so going."

"No way. What for?"

"To try out, naturally." George jetés to the far corner of the room. When the wall in front of him forces him to stop, he spins around. "I'm good, and so are you. I think it's about time we took our place in the limelight." He stops short. "Wait. You're not scared to try out, are you?

"Definitely not scared." I bite down on my bottom lip. "Scared of what?"

"Then it's settled." His grin swallows his whole face.

I can't even imagine what it'd be like to smile that big. It must feel so freeing, like being able to extend your leg straight up during arabesque, no ligaments or skin to hold you back. "No way," I say. "You know Rose and I already live under a microscope. Why would I want to make us even more seen?"

"Because. For once, it'd be the good kind of seen."

I grab my bag and join Abby and Quinn and Mark in the waiting room.

George follows behind me, whispers in my ear. "Working with Gia Gianni, Mags. Can you even imagine what that would be like?"

I take off my flower-studded earrings and slide out the four inches of cut pillowcase I've concealed under my bra strap. I poke the posts from my earrings through the cloth and replace the backings. Then I shove it in the pocket of my bag before George can see.

I know exactly what it would be like to work with Gia, to be in the presence of a legendary choreographer like her for any length of time: like the fourteen years I've spent getting up early and getting here before school and on weekends and working and sweating, every single day, has all led up to the kind of grand finale that makes every single minute of it worthwhile. Like I really am flying.

Then I think of doing it on TV in front of thousands. In front of every damn person in this damn town. "There's no way I'm going."

"Why?" George says.

"You know why."

"But you're gorgeous. Totally *Live to Dance* material."

"I'd also be like the world's biggest target if I went on that show."

"It doesn't have to be like that." George rolls his eyes and then, when a group of skater boys passes by the window, he rolls up the front of his T-shirt, exposing abs cut like a New York steak. His gaze zeros in on the boy in the middle—the tallest of the three—the one with blacker hair than my toes after three back-to-back pointe classes. As much as I don't want them to, my eyes follow George's every move. Up his smooth, pale chest. Down to the menacing little V peeking out on both sides of his hips from the top of his shorts. My own stomach muscles tighten, but for a very different reason than his. I may be *Live to Dance* material, but I'll never be what he wants.

"Hey, George."

George swivels around and, mercifully, releases his T-shirt just as a redheaded freshman girl and two of her dancer-wannabe friends scoot through the door. She flutters her eyelashes at him in this absurdly cartoonish way that makes me think of Betty. No, Veronica. Which is worse. Way worse.

"Oh. Hey, you." He smiles that smile back at her, this time showing both rows of his naturally sea-bleached teeth. By the look on her face, it's like the girl's going to pee herself right here in the foyer of Katina's studio.

George turns back to the window, the boys' backs still slightly in view. While his head is turned, the freshman narrows her eyes at me and mouths all five letters of the word that's become like a second name to me: T-R-A-S-H. But it could be worse. It could be the *other*, newer name some folks have taken to calling Rose and me instead. The one that'll never let us forget what we did. Not like we could forget it if we tried.

It echoes in my head: *Murderer.*

"See you after class, George," the freshman says, though she doesn't take her eyes off me.

George waves over his shoulder but keeps his eyes on that window. The freshman ducks into Studio B, the class next to ours.

When the boys are totally out of sight, George looks over at me. Me, who never left him. Me, who never would.

"Think about it, Mags. Mikhail Baryshnikov. Aimee Bonnet. Michael Jackson. They all got their big breaks somewhere. This could be our somewhere. Just think of it as a chance for us to get out of here." He mumbles, "Maybe our only chance."

"Get out of here and go where? We're good, but Mikhail Baryshnikov good? Fat chance."

"But think of the recognition we'd get."

"I'm already too recognizable." I sink down on the bench and stretch the toes on my right foot, the bones squeezing together till they feel like they'll crumble. When I try to do the same with the left one, this small pain shoots through my toes and up my ankle. I wiggle my toes a few times and it goes away.

George does a couple of flawless grand battements. His legs kick dangerously close to my face. "But you love performing. You said so last year during spring recital."

I think about the spring recital and what, exactly, I had said about it. Love? I don't think so. But I do remember being backstage and hearing the warm purr of the crowd as we waited to go on. I do remember Katina telling us all to dance like we needed it to breathe, love, live. I do remember thinking that dancing was the only place I felt completely, totally myself.

But I also remember that that night, I watched as George threw down an almost perfect solo. When he finished, the whole audience clapped and whistled for him, making so much happy noise actual car alarms went off all over town. He was good, so he deserved it. But also, the cheers were there because he's George Moutsous, enough said. When I performed my solo just minutes after him, there were only five people in the audience clapping for me: Mr. and Mrs. Moutsous; Katina; George's archrival and the only other friend I've got left in Summerland, Mark McDonald; and, of course, Rose.

But the absence of clapping, replaced by the occasional boo and hiss, had nothing to do with me sucking or not sucking— that much I know. 'Cause when I came off the stage, Katina was there waiting. She cupped my cheeks in her hands and lifted my head so that I had no choice but to let my eyes gather in hers.

"Forget about them. You're going places. You're going to be the one that makes it." Then she turned around and told the rest of the dancers how I had demonstrated what it means to dance like no one's watching. But it didn't matter what she said. The Thing That Happened had already happened, two weeks earlier, and was there, hanging over my head like an ax waiting to fall. But I couldn't forget about those hisses and boos. They came from my people. They were my town. What they thought of me—of us—it mattered. No matter what Katina said, it mattered.

I twist the end of my waist-length ponytail around my index finger. "I said I like being on stage. I didn't say I liked performing in front of that many people and I sure as shit didn't say I wanted to do it in front of the whole entire nation."

George grabs the end of my ponytail away from my fiddling fingertips. He lets my hand linger in his, a nest cradling a robin's egg, before slowly placing it at my side. "We've got to do this, Magnolia. We've got a real shot at this."

"I know. But I'm still not doing it."

"Why? Because you could actually make your dreams come true? As if you don't need that cash prize. You could buy a car. Go to college. Think of this as an opportunity."

"You mean a *dancertunity*, right?" I try to shake off George and his penchant for dreaming solar-system big, most of the time, without any thoughts of reality bringing him back to earth. Do we actually have a shot at this crazy thing? Yeah, maybe. But what I won't tell George is that having a shot is actually the one thing that scares me the most. Yet somehow, his words stick me, like pins in a voodoo doll.

Opportunity.

Recognition.

Ten thousand dollars.

Not for college, or a new car. But maybe . . .

Maybe once they saw me on the show—the only show Mom and I watched together and loved together for six glorious weeks every fall—they'd see. See that I'm not her, not any of the things they whisper about Rose and me when they think we can't hear them, and even when they know we can.

And once I won that money, I could give it to Rose so she could step away from the road she's strolled dangerously close

to every single day since last year. Since the day The Thing
That Happened happened. And maybe even Mom would see
me up there on TV. See us and want to come home and try
one last time. Maybe then we could take her to one of those
fancy places. Not like the ones here in Summerland. Good
ones. Real ones. Ones where no one knows anything about
Woodson girls or what it's like to be one. Like the kind I saw
online that swore up and down its glossy site that, with the
right amount of money, they could change anybody's life.

Even mine.

Katina pops her head out of her studio and sighs super loud
when she sees us. Her hair is slicked back in her usual tight
bun, which stretches her skin like Saran Wrap. George has
always said she does it to get rid of the three rows of forehead
wrinkles she developed when her former protége, Mickela
Ray, went and got herself pregnant by a guy who pumps gas
at the Pic 'N' Pay and then quit dance to "start a life" with him.
I always laugh, but only because it's so not true. Katina may
be pushing sixty, but she's gorgeous in that Eastern European
prima ballerina way. All musk and mystery. Not to mention
she's the best damn teacher on the Oregon Coast.

"George. Magnolia. You two are already late, yes? Quit gab-
bing and get your lovebird derrieres in here."

Katina's words freeze my limbs while I know my face
transforms from the perfectly pecan color I'm usually blessed
with to hot, hot red.

I stare at her with bulging eyes. *Save me here, Katina.* She
winks at me before disappearing behind the door to her studio.
George grins at me and then pulls me into Katina's studio where
Abby, Quinn, and Mark are already warming up at the barre.

In the fourteen years I've been dancing here, Katina's studio hasn't changed a bit. Not one of the chipping lilac-painted walls has been retouched. Not one square of the cheap laminate floor has been replaced or repolished. And in a few select places, the floor is so worn that little pink pieces of concrete foundation are peeking through. It even smells the same as it did when I was four, when my mom first brought me here. Like a slightly raunchy, slightly enticing combination of vinegar, rotting peaches, and chalk.

Katina walks past us, adjusting our bodies, pressing our backs down down down so that they get an inch closer to the ground.

"Push yourself, Magnolia. I know you can reach further than that."

I sink lower, lower, trying my best to flatten my back and raise my leg until the muscles underneath feel like they're tearing in two. I don't care if they tear in two. I take a deep breath and push once more and I know I've never gone lower than this.

"Good, Magnolia." She lifts my leg a half-inch higher. "Fabulous, George."

When she's past us, George pokes my thigh with his pointed foot. "If you won, you could finally quit Deelish."

"Why would I want to do that? Your mom and dad would kill me. Plus I love Deelish."

George kicks his other leg over the edge of the barre and rolls his upper body down his leg, his chest becoming one with his thigh. "Whatever. Do you really want to be scooping PB and J-flavored ice cream to summer brats for the rest of your life?"

"It's not that easy."

"It's totally that easy. There's more to life than Summerland, you know."

"I know." It's not what I meant, but he doesn't get it. Doesn't get that me landing another job in Summerland isn't the same thing as him landing one. Not the same thing at all.

"I mean, you really think everyone would still hate you guys so much if you made this town famous for something other than digging?"

"Okay, my people!" Katina runs her hands over her gelled mane. "Take a small break and we'll start with our pointe exercises first today. Let's get the hardest out of the way, and then we'll learn some new choreography, yes?"

Mark and Abby and Quinn sidle off to the left of the room, arms linked, like the three musketeers they are. Mark gives George this wide-eyed little stare, one I know I'm not meant to see because when he sees me looking, he looks away. It kind of hurts because Mark's always been nice to me when not many people still are, but I know what Mark's thinking. And to be perfectly honest, he's right: George *should* be hanging out with them instead of always with me.

Even though George and Mark have been competing for the male lead roles in Katina's productions for as long as I can remember, and even though Mark and I have been dancing together almost as long as George and I have, George has always been more in Mark's league than mine. And the rest of them, too. They belong together. Them, born into perfect families. Them, raised by mothers who'd never, ever hurt another soul.

Still, George heads left, away from them, like he's got total blinders on, so I follow.

Mark opens his mouth like he wants to say something, but then shuts it. I know he wouldn't say it outright. I know he cares way too much about hurting people's feelings to say anything to my face about why George still hangs out with me when almost no one else does, but he's got to be thinking it. He may be the sweetest thing in Summerland, but he's still a Summerland local. And being my friend doesn't make him immune to the poison this place perpetuates. At least when it comes to me.

And technically, Mark should be used to George for- ever choosing me over everyone else. Pretty much all of Summerland knows we're inseparable, like two halves of a razor clam shell, his half shielding me, keeping me safe, mak- ing me enough. It's the way it's always been. And ever since The Thing That Happened happened, I've often wondered if everyone just prefers being away from us. Or me, anyway.

With my back to the wall, I sink down to the floor and then reach for one of my toe shoes. I slip it on my right foot. The cool canvas surrounds my toes, encasing them, protecting them. I hold the smooth ribbons with two hands and cross them in front of my ankle. Then I loop them around the back twice before tying a strong knot—one that won't come undone during whatever new choreography Katina's got up her sleeve.

I tuck the knot under the flat piece of ribbon against my ankle and then grab the other shoe to begin the whole process over again. But instead, I rest the shoe in my lap and peer out the window. The sun is starting to fade behind Mount Hood, causing Vine Street and probably the whole darn town to be smothered in the golden glow of twilight. It's my favorite time of day. And being here, confined in these walls of this studio, is my favorite place on earth.

I've done this a million times before, this shoe-tying business. Could do it even before I was six. But as George drones on about "seizing the day" and "grabbing life by the reins," all I can think of are his other words. Taunting me.

Nobody could hate you if you made Summerland famous, could they?

"Hey George," Abby calls from across the room. And just like that I'm back here again. "We know you took the sign off the door," she says. "We saw you stuff it down your pants. You can't stop everyone from trying out."

"Yeah." Quinn eyeballs George's crotch. "And we've got no problem going in there and getting it back if it comes down to that."

When Abby and Quinn take three seductive little steps toward George and grab Mark's arm to do the same, Mark shrugs them off. "No way," he says. "You two are on your own with that one." But then his eyes lock on me. His eyebrows push together and he studies my freckle-dusted cheeks. My bulbous nose. My forehead, dotted with tiny pimples like some kind of unknown, yet undesirable constellation.

I give him a little smile to remind him of all those other times we had together. Long before The Thing That Happened happened. Like the time when we were nine and his mouse costume got lost so we raced all through the dressing rooms looking for it until we found it—both of us grabbing the giant mouse ears from a trunk of old costumes at the exact same time, which sent us tumbling backward into a giggling heap. Like the time we were freshmen and neither of us could find

our classes so both of us ditched and hung out together—
huddled behind a bush because we were so afraid of getting
caught—instead of going to class at all. I hope my smile will
remind him of it all. Remind him that, I swear to God, I'm
nothing like her.

He takes a step toward me, his eyes wide and clear like
magic windows leading into a warm, warm world. A world
where I'm wrong. A world where he won't look at me in this
new way he looks at me these days, all silent and scrutinizing.
A world where none of them do.

George plunks himself next to me. He wraps his arm
around my waist. I lean my head on his shoulder and close
my eyes. When I open them, Mark's still staring at me.

"What?" I cross my arms.

"Nothing," Mark says. He spins around and does a series of
jeté entrelacé over and over on the far side of the room, even
though they were perfect the first time around.

I want to get up and give him a piece of my mind. Tell him
to stop staring because I hate it and always have. But George
pats my leg. "Leave it alone," he says, so I do. Instead, I breathe
in and out, inhaling George's scent, the mixture of boy and
salt I know so well. At least I'll always have him. At least I
know he'll never leave me the way the rest of them have, one
by one by one.

"So what do you say about the competition?" His voice is
soft, threading its way in and then out of me.

"I say it's a total long shot. You know how many people go to those things, don't you? Everyone will be there.
Everyone thinks they're good enough to be on that show." I
watch Mark and Quinn and Abby practice a series of ronds

de jambe en l'air at the far side of the studio, their legs extending at perfect ninety-degree angles. All of them look good. All of them look strong. "Katina's entire studio will want to try out."

"They say they'll go, but they won't. No one ever leaves this town. No one ever does anything around here except shun you if you're different and snub you if you're not. Unless we do this, we're going to end up just like them."

I stare straight into his eyes, and in them I see the reflection of my own soul. It's all there between him and me and has been since we were four. That was the day our moms met on our beach, Wick Beach, the last day of Season.

We were there, me and Mom and Rose, just doing our thing when up rocked Mrs. Moutsous carrying one very squirmy George wearing a tangerine tutu and a pair of red fire-truck gum boots with little blue wheels painted at the toes and heels. It was thundering and lightning something awful out that day. Flashes thrust into the sand all around us, warning us with every crackle and every ominous boom. I remember thinking that it wasn't safe for any of us to be so close to the ocean in that kind of weather.

All George says he remembers is that he had peed his pants hours before but didn't want his mom to know for fear that she'd make them go home.

That's how George goes through life. Even though we're as different as Deelish's flavors—him being Magic Marshmallow and me vanilla—George sees and feels everything I've felt, and vice versa. And today is no exception. As usual, he sucks away all that nasty cynicism I'm prone to, leaving me with no choice in the matter but to go with his flow.

He grabs my hands. Eyes on me. Baby blues shimmering. For me. "I'm going to be there. I just want you to be there with me."

I don't know why he does this. Maybe it's because he can't stand to spend his days with someone who doesn't overtly *believe* that people can change—that the world can change—the way he does. Or maybe he only looks at me this way because he feels guilty that he'll never love me the way I love him. Not because I'm not pretty enough or smart enough or even good enough at dancing to be his girl. But because he couldn't love me that way even if he tried.

I'd always had my suspicions. When I was eight and ten and twelve, I knew something wasn't quite right in the story of me and George that was supposed to end with happily ever after. But I never knew *for sure* that George didn't play for my team until the day I saw him on the beach with Sammy Baker on the first day of Season, the summer before we started high school.

Still, loving on me or not, George has stuck by my side when not many others have. Even through the hard stuff when my mom first started using and the harder stuff that came later, with The Thing That Happened. I'm the yin to his yang, or at least that's what he's always said.

I throw my hands up in the air. "Fine. I'll go with you." I flip my head over and gather my mass of hair into a firm bun on top of my head. I secure it with four bobby pins, twisting and sticking, twisting and sticking. "But you know getting Rose to agree won't be easy."

George smiles and bends down to tie my left shoe for me, which sends a twinge through my ankle again. "Don't you worry your pretty little head about your alpha sister. I'll take care of her. You know I always do."

I let my eyes meet his and stay inside his for what seems like forever. Because what if he's right? What *have* I got to lose by trying out for the show?

What if I actually won?

Two

Rose digs her nails into my right leg and gives it a little shake.

I don't move an inch. I don't grunt or roll over onto my back either. Nothing to acknowledge the fact that she's huddled next to my bed at 5:16 a.m. On a Sunday. The one day a week during summer when I don't have to get up early for pointe class.

I'm not ready to let the light in or give in to the early-bird-gets-the-worm mentality of the first day of Season. And I'm sure as hell not ready to be reminded of The Thing That Happened, a year ago today, bursting through my brain the second I open my eyes. No. Not yet. Lie still. The trick is to lie still and maybe it will all go away.

"Magnolia, come on." Rose shoves my legs over and squeezes her round butt next to me on the bed. The mattress that I've had since I was three wilts under her weight like a flattened flower, but I still don't budge. Instead, I lie there smelling Rose—the 24/7 scent of Virginia Slims and spearmint gum that reminds me so much of *her*, it's sickening. And intoxicating. I inhale it. It jolts me awake awake awake.

But there's something else in that smell. I scrunch up my nose, trying to place it. Resignation. That's the smell that is my sister and that was *her*, too.

Is. Is my mother.

Rose leans forward and shakes my arm. I can't help but stretch my toes and then calves, working my way up my body, my thighs, my glutes, my abdominals, isolating each muscle group the way Katina taught me to. The movement of my limbs breaks my pretend-sleep spell and Rose and her smell are on me, sticking to me with the force of Gorilla Glue. I deliver her one gratuitous moan, roll over, and pull my sheet up so that it covers my ears.

She grabs a fistful of sheet by my feet and pulls. "Mags, please? I have to be at work in two hours. We've only got one good hour before I have to go and that's if we get out there pronto."

I open one eye to sneak a peek at her. "Did you just say 'pronto'? I'm not getting up this early for anyone that uses the word 'pronto.'"

Rose lets go of her end of the sheet and swipes the pillow out from under my hair. My face makes a *whap!* noise as it bounces off this old mattress, sending Rose into a fit of giggles. I burrow under my covers. I can't help but smile at the sound of Rose's girly laugh because she almost never laughs anymore. She may have to be at work in a couple of hours, but she's never been able to resist a good pillow fight. I roll over and in one swift motion swipe the pillow away from her grip and then swing it around toward her face. "Ha! Take that!"

Rose jumps back and grabs the pillow out of my hands. "You're pretty slow in the morning, you know that?"

I swipe the pillow. "Faster than you."

She pulls it back. "That's what you think."

"It's what I know." I grab it once and for all and then smack her over her head three times, like I'm hammering a nail. Her hair gets super frizzy and stands up all over her head like she's being electrocuted, which sends me into a fit of giggles, too.

"Stop it!" she shrieks, but it's a happy shriek and I know she's loving it. "I can't go to work like this!" She bolts to the door and grabs my dance bag.

Ha. Sucker. Rose may love herself a good pillow fight but I love my bed more. While she's at the door, I crawl back in and pull the covers over my head. Let it be known, I am not a morning person. So while she may be swifter than me before 9 a.m., I have my principles, one of them being *don't get out of bed before nine unless you have to.*

But then she's back and dangling my bag above my head. "I know your shoes are in here. I wonder what it would feel like to have these come down on your head. What are these things made of anyway? Wood?"

I open both eyes. Prop myself up on one elbow. "Canvas, actually. And paper. And really strong glue."

"So they'd definitely hurt if I dropped them on your face."

Now she's getting serious. That's the other thing about Rose. She can be fun and silly and totally carefree when she wants to be, but it never lasts. At least, it never lasts anymore. "Touch my shoes and you're dead," I tell her. "Put the bag down, and back away from my shoes."

Rose huffs in this real exaggerated way, which is how I know the fun's over for real. She's getting close to going out there without me. I know it because she's pulling down her sleeves and tying up her hair and putting her game face on. Fact is, she was probably ready long before she came to get me, wearing about a billion layers of baggy clothes and carrying her thermos of deep black coffee.

"We gotta get out there before Perkins nabs all the biggies. Remember last year? We lost about six big ones because of your lazy ass."

Last year.

She said it, not me.

Last year. The words hang above us now, thick and heavy, like the fog that rolls in on Wick Beach every morning by seven, gone by noon.

July tenth, *last year*.

The words are out now so there's no use staying nestled between the warmth of my mattress and sheet. And even though she knows full well that my lazy ass has nothing to do with why Mrs. Perkins got first dibs on all the big clams last year, I sit up straight, obliging the eager beaver that is my older sister.

"Fine. I'm up. Happy?" I snap, but I can't really be mad at her. After all, without her, where would I have spent the last year of my life? Two words jump out at me like grating little no-see-ums on my thin skin: foster care.

"Not quite. I'll be happy when you put some clothes on."

"What do you call these?" I hold my plaid pajama pants and tank top away from my body and give them a once-over.

"You can't go out like that. It's still subzero out there, and you've got no meat on those skinny bones of yours." She chucks me my old hoodie, heavily worn and loved, from Summerland's local surf shop. I pull it over my head and weave my hair into a side braid and hide the whole mess of it under my favorite faded, barely orange wool beanie.

Rose grabs the knee-high gum boots from my closet and jams one on my right foot.

I laugh as she holds me down, cramming it on my toes like it's two sizes two small, when we both know that Mom's feet were always bigger than mine. "Hey, watch how you treat my feet. I need those." I lift my sheet and rummage around until I find one of my socks. It takes me a second to find its match, but when I do, I put it up to my nose to give it a quick smell check. Semiclean. Good enough. "Can't I at least use the bathroom before you drag me out there before the sun's even up?"

"No. Time's a tickin'. Anyway, I'm dying to test out the new gun Mrs. Moutsous got us."

"Got *me*, you mean. I didn't see your name on that card." I remove the lone boot that Rose shoved on my foot, slip the first torn sock over my toes, and replace the boot. "*My* birthday gift. Remember?"

"Whatever. Aren't you dying to try it out? It's going to work so much better than that stupid shovel." She does a little happy dance around my room, shaking her tush and rubbing her belly. "I can almost taste those fritters now."

I turn my head away. Five minutes ago, she was funny. Now, not so much. "The shovel's never let us down in the past."

"Hey, you should consider yourself lucky that Mrs. Moutsous got you this at all. That woman's so your Santa Claus." Rose holds the clam gun to her chest and rubs it a couple times like one would a poodle, not a three-inch metal tube. I pull my bedroom curtains away from the window and scan our wide sprawling beach. My eyes zero in on the specks of brightness poking out behind the sheet of gray sky. That's how the sun rises here in Summerland. No grand streaks of pink or magenta. No friendly fluffy puffs of cloud either. Just microscopic bits of light over the sea to let us know that yet another day on the Oregon Coast is about to begin.

It's so beautiful. My heart swells with all the love I've got left in the world. I turn back to Rose. She's staring at me like all *her* last bits of love rest on me, which makes me feel guilty, and awful, and so very guilty. Because it's been twelve hours since I told George I'd go with him to try out for *Live to Dance*, and I still haven't mentioned it to Rose.

She'll think he talked me into it. She'll know I've got some other reason, some ulterior motive for finally agreeing to it. Which is the best reason of all to not tell her. Nope, decision made. No point in giving myself one more reason to completely loathe a day that's barely begun.

"The sun is almost up," Rose says. "Can't we just get out there?"

I exhale, the morning magic slipping in time with my breath. "Okay. Let's go."

She bounds out of my room, vindicated. I wait until I hear her meaty feet plodding down the hall before I grab the pillowcase piece out from under my bed. I fold it into a neat square, place it under my bra strap for safety, and meet her in front of our hall closet. She tosses me the newer of the down jackets, grabbing the one with two torn armpits for herself. Side by side like sausage links, we tumble down the three steps of our driftwood front stoop till our toes meet the packed sand of the beach for the first day of clam digging season.

For as long as I can remember, the first day of Season has always been on July tenth. But this July tenth is different. This July tenth marks the one year anniversary of the day that The

Thing That Happened happened. The day my mother crossed the line from being your run-of-the-mill junkie-loser mom to murderer.

Rose was right.

We were too slow getting out and now there are about a gazillion people combing our beach for the telltale little feet that pop out of the sand and then disappear without warning.

"I told you it was going to be packed early," Rose mutters. "Come on." She grabs my arm and pulls me away from the circles of people milling around the sand outside our house, toward the shoreline where the tide has left the beach still wet and glistening.

That's the thing about Summerland newbies—people who don't know much about digging for razor clams—they usually stick to the dry, powdered sand and then wonder why they only pull one or two clams all day. But we know that razors like the sand where the tide's just left. The hard, packed stuff that shimmers under the morning sky, even on the grayest of days.

We reach the water's edge and drop our gear ten feet from Abby, Quinn, and Mark to the right of us, a bunch of local kids who graduated with Rose to the left. Both groups flick their heads in our direction and whisper way too loudly to be considered whispering. As usual, Rose and I pretend they don't exist. Pretend that not seeing them will somehow make them go away.

Rose stomps around the sand in a circle, creating strong vibrations all around her. She's always been good at this part, so I hang back and let her work her magic. Within seconds a foot pops out of the ground next to her and then is gone, digging itself deeper for safety. Hiding itself away from a world that wants to eat it alive.

"There's one!" I shout, as if Rose hasn't seen it. I peek over my shoulder. The kids Rose's age are gone, replaced by a family I know I've seen in Deelish before. But they're doing their own thing and not watching us at all, so I relax my shoulders and just let my insides feel the excitement at the sight of that clam. Just as I'm about to pounce on it with the narrow, curved metal blade of my shovel, Rose grabs it from me.

"No, Mags. The gun! Use the gun!"

"Yeah. Okay."

I hesitate. Mom never used a clam gun. In fact, she always said that real clammers—like her mom and her mom's mom—never, ever used clam guns. And when George's mom gave me the gun last week, I mentioned this fact to Rose.

"That's because they didn't exist back then," Rose had said, flashing her sharp blue eyes at me. "If clam guns had been around then, trust me, every member of the Woodson family would have used them."

But she's lying and we both know it. Mom never would have used one. She liked the simple things in life, like brushing with normal toothbrushes instead of electric ones, and making fritters instead of buying them at Miller's. There's just no way she would have used one and she *didn't* use one the last time we were here. I remember it clearly. Two years ago, on the first day of Season. She had just gotten out and was feeling good, and looking good, too. She even went along with the whole charade, the mock fight me and Rose engaged in every year to be the one to use the shovel first. She loved the thing. Treated it like it was the freaking Hope Diamond. Or better. Like the stuff she pumped through her veins for happiness. No clam guns involved. No way. No how.

"The gun, Mags, use the gun!" Rose shouts again.

I drop to my knees and thrust the pipe deep into the sand with all my might. Dance has kept me thin but strong. Much stronger than you'd think just by looking at me. Without much effort, the gun makes suction, and I pull, pull, pull the tube out of the sand.

"I don't know if it worked," I say, breathless.

Rose takes the gun from me and twists the handle to release the suction. A pile of caked mud and sand tumbles out the tube at our feet, covering the toes of our boots. She tosses the gun to the ground, bends down on one knee, and sifts through the mound with her bare hands. I stand next to her, praying in the only way I know how that my mom's old shovel won't be replaced so easily.

And then it happens. Rose jumps up and screams at the tops of her lungs, "Would you look at the size of this sucker? That took a total of ten seconds! Magnolia, would you look at this guy? It's probably the biggest one anyone's caught here all morning!"

"Let me see."

She tosses a heap of sand at me and I run my gloved hands through it. Sure enough, there it is, and it's huge. Most likely the biggest razor that anyone's going to see all day. A few feet from us, the two little girl members of that family tug on their mom's jacket and point at our score, jumping up and down, celebrating our good fortune with us. Suddenly, the gun looks brighter. Shinier. Like, not only are we going to pull more clams than we ever have before, but we'll show every one of them that we don't have to do it her way—do anything her way. Show them we can be Woodsons, without being her.

"Hey."

The hoarse voice startles me. I lose my balance and then catch myself with one hand, digging it into the sand. My head shoots up. The mom part of that family is here, towering over me and Rose, frowning at us. "You're those girls," she says.

"What?" I stutter the word.

"You're her daughters, aren't you." She crosses her arms. It's not a question.

I stand up. "Whose daughters?"

"You were there when it happened." She turns to Rose. "I know you were. Everyone says so."

"I didn't—" Rose starts. "I wasn't—" She closes her eyes. Sits back on her haunches. Swallows, and then again. Shakes her head but in a totally different way from the lady.

"Leave us alone," I say.

"No. You leave *us* alone," she says. "This is a good town. A safe town. You've got no place here."

I get up and point to her bucket. Inside, she's got one pathetic clam. "Looks like you don't belong on this beach, either." Behind her, her girls are watching her. Watching us. No matter what she says—what they all say—we're not the ones that put that needle into Colleen's arm. But Mom is. To them, it's the same damn thing.

About fifty feet away, Mark stands up from where he's sitting on fold-up beach chairs with Abby and Quinn, their own guns and pails plopped in the sand. Their eyes are all on us, giving us these sympathetic kind of looks. But it's Mark that pushes off his chair and strolls toward us, his arms crossed against his chest. His shoulders are back and square. Even from here, I can see how dark his eyes are.

"Mags, you guys okay?"

"I'm fine," I say. "We're fine."

But he doesn't stop walking. I shake my head. It slows him down. I don't need him to come here and rescue us. I thought he was mad at us too, but it doesn't look that way anymore. It doesn't matter. There's nothing he could do for us, even if he wanted to.

The woman glares at me and then Mark. She turns her back on us and picks up both kids, one in each arm. Mumbles something to her weaselly looking husband, who didn't budge when Mark jumped up. The four of them stomp off to the far side of the beach, as far as they can get without smacking into the cliffs.

"Magnolia," Mark says.

I wave him away. I am fine. We're fine. We took care of this like we always do. He stands there a second but when I don't say anything else, he jogs back to Abby and Quinn, and the three of them resume whatever they were talking about before we Woodsons made things interesting.

I put one hand on Rose's shoulder. She opens her eyes. Still clutching Mom's shovel with one hand, I try to smile. I shake the gun in front of her because maybe it will make her happy like she was a few minutes ago. "You were right about the gun. I can't believe how fast it is."

She blinks a few times, the spell mostly broken. It should relieve me. It doesn't. She can't keep zoning in and out when it suits her. That's what Mom did. Participated in life only when she felt like it.

"We're going to have a feast tonight," she says. "You and me. When I'm off work, we'll make a big batch of fritters, and I'll get some beer bread from Millers and—"

"I work today at six."

"Oh. I guess we could do it before that."

"I have dance before that." I pretend to check my watch. Across the beach, the woman chases her screeching kids, tackling them with tickles. My jaw flexes. "I have to be at Katina's soon. You know how she is about us being late."

"But it's Sunday. You don't usually practice on Sundays."

"Now I do. Katina thinks George and I should bump rehearsals up to seven days a week, morning and night, to get ourselves in prime shape this summer." I stare at my feet. Unlike the other kids around here with college plans and backpacking-across-Europe plans, I have absolutely no idea what I'm going to do with my life come fall. "I won't be home until at least ten, but you could make the fritters without me."

"Oh." Rose stares at our clam for a long time. I watch her gaze dart toward the family, halting just feet from where they are. Stopped by the wall she's building to keep every one of them out.

She walks a few steps toward the lapping sea and rinses off the remaining globs of mud, tossing the clam into our metal bucket. "I guess you'll just have to eat when you come home." Her smile sags and my insides ache. "I'll save some for you. It's no biggie."

But it is, and we both know it. That's not how it's done on the first day of clam-digging season. On the first day, you're supposed to flour-n-fry your first batch of clams together. As a family. Like that family. Like any freaking family in Summerland but ours.

But even when we had one, ours was never like the kind you see on TV. Rose and I were both born when Mom was back on the streets in Portland, "working" for money to buy the kind of things she needed to keep her alive.

When we were little, we used to beg and plead for Mom to tell us what our daddy was like. If he was tall or short or fat or thin or if he liked working indoors or preferred building things in the cool, salty air, like the air in Summerland. As we got older and our relentless pleas turned to the occasional careful inquiry, Mom still refused to talk about why one of her daughters was tall and lean with caramel hair while the other was short and curvy with black hair that swooshed around, silently, like total darkness. Still, even back then we always sort of knew that it takes two pretty different sets of genes to make sisters look this opposite.

Sure, we had Mom for a lot of our years, and Grandma, too, before she died. But we still knew what was missing.

"Come on," Rose says. "Let's get out of here." Rose grabs Mom's shovel, still tucked under my arm, and drops it at her feet. I go to pick it up but she says, "Leave it for the tourists. They need it more than we do."

I grab the magic gun and walk—half a step behind her—away from the shore where the tide's already withdrawing from us. I glance over my shoulder at the discarded shovel that lies in the sand, but I don't go back for it.

I'm sort of grateful for my sister's commute to Portland. I'm almost glad she'll spend nine hours working her lame job at Urban Outfitters because most of the "fine Summerland folks" wouldn't dare hire a Woodson girl. Because I know that when she's gone, I'll sneak back out here and pick up the shovel.

It's worth nothing to the other clammers around here with its rusted tip and rotting handle, so I know no one will take it. And it means nothing to Rose, either—that much is clear. But I'll take it anyway. Because when I win that ten grand and make our town famous, no one's gonna care that the shovel I'm using to pull my clams used to belong to the biggest disgrace Summerland's ever known.

THREE

George presses his nose against the glass case that holds our newest flavors: Mac 'n' Cheese and Buttered Popcorn. "Come on, Magnolia, just one taste. Please?"

I toss my ice cream scoop in the container of warm water and wipe my hands on my apron. "No way. Forget it. You know the rules: no freebies during Season."

George's bottom lip juts out and I can't help but see four-year-old George all over again. It's still adorable. He still knows it. "When did you become such a stickler for rules, anyway? It's so not fun." He clucks his tongue. "No fun at all."

"Your mom gave me strict instructions to limit you to one free cone a day, which you gobbled up precisely fourteen minutes ago. If she told me to limit the freaking president to one cone a day, I would. I like my job. And I need it." I brush a piece of hair off my face. "We both know that."

George gets so pissed whenever I talk about the horrible job-hunt ordeal that Rose went through last summer. Old Lady Miller, who owns half of Main Street including Summerland Liquors, the Pic 'N' Pay, and Xanadu Mini Golf, was not shy about letting Rose know that we Woodson women were not to be trusted.

"Those people suck. My mom and dad know that. That's why they hired you and would have hired Rose too, if she would have let them. They love you guys to pieces."

I squeeze my mouth shut, never having much to say about love when it doesn't involve George and me living happily forever, bound by law in holy matrimony.

He tilts his head to one side. "You're nothing like her, you know."

George's words make my limbs limp. He stares at me like he's not just reading my mind, but reading my breath and blood, too. But when his phone bellows out some Taylor Swift song in lieu of a respectable ringtone, his eyes free themselves from mine all too easily.

Fact: George has other friends. Unlike me—who only has Rose and him and sort-of Mark unless he's with Abby and Quinn, which he almost always is, ever since they bonded over adjoining lockers in eighth grade and became this inseparable trio—George is friends with pretty much every other person in Summerland. So it's not weird when other people call him like other people do. It's only weird that he's studying the name scrolling across the front of his phone like he's studying for his SATs. Across the counter, I stand on my toes, straining to see what—or who—has captivated him this way. The name starts with an "M," that much I'm sure of. And I'm positive the next letter is an "A." But just as I'm trying to confirm the "R" that follows, and the "Y" that I'm pretty sure comes after that, George spins away from me so there's no way I can see his screen. "Sorry, Mags. I gotta take this. Private call, if you get my drift."

I shrug my shoulders like I so don't care and pretend to restock the taster-spoon cup. Pretend to wipe the back counter. Pretend that I'm doing anything but listening in on

George's "private" call.

"Hey, babe," he breathes into his phone. "I thought you might call tonight."

I watch as George's whole body warps. He stands up straighter and puffs out his chest. Fiddles with a rogue piece of hair that's fallen in front of his forehead. Licks his lips, after each and every sentence.

Blinding stars blur my eyes. I mean, what's happening here? *Hey, babe?* I've never known George to be a "hey, babe" kind of guy. And definitely not for any Mary.

Competing with guys seemed bad enough. Impossible, really, when I don't have that anatomy. But the possibility that I may have to fight for him with *girls*, too? My insides cringe while, five feet away from me, George is all over his phone, cupping his hand around it so that his words are totally inaudible to me. But I can see his face. His eyes are all twinkly and dancing while his mouth stretches into a grin, true and beautiful and alive.

"Really?" he says. "You're not seriously going to do that, are you?"

He pauses. One. Two. Three seconds. Smiles again, his eyes rounding and widening and clearing like a June moon in Summerland. "Promises, promises!" he says in this awful, *awful* singsongy voice. And every time Mary says something to him on the other end, George *giggles.*

I creep back to the tables and feign like I'm scraping old gum from under them, needing to get closer to George and that conversation. But he knows me and knows what I'm up to. He wanders over to the farthest end of the shop, almost totally out of earshot. Almost.

"No way. I've got to see you before you do." He slaps his phone off, stares at it for another two seconds with flushed cheeks.

"Who was that?"

"No one," he says. "What were we talking about before?"

I shrug. Slink down, crouching behind the counter so he can't see my own cheeks, burning like a clambake fire. "Something about me not wanting to get axed on account of your freeloading butt, I think."

George leans over the counter to flash me one of his killer grins. "How many times do I have to tell you? You're not going to get fired for giving me the occasional tester. Or for anything else for that matter. My parents love you like you're their own."

"You don't know that." I check the cake order sheet, hiding from him and that hideous phone call, still wafting through the air like the world's greatest fart. I touch my left shoulder to make sure my pillowcase piece is still securely tucked under my bra strap. Then I hoist myself on the back countertop and rest my feet on the ledge below. We've been totally packed in here since my shift started at six, but now the place is empty except for George, and me, and eighteen delicious cream-and-sugar varieties. Which is a good thing because whenever he's here while I'm working I get all rattled and thrown off my game.

The truth of it is, half of me wants him here, wants him anywhere I am. But the other half of me wants him gone so I can put my head down and work, undistracted by the kinds of things I thought couldn't change. Her name pricks my eyeballs, like needles—no, knives. Mary. Ugh. *Mary.*

"Okay," George says. "I'll make you a deal."

Armed with a bottle of Windex, I push myself off the countertop and begin wiping the tables at the far corner of the shop.

He follows on my heels. "You want to hear it or not?"

"Yeah, yeah. I'm listening."

"If you give me one more cone, the plain kind, not even a waffle one, I promise never to ask you for another one. And I'll give you the one thing on earth that's going to make you happy."

I stop dead in my tracks. Turn around, slowly. "What are you talking about?"

"You know. The thing that'll make this all go away. I'll go to Mayor Chamberlain's house. I'll tell him you had nothing to do with Colleen's—"

"George, no."

"Why? I'll tell him Rose had nothing to do with it, too. Tell him that he can't ostracize you guys like that forever."

"It's not even him that does it." I swallow. "He probably doesn't even know. He's been gone since it happened, remember?"

"He's back."

"What?"

"I heard my dad say it yesterday." He shrugs. "Or maybe it was a couple days ago."

I shake my head, stunned. "Even if you go, he won't listen to you. He probably won't even open the door."

"He will too. I've known him since I was like twelve."

"She was his *daughter*. You think he actually cares how anyone in this place treats us? She died in our house, because our mother gave her the drugs. Got her hooked. Killed her. That's all that matters to them." I kick a tester spoon that's fallen to my feet across the floor. "Everyone loves Mayor Chamberlain. And they loved Colleen, too."

"Um, hello? Are you actually working here, or are you like on a break or something?"

Both of our heads shoot up in time to see the same little freshman from Katina's, smooshed between two other girls I recognize, gawking at me. I can't believe I didn't hear the bell ring when they came in. I hate it when I'm too preoccupied with George and all things George to hear a warning bell when it practically hits me over the head.

"I thought you might be in here." She says it to George but she narrows her eyes at me. "You're always in here, when she is." Under her breath, she says, "Even though all my friends say I'm hotter."

I give the girl a once-over. She's pretty for sure and not afraid to show it. Her jeans are so tight it's like they've been pasted to her legs, sticking to her curves in all the right places. And her boobs. That must be some push-up bra. Her boobs are spilling out of her sheer tank top and, let's face it, dancers aren't that well equipped.

She plops her hands on her hips. "So if you're not on a break, we'd like to order something. Now."

I have no idea how it became acceptable for a not-even-sophomore-yet to talk to a no-longer-senior like this, but somehow it happened. Then again, I'm no ordinary postgrad. I tuck my bottle of Windex in my apron. "Sure. No problem. Let me just get back there."

"I'd like one low-cal vanilla with sugar-free gummies on top. In a cup." She eyes me up and down. "Hey, Magnolia, your sister eats here a lot, doesn't she?"

Her two little friends who stand behind her erupt into hysterics. I bite my lip, hard, so that the all of the murderous words that rage through my mind don't fly out of my mouth.

"So, is this like your other job?" she says.

I look up. "Huh?"

"You know, what you do when you're not messing up people's lives."

George glances up from where he's rummaging through the row of containers filled with various nuts and sprinkles and chocolate chips, his eyes bouncing between mine and the freshman's. "Hey. That's a little harsh."

She turns to George, her voice changing from demonic to downright sugar. "George, have you been working out?"

"I, uh. Only at Katina's but, you know." He stretches out his right arm. Bends it forward, exposing the hard, rounded ball that pops from his skin, under his shoulder. Examines it like he's looking at some miracle of nature, a brand-new planet. Planet George. The freshman soaks up every inch of him. When he's finished inspecting his muscles, she walks toward him. Close enough to make my heart beat fast, and not in a good way.

Her lips part, but no words leave them. Maybe she's waiting for him to praise her back, something about her body or her dancing. Something about her *having* a body and knowing how to use it and using it, apparently, to woo my George. But when he plops down in one of the chairs and opens someone's forgotten gossip mag, the freshman turns to me and mouths that hateful three-syllable word: *Murderer.*

She turns back to George, who flips the page of his gossip mag, obviously engrossed in the failing relationships of stars.

"So, are you waiting for someone in here?" Her tone is so sticky-sweet, it makes me sick.

"Nah," he says. "Just Magnolia."

She purses her lips and gives me the once-over. I smile as big as I can and pass her her ice cream. Too bad that while she was attempting to chat up my main man, I tossed on full-cal gummies instead of the sugar-free ones. I hold out my open palm. The girl chucks two rolled-up dollar bills at me. They land on the ground and I crouch down to pick them up. Along with my dignity.

She touches George's shoulder. "Well, you can come to the disco bowl with us, if you want."

"Yeah? Who's going?"

"Just us and a couple of others from the school dance team. Liz and Tianna Bakerman and maybe Dee Potter, too. Mark said he'd probably go. Oh, and you know Caleb and Bo, right? The new lifeguards at Cannon?"

George sets the mag down. "They're going to be there? And Mark too?"

Freshman's eyes ignite—fish caught. She sits down across from him. "Definitely. So you want to come with us?"

"You might see me. If I can talk Mags here into coming along. If not, maybe I'll just keep it mellow and hang with her here." He laughs. "Not too riveting, I know."

Freshman's face falls. "No. Not riveting." She leans forward, pushing her bazookas together, making them full, and round, and touching. Across from her, George smiles. *Smiles.* I mean, by all laws of plausible reason, he should be squeamish about a girl basically shoving her boobs in his face. But instead, his baby blues light up, bright, like he just pulled twenty clams out of that smart ass of his.

"I heard you might try out for *Live to Dance*," Freshman says. "You totally should. Your fouettes are amazing and the first time I saw you do a switch leap, I almost died."

"I'm trying out. Mags is, too. You?"

She looks at me with dagger eyes. "No. You have to be eighteen." She motions to her friends behind her. "But we would if we could. I mean, Katina needs to have more than one good dancer there. That is, one who won't totally destroy her studio's name."

"Are you serious?" George says. "Have you even *seen* Mags dance?"

The girls' mouths drop open and, I have to admit it, mine does too. While I can hold my own with these little dance rats, George defending my honor isn't what I'm used to from him. He's never said much about my dancing, at least not to anyone but me. And I know he was all over how good I was in Katina's studio, but I also know he got an A in Buttering People Up for Personal Gain every year in school. But this. This is something totally different.

Freshman plays with a piece of her hair, twisting it around and around her finger until it's so tight that her finger looks a little blue. "I've seen her," she mumbles. "I see her every week."

"You mean you watch her every week," George says.

Freshman shrugs. "Same difference. Whatever. We have to be there early anyway."

George smirks. "So then you already know that Katina will have at least two dancers to represent Summerland—"

"Two dancers representing Summerland where?" Rose says.

My head snaps around toward the door. She's standing there holding a tray of freshly made razor clam fritters against her chest. I rush to her side, grabbing the tray from her clutches. "Rose! What are you doing here?"

"I thought you'd be hungry after dance. I didn't want you to have to work on an empty stomach."

The girls lick their lips, salivating over the fresh meat that's just walked through Deelish's doors, and I don't mean the fritters. Freshman's eyes travel over Rose's body, all the way down, then up. "I bet working on an empty stomach is something *you've* never done before, right, Rose?"

Rose winces. It's low—like, *real* low. And although she should be used to these types of slams, I can see it all over her face that it still hurts.

George shakes his head at the freshman—his eyes cool and warning—but then turns to me and scratches his head. "Dance practice? We don't have dance tonight. It's Sunday."

"You said that you had dance on Sundays." Rose's gaze pinballs between George and the freshman and then me before it rests decidedly on George. "What were you guys just talking about? Where will Katina have dancers representing Summerland?"

"On TV, of course," Freshman says. "George might get to be on a reality dance competition."

Rose's eyes widen. "Really?"

"Mags," George whispers. "You haven't told her yet? You totally should have."

"You mean you haven't heard?" Freshman says. "Oh that's right. You've been too busy getting people hooked on junk." She smiles in this thin way that makes me nauseated.

Rose's face is motionless. Emotionless. Frozen by the words spewed out by this eighty-pound little freak. One Rose could totally take, if she wanted to.

George's pupils ignite with flames. "Colleen had issues before she hooked up with their mom. She was always looking for a way to piss off her dad. Everyone knows that." He curls his arm around Rose's shoulder, making Freshman grit her teeth and glower at both of them. Then he mouths the words, "Tell her."

I mouth the word "No" back.

"Isn't it great, Rosie?" George says. "Mags was just about to tell you that she's decided to come with me."

"Rose doesn't want to hear about your drama, George." My voice is all screechy like a total maniac, I know, but I can't help it. I grab Rose's arm and lead her away from George before he screws everything up way beyond repair. "You know him. He just babbles about nothing all the time."

"Actually"—Freshman wets her lips in between licks of ice cream—"he wasn't babbling. It's for *Live to Dance*. You might have heard of it? He's trying out with your sister. In Portland. Live."

"Magnolia," Rose says. "You better tell me what this little imbecile's talking about right now or the shit's gonna hit the fan."

I narrow my eyes at the freshman. She smirks back at me.

George gently pushes the girls out the door. But Freshman glares at me the entire way out.

He closes the door behind them and flips the lock, though Deelish is still open. "Come on, Mags. Look at her. She's already turned a million shades of purple in the last minute. Just tell her already."

"Yes, Magnolia. Tell me," Rose says, her face rigid.

"Fine," I say. "I'm going with him. To Portland. I want to be in that competition. I *deserve* to be in that competition."

Rose's face softens. "Are you serious? Why would you be afraid to tell me that?"

"You're not mad?"

"No way. It's awesome. And you're right, you deserve to be there. You've worked so hard for it. It's who you are."

"Better than who I am," I say. "It's who we can be."

"What?"

"It'll be great, Rose. Once I win that money and get our name on TV, it'll change things for us here. We'll be famous." I grab her hand. "They'll have to love us because we'll be stars. We'll be the only ones that ever came out of Summerland."

Rose blinks. Her eyes turn from sparkly to sad. "That's why you want to go? To try to change our rep? Fame won't do that."

"It will. Once they see me on TV, they'll be so proud of us for a change and then people all across the country—not just Oregon—will see that I'm—that *we're*—good at something."

Rose's face falls. She closes her eyes. Opens them. Stares out the window, across the street, to the flashing sign hanging above Miller's Bakery. Seconds pass. I feel this all crumbling at my feet.

I know what she's thinking. The last time we ran into Old Lady Miller outside her shop, Rose and I were walking arm-in-arm en route to the Summerland Public Library in search of movies and books and anything else to fill time during spring break.

Colleen had been dead six months already. Mom had been AWOL five.

As we passed her, Old Lady Miller crossed her arms and whispered, her sharp tongue flickering in and out her mouth like a snake's.

"Lowlifes. Losers. Trash. Just like your mother."

Her voice was hushed, yet just loud for us to hear her words clearly and never forget them.

Now, as Old Lady Miller backs out of her shop and locks her door behind her, Rose's face snaps to mine, her skin a shade whiter than it was before. She swallows. "You can't do this, Magnolia. It won't change things. It can't turn back time."

"You already said I could. You said I deserved it."

"You do. But I changed my mind. You're not going. Not for those reasons."

I squeeze my lips together. Picture myself on that stage in front of every single one of them. Imagine myself doing it. Doing it great. Like no one thinks I can. Not even Rose.

"Yes, I am. It's a once in a lifetime chance. And there's nothing you can do to stop me."

She grabs the tray of fritters away from me and stares me dead between the eyes like lasers slicing me in two. Her hands grip the tray so tight, they tremble. But her words come out slow and so very scary. "You're not going. Not like this. Not at all."

Four

Rose storms out of the shop. I can almost see little puffs of steam shooting from her ears like she's a cartoon character. She's that mad, all right. Mighty Mouse mad.

George tinkers with the top button on his shirt. "That didn't go exactly how I'd hoped."

"You think?"

"I told you, you should have let me handle it yesterday after dance."

I put up one hand in front of his face. "Drop it, okay? There's nothing you could have said to make Rose change her mind. Although, I'm sure it didn't help any when that freshman started in on her, too. What a piece of work."

"No kidding. You'd never know Becca was like that by looking at her, right?"

"Like what? Wait. You know her name?"

He looks away. "I just mean, you know, she's pretty hot and all. You wouldn't think she'd be such a nightmare."

I squint at him. It's one thing that that he knows the little mosquito's name. One thing that even *I* half-admired the boom-boom-pow thing she had going on. One thing that he called her a nightmare, when I can think of a million words I might have chosen to describe her instead. But it's something totally different that he's just admitted her hotness. Decent?

Maybe. Just-barely-over-the-totally-hideous mark? Now *that* I could get on board with. But *hot*? I think of George and his—let's just be honest here—flirty phone call with Mary.

George jumps up. "Well, I'd better hop to it and fix things while the wound is fresh, right?"

"Who are you fixing now? And for the record, I think you should keep your day job. You kind of suck at fixing things."

"I'm going to your house."

"You're not going to my house."

He rests one hand on my shoulder. "I'm sure that once I explain to Rose about the money you'd get if you won, she'll change her mind. I mean, seriously. Is she really going to deny you the chance at a truckload of cash like that?"

I lean back in my chair. George can be so naive at times, it blows my mind. I guess it's because his life has always been perfect. Perfect mom and dad and big brother, Malcolm. Perfect "little" seven-bedroom house on the cliffs. Perfect son, who's always been perfect at everything he does. Hell, he's even perfect at driving me bananas.

"Do you even know my sister, G? Rose will pulverize you. She won't care about the money because she hates the reason why I want it."

"That doesn't make sense. What's the point of taking dance all these years if you can't do something with it? I would have stopped years ago if I didn't think it would take me some-where eventually." George studies me for a couple of seconds, his eyes and mouth softening like our summer sea. "Look. I know she's all high and mighty about taking care of you guys, but you'd think that once you told her your game plan, she'd be into it."

I rest my head in my hands and picture Rose's pale face staring at Miller's Bakery. It all makes sense. Why she wanted me to go and then, suddenly, didn't. She's never said so, but she doesn't have to. "Rose blames us for what happened to Colleen. She thinks we could have prevented it. Thinks we deserve how they treat us."

I scan Deelish as the memory bleeds through me. It was one of those days, locked somewhere after the morning with the ambulances and screaming, after the day Mom actually left us for good. Rose and I were sorting out bills on my bed. I remember feeling like we were on an island—all on our own, and no one even knew we existed—but then, when we were in public, also like we were made of neon colors and flashing lights. Bull's-eyes.

Up until that point, Rose hadn't talked much about what happened, but that morning she wanted to.

"I never should have brought Colleen to this house," she said, tossing a stack of unopened envelopes to the floor.

"You didn't know that was going to happen."

She rested her head against my bed. "I should have seen it coming. She was so excitable. Impressionable. Wanted to do everything and try everything she knew her dad would hate."

"You didn't know she'd try that."

"I could have stopped her. I could have told Mom to stay away from her. Could have told her to stay away from Mom."

She kicked my side table, hard, and the one pretty framed photograph of Mom and me, taken four years before, fell, smashing to pieces on the floor below.

I stare at the shards of glass and whisper, "I miss her."

"Don't waste your energy on her," Rose said, scrambling off my floor. She stepped toward the door, the sharp pieces around and under her bare feet. "She's not worth it. None of this is."

After she left the room, I picked through every flake of glass, cutting my fingers in three different places, just to make sure I saved that picture. To make sure not one inch of her perfect smile was harmed.

George taps on his cell phone. "It's eight forty-five. You gotta close up in just over an hour."

"So?"

"So that means I've got an hour to get to Rose and tell her you have to be in that competition. An hour before you get home and spoil everything with your undying need to please the whole goddamn world."

I groan. "Please, G. Don't, okay?"

"No. You're trying out. Not for the money or to clear your family name, but for yourself. And for Rose."

"Rose said I can't. And I can't go against her."

"You can and you will. Do it for me."

"Ha. And there we have it. Should I even ask what you get out of all this other than having a wingman by your side to make your extensions look better than they already do?"

"It's not about that."

"Pretty sure it is about that."

He stares out the window. "Maybe I'm sick and tired of watching you and Rose barely tread water, ever think of that? Maybe for once I want good things to actually happen to good people. I'm sure as hell not going to sit around and wait for the universe to be good to you Woodsons. No way." He grabs my hand. Pulses zing through me and I can't pull my hand away. "We've been given this gift. This talent that's unstoppable. It's all settled. We're going to Portland. You and me. Tomorrow."

"But Rose—"

"No buts." He heads for the door and then turns around and slaps his own ass. "The only butt worth talking about around here is the one you're lookin' at."

Two hours later, I've cleaned every table and restocked the ice cream and the last of Deelish's customers has eaten and left. I lock the door and bike on home. The lights are all off, so I tiptoe through my front door so I don't wake Rose up.

Not like it matters, though. Just like my mom, Rose is usually in bed by nine, especially during Season. She swears that it's her true love for clamming that drives her to her early nights, but I know that's nothing more than a big fat lie. More like she's so exhausted from all of her overtime at work that she needs to hit the sack early on the nights she can.

I sling my jacket and bag over one of the fold-up kitchen chairs and open the fridge. There's a container of cottage cheese, three ripe tomatoes from George's mom's garden, and a jar of peanut butter—the healthy kind—next to the tray of Rose's fritters. There are at least twelve of them in here, which is how I know Rose went back to the beach after she and I clammed this morning. I lift the cling wrap and pluck two of the smaller ones from the tray. I grab the handle of the toaster oven and prepare to plop them both inside, but then pull my hand back, quick, like something's bitten me. The oven's still hot, I guess, from Rose's recent use, and now I've burned my index finger and thumb, bad. My skin is red and the heat is fierce, so I shake my hand through the air. With my forearm, I flip on the tap and stick my fingers under it, waiting for the cool relief to come.

The water pours over my burn, dimming the pain, but the second I take my hand out the hurt returns with a vengeance. I pull the freezer open with my foot and reach for the bag of frozen peas I know will be there. It cools my hand in seconds. It brings the memory back to me like it never, ever left.

I burned myself when I was little—same fingers on the same hand. I think I was three. Four, tops. It must have been the toaster oven that got me that day, too. Mom was by my side in a flash, hoisting me up so that my small legs straddled her bony hip. She ran my fingers under that water for what seemed like forever and then pulled out a bag of frozen peas or carrots or something from the freezer and pressed them to my skin, wrapping the bag around my fingers, like a shield.

At some point, she sat down. Just me and her and that bag of frozen vegetables, curled up in her lap like we were always meant to be there.

One of Mom's friends came into the kitchen to sit with us. He touched my cheek. "You're lucky to have such a good momma. Got so many fine skills, she does."

I drop the peas back in the freezer. My eyes dart to the clock on the stove. Eleven thirty.

George has been here and gone. I can only imagine how it all went down.

I slide the two fritters in the oven. When the toaster dings, I hover over the sink and scarf down both fritters using my uninjured hand. My mouth barely registers the familiar salty, crispy taste. Usually, I prefer to douse them in hot sauce from the Taco Stop, but tonight I don't bother. I think about grabbing another fritter from the fridge, but then decide against it. I don't want to eat them all by myself when I didn't help make them and barely even helped pull them. So instead, I replace the cling wrap over the tray and close the fridge. I tiptoe to Rose's room and peer in, expecting to see her body curled up on her bed. Expecting to hear her snore reverberating from the walls like thunder. But she's not there. And as much as I don't want to think about where she is, I can't help it. I stride into her room, staring at her unused bed. I sit down. Open the bottom drawer of her bedside table.

It's still there. Not that I thought it'd be gone. Not thought but hoped, maybe.

My fingers loiter above the pipe, air-tracing its curved base and long, slender handle. Its sour stench attacks my nose, so I slam the drawer before it wins. I won't let it seduce me, too.

From the bathroom across the hall, I hear a noise. A kitten's mew. A balloon, deflating. She's home, after all.

I creep to the door and push it open. She's there, sitting on the lid of the toilet, head resting in her hands.

She doesn't look up, but I know she's heard me.

Our house is old and no one's really given it much love in the last few years. Pretty much all DIY projects around here died right about the same time that our grandma did. Grandma loved this house with her whole heart—loved tinkering with loose doorknobs and stuck windows, creaky doors and slack floorboards. Loved planting gardenias in the front window boxes overlooking our beach, that kind of thing. But not us. Rose and I just sort of wander through this house with our arms tucked to our sides, trying not to break anything. I guess we figure there's enough fixing to do around here without us making it worse.

I take a step toward her. "Rose?"

She sucks in this huge gulping breath that sounds all mucusy, like it's full of snot and sorrow. The kind of thick gasp produced by hours, not minutes, of crying. "Are you okay?"

"It's been a year. A *year*." She looks up at the ceiling, her face smeared with mascara and melting foundation. "What are we going to do?"

It's not me she's asking the question to.

She reaches for a wad of toilet paper, but the roll is empty, so she just paws at the curved cardboard without looking at it. I pull two sheets of tissues from the box on the sink and crouch down next to her. I wipe under her eyes. Dab the tissue over her cheeks.

"You don't get it," she says. "We can't run away from our problems. You think this will fix things. It won't."

"It will. We can change their minds. When I'm on the show we'll prove to all of them that we're not who they think we are." My head falls to my chest. "*What* they think we are."

"It won't matter," Rose says. "Those people. They formed a picture of us in their minds a long time ago. Even before Colleen."

"That's not true. People liked her. Liked *us*. George says—"

"George?" Her head shoots up. "What the hell does he know? He isn't part of this family. I don't give a shit what he says."

I chew my bottom lip. "Mrs. Moutsous was friends with Mom. She loved Mom. And others. I remember." The faces, smiling faces take shape somewhere inside me. I pluck another tissue from the box and hand it to her. She can blow her own damn nose. "We used to go the Pic 'N' Pay with her. Before the Safeway was built, remember? People said hi to us. Gave us balloons and free cookies and everything. When she was good, things around here were good. We could be like that again. We just have to show them."

"You don't remember things right, Magnolia. Even when Mom was okay, she was like this ticking time bomb. People were scared of her. At least, the ones who knew what she was capable of."

I turn away from her.

"You remember those summers that Mom woke up with us early to clam?"

"Of course I do."

"She was turning tricks. She even did it right here in our house, after we got back with our pulls. She did it with all kinds of men. Men in this town. *Married* men. Mr. Springman from the diner. Mr. Gibaldi, too."

"No way. We know their kids. Their wives. They've lived in Summerland forever, just like us."

Rose stares at the ground. "We didn't know them the way she did."

I close my eyes, trying to retrace the lines of Rose's picture, her version of our life, but I can't. My lines are different. The colors are different. Prettier. I'm sure of it. When I open my eyes, I'm staring right into my hand. I hold it up for Rose.

"She took care of us. I burned it once a long time ago, too. Mom kept it cold and hugged me for hours after."

"That's right. I remember that time. I saw you guys in the kitchen. I watched the two of you while I was still in the living room with her friend." Rose shudders. "He got up. Went to sit next to you and Mom."

"See? You saw her holding me. You saw she had friends who liked her. You know she was a good mom." I stare down at my skin, pink and angry. "Everyone else did, too."

Rose grits her teeth. "Is that what you really think?"

"It's what I know."

She grabs my wrist and holds my burnt hand in front of me. Her face gets red, redder than my skin. Her eyes go this kind of blue I've never seen on her before. Dark blue, like the hottest part of a flame. "Do you even remember how you burned your finger that day? Do you even know who that guy was?"

I try to pull my hand back but she doesn't let go. "The toaster oven. I remember its fire. I remember her friend."

Rose flicks my wrist away from her. "You burned it on a fire, all right. The flame from Mom's crack pipe being lit. She was holding that flame, Magnolia. She was holding it, lighting her drugs. You were by her side coloring pictures. You were so damn proud of whatever it was you had drawn. You just wanted to show it to her. You grabbed at her hand, but your fingers got that flame instead. The burn was bad. You screamed so loud."

My breath stops. "No. That's not how it happened. I remember."

"You got it right about her holding you. But later. Too late. And after a couple of minutes, she dropped you straight into his lap and locked herself in her room for the rest of that day, and the night too. I don't know why." Rose squeezes her eyes shut. "Maybe she was high. Or maybe she was sorry. But you should have gone to the hospital to have that burn checked out. But instead, *she* checked out. When we needed her, she left us alone with him."

"I don't remember that."

"Well, I do. We sat outside her door, waiting for her to come out, to make us dinner, to give us a bath. We sang songs through the night while people came and left and came and left. None of them asked if we were okay, even when you wouldn't stop whimpering about your hand. They didn't care. They were like that, too. Lowlifes. Losers. Trash."

"I don't remember."

"Of course you don't. How could you? You were four. I was six. We were babies."

I swallow, hard, trying my best to summon the picture of small Rose and small me, crumpled together, holding on to each other on the outskirts of Mom's life. But I can't. The images just won't form.

"But she came out," I say.

"Yeah, *days* later. In the meantime, we had no milk. We had no anything. I took your hand and we walked to the Pic 'N' Pay. I don't know why. It's not like we had any money. The guy from produce said hi and gave us a balloon. The woman in the bakery asked us how we were doing and gave us cookies. But none of them tried to help us. Because to them, we were an extension of her. To them, we still lived in her gutter."

"You're making that up." My voice cracks.

"I was six. I remember more than you."

"No. You're lying!" I kick the side of the bathtub. It doesn't satisfy me, just sends tingles up my left leg. I need to throw something. Smash something to pieces, the way Rose smashed Mom's picture, my memories.

My gaze crawls from the vase of fake pansies to the vanity and the ceramic soap dish on top. There's just no way it was always like that. Rose is making it all up so that I hate Mom, too. I mean, why would she have stayed here—kept us all here—if they always wanted us gone?

But the truth is, she didn't stay. She didn't.

I'm so pissed. So I know I shouldn't say this, not now, but I'm going to. I've held on to it for too long. "Then why are you doing everything in your power to be like her?"

Rose shifts on the seat. "What?"

"How can you hate her so much when you're doing the same crap that she did?"

Her voice shakes. "I don't know what you're talking about."

"The pipe. And your boss."

"Mags, no. It's not what you think."

"I know what you do with him."

Rose's eyes widen. She leans away from me with this real scared look on her face like I'm a stray dog. Unpredictable. Rabid. How she said they looked at us at the Pic 'N' Pay. "You think I—" She swallows. Breathes deep. Her eyes fill with tears. So much water, and so much shame.

"Don't you dare try to lie to me about this," I say. "I know why we have enough money to pay the phone bill and buy the good brand of cheese. And my dance classes. I know how you get the money to pay for those, too."

"Mags, stop. Listen to me—"

"No. You stop. You listen to me for once. You're the one doing this. Selling yourself. Making them hate us worse, on purpose. Just like she did."

Rose folds herself in half, but I don't stop. Can't stop. "I can't be here with things like this anymore. I'm going to win that money and make us famous so they see we're not like her. I have to do this. You know I do." I squeeze her hand. "It's our only chance."

Rose stands up and splashes water over her blotched face and then dabs it with the guest hand towel—the one adorned with little pineapples across the top. When she's finished, she lets the towel fall to the ground like she did with Mom's shovel.

It lies, crumpled and discarded, on the floor of our unwashed bathroom. I remember the morning it had mysteriously come home with Mom. She thought it was hilarious, that towel. Like the idea of something tropical and almost cheerful in the rainiest, most brooding place in the country was just the right amount of irony for our messed-up household.

Rose turns to me. She's scrubbed her skin, but I can still see the hurt all over her face. "I don't support this. I'm not going to help you change what is. What can't be changed. Don't you see that? It doesn't matter what they say. It only matters what we know."

"It matters!" I shout. "We're the ones who have to live here!"

"We don't have to let what they say to us define who we are." She shakes her head. "I'm not driving you and George to Portland. Case closed. And once Mrs. Moutsous finds out why you two want to go there, she'll put an end to it, too."

I look at her. She's wearing that *my way or the highway* attitude of hers. It dawns on me that she and George, the two people that I love and trust most in this world, are cut from the same stubborn cloth.

Rose rubs her arms. "What are you going to do if your plan doesn't work? What are you going to do if you lose, screw up on TV, and the town ends up blaming us even more than they already do? Or worse. What are you going to do if she sees you on TV and wants to come back here?"

I lower my head. "She's still our mom. If I had the money maybe we could actually help her this time."

Rose's eyes go wide. "You're nuts. Don't do this. Don't allow her to do this to you." She puts her back to me and pushes open the bathroom door. And that's when I know. She doesn't want Mom back. She doesn't care about where Mom's sleeping or what Mom's eating or who it is that's eating or sleeping next to her. She glances over her shoulder at me, her voice measured and says, "Leave it alone, Mags. If you know what's good for us, you'd better just leave this show thing done and dead. Just like her."

FIVE

It's six fifteen and I know I should be out there with her.

Instead, I'm curled up on my windowsill, eyes straining to see her through the wispy beach shadows cast by the early morning light. I zero in on her about ten feet from the water. She makes this perfect little figure eight stomping around the sand, then drops to her knees. She hurls the gun into the sand. I think I'm going to hurl into my lap.

Rose is so gung ho about clamming, like none of it ever happened. Like one summer off was enough to heal our wounds and now it's business as usual. Mom's gone, so she can finally get on with her life. Or maybe it's that darn gun. Maybe she's just so glad to have a new way to move forward, an untainted way to carry on with a timeless Woodson tradition.

But it's still clamming. It's still *our* clamming—mine and hers and Mom's—no matter what means you use to get the job done. It's still the memory of the three of us doing it that makes me positive things really can be okay again like they used to.

Rose pulls up the gun and shakes it a few times. Mud piles out. She sifts. Steady. Methodical. I can't tell from here how many clams she's scored, but I'm sure there are at least two whoppers. She's good at this even in the worst conditions, but today the sea is flat and calm and the beach looks ripe for razors.

I can't watch this for another second, so I hop off my windowsill and change my clothes from my ratty PJs to my comfiest jeans and tank. I throw one of George's old school sweatshirts on and weave my hair into a loose braid in front of me. I grab my beanie and then reach for my dance bag from the corner of my room where I usually leave it. But it's not there.

Then I remember: it's in the kitchen where I left it before I found Rose's pipe and heard Rose's sad noises coming from the bathroom. Before her yelling and my yelling because our memories look nothing like each other's memories at all. Before the mess that is my life got even messier.

I bring my bag to my room and stuff it with my black leotard, a clean pair of tights, and my wallet, equipped with the last thirty bucks I've got in the whole world. Then I rummage around in my sock drawer for the photo with the broken frame, its glass now discarded and forgotten and gone. I haven't looked at this thing in months but now I can't stop. My index finger traces every line.

George's mom took this picture of us, outside the Pic 'N' Pay, the morning I started middle school. Mom had forgotten to get school supplies like I had asked her to a dozen times that summer, but it was okay because once she remembered, Mom was so happy and excited for my big day. She even bought me a new pack of multicolored three-ring binders and a new first-day outfit too, both of which were way out of budget. Mrs. M. said how pretty I looked, right before she snapped the photo. She said how pretty we *both* looked. Mrs. M.'s eyes were all misty but at the time, I didn't really know why.

Now, Mom's still face stares back at me. She's wearing lipstick and smiling but there's other stuff about this photo that makes it unforgettable, stuff that Mrs. Moutsous didn't notice or maybe didn't want to say out loud. Mom's hair is washed. Her face looks like it's got some weight on it. Not much, but enough. Enough that she looks like a real person. Enough that she looks the way a mom should look.

I fold the photo in half and shove it into the clear sleeve of my wallet. I place my toothbrush, hairbrush, a tube of hair glue, two spare T-shirts, a pair of jeans, and a handful of bobby pins into the front zip of my bag. It's not much for a six-week competition, I know, but it's almost too much when you consider the fact that I'm not even on the show. Yet.

I check my bedroom clock: 6:36 a.m. I've got about twenty minutes before Summerland wakes up and that means twenty minutes to bust out of here without bumping into a gazillion people that I've known since I was, like, five, all wanting to know where I'm going, what I'm doing, what trouble I'm possibly causing now.

I glance out the window one last time. The sight of Rose and that gun make my chest all tight and achy.

I hate that Rose blames Mom for what's happened, when *they're* the ones who made Mom relapse again and again and again. I hate that Rose doesn't care anymore what they think, doesn't believe that what I'm going to do will be big enough to change them. Change all of this.

I watch her busy frame as she scoots fifteen feet to her left, makes suction, and then sifts through another mess of mud and sand, gloves off. Her hand must be numb, bitten by the teeth of the Pacific. At this rate, she's going to pull her whole quota before most people even get out there, but that's probably her plan.

I tear my gaze from the window. My right hand slips under my bed and rustles around for my piece of pillowcase. I find it and secure it under my bra strap where it'll stay as long as I'm sporting this hoodie to hide it.

I sling my bag over my shoulder and bolt out the back door—the one that faces *away* from the beach. Rose can't see me from here, and God knows that's for the best.

For both of us.

I hate cycling in the morning, even in July.

The chilly wind whips my neck and nips at my cheeks, turning them this raw shade of pink, which stings like crazy. But this is the quickest way for me to get from A to B around here, and like I said, I don't have much time.

My feet pedal fast—past the Pic 'N' Pay, past Xanadu Mini Golf, past the Taco Stop. Past Miller's darn bakery with those awful cakes that people pay ludicrous amounts of cash for, unlike Mrs. Moutsous's cakes, which are good—no, great—and not just because they're fondant-free.

Every now and then my flip-flops catch themselves on the pedals, but I keep going full tilt until I see Deelish. I round the corner and hop off before my bike is completely stopped. It's how I always do it, how I've always done it. How all of us Summerland kids have always done it.

My hands dig into my pocket for the set of keys Mrs. M. had made for me. Underneath them, I feel the smooth paper of the note I wrote last night after my fight with Rose. The one that says, "I'm sorry, Mrs. Moutsous, I won't be at work today, or tomorrow, and maybe not on Wednesday, either. I'm sorry and I understand that you can't save my job for me for when I get back. I'm sorry." At the bottom of the page, I've signed it Magnolia Grace Woodson. Not that she won't know who I am. Mrs. Moutsous knows my handwriting. After all, she's the one who helped me learn how to do it in the first place.

"Magnolia?"

I spin around.

Mark's there on his own bike, strong arms bent over his handlebars. "What are you doing here?" he says, like I have no business being here at all.

"Um. I work here."

He smiles. "Yeah, I know. I meant, what are you doing here at this hour? Deelish doesn't open this early, does it?"

"No, not until ten." I search my brain for something else to say. Something smart and normal. Something that will allow him to pedal his ass out of here and tell no one about what, or whom, he saw. "I forgot to lock the cash register last night. Just making sure everything's where it's supposed to be."

"But the door's locked, right?"

"What?"

He points to the key I'm holding, already inserted into the hole. "The door. If it's still locked, you should be all good, right?"

"Let's hope so."

He waits, kind of staring at my shaky hand while I wiggle the key, hold the knob, turn it, and push open the door. I scoot to the register and pop open the drawer and, sure enough, it's still full of cash. I laugh nervously. "Guess I worried for nothing."

"Better to be safe than sorry." He walks his bike inside and then glances behind him and then back at me, I guess, to see if anyone's noticed him come in here with me. If they did, I don't know what kind of shit they'll give him later. Mark and I are friends but we haven't been close in a while. Not since we started senior year and definitely not since Colleen. Most of his friends these days are dance friends and cool-kid friends, and though I still dance, I'm not either of those things. The last memory I have of the two of us together and alone is the day with our bungled schedules and our butts behind that bush. But he always makes the time to talk to me whenever we find ourselves in the same space. I know he was only trying to help on the beach yesterday. I don't know how to say thank you and I don't know if thank you is what he's looking for here.

He holds up the bag in his right hand and smiles, his top teeth so perfectly crooked they remind me of the cliffs, the rocks, the smooth edges from the waves lapping against them.

"I should get home," he says. "My mom can't see straight in the morning without her coffee. Good thing the Pic 'N' Pay opens early."

"I'll see you at dance?"

"Definitely," he says. "I wouldn't miss it."

I come toward him, ready to shut the door. But he hops off his bike and leans it against Deelish's window. "I heard you're trying out for *Live to Dance*. I mean, like, for real you are. Not just saying you are like everyone else."

"Maybe. I think so." I fiddle with a loose piece of hair that's dropped from my beanie. "You're not trying out?"

"Nah. I'm not really into the whole competing thing. It's like, if you're lucky enough to dance, you've already won." He laughs, like it comes so easily for him. He's not like George, all peppy and cheery all the time, but he's got a great smile. "Pretty cheesy, right?"

I get what he's saying. About dance being more a way of life, a state of soul, rather than this thing to prove. But I also know that it's *him* that doesn't get it. Of course he feels that way. He's got nothing to prove, has always been a winner in this town for as long as I can remember. He might not be all fire and show the way George is, but he's really not that different.

"I just wanted to say good luck." He shuffles his feet, curling his toes against his flip-flops. "I think you've got a really good shot at making it. You're a harder worker than anyone I know."

My breath catches in surprise.

"Maybe I could come down there with you," Mark says. He lifts his head a little and his eyes meet mine. "You know. Cheer you on."

It's a nice thought, but it's no secret that he and George don't exactly get along. Anyway, I know he's only saying it to be nice.

"Nah, it's okay. George is going with me. And I doubt it's worth missing class for." I laugh. "We'll probably be back before anyone even notices we're gone. Anyway, Katina would kill you if you ditched out, too."

Mark's gaze falls to his pedals again. He tells me good luck again, backs his way out of the shop, swivels his bike around, and starts pedaling without ever looking back.

I shut and lock the door behind me and wait another second until I'm sure he's gone, until I'm sure that he's halfway up the cliffs right now, toward his side of town. The lucky side.

I grab the note from my pocket and smooth it out with both hands and set it on the counter where I know Mrs. M. will see it, next to the cash register and photo of her, George, Mr. Moutsous, and George's brother, Malcolm, smooshed together in front of their floor-to-ceiling fireplace. I bet that somewhere in Mark's house there's a framed photo just like it, with his mom and dad and sister looking happy and loved, too. I close my eyes and try to remember the last time I went to the McDonald residence. I'm almost positive I can see it. Giant and framed and hanging in their foyer, where no one would ever miss it.

I back my bike out of the shop, turning it toward the cliffs too, rising on the right pedal and pushing it down, hard. The way up is slow going and I study the short row of million-dollar homes that line each side. I swallow, and then again. Note dropped at Deelish, check. The one "t" I needed to cross before I could leave for the competition. Now all I've got left is to dot the final "i."

I can do this. No matter what Rose says, I can do this, for her and me and for Mom who'd never come back to this place unless it wasn't like this anymore. Like Mark says, I can do this for real. My feet push faster, faster, around corners, past

shops, past houses that I've known and pedaled past for fourteen years, more. I don't stop. If I'm going to try out and be
on TV and put myself out there for all the world to see, there's
still one person I need to see me first.

Six

It's not like I've never been here before.

To these streets, lined with pretty mailboxes and pretty lawns, pretty iron gates leading up to each and every more-than-pretty house that makes up the cliffs neighborhood. I know people that live here. Like George, and George's family, and Mark and Abby and Quinn, and other people besides Mayor Chamberlain. So it's not like I have no business being here.

Still, I feel all weird and wobbly as my thighs push my bike through the uphill burn, passing house after house, each one equaling about ten of my houses in size. I know which one is his. Everyone knows which one is his. The one with the tallest hedges. The one with the biggest roses. The one with the thickest gate.

I round the corner of his street and squeeze my handlebars even tighter, my knuckles whitening. I thought I could do this. I thought I could just rock on up here and tell him we didn't know and tell him we would have stopped it if we could have. Now, looking up at his sad house with no lights on inside and no people around outside, I doubt he'll even answer. I don't know what I'll say if he answers.

I hop off my bike, just kind of staring through the climbing vines that snake the gate and beyond. My finger hovers over his doorbell, not touching it—an invisible force field between him and me. A chill whips through my chest and then out again. I can't press it. I mean, if he answers, what would I say to him? *Good morning, Mayor Chamberlain, welcome back to town, I'm sorry my sister and I let our mother kill your daughter?* It sounded good in my head on the way over. Now it sounds like the saddest sentence one stranger could ever say to another. Not to mention, halfway through something like that, he'd probably kick my butt out of here faster than you can say Summerland.

I stare through the bars, the thick foliage. It's too dense to see anything. I creep around the side of the house and shimmy halfway up the gate, peering over the stacked hedge and into their sprawling yard. There's patio furniture there, a croquet set that looks like it hasn't been used in ages, and a pool that's still covered, even though summer in Summerland never gets warmer than this. I know George said the mayor has been back a whole week, but it looks to me like he still isn't back. Maybe he never will be.

The chill threads through me again. This time, it's like a shadow. A spirit. Telling me what I should have known long before I came here: that I can't disturb him or his wife or his other, younger daughter, Annie, who's going to be a freshman this year at my old school. How I can't intrude on their perfect life anymore than I already have.

Behind me, the quick whoop of a siren sounds.

My fingers release the gate and I fall back, landing on the soft bed of bushes, flattening a rose with my butt. I hop to the ground, turning my ankle in the process.

The cop leans out his window. "Hey. What's your business here?"

"I—nothing. I just wanted to say hello." I stand up. Brush myself off, hobble toward him, vaguely aware of my pants, dirtied, from my fall.

The cop squints at me. "You're the younger Woodson girl, aren't you?"

I nod. Swallow. Glance back at Mayor Chamberlain's house. Down to my pants. Back to the cop. *I swear to God, it's not what it looks like.*

But he thinks it is. "Haven't you taken enough from them?"

"I wanted to tell him how sorry I was."

"By trespassing on his property? Like hell you were."

"I didn't mean to trespass. I just thought—"

"We know what you thought. That your actions have no consequences. Isn't that right?"

I stumble back to my bike, leaning against the mayor's gate. I pull it toward me. Even my bike knows it has no business touching anything of his.

The cop watches me fumble around. He runs one hand over his balding head, like it has hair. "Come over here."

I rest my bike against the sidewalk and take five small steps closer to his dusty black and blue car. I raise my head. He's no different than any other cop in town, but there's something about him. His eyebrows rise, daring me to come closer. My heart thuds, banging out a warning inside my chest. I know I shouldn't get closer, but I do.

Something in his face is familiar. A scar—triangle-shaped—just above his lip, on the right. I've seen him before, coming out of Mom's room while I lay flat and still, under my covers, disappearing, unexisting. That's what I usually did when I heard them getting ready to go. That's what I did to make sure they forgot all about stopping in my room to chat, like they sometimes did. What else could I do? *Hold your breath. Hold it till they're gone.*

"Magnolia, isn't it?" His lip curls, beckoning me.

"Yes, sir."

"Your sister is Rose?"

"Yeah."

"Your mom was Patricia, wasn't she?"

"Is."

"What?"

"*Is* Patricia."

The cop picks at the corner of his left nostril. Smiles, revealing wide spaces and yellowed teeth. Canary yellow. Corn yellow. Piss yellow. I don't remember those teeth. But it was a long time ago. Things change. People change.

"You're a real fireball. I remember that about you." His tongue runs across his teeth. My stomach turns. "You know," he says. "I could write you up for trespassing. Or for intention to break and enter. Or for mischief."

I close my eyes. If I challenge him now, blow up on his ass or blow on out of here, he's going to write me up. And if he writes me up, my chance to be on the show is over. Fact is, someone with trespassing or mischief on her record isn't the type to go anywhere in life, let alone on TV.

"But," he says. "This time I won't. I'd rather not bother his family anymore than I have to." His gaze travels down my face, my chin, my neck. Further. "But we've got ourselves a problem here, don't we?"

I nod my head, slowly. So slow.

"Maybe we could think of another way to solve things privately." His head motions me closer still. I inhale, lean toward him. I'm wearing George's sweatshirt, but it's big and it leans off me, revealing my bare shoulder. I don't pull it back up. His smile widens, stretching across his face so that all I can see are those teeth, those spaces. He leans across his car. Opens the passenger side and pats the empty seat next to him.

I walk around his car. I don't know what I'm doing. But if it gets out that I was at the mayor's house, doing God-knows-what, Rose and I will be ruined.

I pull my stomach muscles in tight and lower myself inside his car. Shut the door. Hold my breath while his eyes hold on to my skin.

He rests his hand on top my thigh, two inches from the last place on earth I want it.

A smack on my window scares me, makes me jump. Next to me, the cop jumps too. It's George, on his bike, hand pressed to my window. My heart beats so fast when, a second ago, it wasn't beating at all.

"What are you doing in there?" He shouts it through the closed window. The cop presses a button on his console to roll it down. George looks across me, to him, venom in his eyes. "Is she under arrest?"

The cop shrugs. "Not yet."

"Get out of the car," George says to me.

I don't know what to do. He's a *cop*. My whole body is shaking, yet frozen.

"Get out of the car," George says again, this time louder. I open the door. George pulls me out, pulls me into his chest.

Wrapped in the safety of his arms, my breathing slows. I whisper into his hoodie, "How did you know I was here?"

"I was worried about you. You didn't return my calls last night. You weren't on the beach with Rose this morning. I went to your house, then Deelish. I found your note." He breathes into my hat, my hair. His voice is soft. "I was on my way home when I saw you in there. With him."

The cop leans out his window. "She was trespassing. I should write you both up for being here."

I feel George's body tense. See his face twist into something I've never seen on him, even when Mark "stole" his part as Peter Pan in Katina's end-of-year production three years ago. That was mad. This is something else entirely. "I live in this neighborhood," George says. "She was here visiting me. I should report *you* for sexual harassment."

The cop scoffs. "Right. In her dreams."

George rests his elbow on the cop's open window. I see him smile. See him lean into the cop like he's not at all scared the way I was. The way I am. "That's where you're wrong," George says. "If you ever go near my friend again, it'll be your worst nightmare."

SEVEN

The cop turns on his red light and speeds down the hill into town, fake rushing to a fake call. The second he's out of sight, George says, "How could you?" He throws one leg over his bike and pushes down on his pedal.

I grab my bike off the road and do the same. "I don't want to talk about it."

"You're going to talk about it." He rides next to me, his tires inches from mine, like he always does. Except that now it's like there's this wall between us, separating us, keeping me from him, or vice versa. "I know what you were going to do back there," he says.

Shame isn't a pretty color on anyone, and I'm no exception. I turn away so he can't see the heat creeping up my neck. I pull ahead of him, studying the salt-washed beach shacks that line the street on either side of us. "He was going to ruin everything."

George slams on his breaks. "What about the show? *You* would have ruined everything if you—"

"I wouldn't have."

"You got in his car."

"He was a *cop*."

George sighs. "Cops can be assholes too, you know. You think your reputation is bad now? If they found out, they'd eat you alive. And just so you know, doing what you almost did is the fastest way to actually become your mother."

His words stab my insides, hard, but I'm the one who handed him the knife. I rub my forearms with my one free hand, suddenly cold.

George is right. I hate that he's right. I'm not her, but I could have been. My mind wanders to Rose and her boss. Things have been so bad around our house for so long now. The power gets shut off and the water gets shut off and sometimes both are shut off at the same time. But lately it's been better. We've had a bit of money for extras, new tights when mine have too many holes, new buckets when ours crack so bad they won't hold the clams. These little things. It's made it all bearable. Rose has never really admitted it, but she's made it clear that what she does isn't wrong. What she does is just surviving. Isn't it the same as what I almost did?

"Look, can we just drop it?"

He does, but at the stop sign, he glances back at me. I can see my reflection bouncing off his pupils, staring back at me, judging me. But I don't blame him. He lives in Summerland too, after all. He can't help himself.

I push off hard to stay in line with him. Swerve my bike, so my tire's almost hitting his in this in-and-out motion. He hates it when I do it. But, like, love-hates it. Finally he breaks, and laughs. The sound of it is like music, moving through my ears.

"By the way," I say. "That note was for your mom, not you."

"You're not quitting the shop. There's no way I'm letting that poor excuse for an apology reach her." He shrugs. "And anyway, she supports us going to the competition. Quinn's going to fill in at Deelish until we get back. She was psyched to have all the hours. I told you I'd take care of everything."

"You gave her all my shifts for the next six weeks? You don't even know if we'll make it past tryouts." My foot slips from my pedal, causing my bike to waver.

George grabs my handlebar to steady me. He's looking at me so hard. It's not the way I want him looking at me at all. "What were you doing in the cliffs?"

"I just wanted to talk to him. I told you that."

"It wouldn't have changed anything. You have to know that."

"It was your idea."

George throws his hands in the air. "I never told you to go there alone! It's a stupid idea!"

"I meant the show. Proving it to the whole town, the whole world. Showing everyone that being a Woodson isn't what they think. I just—" I close my eyes, let them stay that way for three seconds until I feel my bike swerve. "I shouldn't have gone there. You're right. Okay?"

George rests his feet on the middle bar of his bike, his toes—tanned and peppered by soft blond hairs—level with his chest. "People think what they want to think. Sooner or later, you just have to stop caring."

He lets go of my bike and pushes down on his pedals, so I do, too. I wish I could live like that. Unbothered by what they thought of me, of me and Rose. But I can't. Getting on the show is the only way to change things for us. The only way to prove to them who we really are. Not whores. Not murderers. Not like her. No, never like her.

Outside George's house, we ditch our bikes next to the shed. George ducks behind it and grabs the backpack he's stashed there. I clop up his front steps two at a time.

"What are you doing?" he says.

"Going in. I want to see your mom."

"No way. If we go in there now, she'll never let us go."

"You said she was on board with us going."

George stammers, "She is. Or she will be. But we've got to get down there. My mom will only slow us down."

I narrow my eyes at him. "Why am I getting the feeling you haven't told her we're going yet?"

"I did tell her. Sort of." He shifts from one foot to the other. "I almost told her."

"George? Magnolia? Is that you?" Mrs. Moutsous's voice floats out the upstairs window.

"Shit!" George whispers. "She knows we're here." He grabs my hand and pulls me down the steps and around the back of the shed. "Run!" he yells and doesn't let go of my hand until we're halfway across town.

I slog up the steps of the overpass bridge after George, our feet making loud clanking noises under the metal walkway. I'm out of breath and steaming. George pulls a stick across the bars, which magnifies the noise by a million. It's like he doesn't even feel the magnitude of what we've just done.

"You never told her we were going. You lied to me. You lied to us both."

"Get over it already. You're acting like we just committed murder or something."

"Exactly. What do you think will happen when you don't come home tonight? Your mom will murder both our asses."

"She'll be fine." George shrugs. "She always is."

I place one hand over my stomach and groan. "I think I'm going to throw up all over those cars below us."

George hands me a stick of gum. "Chew up. You don't want ralph breath for tryouts." He bounces up and down on his toes. "I can't believe we're actually going to meet Camilla Sky. Like, in person. I wonder if she's really as tall. I mean, how can one person be that tall, toned, tanned, and hot?" He turns to me. "You should only get one of those things in life. Don't you think?"

Hot. There's that word again.

My brain flashes to the sultry Australian host of *Live to Dance*. Hot? Yeah, well, pretty much everyone on the planet thinks she's hot. I guess I just never knew that George did, too. Glamorous? Maybe. Stylish? That goes without saying. But hot? This is definitely something new.

I press my palms against the sides of my head. "Your mom's never gonna forgive me for leaving without telling her."

"You know she will. Rose will too. Eventually."

Shit shit shit shit. The fact that George and I are *both* total assholes for lying to our loved ones comes flooding back to my brain, like a tsunami. A tsunami made of lies.

"If we make it on the show, no one will even care about the little white lies we told." He looks at me with shimmery eyes. "We're going to be famous. In six short weeks." He grabs my arm. "If we win, I bet we'll get movie offers and everything, don't you think?"

I flick his hand away and rest my hand on my collarbone, feeling for the place where my pillowcase piece is still tucked under by bra. "This isn't about being on TV. Not for me, it's not. You know that."

He waves me away. "Well, I want to see my face on that screen." He runs his fingers along the handrail of the over-pass like he's playing a piano. "I want to see what I look like as George Moutsous, superstar, not George Moutsous—"

"Summerland heartthrob that every single person in town loves? Yeah, I can see why you'd want to shake that."

George's face clouds. "I'm going to win. I'm going to win it all and then never look back at this place."

I blink twice, letting the magnitude of my best friend's words sink in.

Win the show. Win. It's the first time I've really thought about the fact that I need to actually *win* for my plan to work. Runner-up won't work. Nothing will work if I get kicked off during tryouts. And if I lose . . . fact is, if I lose I'm still nothing more than a loser.

"They'll change their minds," George says, wrapping one arm around my waist. I don't know how he does it, but some-how, he always knows when my thoughts are going down that very dark road. "They'll see how awesome you are. Plus they're going to announce our hometowns like a million times on TV. Everyone around here will treat you like a goddamn hero. You and Rosie both. All of us."

"We should have told Katina about it."

"She'll hear about it anyway. Everyone will."

"She should have heard about it from us. You know she'd want us there." I think of Mark and his offer to come with us. Even if it was just small talk, it was still pretty sweet of him. "Maybe Katina would have come with us to cheer us on. And your mom would have been so proud. Even if we don't make it on the show, they'd at least be happy we tried."

"We *will* make it on the show," George says again. But this time, he's not smiling. "And yeah, Mom would have been proud all right. So proud, she would have blabbed about it all over town. Hell, it probably would have made the *Summerland Sun*." He cocks his head. "Is that really what you wanted?"

He's right. I hate it when he's right, which is more often than I'd like to admit. If news got out, it'd be over for me before I even started.

I let George pull me to the side of the highway, Route 26, which goes all the way to Portland and away from Summerland. It's about eighty miles to the city from here—eighty miles and a world away from clamming, Katina's studio, Deelish, my life. I've been to Portland before with Rose and George and Mrs. Moutsous for errands and shopping and fish and chips at the wharf. And once she even took us to see the Oregon Ballet's rendition of *Giselle*, which was so awesome that I held my breath from the second the curtain went up to the second it fell back on the stage, because no matter how good Katina's studio is, it'll never be that. Portland's not that far in distance, but it's practically another planet.

Once we're on the highway, three cars zoom past us. I keep my head low, careful not to make eye contact with any of the drivers in case one's a Summerland local. But almost no one from town goes into Portland these days. Not since we got a full-sized Safeway and Home Depot just outside of town.

Two more cars pass, but no one seems to notice us. "So now what? We're just going to wait here for someone to give us a lift?"

"I thought about borrowing Mom's car. It probably would have been easier."

"It definitely would have been easier."

"But less of an adventure." He stares down at the road like it's the road to salvation. "Nope. The only way we're going to get this done is to put a little elbow grease into it. You think the universe is gonna hand us our dreams on a silver platter?" He grins, his smile taking up most of the space on his face. "We've got to take steps to make that happen."

At first I think he means steps, like in a figurative way. Hoops we have to jump through to make our dreams come true. But when George *actually* steps onto the road, stretches his arm out, and extends his thumb, I burst out laughing. "There aren't even any cars coming!"

George waves his thumb at me. "But there will be. And when they come, you and I will be ready."

"When they come? Seriously? You're quoting *Field of Dreams?*"

"You got it, babe. I'm your Kevin Costner. This is our field of dreams. If we get a ride now, we'll make it there by noon."

As soon as the words leave his lips, three cars round the corner and speed their way toward us. I know I shouldn't be surprised, because George does stuff like this—makes stuff like this happen—all the time, but I still am.

The last vehicle of the three, a rusty old pickup, idles up to George and me. I try to peer into the truck at the driver but his front windows are tinted and really dirty. George saunters over to the truck's cab, leaving me standing on the edge of the road. Although neither of us have done this before, George leans into the truck and says something to the driver that I can't even hear. He's so calm, casual. It's like he's been doing it all his life.

"Where you two headed?"

I hear a woman's voice. Although this little fact should theoretically make me feel better, it doesn't. At least, not much. She's still a stranger. A stranger with smoky-sounding lungs. A stranger with smoky lungs, driving a really unsafe-looking vehicle. I take two steps back toward the safety of the ditch, hoping it hides me away.

"Portland. You got room for two of us in there?" He points toward me. "We're a package deal."

The woman chuckles, which sounds more like a truck wheezing—*her* truck wheezing—than a laugh. "I kind of figured that by the way you two were standing, glued together. Not like I'm gonna leave your friend out here. No telling what could happen to a sweet little thing like her." She strains to look at me, still edging backward toward that damn ditch.

Even though I'm pretty sure she's not at all joking, George laughs, and the woman laughs, which pisses me off, because I know they're both laughing at me. *Sweet little thing.* She doesn't even know me.

"Climb on in," the woman says.

George jogs back toward me.

"I'm not getting in with her."

He glances back over his shoulder at the driver. "She seems okay. Anyway, you can't back out now. This is our chance."

"You don't even know if she's got a gun in there."

George folds his arms across his white polo shirt. "You sat in a car with Officer Awful, but you're scared of her? He had a gun, you know."

"He was a cop. He has to carry a gun."

"Some cop."

"That was in the cliffs. This is the *highway*. This is no-man's-land. This is—"

"Hey, girlie," the driver calls. "I ain't got all day for you to mull it over. You in or what?"

I gulp, my mind stuck on the image of that cop. His miserable car and his miserable words. His mouth, moving, forming sounds about me being exactly what everyone thinks I am.

I scan the highway. There aren't any other cars in sight, but there will be. If anyone sees me here, alongside the highway alone, I know what they'll think. Mom and her johns. Most of the time, she found takers right here in Summerland. But when Season ended and the tourists packed their shovels and pails to reclaim city life, Mom had no choice but to take her business to Portland, too.

A car zooms by with a couple of kids around Rose's age inside. I'm pretty sure they're locals, and if they are, Rose will hear about my being here before another car—safer, cleaner, driven by someone who doesn't look like this—will come along to pick us up. I nod to George and let him take my hand and let him lead me to the passenger side of the pickup. He opens the door and motions for me to slide on in, next to the woman.

Up close, she's even dirtier than she looked from afar, but it doesn't matter. She starts the ignition, and I do up my belt

and then slide down in the seat so no one will see me in here,
so no one will see me leaving.

EIGHT

I wish I could say that we ride in this comfortable silence that's both peaceful and thought provoking, but we don't. So I can't. My head feels like it might ignite from the endless stream of pointless noise emitting from this woman. It's outrageous.

While occasionally checking the road to make sure she's still on it, the woman blabbers on about her truck needing a new transmission, the fact that we've had one of the rainiest summers in Oregon history, and about the president's new plan for whatever, which is apparently not working.

I zone out.

G makes a few obligatory uh-huhs and oh yeahs, but I don't bother. I close my eyes and pretend to sleep. My eyelids get heavy and for a second I think I might actually drop off, but when the woman elbows me in the ribs, I wake up and fast.

"Here," she says. "You want these?"

I stare down at her calloused open palm. Resting there is a roll of butterscotch Life Savers. I stare at the familiar caramel wrapper, already torn open. "Where did you get these?"

The woman shrugs. "The general store in Astoria. I meant to get the butter rum ones. Guess my old eyes aren't as good as they used to be. You like 'em?"

"Yeah. Almost no one carries them anymore. I don't even remember the last time I had one."

I stare down at her hand, the roll in her palm. I just told her a total freaking lie. I know the *exact* date of the last time I had butterscotch Life Savers. Two Christmases ago.

There it was. The gigantic box wrapped up in sparkly red paper with a delicate gold bow, leaning against the wall in the living room next to the elephant palm that nobody ever watered. That's where I found it on Christmas morning. I rushed over to it and unwrapped that box, only to find another smaller box inside. So I tore the paper off that one, and again there was a smaller box inside of it. And then another, and then another, until finally I came to a last tiny box, and in it, the Life Savers. I remember staring down at the mess of glittery paper sitting at my feet and thinking that the wrap job must have been expensive. Way more expensive than the actual candy. But like I said, not many stores sold butterscotch Life Savers anymore, so this present was special. Mom worked hard to get me something I'd really love.

Funnily enough, Mrs. Moutsous gave me a roll of butterscotch Life Savers too that year. But not in a million boxes all made out to look like something bigger than it was. Mrs. M. just nestled them between the other little presents in my stocking, which I always opened at her house, with her family, like it was no big deal at all.

"Well, they're yours." The woman smiles big, exposing the two or three gaps in her mouth where teeth should be. "Hell of a lot better than finding them under my seat a month from now."

I take the roll, lift the top off the wax paper, and pop one in my mouth. They taste so good. Smooth and buttery. Just the right amount of chewy versus crunchiness. Familiar. Perfect.

I glance at the woman, watching me with this satisfied look on her face. "So where you going, anyway?" I ask. "Home to see your kids?"

"I'm on my way home all right," she says. "But no kids. Just me and my truck these days." She taps her dashboard, kind of loudly. I think it's going to rouse George, but he just grumbles and repositions his head against the window.

She sticks the corner of her thumb in her mouth and begins working a hangnail out of her dirty hand. "I live outside of Portland, but I need to drop off some new condo plans in the city, so you kids lucked out."

I pop a third Life Saver into my mouth. Then I stare out George's window. The sky is darker than it was ten minutes ago, which means the daily drizzle is going to start—and not stop—soon. I smooth my hair, so very thankful that I remembered my hairbrush. Coastal weather has the potential to frizz my locks in mere minutes, which I don't want to happen today, and especially not on national television. If I even make it that far.

The woman abandons her thumb and fiddles with the FM dial on her radio. She passes two country stations and one gospel but doesn't stop turning until the dial rests on some pretty hard-core hip-hop station. The artist hollers about lovin' "the big booty tang." I cover my mouth with my hand.

She chuckles. "I know. I never thought I'd get into this stuff, either, but after fifteen years on the road with limited options, I gotta admit, now I kind of like it." The woman taps her steering wheel in time to the music. "What did you say your name was?"

"I didn't. It's Magnolia."

"Like the flower." She shakes her head. "Don't grow in this kind of weather, do they?"

"No. I guess they don't. Roses like rain though. I have a sister. Her name's Rose." I rub my forehead. "At least I think they do. My mom told me that once. I'm not sure if it's true."

"Magnolia and Rose. Two flowers. Boy, your momma must have really liked growing pretty things."

"She used to say that there must be something magic about flowers, the way they make everybody feel better about stuff."

"What do you mean?"

I glance at George. His eyes are still shut tight, sleeping like he's snuggled in his own bed, not in some rap-blasting pickup. It's full-on pouring out now. Thankfully, it mutes the sound of the music and our words. "You know. Like, if someone dies, you send flowers. If they're sick, you bring flowers to the hospital. New baby? Flowers. Birthdays? Flowers. I guess maybe she was hoping that if her daughters were flowers that we would fix things for her, too."

"That's some deep stuff, kid. All I know is that if God had it in his plan to give me a daughter, I'd never let *my* flower girl hitchhike out here on this highway. Like I said, no telling what could happen."

I shift in my seat, thinking about this woman's words about God and his so-called plan. I never really think about God—don't even know if I believe in one or not. But I remember what I overheard George's mom say once after one of Mom's earlier disappearances. Rose was still in school back then and neither of us had jobs other than paper routes and the occasional ice cream delivery from Mrs. Moutsous. We hadn't eaten in over twenty-four hours and Rose got worried and called Mrs. M. She came right over with bags and bags of groceries. Shooed us out to the beach while she stocked our fridge, but we knew she was crying anyway.

"Thank goodness we have your mom." That's what Rose said to George as we plodded down our steps. And that's when I heard Mrs. M. say it, even though she didn't know we could hear her and didn't know, I guess, that I'd think of those words every time anyone ever mentioned God again. That if there was a God, he'd given up when he came to my family.

The woman rifles around by her feet for a box of tissues. "So what's in Portland for you two, anyway? You got somewhere to stay when you get there?"

I pop Life Saver number four in my mouth and shake my head. "We're not really staying. There's this dance show thing. We're on our way to try out. It's no big deal."

The woman turns the music down just as the singer belts out something about bitches and hos and gin and juice.

"Your momma must be so proud. Hey, how come she didn't drive you kids to Portland herself? She have to work or something?"

"Or something."

She nods her head, just as George opens both his eyes, catching the tail end of our little chat. He gives me a weary little smile, like he feels bad for leaving me alone with this stranger when it was his idea to ride with her in the first place. I smile back. I'm fine. She's not so bad.

The woman leans over and whistles. "Well, look at you. Damn. Just when I thought a face couldn't get any prettier, you went and got yourself some beauty rest. Would you look at those lips? Honey, are you wearing lipstick or are your lips really that pretty?"

"No." George grins. "It's all me."

"Good for you, son." She winks. "Gotta look your best for those TV cameras, right, honey?"

George rubs the sleep out of his eyes and grins at the woman. I turn my head toward the window. I mean, why does George have to do that all the time? Although, it's kind of nice to know that he's a whore for all compliments, even ones from friendly strangers and not just ones from freshman brats and girls named Mary.

George points to a sign on the side of the highway. "Hey, we're almost in Portland. Do you know how to get to the Heritage Building? I think I wrote down the directions here somewhere." George leans down to grab his backpack, but the woman waves a hand at him.

"You bet I do. Used to drive truck for the Dairy Queen all over the place. So there ain't a lick of this state that I don't know." Without signaling, the woman takes the next exit off the highway.

Within fifteen minutes and two remaining Life Savers, we're in front of the Heritage Building. She drives up slowly. My heart starts beating really fast. Next to me, George and the woman's mouths are gaping.

Already lined up, there're at least three hundred people, long and lean and gorgeous, all around my and George's age. Some are stretching, some are tumbling down the grassy area next to the spots in line. Some of the larger groups have signs pitched around them, showing their home states' names. And there are cameras everywhere. Tall ones and short ones and ones on wheels and ones on the shoulders of official-looking people who jog up and down the line, filming faces and feet. I've never seen anything like it. The only kind of cameras I've ever been on are the ones from George's phone and Mom's old Sony. I watch one photographer smooshing a group of kids together so he can get them all in the shot. Then another comes over and takes the same picture, his shutter snapping twenty times.

My heart races. There is so much happening and everyone seems like they're part of it except us. "We should have got here earlier," I say.

"I wanted to get here earlier," George says.

I scan the line but I can't even see the front. "There must be five thousand people here."

"It won't matter where we are in line once they see us."

The woman drives past the line, then doubles back to get a better look. Most of the kids at the front have rolled-up sleeping bags with them. And even the ones near the back of the line seem sleepy, like they traveled days and nights just to be here early. Everyone has umbrellas to shield themselves from the drizzling rain.

"So what do you kids want to do?" The woman's forehead wrinkles. "I can drop you off at the bus station so you can get back to Summerland, if you want."

"No way," George says. He grabs his bag from the floor and my bag from the seat between us. "You can let us out here, Dolores. We better get in line before another hundred get in front of us."

I blink. I have no idea how George knows this woman's name. I mean, I'm pretty sure she never told it to us. Positive she never told it to us, actually.

"All right, doll. You two go get 'em. But take this with you." She reaches behind her seat, fumbling in the junk until she finds what she's looking for. She tosses us a weathered maroon umbrella. "It ain't pretty, but it works."

"You sure?" I point to the sky. "It's not going to let up anytime soon."

"Won't need it. I'm going home, remember?"

I nod and climb out the truck after George. "Thanks for the ride and for the Life Savers." I want to say more, but my throat catches.

Dolores grins. "You bet, honey."

I survey the mass of people drinking piping hot whatever from thermoses and turning pirouettes. The crowd has this vibe about it. This combined stench of excitement and nerves and terror that's pungent, and awesome. I feel my limbs soaking up the energy. I wonder if George is feeling it, too.

Maybe they think I'm out of earshot, or maybe they just don't care that I can hear every word of what they're saying. "You take care of this girl now, you hear?" Dolores is saying. "She's a keeper. Don't let her out of your sight for a second."

I peek at George, sure as shit he's gonna laugh out loud at her sage words of wisdom but instead his gaze locks on hers. "You know I won't," he says. "Couldn't, even if I wanted to."

NINE

The second the woman's truck is out of sight, I eyeball George. Sometimes he's so mysterious, and I know it's on purpose. Sometimes I think he's gotten so good at hiding things from me, he doesn't even know he's hiding anymore. "How did you know her name?" I ask him. "Have you met her before or something?"

George pushes us through a circle of break dancers, all styled out in wristbands and high-tops in every array of neon colors. He shrugs. "Simple. I asked her."

"When? You practically slept the whole trip."

"When she first pulled up." He raises one eyebrow. "You don't really think I'm stupid enough to climb into the car with someone without even finding out their name, do you?"

George places his hands on my shoulders and spins me around to face some dancer, now taking center circle. A camera pushes past us, zooming in on the guy who's shaking his thing to the beats blasting from an eighties-style boom box. George bobs his left knee up and down and shimmies his shoulders forward in perfect rhythm with the breaker's and the camera swivels around to film him, too. I scoot out of the way. If I did that, I'd look like a total fool. But George looks normal. Like he's one of them.

I watch a B-boy standing next to us wearing and totally owning an acid-washed bomber jacket and a half-shaved head, the rest of his hair flipped over to one side. He's not dancing, just smiling at George and eyeing him up and down while George shakes his shoulders and pops his knee. At first George seems oblivious to the boy's stare, but it doesn't take him long to notice that someone's watching him, which doesn't surprise me at all. Their eyes find each other and hold each other for three whole seconds. The B-boy bites his bottom lip and I can't help but bite mine. It feels weird to be standing so close to them when it's obvious there's some kind of heat exchange happening between the two of them, but I can't help it so I stand closer to George. This guy's a stranger. And George is mine.

The B-boy takes one small step toward us. He pulls a mangled cigarette out of his high-tops and lights it, inhales, and blows a cloud of smoke toward George. George breathes deep, like that smoke isn't filled with addictive carcinogenic chemicals and tar but the freshest air he's ever smelled. It makes my stomach turn.

And then George turns around. Literally puts his back to the guy as if none of it has even happened. He grabs my hand and drags me away. From over my shoulder, I see the boy still watching us as we walk away.

When we're definitely out of earshot, I drop George's hand. "What the hell was that?"

"What?" George blinks, his face totally blank.

"What just happened with you and that guy back there?" I fold my arms across my hoodie. "Seriously. I'm not going anywhere till you tell me what's going on with you acting like you know all these people when I know you don't."

"You're right. I don't know who that guy is." His face turns to the crowd, searching, but the boy is gone. "Yet."

"And what about the woman? Dolores."

George shoves his hands in his pocket. "Not everything is as complicated as you like making it. That guy was hot. And when I walked up to Dolores's truck, I could just tell she was okay. I don't know, maybe she just seemed like she needed the company." He tilts his head back toward the clearing sky. "Maybe she was an old soul. You know, put back on earth for the sole purpose of getting us here."

I've heard people say that George is an old soul about a billion times before. There was even this one time, at the state fair, when the two of us went into a psychic booth to have our fortunes told. Within five seconds this withered woman was marveling at George's old soul. The psychic then turned to me and said that I was brand new. Fresh as a baby's bottom.

So now George shrugs it off like it's all totally copacetic. Like he can just tell me "he feels her" or whatever and that I should get it. But I can't help but feel ripped off. Because when I meet someone new, it takes me for forever to decide if they like me or not.

I let the conversation drop because I know this isn't one I'm going to win. Instead, I scan the line we've joined, twisting around the building and the whole block like a maze of human dominoes. "We're way at the back," I say.

"I know."

My eyes dart left, right. There are kids still lining up behind us, but there are at least two hundred in front. "What if there are so many good dancers here, the judges don't even get to us today?"

"Then we'll try out tomorrow."

"What if there *isn't* a tomorrow?"

"The sign said tryouts were for two days. There'll be a tomorrow."

I know George thinks I'm being all negative because he says I'm like that sometimes, when really I don't think I'm like that at all. I just like to know the facts and the fact is we're at the back of this really huge line. During clam season in Summerland, we're only allowed to pull a maximum of sixteen clams per day. That's a fact too, plus it's the law, and everyone knows about the hefty fines that go with breaking it. So when we've pulled our quotas for the day, there's nothing to do but go home.

George starts to say something else. Something about embracing blah blah blah and how I project blah blah blah, but I'm barely listening. My hand goes up to my pillowcase piece, still tucked under my bra strap. I feel its thin cotton between my thumb and index finger. Being here. Doing this today. It's my only shot. I grab the sleeve of George's hoodie. "We need to get to the front of that line. We need the judges to see us. Today."

I pull us out of place and drag him toward the front of the building where there are like fifty cameras instead of ten. George waves at one as we pass, and the cameraman swivels around and zooms in on George's face while I keep my head turned and away. We inspect the other dancers, passing two tappers doing some mean a cappella stuff for a camera on wheels alongside a third guy who's holding their place in line. They're incredible; I'm not kidding. Their feet shuffle faster than razor clams digging themselves to safety, and I wonder what Katina will think when she sees them on TV—if this stuff will even make it to TV. Her only tap teacher left Summerland last year and she never found a replacement, so most of the kids in Summerland have given up tap. In front of those two, a boy who's made of muscles practices back tucks. Standing. Back. Tucks.

My heart beats fast because every single dancer around us is awesome and they're all being *filmed*, like all the time, and they're smiling like they're fine with it. Happy about it. George's eyes lock on every one of the dancers and cameras but he trails behind me for once, silent. We keep walking. Searching for what, I'm not totally sure, but the deep pounding from inside tells me to keep going. Keep going, if I want this to work. And then, like a magical oasis appearing from a never-ending walk to nowhere, there it is. Or rather, *she* is. I stop. Behind me, so does George, bumping into my back because his head's down and he doesn't seem to see what I do. This skinny blonde girl with impossibly long legs is blabbing loud enough for the whole damn line to hear. She's about number twenty-five in line and alone, and by the looks of it, annoying pretty much everyone around her. The girl in front of her turns around and folds her arms across her toned, petite frame. Her teased-out afro bobs around her heart-shaped face. She flicks it away from her forehead, revealing the greenest eyes I've ever seen. I take a step back. Next to me, so does George.

"And you know what else I heard?" Legs says.

"No. What?" Eyes says. Her voice is flat and her body language just screams serious loathing for the leggy girl.

"I heard that they're not looking for any small people this season. They want tall dancers. *Womanly* dancers. Not little girls. And I heard they said tall girls just look better on camera." The second she says it, a girl with a camera spins around to film her. "But who knows? You might get in. Depending on how good you are."

Wow. Legs does not seem like a good person. Eyes must think so too because she says, "What did they say about girls with really big mouths? Because if they're looking for girls with super big mouths this season, you're a shoo-in."

Legs ignores her and does this grand plié down to her dance bag to retrieve a tube of pink sparkly gloss to smother her super-big mouth with. Eyes flutters her eyelashes. When the two of them suddenly notice George and me just standing there, horning in on their femme fatale conference, George nudges my side. Whispers, "Mags, what are we doing here?"

The thing is, I don't know. Don't know why my body chose these two girls to stop next to when, really, getting between them seems like a very bad idea. I look up at the sky, the sun peeking between two skyscrapers. Behind me I hear noises. Not town chatter but city noises. Cars beeping. Music blasting. Garbage trucks and delivery trucks moving and moving and moving. I don't know what I'm doing here. Until, suddenly, I do. This isn't Summerland. These girls don't know me, know who I am or what I've done or what I'm capable of doing. I'm not a no-good Woodson girl. Not here I'm not.

I peer into George's eyes, and it's all there. It's all perfect. It's all very un-me.

I turn around and feign like I'm having some kind of coughing attack. While my back's to them, I wrap my pillowcase piece around my index finger. Then I face them and smile at both girls.

"Thank God you're not in yet," I say to Eyes. I hope she gets it, knows to play along with what I'm about to do. "So, hey, thanks for saving our spot."

Legs's mouth drops open. She stares at me like I'm a lunatic while Eyes stares at me like I'm Joan of freaking Arc.

"Man, I'm so glad we made it back from the hospital in time." I hold up my finger for both Eyes and Legs. "See? Only one little stitch." I smile and then muss George's hair with my non-wrapped hand. "I'm never going to let you borrow my eyebrow tweezers again if this is what happens when you do." He gawks at me, but says nothing. I'm not sure if he's not getting it or if he's just too shocked to talk. I turn to the girls. "I'm just glad we made it back. I would have died if we missed this. Thanks again for saving our spot."

I wedge myself in behind Eyes and in front of Legs. Then I pull George in with me and two cameras swivel over to film us. I keep my head up, looking straight at them. I swallow but I smile and they slide on past me to film someone else. There. Easy-peasy, mac and cheesy. I can do this. I can even do it on camera.

Legs holds up one stiff, perfectly manicured hand in front of her body. "No way. You can't save spots. I came all the way from Arizona. I've been here for six hours."

"The spot's theirs, fair and square," Eyes says. "They were here a good hour before you showed up. And anyway, it was an emergency. You can totally save spots in crisis situations. Everyone knows that." She turns to George and me with this humongo smile, her eyes glistening. "No problem. Just glad your finger is going to be okay."

"Whatever." Legs flips her hair and then turns around to focus on whoever's behind her, the new target of her verbal abuse.

Inside of me, my heart swells. I did it. I'm the one who got us to the front of the line. Me, not George. *Me*. And I know why I did it, or rather, how: here, no one knows me. Here, I'm not one of the loser Woodson girls, daughter to Patricia Woodson, town whore, town junkie, town killer.

Here, I can be anyone I want.

"What sky did you two fall out of?" Eyes says. "I was praying for a divine intervention when you two rocked up out of nowhere." Her eyeballs bounce between me and George, who still hasn't said a word. I nudge him with my foot. Gawk at him like *What the hell is going on with you?* He stares at me and then back at Eyes. He doesn't speak. Because of her? Sure, she's gorgeous. But more importantly, she's also a *she*.

"Hey, are you guys ballet dancers?" Eyes says.

"Yeah," I say. "Contemporary ballet."

Eyes's hair bounces around her face, like it's dancing the cha-cha. "Me too. It sucks. Fifty percent of the people here are contemp. Guess we'll just have to blow their minds, right?"

I think of how much she sounds like George. He's always like that, all gung ho and rainbows, fluffy kittens with pink satin bows. Except for now. It's like we've changed places. Sure, George may have grabbed the sign and made me come and found us the ride, but I'm the one that got us in line. I smile at Eyes. "Then they'll have to pick all three of us."

Eyes holds out one hand. "I'm Rio."

She makes me think of Rose. Rose who, in all likelihood, is totally sick with worry about where I've gone and why I haven't called. And it's not like me not having a cell phone is any kind of excuse. George has one, along with pretty much everyone else on the planet, so I could have called. If I wanted to.

I remove my pillowcase from my finger, tuck it back under my bra, and shake Rio's hand. George's B-boy slides past us, his eyes on George the whole time. I nudge George in the ribs and whisper, "There he is again," but George doesn't answer me or look at the boy or take his eyes off Rio, not even for a second, which makes my mouth feel dry and prickly.

"Where are you from?" I ask Rio, and I hope it's somewhere like Missouri or Idaho.

"New York City," she says, and a little piece of me dies. George has always wanted to go there. He says it's where anyone who's anyone comes from.

"Are you two a couple?" Rio asks.

"Uh, no," I say, for both of us.

"Oh." Her eyes shift from George, back to me. "I should have known, I guess."

I glance at George. Gay George. Gay George with great style and great hair and moves to match. Gay George, whose eyes swarm every inch of her. Like he's no longer Gay George.

"That's the way it usually is, isn't it?" Rio says. "Partners end up being the best of friends instead of lovers."

"I guess that's true." I elbow George. "Right?"

George shakes his head. Opens his mouth like he wants to say something, but no words come out, which is weird and strange and entirely embarrassing for both of us.

Rio grabs a can of Coke from her backpack. She cracks it open and offers me a sip first.

"Then again," she says. "Some of the greatest dance partners of all time have ended up being the most fantastic couples. Like those two hip-hop choreographers. You know who I mean. They seem so in love, don't they?" She points to George. "So anyway, does he speak?"

I elbow him in the ribs and then wait for him to flash Rio one of his killer smiles and charm the pants off her in two seconds flat like he usually does. Has, with nearly every guy and most of the girls in Summerland. But he's not saying a thing. Instead, he's just kind of staring at her like she's this new little planet inside a solar system he's seen a thousand times before.

He's totally silent. Deafening. Alarming. Scary silent.

In fact, I've never seen George so at loss for words in my entire life.

TEN

I never would have thought that it would take a six-foot Australian brunette with a bob to break George's spell, but apparently, that's exactly what it takes.

The second Camilla Sky trots on to the wooden outdoor stage, George is George again, waving his arms in the air and shouting for her—*to* her—like they're long-lost friends. Although I can barely hear him because all five hundred kids next to us are yelling the same thing, along with a bunch of shouts of "Camilla, I love you!" to go with it. There's a huge screen behind Camilla and about a gazillion cameras filming her and filming the audience and blasting it all on that super-sized screen. The screen flashes from Camilla to her adorers, the ones at the front who are almost crying and the ones at the back who are climbing on each other's shoulders to get a better view. The whole thing is totally manic and I feel my whole body getting hot because I can't believe we're really here. I can't believe we're really doing this.

Camilla raises the roof, lifting her hands above her fedora, and so does the crowd. I mean, it's pretty impossible to *not* do whatever she wants you to. Something about her cherry-shined lips and smooth skin—smoothest I've ever seen in real life and not some airbrushed mag—makes you want, no, *have* to obey.

A group of breakers circle around her, jumping up and down, and cameramen swarm them. To anyone else—present company included—they'd be totally cringeworthy. Camilla loops arms with them like she's the one who worships them. Then she wipes her brow and spins around to face her cameras, her audience.

I wish I could hate this woman.

I mean, I bet she guzzles beer at baseball games without some dude even asking her to. I bet that when a girl tells her a secret she takes it to the grave. I bet that when she goes back home to whatever small Australian—maybe even clamming-obsessed—town she comes from, everyone treats her like the goddess she is. Then again, I bet that in *her* hometown, the name Sky isn't totally synonymous with trash.

She coos into the microphone. "Welcome to Season Six of *Live to Dance*! I can already tell that you guys are going to make this show the best, most competitive, most heartstopping season yet!"

I glance over at Rio. Her eyes are smiling with this shimmery kind of light, blinding me with all the hope and joy she's radiating. George is smiling, too. One of his big, awestruck grins that makes it impossible for me not to smile. Even though my stomach feels like it's going to jeté out my throat.

Camilla presses the air down in front of her with her hands and the crowd cools, cameras panning out. "Okay! Listen up. I know you're all dying to show our judges your stuff, but before you go in, let's go over the rules." She takes a clipboard from the guy next to her. "Rule number one: Every competitor must be at least eighteen years of age. For everyone who is eighteen or older, there's a table set up by the front doors.

Once you've got your number, head to that table to show the staff your IDs so they can verify your dates of birth." She smiles, but it doesn't reach her eyes. "Anyone who's not at least eighteen, better luck next year."

A couple of boos emerge from the crowd, and two kids actually slink out of line, shoulders sagging. Two cameras follow them out and their faces flash on that big screen. Both of them look completely mortified. One gives the cameraman the middle finger, and the crowd boos louder. But then a guy with a pencil behind his ear whistles and the cameramen let them go. But other than those two, everyone else stays put, even though every tenth kid here looks about fifteen. Rio leans forward and whispers, "You guys are eighteen, right?"

"George turned eighteen in February," I say. "Valentine's Day. I turned eighteen last week." I shut my eyes, trying to listen to Camilla's explanation on the age thing—something about legalities in case of injury—but I can't.

All I can think about is my birthday. Mrs. Moutsous, her kind face proud as she handed over the present she picked out, just for me, because she thought I'd love it. The clam gun, wrapped in sparkly paper, waiting for me to open it, waiting for me to own it.

My mind morphs, swirling with other pictures—worse pictures, uglier pictures. That cop in Summerland, his teeth grinding against each other, his voice calling me forward, his hand, touching me. Colleen's body, limp, lifeless, covered in a sheet so thin I could still see the slope of her nose, the curve of her cheek through it as they wheeled her away.

My arms grow cold, heavy. I rub my eyes but the pictures won't leave me, no matter where I go, what I do. I push my fists into my sockets.

"Mags?" George touches my shoulder, his palm warming me.

When I open my eyes again, everything's the same, but different. I scan the crowd, focusing on everyone and no one. Dancers, they're all dancers. Everyone here's just like me, loves what I love. Summerland feels far away, long ago. Even this morning outside Mayor Chamberlain's seems a lifetime ago from where I am now. I nod at George. His face relaxes. When he turns away, I rub my arms. I can't believe how far I've come. I can't believe I'm here.

"Rule number two!" Camilla shouts. "All dancers must wear proper attire for your style of dance. That means all you hip-hoppers can wear your trackies and denim. But ballet dancers, you must be in leotard."

I bend down to loosen the drawstring of my tie-dyed dance bag and feel around inside to make sure I haven't forgotten anything. Then my hand goes up to my collarbone to make sure my pillowcase piece is still there, too. It's all I've got. Right here, right now, it's everything I need.

Camilla grabs another stack of papers from her assistant and pats him on the head, like a puppy. "Okay. Now that those little tidbits are taken care of, Billy here's going to walk down the line and hand everyone a number to pin to the front of you." The screen behind Camilla flashes a huge picture of Billy's face, though I can't see him in the crowd anywhere. He's not a star like Camilla. Just a regular dude in jeans and a tee and baseball cap that reads LTD on the front, but maybe that's the point. Maybe they don't hire anyone to stand next to Camilla who won't make her look good.

"Underneath that number," she says. "I need you guys to write down whatever state you're hoping to represent if you make it on the show. I'm going to take down your name and a few fun facts about you so that the judges and I can get to know you better."

Fun facts? I poke George. "What do you think they're going to ask us? Do you think it's going to be, like, personal stuff?" I bite the inside of my cheek. I can only imagine how the Hollywood staffers at *Live to Dance* would love to have a murderer's daughter on the show. Good for ratings? Maybe. Good for getting the Woodson girls a brand-new life? Definitely not.

"No clue, but who cares?" George says. "I'd tell them where and when I lost my virginity if it would help me get on the show, wouldn't you?" His words make me flinch.

I never knew that George apparently lost his virginity somewhere, sometime during our symbiotic friendship. Mercifully, my mind has always blocked out those kinds of images. Now, it's all here. His chiseled body, meshed with someone else's. His lips, pressed against another set of lips. My stomach wrenches at the pictures that seep through my brain like toxic, poisonous sludge. And then an even bigger reality sets in: while I've remained pitifully pure, hopeful that one day it would be me and George together in the holy sense of things, George was slutting himself out around town. And even though the fact that George was getting freaky with *guys* shouldn't make me sad, or jealous, it does. Suddenly, gender has nothing to do with it at all. It's more a case of him wanting someone that isn't me. Maybe even multiple someones.

I drop his hand and step closer to Rio.

Camilla adjusts her fedora and the cameras zoom on that, flashing other pictures on the screen behind her, Camilla in a dozen different outfits on a dozen different occasions, but always, always in that fedora.

"Now, I assume you all know the basics of how this competition works. You've all seen our show, right? You'll do a one-minute solo to your own music. One minute—no more, no less. If you go over time, the judges will cut you off, okay?"

My mouth drops to the floor.

Holy. Crapola. The solo.

I always knew this was coming. I mean, of *course* I'll have to do a solo if I want to land a spot on the show. But I've been so busy obsessing over this morning's almost-arrest and Rose, then Dolores, and now this hideous George-minus-virginity topic, that I think I temporarily blocked out the *performing* part of this competition. I feel my fingernails dig into something, but it takes me a second and a high-pitched yelp from George to realize that it's his forearm. "I don't have a solo." My eyes meet his. I must look like hell because George starts laughing and shakes his arm free of my claws.

"Yes you do. Do the piece you've been working on with Katina since the beginning of the summer. It's perfect."

"It's a work in progress, not perfect." My voice shakes. I hate that it's shaking.

"It's beautiful. You know it is."

"They'll laugh me off that stage." I stand up straight. I'm not whining. It's just a fact.

"They won't." He touches my cheek. "We're not in Summerland."

I feel my stomach muscles clench, but I bend down and open the front zip of my bag, hoping the second I see my disc, my music, it'll all come back to me. I grab the CD, but as soon as I see the word scrawled across the front, my knees turn to mush. *Me and G.* Pictures. That's what this disc is. Pictures of George and me from our last days of high school. The scavenger hunt. The prom I didn't want to go to until George said I had to and Mark seconded that motion. Pictures. Not music. The disc falls from my hands. It slaps the ground and I'm sure I hear it crack.

George swoops down to pick it up. "You're going to break it before you use it."

The world in front of me, next to me, around me blurs into a muddled blend of colors. "It's the wrong one."

"Huh?"

"I brought the wrong disc." I take it from him. "Pictures, not music."

"Didn't you double-check your stuff?" I can hear the disbelief winding through his voice.

"I didn't have time. There was so much to do."

"Yeah, like writing crappy-ass resignation notes to my mom. Like making deals with the devil."

"Almost-deals." I feel my jaw clench. "Not the same thing."

Rio's head swivels back and forth between me and George. She eyes us curiously, but she doesn't ask a thing about what we're talking about and I'm glad. That's one can of worms I don't want to open.

"It's okay." Rio unzips the front pocket of her own bag and then hands me her iPod. "I've got unlimited music on this thing. Find your song and the judges can download it into their system." She shoots George a look. "They'd rather have this than CDs anyway. And you've probably got a while before you're up, so there's time to work the kinks out of your solo." She closes my hand around the iPod, tight. "And listen. No one will laugh at you. Don't worry."

"I'm not worried."

"I'm just saying," she says. "We'll be in the audience cheering for you, okay? Just find our faces, close your eyes, and do what you do best."

We.

Rio's words float through the atmosphere, autonomously. Disjointed from others that follow. Words that were never there before. *We. Us. George and Rio.* Five minutes ago there was no *we*. Now there suddenly is.

And then he's touching her. Saying things like, "I've never even seen hair like this in real life," and "it's so gorgeous," like it's the most normal thing in the world, him playing with the thick, tight curls that frame her face.

My eyes are glued to the two of them, cemented, like it's permanent. I mean, he's touching her *hair*. With both hands. As I pry my stare away, I notice that a bunch of other contestants are kind of staring, too. And not just contestants. Cameras. There's one right next to us, filming as George twines her hair in his fingers and Rio closes her eyes. My breathing gets heavy. Are they going to put this on TV? Is that the kind of thing people want to see? I'm not sure if it is or isn't but all I know is that I don't even want to see it. I reach over and pull on George's shirt. "Stop it, G."

"Why? Jealous much?"

"No." I glance at the camera. It's now filming me. I hide my face with my arm. "You're making a scene," I whisper. "You're supposed to be thinking about your solo."

George rolls his eyes in my direction. He acts like he doesn't know they're watching him. Twenty eyes. Fifty. More. But he totally does. He's putting on a show. He taps his temple. "Whatevs. It's all up here. Once the audience sees me dance, it's all over for everyone else."

Camilla waves her arms for the crowd to settle. "All right. Here's the last thing on my agenda this morning. Everyone numbered one through one hundred will compete today. Anyone numbered one hundred and one through two hundred will compete tomorrow. After that, you may or may not get to try out for Season Six. That much will be up to the judges. Does everyone understand?" She glances at her assistant. "Okay, Billy, don't keep them waiting out here a second longer than you need to. Give them their numbers already!"

The crowd explodes in cheers while ten cameras fly toward her and Camilla makes this big show of doing some mock twirls and leaps with a few of the contestants. Billy walks down the line with his numbers and kids scrawl their home states underneath with Billy's black marker. I see kids from places way across the country like North Dakota and Maine. Places I've never even considered until now. Every time a kid from a new state is noticed, that state flashes on the screen behind us in giant black letters. Wyoming. Utah. Mississippi. New Mexico. There are people here from everywhere. The only other state I've ever been to besides Oregon is Washington, the one right next to us. It makes me feel small. It makes me feel like they'll never remember who I am and where I came from.

When Billy's about ten people in front of us, I turn to George. "Do you think they're going to show our auditions on TV? I don't know if I can do this in front of everyone." I swallow. "In front of all these cameras."

George grabs my hand and squeezes, once, twice, three times. "You can," he says. "You have to. You remember why you want everyone to see you, don't you?"

I study his fingers entwined with mine. I know I have to do this if I want to change things. But the crowd. The people. What if I make it all worse?

Rio takes a step closer to me. "Hey. We all have our reasons for being here. Try to remember what yours is. Keep your eye on the prize, whatever your prize is, okay?"

"Okay." I exhale. I force a smile which makes me kind of smile for real. And then, just like that, I *do* feel better. A little. I can do this. I have to do this. I mean, without me we wouldn't even be this far in line. We wouldn't be trying out at all. And dancing. I think of the way I felt watching *Giselle* with George, my stomach filled with this mixture of wanting and needing and knowing that I could have everything up on that stage if I just kept working. The next day at Katina's, I felt myself channel her, be her, feel the immobilizing pain she felt as her love left her for another. My legs lifted higher that day, my leaps reached higher than they ever had before. Katina's eyes never left me. After class, she said that I looked like a star out there. Even if no one else said anything, I know they noticed, too. Dancing. If nothing else, I can do at least that.

Camilla and her crew make their way down the line. They work fast, passing out numbers and firing off questions, while the cameras stop at every single person to record it all. Ten minutes later, they're in front of us, handing us numbers thirty, thirty-one, and thirty-two. I scan the back of the line where we would have been if we hadn't pulled my move. They're so far back, I can hardly see them. No way they're auditioning today.

Camilla wraps her arms around George, Rio, and me at the same time, as though we're a single unit. The cameramen wave everyone around us to stand back because they need to room to get it all. "I love it! You're like the three musketeers," Camilla says, and I can't help but think of Abby and Quinn and Mark at home. They're the three musketeers, not us. George and I have always only been two.

She turns to Rio. "Did you all come here together?"

Rio motions to me and George and the word OREGON scrawled underneath our numbers. "No. They did. I met them here."

"Love at first sight. I just adore that!" Camilla removes her fedora and smooths a strand of her glossy hair across her forehead. She smiles for her cameras and turns to George and pouts out her lips. "Okay, you first. What's your name?"

George puffs his chest out. "George Moutsous."

"George. What a great name! I might just call you Georgie Porgie, if that's okay with you."

Rio and I can't help but bust out laughing at Camilla's ability to make everything sound sexy. Even Georgie Porgie.

"Georgie Porgie," Camilla says. "Tell us something about you. What's your favorite activity? When you're not dancing, of course?"

George digs his hands in the front pocket of his ripped jeans and bows his head. He looks up at her, just with his eyes. It's pretty hilarious. George has, like, no shyness in him whatsoever, but he sure as hell does a good job acting the part when the cameras are on and rolling.

"I like to just hang with Mags here, you know?"

"Oh, absolutely!" Camilla nods, satisfied. "Who wouldn't want to hang with beauties like these two." She turns to me. "And you, young lady, what's your name?"

I tell her my name but I leave out the last part and she squeals and says how it's the sweetest name she's ever heard. She shoves the microphone in my face. "Tell me, Magnolia, who inspired you to be a dancer?"

My own gaze drops to my feet. There's just no way I'm going to tell Camilla Sky that Mom put me in dancing to get me out of the house and give herself a break from me always wanting something. And on some level, I guess she knew I needed the break from her always taking. I clear my throat. "Nobody did."

Camilla stares at me, deep and unblinking. Her burning stare reminds me of the people in Summerland. Always looking. Always searching for some kind of sordid truth behind my eyes. "Come on," she says. "There must be someone out there who made you want to dance."

George pulls me tighter toward him. "Mags doesn't need role models. She's always found her own way. We both have." He grins at Camilla's crew. "You can write that down if you want to."

Camilla turns to Rio. "So. You've seen a lot of kids practicing out here today, right?"

"Right," Rio says. "It's hard not to eye your competition."

Camilla's eyes light up. "Well then, here's my question for you." She motions for the three of us to come closer to her, which we do. The cameras slide closer too, and I feel their lenses all over me, like they're drilling holes through my cheek. "Who do you think is the one to beat out here?" Camilla says.

Rio's smile fades. Her face drops and her eyes seem to actually dim. "I don't know. I've only seen everyone warming up."

"But if you had to guess," Camilla says, tapping her foot. "If you had to pick someone that just shone. Who would you say that person is?"

Rio's eyebrows gather. She pauses for a full three seconds. "These two. George and Magnolia. I'd say they're the ones to beat."

Camilla throws her head back and laughs. "Oh, you two are lucky ones! You seemed to have found yourselves a true friend in this pretty little thing. What did you say your name was?"

"Rio."

Camilla straightens, suddenly serious. "I know, sweetheart. Rio *what?*"

"Bonnet," Rio whispers.

I turn to her. "What did you just say?"

A cameraman flips his machine off his shoulder. "She said it too quietly. I didn't get that." He turns to Rio, his eyebrows furrowed. "We need to get that again."

Camilla rewinds herself as if on autopilot. "Rio what?"

"Bonnet." Rio pushes her shoulders back.

"Rio *Bonnet*," Camilla says. "Granddaughter of the original prima ballerina. One of the greatest ballet dancers of all time."

Camilla flutters her eyelashes for the millionth time and the screen at the front of the stage switches to show Rio's face, big and blushing. Which is how I know that we've been set up. Rio's been set up. Camilla's known who she is the whole time, while George and I carried on with her like she was a normal person. Like we're all in the same league.

"Aimee Bonnet was your grandma?" I say.

Rio shrugs. "So they say. I never actually met her. I'm from the States. That side of my family's all in Paris. Anyway, I think she died before I was born."

"But you're still blood," George says. He cocks his head and stares all around her face, her hair, her body, like he's seeing her in a whole new light. A darker one. Scarier one. The cameras zoom in all around us, but for the first time, George seems oblivious to them. "Why didn't you tell us who you are?"

"Because it's not important. Like I said, I never met her."

Camilla gives Rio's cheek a little cheek pinch. "Or maybe she was just too modest to tell you that Rio Bonnet is exactly like her Parisian grandma. From what I've heard, there's no one here that you need to worry about more than her."

Eleven

Rio follows on George's heels, her arms dangling by her sides. "I told you, it's no big deal, okay?"

"Not okay," George says. "That's the kind of detail you should have told us the second you met us."

I put myself between them to keep them moving, walking toward the auditorium, in time with the other ninety-seven kids auditioning today. Fact is, I don't want them to gouge each other's eyes out before we even get in there.

"Right," Rio says. "I should have said 'by the way, I'm awesome and it's because of my dead grandmother who I've never even met'?"

"That's exactly what you should have said." He glares at her. "If I would have known you're a Bonnet and could actually dance worth shit then I never would have—"

"Never would have what? Made friends with me? What does that say for Mags here?" She pushes her way into the third row and takes an aisle seat. George skips the seat beside her and slumps down in the next one. I slide in the middle. The tension between their seats is electric; I'm not kidding. Little neurons are actually firing from George through me to get to Rio.

Mercifully, the lights dim, and Camilla Sky flits on stage. She fumbles around with her microphone but when she can't get it to work, she drops it to the ground and stamps her foot until one of her assistants climbs on the stage and pins it to the neck of her tank top for her. "I need numbers one through ten to go backstage," she says. Her lips are thin and her eyes seem much smaller than before. Not exactly the bubbly cheerleader we saw when the cameras were on us. A cameraman slides his equipment to the front of the stage and gives Camilla a *we're rolling* hand signal. She fluffs herself and brightens. "Ladies and gentlemen, please welcome judge number one, Executive Producer Elliot Townsend!"

On all sides of me, people clap and hoot while reality TV mogul and creator of the show, Elliot Townsend, queen-waves from his seat.

Next to me, Rio elbows me in the ribs. "Magnolia, did you hear me? I said, is he always this much of a baby?"

"Who? Elliot? I don't know. He seems okay and the last time I saw him on TV—"

"No. *George*." Rio's eyebrows smoosh together like one long caterpillar, inching its way across her forehead.

"Oh." I shift in my seat, the picture of George pulling me from that cop's car swarming my head. I mean, I know George can be kind of righteous from time to time, but he's still my George. I might have gotten us into this audition, but I might never have left Summerland without him.

Instead of answering, I point to the judges' table, where four cameras are filming them from the back, front, and both sides. Elliot Townsend adjusts his leather jacket. He must be used to all these cameras all the time. They all must be. "Don't you guys think he looks shorter in person?" I wipe the sweatiness of my palms on my lap. "I heard someone say that he wears shoes with three-inch soles on them, you know, to appear taller on film. You think that's true?"

Rio snorts and totally skips over my Elliot-plus-heels comment. "You know what, Magnolia? I really thought you were going to be cooler than this."

Cooler than this? This girl doesn't know me—doesn't know either of us—at all. If she did, she'd know that I'm the least cool person that ever came from Summerland. Next to Rose, of course. And my mom. We've always known that. Everyone's always made sure of it.

In front of us, Elliot Townsend writes something down on his notepad while I study his leather-clad back. When you first look at the guy, you can't help but assume he's a royal pain in the butt. But actually, I have to admit, he's got some swag. But something's different about him this season—different from the last time I saw him, nearly three seasons ago, when Mom and I were still watching, still together. I squint my eyes.

Now his hair is longer. And sun-kissed. And his eyes seem less tired, like maybe he's had some work done. I glance at George to see if he's looking. But it seems as if he hasn't noticed any of this. Which for George, is so not normal.

As if he's heard my thoughts, Elliot Townsend swivels around in his seat and stares right at me. The cameras zoom in on his face and it flashes up on the large screen on stage. It doesn't show me, show who he's staring at, but I know and it's enough. My heart thuds with the power of a thousand clam guns. Maybe he heard what my mind said about the heels and the hair and the tan and the work. Or maybe. Maybe he's looking at me because he knows I've got something special.

Something to prove. Something that's going to make me shine right here, right now, like Camilla said.

But then other thoughts follow. Like maybe he knows who I am. Colleen's death made news all over the state of Oregon, in papers and on TV. In each one, Mom's name. Our name. Maybe the news made its way to California, too. I scan the other contestants, their numbers, states, pinned to their leotards. Georgia. New Jersey. Rhode Island. Maybe it even made it further than California.

I close my eyes again. But when I open them, Elliot's not looking at me at all.

Onstage, Camilla adjusts her fedora and the screen flashes with her face instead of Elliot's. I feel myself relax. I'd hate to be him and on that screen all the time. It's no way to live. "Ladies and gentlemen," Camilla says. "Please welcome our second judge, Astrid Scott!"

The rooms blows up with more cheers and whoops. Astrid leans forward to accept her applause and then it's her face that's on that screen. Although every single one of us can see down her blouse at the two melons she probably paid darn good money for, it's kind of okay. Sure, that screen makes them seem bigger than they are, but I mean, she is the one and only Astrid Scott, awesome pop star turned slightly over-the-hill mother of some cute little baby from Uganda.

At first, the paparazzi was all over her "transformation." I saw it all over the tabloids in the Pic 'N' Pay and at the gas station. They said she had a fat ass and called her a has-been. But when she came up with the concept for *Live to Dance*, all her sins were forgiven. That's how it is when you're a star, I guess. They only hate you till they find someone new to hate instead.

"You can't be mad at me for this," Rio says, leaning over me to George. "You have no right."

"Come on, Mags." George pulls the shoulder strap of my leotard. "Let's sit somewhere else. We came here to throw down, not get played by the competition."

"Fine, go," Rio says. She flicks her head at me. "I should have predicted you'd be loyal to him like that, the way you're always hanging off him. Loyal like a lapdog."

That's it. That's *so* it. I've got real reasons to be here, yet these two are acting like Rio's family tree is the biggest newsflash we've ever seen. But newsflash to both of them: it isn't. And Rio? Where does she get off acting like she knows me, knows anything about me and George when the only people that knows us—me and him, not *her* and him—is us. Fact is, I may love George through and through, but I'm not his labradoodle. I flick George's hand off my leotard. "You're both acting like babies."

Rio blinks.

George stares at me like I'm missing a limb.

"G. Rio's right. It shouldn't matter who her grandmother was or how awesome she is because of it. And it definitely shouldn't make us hate her."

Rio leans across me again. "I've worked hard for what I am, regardless of what he seems to think."

I hold up a hand. "And Rio. I get where George is coming from. It's kind of like, knowing who you are changes things. Whether you want to admit it or not, it just does."

Rio turns her head and, with one hand cupped against her cheek, hides her face from me. But even though I can't see her—see those eyes that somehow say so much—I know that she's crying. Her shoulders are trembling. She's breathing so fast, in and out, like she's struggling to breathe at all.

And then I feel like I'm going to cry, too.

My hand goes up to feel my pillowcase piece, still tucked under my bra strap, molding into my shoulder blade. I try to refocus on Astrid, but my eyes are blurry. I try to go over each and every step in my solo, but it's like I can't even picture one single sissonne or chassé.

Instead, I think of home.

By now, Rose will definitely know that we've skipped town, and there sure as heck won't be any mystery as to where we've gone. A pit forms in my stomach. Because maybe she's heard about the cop, too. In all likelihood, she and Mrs. Moutsous are on their way down here now to drag our butts back home to clamming and Deelish and everything that is Summerland. Everything I've ever known and loved.

Everything that chains me.

Rio sucks in a slow breath. "You're right. I should have told you guys who I was, but I wish it didn't matter. In Brooklyn, my dance studio even wanted to put my face on their sign out front to drum up more business. Can you believe that? They expect more from me than they do from everyone else. I was en pointe before I was ten. Before my feet were even fully grown or before my bones were strong enough. Just because they thought I could handle it." Rio's gaze falls into her lap. "Everyone expects me to dance like her, and act like her, and be her."

I keep my eyes forward. I can't deal with this right now. Can't deal with Rio's grandma drama when really, I'd kill to have that kind of name following me around. That kind of legacy. The kind people associate with beautiful dancing, not terrible death.

But the thing is, deep down, I know the way we judged her for who her grandma was isn't any different from the way Summerlanders judge me and Rose because we're Woodsons. I don't blame her for leaving out her last name, when really, if anyone here knew who my mom is, I'd do the same thing. Rio's no different than me. She's still got those same chains and same shadows, weighing her down, darkening her light.

I want to say all of that to Rio. But I can't. It might be the same, Rio's life and mine, but it's different, too. She's never even met her shadow, while mine, at some point, always comes back to live with me. And most of the time, I want her to.

As usual, George says everything I can't. "We get it. You're here to make your own mark. We respect that. Right, Mags?" His voice is soft, all the anger that laced it a whole fifteen seconds ago blown away, like a snowflake in the wind.

Rio exhales. "Thank you," she mouths to me, even though I haven't done a thing.

Because things seem okay between them now, I turn my focus to judge number three. Keep my eyes steady and non-blinking as I study Gia Gianni, the most terrifying judge of them all. After Camilla runs down Gia's repertoire of Tony awards for choreography while the screen plays these clips of Gia's successes with seven different dance styles over what looks like the last twenty years, Gia stands up to give this monumental speech about how pleased she is that try-outs were held in Portland this year because, according to her, some of the best dancers she's ever worked with have come from Oregon. When she says it, the screen changes to pictures of Oregon. Portland, the Heritage Building we're sitting in, and pictures of the coast. There are the beaches I know, like Cannon, and the sprawling highway, lined with trees on either side. I see pictures of the Oregon Caves that Mom took Rose and me to once when we were really little, and then there's a picture of Mount Hood. My chest aches. I know we're still in Oregon. But it feels like we're so far from Summerland.

Gia says how honored she is to train us and help mold us into the dancers she knows we can be. She says we ought to abandon everything we've ever learned and just dance through our hearts. Feel the music. Forget the steps. Find the place inside our souls that makes us want—no, *need*—to be here. Her words pour through me. My heart beats with a fire I've never known. But now I do. I'm from this place with good dancers and I'm one of them and I'm going to make it through this round. And then I'll show them. Prove to them that these chains can't shackle me, not for one more day.

As the lights come on and the competition begins, my eyes shift to Rio and George one last time, hoping that they see it, feel the excitement, the sheer goodness of what we're about to accomplish, too.

But they're staring across into each other's eyes, all serious and starry like they're I don't even know what.

It doesn't make sense. After our kiss that day, George made it clear to me that doing that, leaning into me, his hand covering mine and his breath close to mine and then his lips against mine, was nothing more than an experiment.

"I needed to know how it felt," he had said. "I wanted to try it with a girl so that I'd know either way. I wanted it to be with you." He looped his pinky finger in mine. "Friends till the end."

I didn't say anything after that. I guess I should have been honored that I was the chosen one, the one George trusted to test his possible straightness, probable gayness with. But all I could hear in that moment, there under that bridge, was *friend*. Friend. Friend. It crushed me, like the weight of a thousand disappointments. Friend. Friend. Friend. George never had feelings for me. At least, not the kind I had for him. Have.

Now, looking back on that time, the whole thing feels like pieces of a puzzle I'll never put together. George made his intentions perfectly clear. And now, right here, looking from George to Rio to George again, a different thing is totally clear: all George and Rio see is each other.

TWELVE

The first dancer's solo totally blows my mind.

Which is crazy because he's that same B-boy George and I saw in the breakers' circle when we first got to Portland. Same boy who stripped George naked with his eyes. Same boy who was at the back of the line when we last saw him and now, somehow, isn't.

I never saw him practicing outside like most of the kids were, but watching him on stage now, I know that the guy's got serious skills in more ways than one and I wonder if the judges pulled him to the front—he's that good. He's still wearing that bomber jacket, but even through it I see his limbs ripple like water, like waves, not appendages with blood and bones. He's so into his own routine, he doesn't make eye contact with the judges at all and doesn't seem to notice the cameras moving all around him, zeroing in on his feet, his hips, his face, and projecting it all on the screen behind him. For most of the routine, his eyes are closed. I'd never close my eyes on stage like that. Not when I need to see where the floor is and where my feet connect with it.

"He's beautiful," George whispers. I watch George's face change from normal George to George lit up with this sort of divine illumination. It's like he's in love, either with his moves or the guy, I'm not sure which.

"He's really good," I mumble, and I wish so bad that he wasn't.

"He is," George says. "But I've seen better."

I give George a little *ha* because I've got this sneaky suspicion that the "better" George claims he's seen is himself. And George *is* good—no, amazing—but this guy's more magician than dancer. I think of his smoke, circling George, calling George toward him. I wonder how much of this guy is an act and how much is real, and I wonder if it even matters, because all that matters is what the judges and audience see in him. But there's no denying he's got talent, and the other dancers must think so too because everyone in the whole room is going nuts with whoops and cheers every time he even breathes.

The guy does head spins so fast it's like he's going to drill holes through the stage. George leans forward, rests his elbows on his thighs. "If I'd known he was this good, I might have done something about it while I had the chance."

"Better late than never," I say. Although I don't know *why* I say it. I don't want George all gaga over Rio. But I don't want George all gaga over this guy, either.

"I think I've seen him before," Rio says. She squints at his number which, sure enough, has NEW YORK scribbled beneath it. "He dances outside my library sometimes for money. I don't even think he's had any real studio training."

"Boy," George says. "Have we ever wasted our money."

His words hit me hard, like a grand battement in the face. Everyone knows dance is expensive, but it's never felt like a waste—at least not to me. Admittedly, though, I've never really added up how much it's cost us over the years, either.

Sure, there were months where Mom couldn't pay and Rose couldn't pay and Mrs. M. had to pay for my dance instead, but somehow, always, it all worked out.

Now, my fingers twitch as I count numbers, adding, multiplying, figuring out just how much cash I've spent on my little hobby over the last fourteen years.

Tuition runs around eleven hundred a year. Times that by fourteen plus a couple hundred each year for recitals and costumes. The numbers spill inside my head as I add each one up like I'm a human calculator.

Twenty thousand dollars.

Holy crap. Like I said, I knew dance was expensive—definitely too expensive for a family like mine—but no more than piano lessons or soccer or swim or karate or any of the other activities moms put their kids in to keep them off the streets of Summerland. I knew it was pricey. I just never thought about how truly out of our Woodson league it was. Twenty thousand dollars. I place one hand over my stomach. While that might be fine and good for George's and Abby's and Quinn's and Mark's families, spending twenty thousand dollars on dance is definitely not okay for mine.

My mind scrambles to trace the last five years of my life. We could have used that money to get Mom the treatment she needed before the drugs went from bad to worse. We could have used that money to make things the way they were when I was little, the way I remember it being even if Rose doesn't. When Mom was still Mom and clean and clamming and the clothes didn't hang off her like blankets and the wind made her cheeks pink instead of sunken and we walked through our town and people would say hello instead of the other things they say to us now. We could have used it to keep Rose in school, keep them both away from the demons they think control them. Or we could have used it last year, six months ago, yesterday, to pack our stuff and just leave Summerland. We could have used it for anything. If it weren't for me and dance and everything that leads up to this exact moment.

But I can't think of the money. Not now. All I can think of is this.

George crosses his arms but his eyes never leave the guy on stage ripping out these drool-worthy sequences. "We're fine. It'll be fine," he says, and somehow I'm not so sure I believe him. "He has to be able to dance every style to make it on the show. Even ballet. That's not something you can learn in a week."

"You're right," Rio says. "He'll never win if that's all he can do."

"I've never done hip-hop or West Coast Swing either." I nudge George. "And neither have you."

"So what?" George says. "You already know ballet. Everyone knows it's the hardest, the most technical." He waves one hand across the stage. "You can learn this. Anyone can. You'll do what you need to get through."

"I need to do more than just get through."

George turns his head to me. His eyes meet mine and hold. "Do you think any of these kids want this as bad as me and you?"

"I do," Rio says. "I want to win this thing bad. Real bad. Michael Jackson bad."

George breaks my gaze and turns to Rio, awe splashed through each of his baby blues. She holds his eyes, too. It's out of a bad romance novel. A telenovela. A cheap teen flick where everybody falls in love and everybody sings. Call it what you will, but it's still pretty obvious. The two of them look as happy as two peas in a pod again. Two peas, in one pod.

Street Guy finishes his solo and while the whole auditorium is going crazy with hoots and screams, he steps forward to accept the judges' critique. Elliot Townsend waits for the room to quiet. The cameras swivel between Elliot and Street Guy. On the screen behind him, the guy's face is blown up so large I can see his pores. He's not even sweating.

"Your fluidity is amazing, young man," Elliot says. "Where did you learn to dance like that?" He looks down at his folder and up at Street Guy. "James?"

"Liquid," he says. "I'm called Liquid."

"What sort of training do you have, Liquid?"

The guy shrugs. "The only training I have is in living in cardboard boxes for the last two years and eating dog food two meals a day. If you're talking about that kind of training, I got a ton." It totally shocks me that anyone would talk to Elliot that way. But Liquid's face is blank, impassive. At ease up there, even though there are at least a hundred of us in here.

Elliot asks him about dancing other styles, and George and Rio nod at each other because they know how this works, while I can't remember much of it. Liquid just sort of shrugs at all of Elliot's questions, his hands dug in his front pockets, his hair shielding his eyes. Doesn't say he knows ballet or contemporary or even ballroom and, to be quite honest, it doesn't really even seem like he cares. But the judges keep poking and prodding him and asking where he was born and who he lives with and where he learned to dance until Liquid starts talking. His words are slow. His sentences are clipped. I can tell he doesn't even want to talk, but then he does talk about the street. His life on it. And the other kids who live on it with him.

He says stuff about bumming spare change and fighting in alleys and sleeping in dumpsters to avoid getting stabbed by addicts who can't see straight. I don't know where he's had any time to dance at all. I mean, is this how it is for all people on the streets in big cities, this dancing and dumpsters and sticking together and caring about nothing? Because it's not what I picture when I envision my mom there.

I wonder if he ever came across her during his street days. I wonder if she saw him dance and thought of me. New York. Is that how far she went to get away from us?

The judges glance at each other and whisper in each other's ears and scribble on their pads and steal quick glances at Liquid.

Astrid Scott's the first to speak. "That's quite a story you have there. But you won't be sleeping in cardboard boxes anymore, Liquid, because you're going to Los Angeles! You've earned our first spot on the show!"

The whole audience erupts like Mount St. Helens. Everyone's pumping their fists and shouting fake-happy, fake-encouraging words like, "Way to go, man!" because he's good and on the show, and good plus on the show equals fewer spots for everyone else, including me and George and Rio.

But Liquid just thanks the judges, then strolls to stage left, while grabbing another cigarette from his back pocket. Then he drops to the ground and worms himself all the way to the double doors while the cameras hover above him, catching it all and blasting it on the screen behind him. He's probably the coolest thing I've ever seen. And the saddest thing, too.

But the judges are beaming and it's that energy that's projected on that screen, the clapping, the cheers, the waving his ticket in the air. Because they know they've just handed the guy a brand-new life and it isn't often that people will do that for you. Usually all they ever want to do is take it.

I study my number thirty-one pinned to my shirt. Twenty-nine more dancers before I'm up.

"He really was incredible," I say. "Here's hoping everyone's not as good as him."

"They won't be," George says. "I guarantee half the people in here can't dance."

Like always, George is so on the money. Because the next three dancers aren't good, and I'm so glad I almost pee through my sweats. The first one's this girl from Nebraska who says she's contemporary ballet, but it's clear she's never taken a dance class in her life. Her arms flail above her head, jerking to every second beat of some Beyoncé song that was popular a billion years ago.

"Oh shit," George whispers. "I can barely watch her."

"She's brave to get up there and do that, though."

George grunts. "Brave, or really stupid."

The cameras zero in on her, capturing all of her steps, which aren't really steps at all. I think about her Nebraskan hometown and wonder if her people are going to see this. I wonder what it'll be like when she gets home. If they'll be nice to her about it, or if this single moment where she's trying to be fearless and trying to do something different will ruin her.

The judges thank her for coming out and tell her she's not right for the show. She bows, letting her yellow curls fall in front of her face, but when she lifts her head, I can see it in her shattered eyes. She thought she stood a chance.

And so do the other two who come after her—one guy, one girl—both "contemporary," both devastated when the judges send them home. The dancer after those three is this tiny tapper from Montana with killer calves and a high ponytail. Both her feet and her music are so fast, and even though I know tapping's really hard, I don't get it. Don't get how they can feel the music like that when the *click-click-click* of their shoes overpowers the vibrations—the soul of every song.

The girl smiles so hard I think her face is going to crack. On the screen behind her, they blast her face so big I can see inside her mouth, to her molars.

George points to the judges' table. "Look at them. They're eating it up."

George is right. Elliot's and Gia's and Astrid's eyes are all sparkly and kind of moving around in time with her feet. He's so right. They *are* eating it up. And the crowd is digging it, too. Some of the kids are even on their feet cheering and whistling with their fingers in their mouths. Which means she's good. Really good.

The judges call her forward and Elliot tells Happy Feet that she's earned her spot on the show. The cameras slide forward and flash her name on the screen in sparkly red letters. *Hayden Bosworth. Tapper. One to watch.*

Next, this hip-hop guy from Florida, who's as big as a gorilla and is wearing a backward hat and slinky shorts, gets on stage. Behind him, the screen changes to show pictures of

Florida: NASA, the Keys, the clear green sea, yachts cruising up and down waterways. Then it switches to him, his body and face, and I have to admit that his hard-hitting pops and air punches are pretty legit.

But when he thrusts his chest into the ground and pounds it with his fists, I know I don't like him. Or maybe "like" isn't the right word. I lean in closer.

I mean, the guy's got crazy passion and it doesn't take a hip-hopper to know how good he is at his style, but I'm not kidding when I say he looks as though he's ready to kill someone with both his giant hands. His face is red and his teeth are all jagged—it's like he's been in multiple fights, not to survive like Liquid, but for fun. And his top lip is curled up in this unsettling way. And there's a light in his eyes. Not light like George's light—shimmery and everything—but light like fire, ready to set us all aflame. This guy's like that, only scarier because he's here. Like no one I've ever met in real life.

He finishes his routine and then steps forward, his chest puffed out and heaving. He stares into the audience and the cameras focus in on his black eyes. Then he spits. Right there on the stage. In front of all the cameras. On purpose.

Elliot Townsend shifts in his seat. I expect him to yell at this kid for defacing property or being so rude or scary or something. I expect the guy to be embarrassed, regret what he's done because the cameras have caught it and now maybe everyone in his hometown will see what he's done, too.

"Tell us about yourself," is what Elliot says. He doesn't mention the spit and I wonder if maybe I imagined the whole thing. "Mr. Jackson Wiles, is it?"

"Jacks. Not Jackson. Not ever."

"Jacks. Give us something to remember you by."

Jacks shrugs. "What's to tell? I got a deadbeat dad in Miami that stubbed cigarettes out on my arm when I told him I wanted to dance instead of play football. A mom that stayed in bed watching TV as the fire burned through my skin."

All of the judges except Elliot grin, so obviously impressed by his dance and sob story skills. The cameras slide closer to the judges. Astrid adjusts her low-cut blouse. Elliot pretends the cameras aren't there, but I can tell he always knows they're there. They zoom in on Jacks's face. The screen behind him lights up, zeroing in on those broken teeth, wrecked and ruined. It's sick.

"What a difficult upbringing." Astrid sniffs. "And how did that make you feel, Jacks?"

Jacks sneers. "Feel? I haven't felt a thing since I was five."

George and Rio and I exchange glances because it doesn't make sense. How can a guy with veins pulsing through his neck and little scars the size of pennies all over his arms not feel anything? Or maybe he does feel and what he really means is that he doesn't feel anything good.

Jacks cracks his knuckles and the sound magnifies by a million, echoing through this auditorium. No one says a thing. The whole place is silent save for the sounds of cameras wheeling all around us and the deep breathing coming from Jacks.

The judges hand Jacks his ticket to LA and he grabs it and storms off stage like he's doing them a favor when really, if you ask me, he's done them anything but.

Next this awesome ballroom couple from New Mexico dance a fox trot to an old Prince song and make it through, as does as a West Coast Swing guy from New Jersey named Lawrence. And then a hip-hop girl from Illinois, called Zyera, who wows the judges with her "crisp popping abilities," plus another contemporary girl from Georgia named Juliette, whose leaps literally defy gravity, make it to the show. The screen flashes all of their faces and their families in the audience, holding signs that cheer them on and wish them good luck.

I think of home and Rose and imagine Rose watching the show somewhere, her nails getting chewed to death because she always chews them when she's nervous. I imagine her getting a poster board from the Pic 'N' Pay and using a sharpie to draw those thick black bubble letters she does with my name and George's name across the front. I imagine seeing her face on that screen, holding it up.

But I know that won't happen. Rose is always working. I don't know if they have a TV where she works. Don't know if she'd want to watch it even if they did.

"They've just let eight people on the show," George says. "Eight people out of thirteen and we've only been here a few hours."

"How many do they pick in total again?" I say.

George shrugs. "It's different for every season. They usually just stop when they have all the talent they need."

I shift in my seat, my knees jittery, my toes tapping. At this rate we'll be lucky to audition at all today, no matter what number we have. The way it is now, my whole cutting-in-line super-plan seems almost for nothing.

But after Juliette, six terrible dancers are sent home while the audience boos and pretends to throw stuff to get them off the stage. Elliot tells them they make a mockery of dance. Astrid tells them to take dance lessons and lots of them. I sit up straight and push my shoulders back. I'm not like them. I've been training for this exact moment my entire life. I can do this. Only eleven more dancers until it's my turn to prove it. And then that realization sinks in, too. Only *eleven more dancers* until I'm up.

A classical ballerina takes the stage.

"We gotta get back there," George says. "We're up in fifteen."

Next to me, Rio squirms in her chair. But she doesn't get up or say a thing while, on stage, the girl rises on her toes and extends her leg in attitude. She's really good and her legs are long and her hair is beautiful and it actually looks like golden droplets of rain when she pirouettes.

Wait. I lean forward to read her home state.

At the same time, Rio says, "Hey. Is that who I think it is?" She blinks a couple of times and then it clicks. Arizona. I've met someone here from Arizona already. I know that hair and those legs. And Rio does, too.

"She's not terrible," Rio says. But I hear it in her voice. Legs is definitely not terrible. She's amazing. Better than any of us thought she'd be when we cut in front of her in line. Better than any classical ballerina I've ever seen in my life.

The screen behind her changes to show colors, swirling pastels—pinks and greens and cool blues—shades that match her flowy hair and movements. They didn't do that for any of the other dancers. Then again, no one before her danced ballet like this.

When she's finished, the judges toss her bucketfuls of praise and with it, a ticket on the show. But Legs doesn't jump up and down as she accepts it. She scans the crowd until she reaches our row, and stops. The colors disappear and the screen changes to show her face. Which has this really smug, you-guys-are-so-gonna-eat-my-shit smile on it.

The world looks totally different from backstage.

People are crazy bouncing up and down as they breathe and stretch and come offstage smiling these ear-to-ear smiles. Or don't. The few who make it bound toward us, eyes gleaming. But the ones who don't stumble back, skin sallow, clouded by the words they've heard. *You're not good enough.*

These ones have tears hiding behind sockets. Some don't even try to hold them back. Some let them free, falling, unobstructed, dreams crushed.

Total elation.

Or heartbreak.

George comes out of the restroom, changed and ready. His hair is freshly gelled and swooped over to one side and he's wearing a clean white tank and a pair of fitted gray calf-length sweatpants that accentuate his lean torso, tight butt, small waist. He's washed his face and it looks so good—clear and poreless and perfect. Everything about him is chiseled and styled except his eyebrows, which are messy, but manly messy. A camera swivels around to film him and he laps it up, rolling his shoulders back and smiling. He's like a blond

Channing Tatum, only better because he's real. The audience is going to love him just as much as the cameras seem to.

George hands some backstage assistants Rio's iPod with our music on it while I duck into the bathroom to swap my own clothes out. I give myself a once-over in the mirror, hoping I seem half as self-assured as George. I can feel the cameras on me even though there aren't any in here. I can feel the heat from their lights and I'm sweating and my face feels so warm and yet is so white.

I grip the sides of the sink and squeeze until my knuckles are white, too. I close my eyes. Say the words I've said inside my head every minute since we left Summerland: You can do this. If you want to fix what's been broken for so, so long, you have to do this.

When I open my eyes, my reflection's all blurred and out of focus and my body is outlined in a thin black line, my insides colored in with brown—no—gold. Shimmery, blurry gold.

This happened once before, three summers ago. Before Colleen died. Before things got worse than we ever knew they could.

Mom was home and she and Rose and I went for breakfast at the Pig 'N' Pancake—Mom's treat, which didn't happen often, if ever. While they grabbed us a booth, I excused myself for the bathroom. I guess no one knew I was in there, though, because seconds later Mark's mom and little sister came in, breathless and giggling over the bad smell the Pig 'N' Pancake had. They talked about going elsewhere. They talked about how Mark liked the Pig 'N' Pancake and wouldn't go elsewhere, which made them both giggle harder. They talked about how the restaurant should hold its standards higher, the way it used to.

They didn't have to say it, but I knew what they were talking about: the smell, the buzz in the air, like the hum of an old refrigerator. It was because we were there. And even though Mark never said it either, I knew it's how he must have felt about me, too.

So I waited in my stall until they did their thing and left the bathroom. When I came out, my reflection was hazy, distorted. There, but not really there. Me, but not really me.

Now, I cover my eyes with my shaking hands.

When I finally let my arms fall to my sides, the gold is gone and the black outline is gone, too. I look exactly like I always do. And then I know: This isn't like that last time. Here, no one's talking about me. No one, save George, even knows who I am.

I swing open the door and smack directly into Rio and George. Behind them are a few dancers who have already auditioned. The ballroom couple and the tapper and Jacks and Liquid, who are sizing each other up, like they're about to throw down. Jacks's face is all red and heated again. Liquid's laughing at him, though I don't know why.

George looks at both of them over his shoulder. Back at me. Frowns. "You take a nap in there or what?"

"I couldn't find my tights."

"Fix your hair at least." He licks his palm and smoothes out my wispies with his spit while Rio watches, her smirk covered by her hand, but not well enough. From on stage, we hear this weak round of applause and then number twenty-eight, a guy from Texas, comes off the stage. He's clenching his stomach with his fingertips, kind of digging into his middle, tearing at his own skin.

George pats the guy's back halfheartedly and then straightens into a perfect exclamation mark. "I'm up next. It's now or never." He kisses my cheek and Rio's and we tell him to break a leg, and then he runs toward the wings. We follow behind him but stop when we get to the wings and let George take center stage alone. The cameras from the ceiling lower to follow him and I wonder if he can feel their heat, too.

He crouches down in a half-man, half-moon position.

I know his stance. Know his routine like I know every pine-lined street in Summerland. Yet I never get bored of the sight of George's perfect back, rolled into an enviable sphere. His natural roundness is what makes him flow like some smooth, space-aged machine. It's what sets him apart from everyone. The music starts. But it's not the usual pop-princess song I'm used to hearing him dance to.

My breath catches and holds.

I know this song.

Last August, a month after my mom left, George and I heard it in Washington. We were all there. Me and him and Mrs. Moutsous and Malcolm and Rose, all of us on this little weekend getaway to take Malcolm back to college after summer vacation, when George pulled me away from them.

"Come on," he said. "Let's get out of here."

Before I had the chance to protest, George pulled me into a yellow cab that stopped in front of us, suddenly, as if it knew.

"The Gorge," he told the driver who nodded and flicked his meter on.

"Of course you're taking me someplace that sounds almost exactly like your name," I said. "So predictable."

But George didn't laugh. Instead, he got all quiet and then turned his head to stare out the window. "You ever feel like you know every person in Summerland, but nobody knows you?"

I wasn't expecting these kinds of words to come from George. The fact was, it wasn't like him. It made me feel vulnerable. More than that, it made me feel afraid. "Maybe. I don't know. What do you mean?"

"Like you can never really be yourself. Be the person you are on the inside."

"Yeah. I pretty much wish I was someone else on a daily basis."

"I want to get out of here," he said, his head glued to the window. "Where no one knows me. Where I can be the person I'm destined to be without all this stuff dragging me down."

I didn't know what he meant. No one in our town ever dragged his name through the mud. He was George Moutsous. Everyone knew that and loved him for it.

Fifteen minutes later, we got out in front of this place on the edge of the Columbia River. It was called the Gorge, like George had said. But no sweet name came close to describing this thing, this amphitheater, smack dab in the middle of an epic canyon. A concert was just ending there. But everyone was still seated all over the stadium's grassy area, listening to the band's last song. The acoustics bellowed in and out of the Gorge's walls. Echoing. Exhaling. Breathing out the breaths of angels.

We sat in a patch of worn-away grass and inhaled the music.

We closed our eyes. We went outside of ourselves. We imagined.

I never did know the band's name, but I'll never forget the song they played—the only song we made it in time to hear. There was this line in it that made me feel something I hadn't before. Made me feel like it was me they were singing for. Me they were telling it to. *Dance yourself clean. Dance yourself clean.*

And in that moment, I dreamed. Dreamed what it would be like to really to dance myself clean. From the picture I still see every single night, behind my eyelids. My bike, pulling up to my house after my shift at Deelish. Paramedics leaving, two of them, three of them, more, pushing her lifeless body strapped to a stretcher, dried blood still caked on the stiff corners of her mouth.

That day at the Gorge, we lounged on the outskirts of greatness, the music flowing through our veins, more potent than blood.

And now, watching him on stage, leaping, turning, gaining momentous height, creating impossibly clean lines with his limbs, I know that George must have felt it, too.

His tilt jumps are endless. His pique en arabesque stops time. I've never seen his legs extend that high. I've never seen George dance himself clean. Until now.

And then, as he nears the front of the stage, his upper body ready to take one final leap, his left foot misjudges the firm ground below him. And then George is down. Crouched down, crumpled, in the same position he started in.

Half man.

Half moon.

THIRTEEN

George stays balled up in this shape, his head buried between his knees, while the song plays itself out. Seconds pass. Cameras swoop, moving past him and behind him and in front of him.

His body heaves.

Get up, George. Please, get up.

The crowd is completely silent.

My body is shivering while my eyes dart back and forth between his crumpled figure and the judges' faces. They exchange glances. Lean back in their chairs. Whisper. Flip through the sheets in front of them.

"Excuse me, young man? Are you all right?" Elliot calls. "Do you need me to call for assistance?"

George's head swivels from side to side, slowly. The rest of him is still, except for the rise and fall of his back.

Get up, George. Please, get up.

Next to me, someone's elbow jabs me in the ribs. "Is he dead or what?" My eyes slide left to meet hers. Happy Feet. She's smiling with that same plastic grin.

"Why isn't he moving?" Rio says.

"I don't know." My hands press the sides of my cheek. "I've never seen him slip. Never. Not in fourteen years."

Rio chews on her thumbnail. "Maybe if he gets up now they'll give him another shot. Come on, sweetie," she whispers. "Get up."

My eyes burn through Rio's, but she doesn't notice.

Fifteen minutes ago, she thought he was hot. Hot I could deal with, or sort of deal with, at least. Now, she's watching him—his body rolled into this ball that makes him look so small—with something entirely different in her eyes.

Next to Rio, someone spits a piece of their own chewed-up nail to the ground in front of me. I glance left. Jacks.

"He better get up or it's game over for him," Jacks says. "Not that I'd care."

"He's going to get up," I say.

"Nope. Doesn't look like it."

"You'd like that, wouldn't you?"

"I wouldn't care either way."

I get close to him. So close that my face is inches from his, even though I'm a good foot shorter. Scars. He's full of them. Not just on his arms but all over his face. There's a big one under his right eye, sloping from the bridge of his nose to his temple. And another one under his lip. Puffy, and in the shape of two semicircles, like teeth marks. I wonder how many fights this guy must have been in to make his face like this. I don't want to know who he was fighting. My face is so hot I can feel it. I ball my hands into fists.

He laughs. "What? You think I wouldn't hit a girl back?"

"I think you would. I think you'd hit anyone if you thought it'd earn you points somehow."

"Magnolia, come on," Rio says, softly. She pulls my arm away. "It's not worth it. He's not worth it."

Jacks laughs again but he backs off. He turns his head but I see him touching a fresh-looking cut on his neck, just over his collarbone. He sees me staring. Turns away, covering the cut with his hand. I think of what he said about his dad. I wonder if those marks and scars are from him. I wonder how far Jacks went to provoke them.

It's not my problem. I turn back to George. "The judges will give him another chance. You'll see. You'll all see." I open and close my hands but it doesn't relax me any. "He's good. You have no idea."

Rio digs her hands in the pockets of her hoodie. She flicks her head toward the judges. "They look like they don't know what to do next."

I stare at the screen. It's frozen on George.

"What is it you're feeling?" Gia says into her microphone. Her usual bluntness is freckled with a kind of softness I've never heard from her before. The cameras zoom in on her face and then it's her face that's plastered on the screen next, alongside George.

George raises his head. "It's just so much."

Gia glances down at the paper in front of her. "What is, George? What's too much?"

"I just can't take it anymore." He motions across the silhouetted audience, blackened by dim lights. Silenced by the slip of his foot and the surrender in his voice. "We all want this so badly," he says. "Everyone in here. But my friend, Magnolia. Magnolia Woodson. She needs this more than any of us. It's why we came. But I just couldn't do it out there. Couldn't dance knowing that if this didn't work then maybe she'd never dance again."

Wait. What is he talking about? Why did he say my last name? I look at Rio. Her stare flickers back at me.

Even from behind, I can tell George's shoulders are shaking. So this big part of me wants to run out there and pick him up and fold his body into mine. But then there's this other part of me that's confused. Didn't they see his foot slip? Why aren't they asking him about it? And my last name. Why did he say my last name?

George lifts his head. "If this doesn't work for her, if she doesn't make it on the show, then she can't fix her reputation. If that happens, well, I don't know what she'll do."

My mouth drops open. *What?* The cameras move closer to George. The screen projects his face in supersize but then it changes to *my* face. Me, standing here shocked and pale and awful.

"She wants them to see that it wasn't her fault," George says.

"Wants who to see that *what* wasn't her fault?" Gia says.

"Our town. The mayor's daughter's death," George says. "She thinks she's responsible for what happened."

"Oh my God," Rio says under her breath. She steps into the wings and out of the camera's shot.

"Oh my God!" Jacks and Hayden say, much louder, and in unison.

Next to them, Liquid stares at George on stage. He shakes his head. Flicks his hair away from his face. "I'm not watching this," he mumbles. He pushes on past us, disappearing somewhere backstage.

Jacks laughs. It sounds like thunder. It sounds like death. "He's selling you out. He's totally selling you out."

No. This can't be happening. There's no way George would do this to me, make me seem so petty and selfish. Tell the whole world my secret. Make it so that I can't escape my name, no matter what I do. George. My George. Who's helped me leap over every hurdle, swim through every river I've ever almost drowned in before. No. There's just no way.

"She wasn't supposed to work that night," George says. "But when she got home, the house was still full of people and there were drugs everywhere. Colleen was dead. They were wheeling her away." He hangs his head. "They blame her family for everything."

"No," I whisper. My palms are sweating and my heart is beating so fast I cover it with my hand. But through my touch, it pounds harder and faster, jolting me with every thud. The screen behind George flickers back to me. My heart. My hand. I drop it to my side.

And then George lets it out. Two last little lines. "I just can't dance. Not while knowing what might happen to Mags if she doesn't prove to Summerland that she's not the garbage her mother is."

"No," I whisper, my knees buckling. "Why is he doing this?" I've known for a long time that the people of Summerland thought my mom was garbage. I just never knew George thought it, too.

This can't be happening. But it is. He's using me. Using me, my name, my story that I thought I left behind—wanted so badly to leave—in Summerland, to get himself on the show.

"Why is he doing this?" I say again, louder this time.

"He cares about you," Rio says.

"He cares about getting on the show," Jacks says.

"He told me. He told all of us." Rio motions to Hayden and to Jacks. Behind them, Liquid's back with a couple of his street groupies by his side. I have no idea how he got them back-stage. I don't even care. "When you were in the bathroom." She turns to Liquid. "You heard him, right? You heard him say how worried he was about her."

Liquid shrugs and blows the hair out of his eyes. One of his friends says, "Liquid's here to dance. Possibly get laid while he's at it. That's it." His groupies bump fists with each other, but Liquid doesn't. He stands off to one side, watching George.

Rio turns back to me. "It wasn't your fault. All that stuff that happened with your mom and that girl."

"Stop. Just stop." I take a step toward the stage.

Rio grabs my arm. "Don't. It won't do you any good."

I turn to her, fire radiating from my limbs. "He slipped! He slipped! Did he tell you that he was going to do that, too?" I shrug my arm free from her grip. Breathe. In. Out. "This isn't his story to tell. Who I am. It wasn't for him to share that with anyone."

But it's too late. On center stage, George is letting it all out.

He tells them about my mom's addictions. He tells them about her leaving us, again and again and again. He tells them every gruesome detail about Colleen's death, even though he wasn't there, even though I never told him the details of what happened because I never want to think about them again as long as I live. He tells them about me. How I rarely go places anymore besides Katina's and Deelish and home. Scared, always scared, of what they'll say if I do.

The cameras zoom in on his face, his body. He takes a deep breath and looks straight at them. And then he tells them about him. Holding me together, every day since it happened.

Next to me, Rio's eyes are watery. "I had no idea it was like that for you in your hometown. It's worse than mine. I should have thought."

I bite my bottom lip, but I don't say a thing. Because if I do—if I open my mouth one teensy little bit—I'm going to scream. At George, at the impossible unfairness of life, at this damn competition and what I need it to be.

"It's just too much to handle. I've carried this weight for too long," George says between sobs. "An entire year."

Gia nods. "I know, George. The world is cruel that way. Sometimes it's good to us. But other times"—she shudders—"other times it feels like it'll kill us."

"But that's why we dance," Astrid says. "To let it all out. For it to be okay, no matter what happens."

"I don't know," George says. "I don't know if she will be okay if she doesn't win. We need to be here, to fix things. We need to win."

I double over, sucker-punched. We. We. We.

We've always been a "we" before—me and George. But this is one "we" I don't want any part of.

Gia strains to look behind George. "Where is this friend of yours that might not be okay if she isn't on our show?"

George shields his eyes from the light with one hand. He turns and points to me. At me. "There. Magnolia Woodson." He says my name, loudly. Revealing me. Exposing me. Stripping me down to bone. "She's on next."

I take two steps forward. Out of the wings. Onto the stage. "I'm here. I'm Magnolia."

Elliot Townsend whispers something to Astrid, who in turn whispers to Gia. Gia nods her head. Then Elliot speaks. "Hello, Magnolia. Good to have you here. You'll have your chance to dance, but first we have some words for your friend." He clears his throat. "Your friend who obviously cares a great deal about you and your family's well-being."

I take a step back.

"We don't need to tell you that you're an extraordinary technician, George," Elliot says. "The quality of your movement is spectacular. You have all the talent we expect from dancers at the *end* of our competition, and to see it on display when the show is only beginning is impressive to say the least." Elliot pauses to take a deep breath. "But what amazes us the most is your conviction. You drew your strength from the passion you feel for your friend, and her plight. It was all quite palpable."

George inhales and his words come out more as squeaks than sentences. "I promised to help her. She needs this to go on. I don't think she'll dance anymore without this—"

"George!" I shout. "Please, stop. Please."

His words halt. His head snaps around. *Take it all back.* My thoughts burn and I hope they're burning through him. *Take everything you said back.* But I know he can't. Won't.

"We're going to give you your ticket to LA, George, because you deserve a spot on the show." Elliot nods at me. "Then we'll watch Magnolia perform. If she's anywhere near as good as you, she'll get her own ticket. But if she's not, well, the next part is up to you. If you're serious about dance and want a career in it, you keep your ticket. After all, getting in this competition is a guarantee that you'll be dancing professionally for a long, long time." He waves the ticket above his head. "But if you're willing to sacrifice yourself to take care of your friend, we'd never want to stand in your way."

What is he saying? The screen behind George shows Elliot talking, saying it in loud words, but I still can't hear it the way I need to.

My brain swells, then shrinks, then swells again. And then it all becomes clear. If I don't make it through on my own, they'll let George give his spot to me. If he wants to. I don't want George's pity place. Yet I don't know if I can *not* take it, either. If he'll give it to me.

George freezes. I can tell it's not what he expected.

Elliot grins. "So that settles it. Let's just watch Magnolia dance, while you think about how you want your own life to play out. Sound good?"

The cameras swoop to the front of the stage. Elliot sits up straight. Pauses dramatically. "Magnolia Woodson. Please take center stage."

I touch my collarbone to make sure my pillowcase piece is still there. Pulling me back. Pushing me forward. And then I walk out to the middle of the stage and turn around so that my back is to the judges, so that I'm facing that huge damn screen.

George slinks off stage. I stare at him as he slides on past me, but I doubt he can see the fire speeding from my eyes to where he stops and stands in darkness. Next to him, Jacks gives me a sarcastic two thumbs-up while next to him, Hayden's smile is paralyzed. But Rio. With sincere eyes, Rio mouths the words, "Break a leg."

I whisper back to her. "If I don't break my own out here, I'm definitely going to break his."

I bow my head and wait for my music.

A million images flash through my mind, none of them clear, but all of them fighting to be. Clamming with my mother. George on our beach. Rose and the clam gun. The money and the names and the drugs and her body her body her empty body, leaving my home, never to return.

I take one gigantic deep breath and close my eyes.

I know why I'm here. To beat George's lying traitor ass.

And to dance myself clean, too.

Fourteen

The music starts with a low hum.

I rise on the balls of my feet in elevé. Close my eyes. Lift further like a doll, an invisible string pulling my head, neck, back, so that only my toes graze earth below. I slide my coiled right foot north, along the strong curves of my left leg. It's stiff and rigid, supporting every ounce of my weight—though here, in this moment, I am weightless.

I hold it there until my music speeds, tempo speeds, heart speeds, and then extend it into the air, staying in that position for eternity.

The beat of my song drops, and I leap. Soar, into the blackness of my own barely pumping heart. But the rest of me. The rest of me stays back somewhere between the wings of the stage and my bed, in Summerland. Warm with the memory of sleep. Safe with the promise of a thousand maybes.

My music plays on and I dance.

I fly.

The shell of my body shatters, releasing my soul from the purgatory of longing. Liberating my heart from pain. My legs are no longer my legs. My arms are no longer my arms. I am a blackbird. I am free. I am clean.

No longer can I feel my neck attached to my head, moving, in any direction.

Can't feel my fingertips—don't know if my hands are open or closed.

Can't hear my music, the rhythms muted by my heartbeat, thumping in my chest heavy and hard and fast and heavy.

Can't see the screen, flashing my picture and pictures behind it. Birds. Trees. Waters. Rain. Summerland. Summerland.

And my brain. Black. Blank. Numb.

But I don't know where it starts or stops or if it comes from my head at all, or my heart or my eyes or my ears or my feet or the stage or the music or the memory of what it is I'm doing here, and why it is I'm doing anything at all.

And then suddenly, the lights come on.

And I'm here.

In the middle of the stage. Staring into these lights above me that shine so bright. They're burning through me. Burning me down to ash.

My hands are open now—that I know. My palms are pressed flat against my chest.

No music is playing, but I can *hear* that no music is playing. Someone out there coughs and I can hear it. Someone sighs or gasps or sucks in air or lets it out—and I can hear that, too. I'm in my position, my final position. I've finished my routine.

A pain shoots through my body, from the toes on my left foot. I've felt it before in Katina's studio. There and then gone. Hurting, but not like this. I don't remember when it first started. If it came last year or years ago. I only feel it when I feel it. Now, it winds its way through all of my other parts. My calf, my thigh, my hip, my spine, my neck.

But the lights are on.

So I pull my head straight. To see what it is I can see.

"Please step forward, Magnolia Woodson," a voice says. And I know, as my heart and head and body know, that the voice belongs to Gia Gianni.

And the pain disappears.

"Magnolia," Gia says. "You have a big reason for coming here today, don't you?"

"Yes."

"We've heard about it from George. But would you like to tell us about it in your own words?"

"No."

Elliot taps his fingers on his tabletop. The noise magnifies by a million in this auditorium and I think they're probably capturing it on the screen behind me, though I wouldn't know. "We want personal stories for our show," he says. "If you have one worth telling, we'd like to hear it."

"He said it all. There's nothing more to tell."

Astrid Scott bites her lip. Her eyes dart back and forth between the other judges. "Elliot means that, well, quite frankly, your solo was exquisite. Look around you. Listen. You've taken our breath away."

I inhale. "I want to dance. George told you just how much I want to be on the show. If I was good enough, then let me. If I wasn't, send me home. Please, just let me go."

Elliot straightens in his chair. He crosses and uncrosses his arms. Next to him, Astrid leans forward and takes a long drink from her bottle of water. Wipes her puffed lips with the back of her hand. And next to her, Gia folds her hands together and tucks them under her chin.

Finally, it's Gia that speaks. "The fact is, there's just no way we could deny you a spot in the competition. Magnolia Woodson, it would be my pleasure—all of our pleasures—to work in your presence. You danced like the name of our show. You danced like you need it to live."

Elliot waves a small rectangular piece of cardboard at me.

I take seven steps forward. My hand reaches out and my fingertips open and then close around it.

"Welcome to the show. We'll see you in LA."

I know there are so many things I should say to him, to them, like thank you. Thank you so much for this opportunity—no, *dancertunity*—to be on their show. But I don't say any of it. Instead, my fingers pluck the ticket. My body turns around. And my feet. My feet walk offstage.

Strong.

Confident.

Finished.

FIFTEEN

I have no idea how I got backstage, but somehow, I did it.

I'm shaking and buzzing, but all I can think about is how George betrayed me. I scan the room but he's not anywhere. Seconds later, I'm surrounded by people I've seen and people I haven't. They crowd me like I'm something special and pat my back and offer me sips of water and say things about me being amazing, angelic, inspiring, perfect.

I touch my cheeks with my fingertips. The cameras are on me, close to my face and surging chest, but I don't care. I'm smiling. Big. Hard. Real. I did it. My plan will work. This is going to change things for me and Rose. More than ever, I know it will change things.

Someone next to me points to the stage and mumbles something about the girl who's on next. Something about how life pretty much sucks for her, having to go after me. *Me.*

Jacks crushes the can of whatever he's just finished and tosses it across the room into the garbage, like a basketball. "I thought you were going to crash and burn. You were like a scared little rabbit out there." He sighs. "You weren't terrible. Better than most people around here." He eyes Liquid. "Definitely better than that guy." Liquid doesn't answer. Just gives Jacks the double middle finger and drops down for a head spin.

Even though it's coming from Jacks—pretty much the last person on earth I'd ever expect a compliment from—I can't help but let my heart feel the warmth and swell of what he's said. I *was* better than most of them. I let it hammer through like a thousand beating drums. I was good. And this will change things.

Jacks sticks one foot out to trip Liquid, mid-spin.

"Hey, man, what's your deal?" Liquid gets up, hands thrown in the air.

Jacks ignores him. Turns to me. "Where'd you say you're from?"

"Summerland."

"Asshole," Liquid mutters. He whips a cigarette out of his pocket and sticks it between his lips, unlit. But then he slinks away with his friends.

"Summerland? Where the hell's that?" Jacks says.

"Here. In Oregon."

"And you learned to dance where?"

I take a sip of my water. Straighten my back and elongate my neck. Say something about my small studio. My strong teacher. Maybe I even say something about the fact that I've danced since before I could walk. But what I won't say is anything about dancing with George next to me. Always with him next to me.

And then suddenly he is next to me again. "Mags."

No. He can't take this from me.

Liquid comes up behind George, grabs his arm, waggles his eyebrows. George shrugs him off. "Not now. Later. Okay?"

Jacks gaze bounces between Liquid and George. "Oh, that's just perfect. Now everything makes sense. You two are a regular Gene Kelly and Rita Hayworth. Question is, who's who?"

I stare at Jacks. I'm not going to lie, the fact that he knows who Gene Kelly and Rita Hayworth are catches me off guard. And I know it must catch George off guard too. But George ignores him, his eyes steady and on me. "Listen to me, Mags."

Like nothing ever has before, earning my spot on the show will change things for me and Rose in Summerland. That's what's important here. I turn my head. Look straight at George. See him like I've never seen him before. Fixing my family's life in Summerland. That's what's important here. Not this with George. Never again.

I take a step back, moving away from George's smothering stare. I used to think it was love when he looked at me like this, his pupils meeting mine like they're searching for something good, and finding it. But now I know that the only love George has ever felt is love for himself.

"What do you want?" I say.

His mouth falls open. "You made it." He studies his feet. "I knew you would."

I shake my head. I don't say a word.

A couple of the other competitors—one guy, one girl, both contemporary dancers, both from Minnesota—walk past us, staring at me and George and the heat that's radiating from us both. They stop, just inches away from us. Waiting.

George steps toward me. Tosses the couple a dirty look. So dirty, in fact, they keep walking. He whispers to me, "Don't be mad, okay? I didn't know that was going to happen. I had to make sure we made it through. I did it for us."

My limbs fall limp, softened and worn, like kneaded clay. "Tell me," I say. "Tell me how you did it for us. Because I want to believe you. I want to believe that you are the same person I've known my entire life." I motion around the room, to all the eyes watching, watching, watching. There are no cameras in Summerland, but it's no different than this. "Everyone thinks you slipped and freaked out because you thought you screwed up your own chances of getting yourself on the show. Everyone thinks you did this for yourself."

"Who cares what they think. What do you think?"

"I don't know what to think anymore."

I turn to go, but he grabs my arm. Sticks his face close to mine. Keeps his voice low. So low, only I can hear it. "Fine. I admit it. I slipped, okay? But who cares? It worked, didn't it? They loved the story. They loved us both because of it."

"I trusted you. You told them who I was. Everything you said is going to make it on TV. Now it won't be only Summerland people who hate me and Rose, it'll be the whole nation."

"They won't."

"You thought I wasn't good enough. You took my past and made a circus out of it. She died, George, and all they'll see is how I whined about how it made me look. You know it means so much more to me than that."

"You're right. I do know. You want your mom back. That's why you're here. You want her back and you can't even see that she's a shitty person but that's what she is. That's what she's been for a long, long time."

"You're wrong. You have no idea. You shouldn't have done that to me. After everything we've been through." I clench my fists and release them. "You're selfish. And scheming." I get close to his face. "You're nothing but a liar."

George's eyes waver on mine as if he's stumbling, falling. "I know you'd do anything to turn back time to before Colleen and the drugs. To before things got so bad in your house. I was trying to help you get there." He steps closer. Closer. Takes my hand and places it against his heart. I don't pull away. Instead I leave it there, nestled in the warmth and softness and safety I know so well. "I was trying to help you fill the hole I know you've felt every day of this year." He flicks his head toward the stage. "Those emotions were real. Everything I felt out there was real. I want this for you. I want you to see how it doesn't matter what they think of you. I want you to know how amazing you are, with or without them."

I jerk my hand away from his chest. "You did this for you, not for us."

"Mags, please," George whispers. He glances left and right but there aren't any cameras near us anymore. "You made it on the show. I did what I had to do to get us there."

"I would have made it on my own."

"Everyone's good out there. Have you seen where some of these kids have come from? They've gone to real dance schools with famous teachers and round-the-clock training. We're from Summerland. It isn't good enough. I needed to make us stand out. Give the judges something to remember us by. It doesn't matter how good we are." He slaps his chest. "Our stories. That's what they want. Something to sell to the crowd."

George's words permeate my brain and spread like anthrax. *It isn't good enough.* I know it's what he said, but I also know it's not what he meant. *You're not good enough.*

Until this very second, I thought we could go back to the place where "friend till the end" is enough because wading through George's thick ego is something I've always been able to navigate. But now I see who he really is. A fame whore. A glutton for the limelight. A sellout, willing to sell me out too if it means selling ourselves to the crowd, piece by piece by piece.

Everything inside me goes black. And then white. And then red, lava red. And then I'm on top of him, banging his chest with both fists.

"What the hell are you doing?" George shouts and people fly toward us. Cameramen on foot and cameras on wheels and kids with phones snapping pictures and cameras.

I feel someone yank the back of my leotard and someone else grab my hair. "Get her off him," someone shouts. Hayden. "She's losing it. Get her off him before she hurts him!"

Tears fly from my face. My hair hurts from being pulled. But the pain is nothing in comparison to this. To knowing that George never believed in me.

"You're dead! You're nobody to me!"

A crowd forms around us, circling, swarming. Lawrence. Zyera. Jacks. Liquid. Screens come closer, forward, around, over, and between George and me. They're filming it all. Another circus. I don't even care.

My head snaps back. I shriek and then whoever it is that has me lets go and grabs my arms instead of my hair. I swivel around. It's Liquid who has my arms pinned behind my back, twisting them so high it feels like they're going to snap like branches, like kindling, not arms. I stare at Liquid, pleading, but I see nothing behind his eyes. Why is he doing this to me? I could see it from Jacks but not from him. Jacks is the brute. Liquid's the one who doesn't want to do anything but dance and get laid. And then I remember. George is the one he wants. And I'm nobody.

I try to lunge forward, but it's no use. Liquid's got a good grip.

And I've got nothing left.

George jumps back but he springs too far, too quickly, his left cheek hitting one of the cameras, knocking over the man behind it. Liquid releases me. The man scrambles up and the light of his camera flashes red, rolling. George doubles over. He glares at me. His hands drop to his sides, revealing the scratch slashed across his face from the bottom of his left eye to the tip of his chin. It's bleeding.

"Who do you think you are?" I never expected to hear him this snarly. I never expected any of this from him. The crowd moves back though the cameras don't budge. I hear Jacks laughing somewhere at the back of the circle, while Liquid stands so close to George, ready to grab me again if I get near him. I don't want to be anywhere near him.

"Just leave me alone, Moutsous. Leave me alone for the rest of my life."

George dabs at his cheek with the bottom of his tee and then holds it out, surveying the blood. "With pleasure," he says. "I've spent the last ten years of my life letting you drag me down. I'm sure as hell not going to spend the next ten doing the same."

Sixteen

I hear the music stop. I hear a bunch of people clapping and cheering. I hear the screech of metal chairs—judges' chairs—pushing back, which probably means a break or a standing ovation for someone out there. And I hear Camilla's voice. Excited. Exclamatory.

The clapping simmers. And then Rio comes flying backstage toward George and me who are still standing, facing each other, locked in the most wicked stare down ever.

"We made it on the show!" she screams and the cameras swarm her. "We're gonna be on TV! We should try to get one room at the hotel, right? We are the three musketeers, just like Camilla said! All for one, one for all! Isn't it awesome? I can't believe we all made it!"

George blinks. His head turns toward Rio, the cameras, but he doesn't take his eyes off me. "What are you talking about?"

Rio jumps up and down all around me and George, making these crazy whooping sounds. She's out of breath but still spurting words that seem empty and hollow and impossible. "I made it through. Did you watch me? They said they've never seen anything like me before. Kind of like what they said to you, Magnolia. They loved us all. Isn't it perfect?"

I take a step forward and Liquid grabs my wrist, but I shake it free and he doesn't reach for it a second time. I rub the sides of my arms where his fingers have dug into my skin and the cameras zoom in on that. One guy shoves a girl out of his way to get a better shot and Liquid stumbles back and I know he doesn't care how he hurt me. I know he's probably hurt a thousand people before me like this, only worse because it was to save his life, not to save some twelve-year friendship.

Rio celebrates through all of it.

I can't believe she's danced and finished and neither George nor I watched her or cheered her on, like we promised we would. Like she did, for us. And by the gallon of glee spilling from her, she has no clue that the term "three of us together" no longer has any meaning.

George must see it too. See how totally oblivious Rio is, because his face softens. He gives her a weak little smile. Squeezes her hand. "I knew you'd make it." His gaze shoots briefly to me, then down to the smooth floor below, avoiding Hayden, Jacks, and the other contemporary girl, Juliette, too. He doesn't look at the cameras. He doesn't even look at Liquid, who's only ever been looking at him.

And me. Most of all, George is avoiding me. "I knew we'd all make it," he says, but his voice is quiet, bitten.

Jacks's jaw clenches. "You hoped we wouldn't," he says. He steps closer to George. "You're transparent. I know you were hoping we'd all fall out there." He head flicks to Rio. "Even her."

The glimmer in Rio's eyes dulls. She stops jumping. Creeps slowly toward George, ignoring Jacks's words. "What happened to you?"

Rio touches George's cheek, stained with the red tracks of deceit. He flinches, but he lets her touch the blood, lets her wipe a drop that's still loitering there at the corner of his nose.

George raises his head and stares me square in the eyes for one, two, three seconds. It's enough for Rio to know. She spins around, her eyes wide and wild. "Did you do this to him?"

"No. I didn't—" Something makes me stop. Like my mouth and brain are out of words. My left hand slides up under my bra strap to find my pillowcase piece. I take it out, hold it against my eyes that sting as though they're bleeding, too.

A month after Colleen died, I came home from dance late to find the house dark and quiet. I thought I was the only one home. Rose had started working at Urban Outfitters only a week earlier and seemed to be gone more often than she was home. Mom was always at her court-ordered counseling sessions in Astoria, every day, sometimes twice a day on days that seemed more bad than good.

So I thought I was alone. Until I heard noises coming from Mom's bedroom.

I pushed her door open. She was there, crumpled underneath her blankets, crying into her pillow. On her nightstand was a small rectangular mirror and the remnants of fine powder that clung to its edges, like a snow that just won't melt.

I climbed on the bed next to her and lay behind her. I wrapped one arm around her thin frame.

I know she felt me, but she didn't roll over. Instead, she whispered, "I'm sorry."

I snuggled in closer behind her back and her bones that poked me in a way I knew they shouldn't.

"I can't keep doing this," she said.

"So don't."

"You don't understand."

"I do. Just give it up. You don't need it. You have us."

Her body quieted for a moment, as if taking in my words. I needed her to know that I'd never give up on her. That I'd fight for her, through anything.

"Everything felt easier when I lived in Portland," she said. "It's big and free and nothing like here. Nobody knows you, no matter how long you've been there."

"We belong here."

I remember wishing I hadn't said it, because something about those three little words made her cry again, harder this time. But it's how I felt. Things had been good for us there at one time. We'd been a family, me and Rose and Mom. I said it again. "We belong here. This is our home."

"She's dead," my mom said between heaving breaths.

"But we're still alive." I nuzzled her neck and she turned away. It's not what I meant. Only that yeah, this terrible thing had happened but it didn't need to keep happening. We could fix things. As long as we were still that family of three, that trifecta that connected us and would always connect us, we could make things better like they used to be.

But Mom couldn't hear me. "I killed her," she said. "She's dead. She's dead. She's dead." Her body shook, the words, shaking her, as if out of some unwakeable nightmare.

Ten minutes later, I felt her body calm and then give in to the desperate pull of sleep. Felt my own body, my breath, slowing to match hers. But I got up. Took that mirror from her bedside table. Dusted the powder into the toilet with my bare hand. Walked back to her bed, and slept.

I woke up the next morning to bright streams of light pouring through Mom's curtains, bouncing off that damn hand mirror, cleaned, but still there. The mirror's reflection flashed prisms on the wall behind us, beautiful rainbows that made the place seem happy and colorful.

I sat up.

Mom was gone.

Somehow, I knew that this time, she was gone for real. She couldn't take it in Summerland anymore. Not after what she'd done.

I placed one hand over her pillow, hoping to feel her warmth. Instead, all I could feel was the wetness she'd left behind. The tears, the release, the realization that she couldn't get better. Not here. They'd never let her.

I never told anyone that I'd cut out that four-by-four square of pillowcase that absorbed her grief in a way we never did. Never told anyone that I've been carrying it with me since that morning, exactly one year and one day ago.

Now, Rio's hand is on mine, pulling at mine. My breath catches in the hundredth of a second it takes for her to grab that piece of cloth away from me. My body lunges toward her, but I'm not quick enough.

She pulls her arm back, hand closed around my scrap of pillowcase. "Magnolia, what are you doing?"

"That's mine. Give it back to me."

"It's just some stupid handkerchief. Can't you see he's bleeding?"

Rio furrows her brows, turns to George. She presses my square to his cheek. The blood soaks through to the other side in seconds, growing from the size of a dime to the size of a silver dollar, the deep red thick and dark and damaging. Her bottom lip trembles. "Tell me what happened to you."

George bows his head. And even though I expect him to tell her every ounce of what's transpired between the two of us, how the earth has shifted, the planets unaligned, he doesn't. Instead George just stares at the ground.

Rio glances over her shoulder, accusing. She wipes the remaining droplets of blood from his face. When she's finished, she walks to the garbage can, opens her palm, and lets my pillowcase piece fall into it.

"No!" I throw myself toward Rio and then Liquid is back, jumping between me and her. I don't know why he won't let me have at Rio when Rio's taken George from him, too. Maybe it's payback, for damaging George's perfectness. Maybe it's all he knows.

"Magnolia!" Rio shouts. "What's gotten into you?" The cameras swing between us and I see our reflections bouncing off them. Rio's face white and open. Mine red and crumpled.

"Give it back!" I turn and snarl at Liquid, "Get out of my way."

"How could you do this to him?" Rio says.

"Don't you mean how could he do this to *me*?"

Rio's eyes widen, shifting around the room without really settling on anyone. "He didn't mean to. I know what it looked like out there." She's scrambling for words. She touches George's scratch, swelling and bluing and looking so much worse than I ever meant it to be. She turns back to me, her bottom lip trembling. "You hurt him."

"He slipped," I say as another cameraman pushes two kids next to him away. He comes closer to me and I know what he wants. To capture my truth. To get it all on film so he can blast it on that large screen later.

"Come on, Magnolia," Rio says. "He didn't do it on purpose. He's your friend. He wouldn't do that to you."

"Screw you." My voice echoes through these blackened backstage walls. "You can believe his lies if you want to. But I know him better than that. Better than you ever will."

One of the show's producers walks backstage. He eyes Rio and George and me, the anger weaving between us. "Everything okay back here, kids?" He nods to the cameras. They give him a thumbs-up because they're still rolling. He walks away. It's all he cares about.

I push Liquid out of my way and march to the benches where George's stuff and my stuff are still stashed. I grab my bag and sling it over my shoulder. Then I pick up George's bag and chuck it at Rio, hard. It hits her smack dab in the middle of her chest. Liquid pounces toward me, ready to detain me again.

I hold up one hand. "Don't bother." I turn to Rio. "Take him. It's pretty damn clear you've wanted him since the second you saw him. So have at him. He's yours." I fling a water bottle at Liquid. He ducks and it hits the wall behind him and all his friends laugh, though Liquid doesn't.

"You too. You can all have your god George. I'm better off without him."

With my left foot, I kick the garbage can that holds my pillowcase. The pain juts through my leg, all the way up to my throbbing head, but the can doesn't budge an inch. So I kick it again. Harder this time.

The wide eyes all around me still feel stuck to my face, my hair. I see Liquid touch George's cheek and I hear Jacks call me a bitch and a psycho and a bunch of other things that I could call him too if I wanted to. I bolt through the bathroom door. A camera tries to follow me in but I pull the door closed, quickly. I hear the door slam against the lens and I know I'm going to pay for that later, but I don't care.

My chest collapses onto the countertop between two marble sinks. I stare at my own reflection in the mirror. Bits and pieces of my mother glare back at me. Her deep-set eyes. Her pointed chin. Her sharp widow's peak. From outside, someone calls my name.

Damn you. I shake my head at the person in the mirror. *Damn you for leaving us to pick up your pieces.*

I flip the lock on the door, desperate to hide the new tears that form and pour—ones that have nothing to do with George's betrayal.

And everything to do with my pillowcase piece.

Bloodied. Discarded among soda cans and fast food wrappers.

A piece of trash, that girl.

Trash.

SEVENTEEN

There are cameras everywhere. Five of them, ten, swiveling in every direction, but all I can see when I push through those double wooden doors is Mrs. Moutsous. Her broad smile and blue-green eyes—endless like oceans—warm me. George has those same eyes, that same smile. I wished that she'd come. I can't believe that she did. The sight of her makes me believe that I can go back.

It's happened between me and George before. We've had our share of arguments about meaningless stuff when we were six and ten, and even had one last year about something I can't even recall right now. We've always made up.

My hand feels my collarbone. The empty space taunts me. This isn't like one of our normal spats. This time is different.

Mrs. Moutsous searches the crowd. She stands on her tiptoes and ducks left and right around the people and cameras in front of her. When her eyes find mine, they brighten with flecks of light. "Magnolia!"

I wave and manage a smile back at her. "Mrs. M. You came."

"Of course I did."

I rise up on the balls of my feet, searching next to her, behind her. Maybe there's someone with her. A shorter girl, younger, with dark hair and silver eyes. Maybe she drove with Mrs. M. to meet us—meet me—outside these doors, too. I take a couple steps toward Mrs. M., but before I get close, Camilla Sky leaps between us and sticks her mic in my face and her cameraman follows. Camilla's still wearing that smug expression. And even though I notice she's changed into a taupe sequined minidress, she doesn't seem to notice that I'm an altered version of my old self.

"Let's hear it, Magnolia Woodson! What do you have to share with our viewers today?"

The camera comes closer to me. I hold my head high. Breathe deep. Smile. If they're going to show this on TV, I need there to be some good stuff, too. "I made it." I hold up my ticket to LA. The excitement is there in the depths of me, somewhere. It has to be.

Camilla tosses her hair back. "Of course you did! When I first talked to you outside I told the crew you'd make it." She winks, like she's sharing some big secret with me. "A woman just knows these kinds of things."

I so badly want to ask her if she also knew something—anything—about how my life was going to unravel, pulled apart by the single thread that's held me together. And if she did, why didn't she warn me that I would likely never feel the same about anything, anyone, ever again. But I don't have time. A second later, the next competitor flies through those same wooden doors.

It's Happy Feet Hayden. Even when a gray-looking man and woman, with tears pouring down their cheeks, leap over the entire crowd to get to her, Hayden's smile, glazed like a donut, never wavers. The cameramen zoom to her, her family, their hugs, her smiling, smiling face.

Two seconds later, the doors open again. Liquid and his groupies. They're huddling around him and then they lift him over their shoulders while he lies back, their arms cradling him. And the cameras are loving it, fighting each other for shots of the street kid turned sort of superstar. The boy who slept in boxes and needs no one, needs nothing except this.

Next Jacks appears, one fist crossed over his chest, one fist pumping through the air. "Jacks has arrived! Jacks will dominate!" he shouts. A few people laugh, I guess, because he's talking in third person and a few more cheer for him. But I don't have time to see who it is that rushes over to congratulate him. A second later, the next two competitors fly out of those doors.

George and Rio.

Their arms are linked together and their faces give away nothing about what's transpired. Nothing other than total elation, which Camilla inhales. Her eyes meet mine for a second before she scuttles off toward them, taking her cameras and that "gut feeling" she had about me with her.

"Georgie Porgie. Rio Bonnet," Camilla coos. "Please tell me that you two will be joining us in LA for Season Six. I just don't think our viewing audience could take it if you didn't."

"We made it," George says, and pulls Rio in tighter. "We blew them away." He turns his face, his left cheek away from the cameras. Rio leans her head against his chest. George leans toward Camilla's microphone. His eyes flicker to the place I'm standing, back pressed against the cold concrete wall. There's nothing in his eyes. Nothing that I recognize.

Mrs. Moutsous makes her way over to George. "You made it, George! My son, my son." She turns around to yell these same words to the crowd and cameras and everyone claps and cheers because, really, there's nothing as precious as a mother whose hopes and dreams for her child come true.

She curls her arms around his neck and then around Rio's neck, even though she's never laid eyes on Rio before this exact moment.

"How did you know?" George asks her. "I wanted to tell you but I couldn't."

"When I went to Deelish and Quinn was there instead of Magnolia, I put two and two together," she says. "And then I ran into Mark. He was poking around outside Deelish. He said he thought you guys were on your way down here." She ruffles his hair. "I got in my car and sped most of the way. I never would have missed this in a million years."

I close my eyes. When I open them again, I'm no longer staring at them, but out the window, onto the street. The truck driver's words—the last ones she said to George before we left—float through me, like a spirit.

Take care of our girl here. Don't let her out of your sight.

And then his.

Couldn't, even if I wanted to.

I lean my forehead against the window. This can't be happening. It can't.

And then I hear Mrs. Moutsous. "George. Where's Magnolia?" she says. The cameras focus in on her, her mouth changing from smile to something else. "Oh my goodness," she says. "What happened to your face?"

Before I can hear another word, I slip out the door.

Eighteen

My eyes dart left and right, searching the world for refuge.

Because at some point, while I was in that auditorium changing the entire course of my life, the skies opened up and it's pouring down something awful now. I gape at the massive drops of rain hitting the pavement while millions of thoughts zoom through my brain, the most important one being: Why on earth did I leave Dolores's umbrella in the auditorium?

Across the street, I see a bunch of restaurants and shops, all with green-and-red-striped awnings over the doors. A few people are already huddled under them. I'm just about to run to get under one too when I hear this voice from behind me, shouting my name.

"Hey! You can't just leave! It's in the rules!"

I turn to see Camilla's assistant, Billy, holding a clipboard in one hand and a pen in the other, racing to catch up to me.

He grabs my arm, too fast, too tight. "I said you can't leave. You've got to go back in there and put on a happy face so they can catch it all on tape." He shows me his list, with my name on it. "You're on the show now."

"I've got to get out of here." I fling his hand away and try to shield my face with my hands but the rain pelts me on all sides, soaking me through to my core. I shiver. Next to me, Billy doesn't seem to care that he's drenched, too.

"No way. They told me to bring you back. I'm supposed to make sure you've got all your flight details, and you've signed all your release forms." He taps his soggy clipboard. "Forms first. Then you can go home and do whatever menial things you kids do while you're not making TV history."

"I can't go home."

The guy sighs. "I don't care if you pirouette yourself to the moon and back between now and tomorrow. But come tomorrow afternoon, if your ass isn't at that airport, I'm going to hunt you down. Got it?"

"Fine." I grab his pen and flip through his pages. "What does all this say?"

"That you know the rules, your rights, and what you've committed to. You're on the show. You're ours now. You've got to do what we tell you to."

My head snaps up to search his eyes. Once upon a time, I did what everyone told me to. *Get out. Get lost. Get away from our families because your family is poison.* I won't be that any-more. This is different. I take his pen and sign my name. My name. Here, it doesn't mean what it used to. Here, I can be anyone I want.

Billy plucks his pen from my fingertips. "You're not off to a great start, you know. Sure as hell ain't going to win any votes if you're not where the cameras are." He turns and races toward the Heritage Building. He's so right. The cameras don't lie. Once they're on me, everyone will know I'm a Woodson, no matter what. I watch him until he disappears through those damn double doors.

I race across the street and squeeze myself in under the awning with the other businessmen and couples, tourists and buskers, all struggling to keep dry. Standing next to me is a woman wearing a trench coat, clutching the hand of a little girl with eyes so big and brown and perfect looking. Her mother's eyes meet mine. Her gaze drops down to my leotard and sweats—no jacket, nothing to cover my arms, which are blue and covered in goose bumps.

Her eyebrows push together as she places one hand on her little girl's curly, damp head and stares at her like she's silently willing her to have more sense than me when she grows up. The sight of them huddled together like everything they want and need in the world is right there between them makes me shake, and not because I'm cold. *I have to get out of here.* I slip away from the awning and sprint down the street, darting puddles and water and mud.

After a few blocks, I'm out of breath. I slow to a quick walk, letting the rain cover my face until I'm so wet I feel like I'm made of water. I pass a few coffee shops and Laundromats but I don't go in any of them, no matter how warm and dry they look. As drenched as I am, none of these places will want me anywhere near their fine establishments. I honestly don't blame them.

A few streets later, I spot a huge electronics store blasting music and flashing lights. We don't have anything like that in Summerland, so I can't help but make my way over to it. The front window is filled with massive TVs, all on different channels. Sports shows and news and commercials and soap operas. And then, on one of the TVs on the bottom row, I see it. *Live to Dance.* I watch as the screen changes from sweeping shots of the crowd filled with blurred faces that I can't make out to the Heritage Building to Camilla Sky to a few of the dancers I never saw audition and a few that I did. I see that ballroom couple and Jacks and I see Legs and the tail end of her ballet routine. Underneath, the words: BEAUTIFUL BALLERINA STUNS STAGE run across it over and over and over. I'm sure Legs will be thrilled when she sees it. Then the screen changes to show Rio, her eyes greener on TV than they were in person, if that's even possible. Under her face scroll the words: GRANDDAUGHTER OF AIMEE BONNET REALIZES HER DESTINY. I close my eyes. Back away from the store. Before it's my face, my name I see on that screen, too.

On the corner of the next street, I spy a white brick building lit by old-fashioned lamps that make the place look inviting, in a homey kind of way. I get closer to it and read the sign hanging above its front door: PORTLAND SHELTER. The next thing I know, I'm climbing the steps two at a time and pressing the buzzer. It's a long shot, I know. Her being here—being anywhere I am is a long shot. But still, my chest gets all tight and achy at the possibility she *could* be.

I press the buzzer a second time. The door clicks open.

Before my whole body is through the doors, a gray-haired woman sitting behind a low desk asks, "Can I help you, young lady?" She raises one bushy eyebrow. So does the younger woman next to her.

I clear my throat. "My name is Magnolia. Magnolia Woodson."

The older woman cocks her head. Exchanges glances with the younger woman. Smiles at me. "Are you looking for a place to stay tonight?"

"No. I mean, yeah. Maybe."

"Okay." She pushes a clipboard in my direction, gently. "Would you mind signing in? Then we'll get you set up."

I take her pen, poise it over the last blank line, scanning the names above it. Most of the handwriting on this sheet is totally illegible, so I can only read like 50 percent of the names here. And the ones I can read aren't what I'm looking for.

"Also," I say. "I was wondering if someone I know was here. *Is* here, I mean." My voice doesn't even sound like me, the words rattling through my ribs and out my mouth.

The older woman sits up straight, surprised. "Oh? It's your first time here, right?"

"Yeah. She's a friend. A friend of mine's mother, I mean."

"I'm Eleanor," the older one says, holding out her hand. She points to the younger one. "This is Chloe. We're the intake counselors here. If your friend's mother has been here recently, we'll definitely be able to tell you."

Chloe opens the top desk drawer and pulls out a notepad and a pen. She taps the pen to her mouth. Her voice is soft, careful. "What's her name?"

I reach into my bag for my wallet and take the picture out of the plastic sleeve. I stare at it. The face I know so well— yet somehow so little—stares back at me with its dead eyes. When I glance at Chloe and Eleanor, they're smiling at me but sort of cautiously. Like I might break if they look away.

I turn the picture around so they can see it. "Patricia. Her name's Patricia."

Chloe nods and flips through a couple of sheets in front of her. "Does she ever go by Patty or Pat?"

"No. Never."

"And her last name is?"

"Woodson."

Chloe's head snaps up. Crap. I've signed my full name on their intake sheet and she's read it and now they know.

"Can I see that photo?" Eleanor holds out her palm. "Maybe we've seen her when we're in the field."

I hand over the photo but my gaze wanders behind them to a door that someone's just opened, leading to a second large room. It must be some kind of common area, filled with at least eight different men, and maybe even more women. Some of them are munching on vending machine snacks, a few of them are chatting with each other, but most of them are solo, huddled up in a way that makes it clear they're not looking for company of any kind. It's these ones that make my insides cold. Knowing that even here, in a place where the warmth and company is free, they'd still rather be alone in the world than with people who want them.

My eyes rest on one lady, standing by herself near some kind of old juke box. She's tall and thin, with the blackest of hair. So black and straight, that I can't help but think of one person, and one person only.

I watch her press a couple of buttons on the box, but no music comes out. But she must hear something in her head, because the next thing I know, the woman's got her arms all stretched out in this perfect, graceful "T."

In front of me, Chloe or Eleanor says something. But my eyes and ears are glued to that woman and her fingers, which are so delicate. She starts to twirl, round and round and round. My stomach rolls over. Underneath her weight, her legs are wobbly like a newborn fawn's.

Chloe hands me the picture back. "I don't think we've seen who you're looking for. Do you have a number where we can reach you?"

I glance back at her. "That woman over there. Do you know her name?"

Eleanor and Chloe exchange these shy smiles when they see who I mean. Chloe's voice gets stronger, bolder. "That's not her."

"You don't know that," I say. "It could be her."

Eleanor moves her chair to give me a better view. "See for yourself. But I assure you, Miss Sunshine-Belle is nobody's mother. And never will be, either."

I take five small steps toward Miss Sunshine-Belle. She teeters toward me, eyes still closed, legs still spinning. I get closer, closer, closer to the woman they say can't be my mom and I don't get why because she definitely could be. Me and her, we're not so different. Mom used her body to get things, take care of things, make things happen, because she didn't know any other way to do it. I use my body, too. Maybe in a different way, dancing instead of turning tricks, but it's still using what I've got to survive.

The woman stops twirling. Just stops and stares right at me, her lip curling up like she's looking so deep inside of me and doesn't exactly like what she sees. I wonder if she knows that both of us are users, that both of us are pulled so deeply by something we can't control. And then I see something else on her. Not just recognition, but a five-o'clock shadow, creeping up her unwashed skin.

I bolt toward the exit and thrust my foot into the metal push-bar of the door. It hurts. I let the door clang shut behind me. It's almost dusk and the streetlights on both sides of the road turn on in succession, like rows and rows of Christmas lights. They sear my head, hitting my tired eyes with the power of thousand-watt bulbs.

But it's nothing compared to the sudden, painful flash inside my chest. We're nothing alike, me and my mom. How could I have been so stupid? My mom never danced a day in my life.

NINETEEN

I rest my head in my hands and close my eyes, my breath heaving, struggling to catch time with my heart. It's stopped raining and the air is still, but I don't even care. I want so badly to call Rose, to tell her I made it, tell her we're worth something, but I know I can't. She didn't even come with Mrs. M. She could have, but she didn't.

I sit down on the last step. Behind me, I hear the metal door push open and then close. I'm expecting to see one of the people from the common room, Miss Sunshine-Belle even, dancing, making me think that dreams sometimes do become real.

But it's Chloe, the younger of the two social workers. She stays on the top step and leans over the railing. She doesn't look at me, just pulls a pack of cigarettes from her pocket and lights one.

"Rough day, I take it." She blinks at me in the subtle darkness, leans across the railing, and blows three rings of smoke in front of her. "You didn't plan on sleeping here at all, did you?"

I sit up straight and shake my head, my wet hair grazing my face. "I didn't plan on any of this."

"No one ever does."

"I'm not supposed to be here. I'm on my way to Los Angeles. I made it on a show. It's called *Live to Dance*."

"I know that show. You're going to be on it? That's awesome." She takes another long drag of her cigarette. "So what are you doing here?"

I open my mouth but nothing comes out. I don't know what I'm doing here, how I got here to begin with.

Chloe stubs her cigarette on the sidewalk and then tilts her head back to the sky, darkening, filling with more stars I ever thought a city like Portland could hold. She pats her empty wrist, as though at one time it owned a watch. "I'm off for the night. Time to make my way home." She jogs down the steps and walks away from the building.

I stand up. "So you're just leaving?"

She turns. "Unless you give me some reason to stay."

I open my mouth to tell her. Tell her that I lied and tell her that the picture I gave her wasn't my mom's friend. Tell her that I *do* know why I came here, why the second I saw that sign, I knew I had to see if she was here.

Chloe sighs long and deep. But then she strolls back to the steps and tugs at my arm. "Come on."

I follow her back into the building, through a second set of doors that I never went through the first time. We pass Eleanor and she sees us, but she doesn't look surprised or anything. The room is just like the common room, but this one must be for staff or something, complete with a large pot of coffee set up and already brewed. She pours us both cups, leaving room for cream and sugar. Then she grabs a blanket from behind a chair and drapes it over my shoulders. "So why aren't you staying in some fancy hotel?" She grins in this way that makes me realize she's pretty young. Not my age, but close. Not much older than Rose. "Don't those shows pay for stuff like that?"

I take a short sip of my coffee. "I don't know. I don't care about the show anymore."

Chloe's eyebrows shoot up. "You know, most people don't ever get to live their dreams out in real life." She adds a third packet of sugar to her coffee and stirs.

"I only tried out in the first place to change what they think of me. It was a stupid idea."

"Change what who thinks of you?"

"The people where I'm from." I hide my eyes behind my cup. "They blame me and my sister for something that happened there."

"You can let people blame you for all kinds of things in life. But the question you really want to ask yourself here is, what do you think of you?" She leans in toward me. "Took me a long time to learn that lesson."

I swallow, the truth of it creeping up, creeping out in a way I never meant it to. I close my eyes. I don't want to cry, but the tears are there. They fall, silently. One by one, into my coffee and into my mouth.

TWENTY

I follow her out of the shelter.

There're a couple of other workers there now—Eleanor included—smoking cigarettes on the back steps. Chloe nods goodnight to all of them. Each one smiles back at her and me but they don't ask her where we're going. It's like their job of fixing people never ends the way other people's do. Or maybe they don't want it to.

Once we're away from the building, though, I ask her where we're going. She's still a stranger. And even though the only *other* stranger I've ever trusted got me to Portland safe and sound, Chloe could be anyone. If Rose were here, she'd make sure I knew that.

"I want to show you something," Chloe says.

We walk another few blocks and make some more turns and walk farther, down a hill that literally looks as if we're descending into hell because it's full of garbage and old liquor bottles and it stinks. The whole way down, I get this bad feeling in my gut. Still, I don't stop. Not even when I see that what we're approaching is the bottom of some broken old bridge with five or six homeless people sleeping there, nestled together on plastic bags and cardboard strips. Everything here is so awful, worse than any place I think I've ever seen.

Chloe pulls out her pack of cigarettes, watching me, watching. "What is this place?" I pull the blanket over my hands. Something about this place makes me colder than I thought I could be.

"Today's my anniversary," she says. "Clean for four whole years."

I search her face. Does she know my mom? Is that why she brought me here? Is my mom *here*? I scan the sleeping bodies. None of them are her. All of them are too old, too dirty, too different from how I remember her.

"Five years ago, this is where I lived. Hard to believe." She reaches into her jacket pocket and takes out a picture of a little girl, aged three or four. "This is my daughter. She's my reason. The reason I needed to get healthy." Chloe caresses the photo with her thumb. "She's the reason I'm still alive today."

"Who stays with her when you're working? Her dad?"

"No. Her daddy left me before she was born." She claps, hard, the noise booming through the silence around us. "The second he knew I was pregnant, *wham!* He was out of there. I thought we'd be okay at first, me and my baby girl, but things got so hard. I needed to live and buy diapers and formula and it was just so much." She exhales. "Too much. Jobs are pretty scarce for high school dropouts." She stares at her feet. "It was rough, but I was doing okay. Until I found out I was pregnant again."

I blink. She seems too young to have kids. Too small and frail. I wonder what I look like to her. "You have another baby?"

She crosses her arms, holds herself tight. "No. Not like that, I don't. I didn't get to have my second little girl. Didn't get to hold her hand and kiss her tears away and be her mom." She sighs. "Not in the way it counts. I don't know what I was thinking that day it all happened. No, that's a lie. I *do* know what I was thinking. That I couldn't do it. Couldn't raise a second baby on what I had. There was barely enough food to eat for the two of us as it was. And those welfare checks?" She laughs and it sounds awful. "Well, those don't feed a growing girl and a growing mom, either. After months of us not paying the rent in the crappy apartment we were living in, the landlord finally kicked us out. Or said he was going to, anyway."

"A pregnant girl with a baby? He should have gone to jail for that."

"See, that's what I thought at first, too. I was angry. I was mad at the whole world for making my life so ugly."

At the far side of the bridge, a man—now awake—is peeling the garbage bags from his shoulders. Next to him, a woman shouts at him for making too much noise.

"I didn't want that kind of life for my babies. I wanted them to grow up all skipping and happy and not knowing a damn thing about how bad our life was. I was just a baby myself. I wanted to finish school. I wanted to do something meaningful for myself. It all got so confusing. On the night that slumlord evicted us, I snapped."

I look Chloe straight in the eyes. I think of the way my mom snapped when she left us. The way Rose snapped when I told her I was leaving Summerland. The way I snapped when George stood on that stage and told them who I was. I don't think Chloe's talking about this kind of snapping.

"I never meant to hurt her. But when life gets so desperate like that, a person can get so damn selfish."

"You're a mother," I say. "Your only job in the whole world was to love your girls."

Chloe smiles, but her eyes are still small and sad. "I know that now. But at the time, all I could think of was that they deserved better than what I could give them. I ran a bath for her. A higher one than normal. It was just the way she liked it. Warm water with lots of shampoo bubbles. Her little green squirt frog floating around, following after her pudgy legs."

My throat tightens. My chest thuds. *No. Please. Just don't say it.*

"And after she played in the water for a couple of minutes, I turned her over, onto her stomach. I kissed the back of her head. Rubbed my face in those little brown curls, all wet and matted to her neck."

I put one hand over my mouth to stop the noises inside of me from escaping, to stop her words from getting in.

"And then I held her whole little self under the water."

Chloe's breath gets slow and heavy, like it's too much to lift. "She kicked around under the weight of my hands for a second or two. But then she didn't kick anymore."

I ball my hands into fists. I want to hit something. Hit her.

"My eyes were blazing and all my mind could think of at that moment was that I couldn't do it anymore. I just couldn't do it anymore."

My voice cracks. "All she wanted was for you to love her. All she wanted was a shot."

"I know that now. And something inside of me said the same thing. So I grabbed her little body out of that water. Fast."

My heart speeds. She tried to undo it. She tried.

"I pulled her out. And I pushed on her stomach so hard she threw up. I wrapped her in the bath mat and shouted downstairs for someone to call nine-one-one. When they came, exactly three minutes later, I told them every truth of what I did to her."

I stand in silence, motionless, the grayness inside me seeping out.

"Longest three minutes of my life, that was." She pauses a moment, then takes a deep breath. "But she was okay. Her body had gone into shock from what I'd done, but she was going to be okay. Another three minutes under that water and I wouldn't be here now to tell you this story." She runs her hands through her scraggly hair. "After she recovered, DCF took her away from me. Said if I didn't get some help, they'd take my new baby away once it was born, too. I pleaded with them not to but when that landlord kicked me out, it seemed like I had no way around it. I spent six whole weeks kind of wandering around, sleeping here and under other bridges, nearly freezing to death and eating out of garbage cans while I figured out what to do with myself." She shrugs. "I guess my body finally gave up on me, because I wasn't getting the proper care and nutrition a pregnant woman needs."

Chloe points to a heap of trash, a mess of rotting sleeping bags and fast-food containers around it. "I had a miscarriage. Right over there. This is where my baby lived. For one brief second, she opened her tiny little eyes and looked up at me." Chloe inhales and then lets the air out in these short spurts that sound like they hurt. "I've never been a religious person, but I'd swear on a Bible that that baby took one look at me and said, 'No. This isn't how I want my life to be.' Because right then and there, she closed her eyes and never opened them again." Chloe closes her eyes, her body swaying back and forth. "I like to think she went to another place with warm beds and warm food and love."

I walk toward the heap of trash where the bridge looks the worst, covered in graffiti and reeking of booze and sadness.

"I can't believe she died here."

"I know it seems like the worst place on earth, this bridge. But this is where I changed. This is where I knew that I'd never have my baby back, but I *could* do something about my first little girl. Not because people told me I was awful and ugly because of what I did, but because I knew I wasn't." She tucks the photo back in her bag. "And the second I got clean and got her back, I knew I wanted to do something else. Something for us. Make myself into the kind of mother she deserved."

"But you did it for them, too, right? To show them you weren't who they thought you were."

"It wasn't as easy as that. You can't erase the things you've done. Once they're done, they're done."

"But you did. You got her back. You changed what they thought of you, so you got her back."

"No," Chloe says. "You've got it all wrong. Before I could get her back, I had to make myself into someone I could love." She bangs her fist with her chest. "*Me.* You can't make other people do a damn thing in this world. Lots of people still blamed me for what almost happened that day in the bathtub. It didn't matter that I'd changed because they saw what they wanted to see, no matter what. That's how life is. You can't be who others think you should be. All you can do is show them that you're human. Show them that you're strong. Show them that while you may stumble, you won't fall. And if they still don't like who you are when you've shown them all that, best to just let them go. Leave them right here, under this damn bridge."

I step though the sliding doors of the airport. It's already close to nine but the place is still bright and bustling with nicely dressed people buying paninis and lattes from the Starbucks and hurrying, suitcases obediently rolling behind them. It reminds me of Summerland. Not the sandwiches or luggage, but the hustle right before night sets in each day. The mentality that, with the break of morning, things that used to feel so wrong can suddenly feel so right.

I'm stiff from my long day and even longer bus ride here, but I make my way to the American Airlines check-in counter because that's what you're supposed to do. Or at least, that's what George did once, two summers ago, when Rose and I brought him to this airport to say good-bye because he was leaving, going to stay with his cousins in Colorado, for half the summer. I remember thinking how I hadn't expected the airport to be that big or that clean or that new or that modern because nothing—*nothing*—in Summerland was.

I remember George grumbling something about there being no meal on the plane and something about hating the middle seat but always getting the middle seat. I remember not really listening to him because I was so busy thinking about how weird it was that at that exact moment, people in this airport from all over the world were in transit. And

I remember thinking that transit, moving from one place to the next, is a lot like being in limbo and not moving at all. Both of them mean not being in the place where you came from. Both of them mean not having arrived at the place you're meant to go.

Most of all, I remember thinking about how much I was going to miss George. But now, those kinds of thoughts sit on the outside of my mind while the pictures of Dolores and Chloe stay in. It feels like it's been days since I was in Summerland. It feels like a dream and maybe I didn't meet any of them at all. And somehow, it feels like they've always been there inside of me.

I glance up at the clock on the wall. Twelve hours. I've got twelve hours to kill before my flight, but I don't even care.

I'm going to be on that show. Not just to kick George's butt and win the whole damn competition so that they'll like us again, but so that we can like us again. So that we can get there. Not stay in limbo. Not be in transit. But be in the place that Rose and I and maybe even my mom were always meant to be. Summerland. But a whole different Summerland from the one we've known for a long, long time.

TWENTY-ONE

I wake up sprawled across two chairs, separated by the most uncomfortable bar jabbing into my hip. It takes a few seconds to remember where I am, why I'm here, who's here (or not here) with me. I sit up straight and stretch and peer out the windows, exposing the clear runways and rising sun. It's morning. I've spent the whole night here.

I search out the bathroom and scrub my face and scour my teeth with my finger, then just roam around the airport checking out gift shops, trying my best to ignore the hunger in my stomach because I haven't eaten in far too long. Before I know it, it's 9 a.m. I check in and pass through security, then make my way to the gate. For the longest time, I don't recognize any of the people who arrive at my gate after me, seemingly in pairs. But I scan eyes and faces hoping to catch some quick glimpse of her flushed cheeks, her long, silky hair.

I remember this one time, a few years ago. It was after auditions for the production of *Coppelia* that Katina was putting on. I'd been so nervous. I told myself I wasn't going to get cast as Swanilda, even though I'd been practicing her part for a month and had it down.

The audition came and went. Ten minutes later, Katina posted the results. Swanilda was mine. Not Abby's or Quinn's or any of the other girls that had tried out with me. I was going to dance the lead. I deserved it.

One by one, though, all their mothers came to pick them up outside the studio, congratulating them for the parts they did get, for working so hard. I waited and waited for Rose to show up but fifteen minutes passed and everyone left and she hadn't come. So I started walking home. The sun had already set and I didn't like walking around after dark, for no other reason than it made me feel like I was all alone.

But then like five minutes into my walk, Rose's old Pinto pulled up alongside of me. It was packed with balloons in every color, filled so full there were no remaining spaces in the car for her or me. On every single one she had written the words GO SWANHILDA in big black letters. I hadn't even called her to tell her that I got the part, but somehow, she knew I would, and that was everything. Sure, she'd spelled the lead's name wrong—adding an H unnecessarily—and sure, she was late, but I don't remember caring about either of those things. The balloons were filled so big that they were all just on the verge of popping. When she pulled me into the seat next to hers, about eight balloons popped and made us jump and cover our ears like we were under siege, but together. We cracked up. She put the car in drive, which popped another four. Every time either one of us moved or laughed or spoke another balloon would burst and we'd piss ourselves and eventually we were just popping them for fun. By the time we got home, there were no balloons left. Just a car full of latex mess. But she had come for me. And it was the best thing ever.

Now, watching this airport get busier by the second, I pray that one of the hundreds of people dashing around me, in and out of doors, to and from departure gates and arrival gates, turns out to be Rose. I'd give anything to see her. I'd fill this whole airport full of balloons just to make her appear like she did in that ratty old Pinto.

But she never comes.

Eventually, a bunch of other people from my flight do though, most of them sleek dance types or cheesy television types, as well as a lot of older, parent and grandparenty looking people. One by one, the cameras start to appear all around me and, until this moment, I'd almost forgotten how it felt to be surrounded by them at all times, watching, scrutinizing, judging, like the eyes in Summerland.

I spot Liquid with his groupies playing Hacky Sack near the big window and Jacks slumped forward in a seat on the other side of the room, sleeping, snoring, his body like a volcano ready to blow. Nobody's really doing much so the cameramen put their equipment down, except for one or two who film the few kids who are stretching and pointing their toes, which definitely isn't me.

And then, out of the corner of my eye, I see someone—*two* someones—walking toward me.

It's George and Rio. I take a series of deep breaths and tell myself that I've judged this all wrong. Maybe the two of them are simply hanging out the way George and I hang out. Have always hung out. Every single day of my life until yesterday.

But then I see Rio grab George's hand and pull him behind a row of vending machines. I lean forward in my seat to watch them, but at this angle, there's no way I'm within spying distance. So I get up. But really, a better view of the two of them, smooshed up against the machine that sells Cokes and

Sprites and all the stuff dancers try to avoid, isn't exactly what I need right now.

They're not kissing. But their bodies are pressed together, her back against the hard plastic of the machine and his knee hitched up between her legs. They're not kissing. But her right hand is spread flat on his chest while he whispers a bunch of God-knows-what into her ear.

"Will you look at the two of them?" a voice says from somewhere near.

"I know," another, different voice says. "The show hasn't even started yet and they've already coupled up. It's so gay."

I search the crowd for the faces that have said it because I hate it when people use that word like that and because I know who they're talking about. It doesn't take me long to spot that tapper, Hayden, coming toward me, with Juliette glued to her side. The girls make eye contact with me. I have to hold myself back from jumping in front of them and yelling, "*It's* not gay, *he's* gay!" so loud, the entire airport will hear me. The entire world.

I want to tell them about that time I saw him with Sammy Baker. I want them to know about the millions of times before the time with Sammy Baker, that were just like that moment he had with Liquid. Hot. Passionate. Full of hormones. And with *guys*.

But I don't yell anything at the girls. Instead, I cover my face with my bag and scream as loud as I possibly can into the fabric. George and Rio. A couple.

These are the kinds of things I would have talked about with Rose, if she were here, with or without balloons. She's the one I would have sat with, so I wouldn't have to be alone.

A couple of the cameramen are on me, probably because of my scream, but I don't care. I let my bag fall into my lap. I feel around inside of it, its emptiness suddenly very real. Two leotards, a couple of T-shirts, my toothbrush, my hoodie that already needs a good wash, and thirty bucks. That's all I've got. Twelve hours ago, it didn't seem to matter. But now, under the airport's fluorescent lights, it feels ridiculous for me to go to LA with almost nothing. At least, before, I would have had George.

Fifteen minutes later, the woman working at the little desk outside my gate gets on her loudspeaker and announces the boarding call for my flight—Flight 201—to LAX. I watch as groups of other contestants line up, hand the woman the same ticket I'm holding, and then disappear through the doors. When most of them are gone, I sling my bag over my shoulder and go. Go through the glass doors, allowing myself to glance back over my shoulder and scan the rows and rows of empty chairs, one last time.

Just in case.

The plane is a lot more cramped than I imagined it would be, and not at all glamorous or luxurious-feeling the way they make it seem on TV.

I study the numbers above every seat I pass, taking extra care so I don't miss mine, 14B. The stewardess puts her hands on her hips and plucks my boarding pass from my hand. "This isn't a Sunday drive, sweetheart." She points to my seat, right in front of her.

"Sorry." I sit down, place my bag on my lap. "This is my first time."

She takes my bag from me, and puts it under my seat. "Your first flight to LA?"

"No. My first time on an airplane."

She steps back. Puts one hand to her chest. "Oh. Oh *my*. That is something. Well. Welcome aboard! If there's anything I can do to make your flight more comfortable, don't hesitate to ask." She reaches into the front pocket of her apron and pulls out a pin in the shape of a toucan wearing a captain's hat, with a cartoon bubble coming from his beak. The bubble says, *Flight attendants are just* plane *great!*

"Thanks." I try to smile. I really do. But when I don't muster the sort of enthusiasm I suspect she presumes I should, she narrows her eyes and saunters down the aisle, hips swaying.

I clutch my armrests, my nails digging into the rubber sides so hard it leaves marks. I search the cabin for a friendly face to make this trip be okay. I recognize a lot of the other passengers. Like that swing guy, Lawrence, sitting with the hip-hop girl whose name I can't remember to save my life. Like Hayden, still lit up and smiling, sitting next to the same tired-looking man and woman I saw cry for her at tryouts. Like Liquid, now without his groupies because I guess they aren't coming with him, but with some girl with a shaved head wearing a fitted tank and low-slung jeans, her arms covered, like sleeves, with butterfly tattoos. And like Jacks, sitting with his knees up and his hat pulled way down over his face, next to some guy who's wearing the same outfit, sitting in the exact same way.

Everyone here has someone next to them. Maybe they're not the same people who drove them to auditions or hung with them backstage, but it doesn't matter. They've all got someone here now, coming with them to witness this moment, maybe even the greatest moment they've ever had in their entire lives. Everyone but me.

Two seconds later, I spot Legs coming down the aisle. She tosses a magazine in her seat, one row up from where I'm sitting.

I bury my face in the safety procedure brochure from the front pocket of my seat. Until, that is, I actually read what could, potentially, happen on this very aircraft. I shove it back into the seat, where it belongs. Now my face is fully exposed, but it doesn't matter. Legs and some woman who looks just like her are so busy bickering about luggage and the importance of "packing light" versus packing "in preparation for all things unexpected," that they don't even notice me.

"Mom," she says. "You're embarrassing me. Can't we just drop it?"

Her mom reaches across her and pulls the shade down. "Fine. But you'll be sorry when you're the only one who didn't pack one nice dress. You should never go anywhere without at least one nice dress. You know that."

Five seconds after that, George and Rio and Mrs. Moutsous come down the aisle. They walk closer and closer toward my seat. I hear Rio's voice all chatty and excited and George's voice, too. He sounds the same as he always does. Confident and calm. I don't know why I expected him to sound different. Nothing's changed for him.

When the two of them reach my row, they swoosh on past me, submerged in their own little worlds like I no longer exist. But Mrs. Moutsous stops. She whirls around, her eyes wide.

"Magnolia, where have you been? I lost you after tryouts and then when I tried to find you to take you back to Summerland with us, you were just *gone*. I've been worried sick."

"Sorry. I didn't need to go home. I had everything with me so I came straight here."

Mrs. M.'s forehead furrows with more wrinkles and lines than I've ever seen on her. "That was *yesterday*. You've been at the airport since then?"

"Yes. I mean, no. I had some errands to run first." My stomach sinks. Such a lame lie. It's not like I've had much practice. Until recently.

"You shouldn't have run off without telling someone. I was frantic when I couldn't find you."

I try again. "I called Rose." I stare at my lap. "She wasn't home."

"Excuse me. *Ma'am*."

Mrs. M. and I look up to see that same chirpy flight attendant, hovering next to Mrs. Moutsous. Her frosted pink lips purse themselves in my direction, I guess, because I'm still not wearing her pin. She flutters her eyelashes at Mrs. M., and not in a nice way. "I need you to take your seat. We're preparing for takeoff."

Mrs. M. nods at the flight attendant, but she keeps her eyes on me. "I'm glad you made it, Magnolia. You and George have danced together since you were so little. Your mom would be so proud. Everyone will be." She tilts her head to one side. "You know, no matter where you two go from here, I'll always be proud of the person you've become."

I inhale, her words feeling like the best, most incredible words a person could ever hear another person say. But when I don't reply—can't find the right words quick enough to say to her, Mrs. Moutsous turns around and makes her way to her row. To George and Rio.

To their shared happiness.

Twenty-two

The hotel lobby is like something I've only ever seen in magazines. It's completely white. White see-through curtains that hang between the bar, filled with lounge chairs, and the front desk. White tables and chairs and rugs that look super soft, though I don't know if they're the kind of rugs that you're supposed to walk across. White ceilings where white chandeliers hang, made from tiny white shells.

I'm so busy staring at everything that I don't even hear the woman—dressed in white—behind the white desk say *Excuse me, young lady* until she's practically shouting it and the guy behind me—another contestant I don't remember seeing try out—sticks his finger in my back and tells me to go.

So I do. "I'm with the *Live to Dance* group," I mutter, though I'm sure it's pretty obvious, what with the cameramen here taking shots of the lobby and the dancers doing twirls and pliés and all sorts of stuff that must seem totally ludicrous to the other, non-dancing patrons mingling in the lobby of this posh hotel. Behind me I hear Jacks's voice cursing something about the pansy-ass something or other that did shitty-ass something or other on the way here. Out of the corner of my eye, I see Liquid doing more head spins while the girl who was with him on the plane does her nails with a bottle of Wite-Out.

The woman stretches her glossed lips into a smile, exposing two rows of veneered teeth. She doesn't say anything about us because I guess she's used to cameras and actors and movie stars and this is normal for her, when it's anything but normal for me. "Welcome to Los Angeles," she says. Her head bobs up and down but I swear her boobs don't jiggle an inch. "Do you have a roommate preference or should I just assign you one?"

Crapola. Roommate? I had no idea we were going to have to share rooms at this place. If I did, I definitely would have chosen George as my roommate. I mean, in the past I would have. "I don't know. I didn't think."

"You can choose your own if you want. Another girl, that is." She presses a few more keys on her computer. "They've told us not to let the boys and girls mix."

So I guess I couldn't have chosen George even if we weren't over. I glance over my shoulder. George and Rio are back there somewhere. I can't see them, but I know they're there. Just like they were there at the airport, on the airplane, and in the shuttle that drove us to this hotel once we landed. But now there're at least two dozen people between me and them, other contestants and their family members, as well as a whole lot of the show's crew. I wonder whom Rio will choose for her roommate and I wonder if, once upon a time, she would have chosen me. I think about how happy Liquid will be because he'll finally get George to himself.

"It doesn't matter," I say. "I'll share with anyone. I don't care."

"Suit yourself." The woman drones on about spa services and continental breakfasts, and then hands me a rectangular card, her huge smile getting huger. Thankfully, I recognize the card as a room key, because I have stayed in a hotel twice before. That time in Portland when we went to see *Giselle*. And again in Seattle with George and the Gorge. On both of those momentous occasions, I remember thinking how cool it was to sleep somewhere where someone brought you fresh towels every day and made your bed and folded your toilet paper into cranes and rosebuds and delicate little fans. I remember thinking it was paradise.

I just don't know why I don't feel that way about it now.

The woman shakes my hand and tells me to enjoy Los Angeles. She's so darn nice, except I can't tell if her kind of niceness is real or not. And I can't help but think of the one good hotel we have back in Summerland.

People were so pissed when it first went up, all decked out in fancy marble and sparse rooms. But when they started hiring all the locals for housekeeping and maintenance, people sort of forgave them for whatever it was that made them mad in the first place. Rose even applied there. They said they couldn't hire her because she was only fourteen at the time, but I bet they heard about us Woodsons pretty darn quick and wanted nothing to do with one, just like everyone else in Summerland.

I wonder if this lady would be as nice to me if she knew who I really was.

When I find my room, I stick the little card thing in the slot and when the light goes red, I push on the handle, but it doesn't open. So I push on the door with my hand and when that doesn't work, I try the card thing again. But the stupid red light just keeps flashing at me so I insert it again and again until pretty soon I'm so pissed off I end up kicking the bottom of the door with my sneakered left foot, which really freaking hurts.

And just as I'm about to sit down and pull off my shoe to assess the damage, the door swings open.

Only I'm not the one who opened it.

TWENTY-THREE

She laughs and it sounds like nails. It's so not funny.

"Oh, it's you," I say.

Legs, from inside what's supposed to be *my* room, rolls her eyes. "I'm pretty sure that's what I should be saying to you."

I stare at this girl, my gaze traveling up and down from her blonde head to her bare feet. She looks a little different from when I saw her a few days ago, having it out with Rio in the tryouts lineup and different from when I saw her arguing with her mom. Now, her thirty-plus layers of gloss have faded, revealing two pale, slightly chapped lips. And the rest of her—the rest of her is off, too. She's wearing sweatpants, an old tank top, and flip-flops so worn even I wouldn't wear them. Which is when I realize she doesn't look different. She looks normal. Like she could be any girl out of Summerland, not the viper she was in that line.

Why isn't this girl staying with her mom when I saw them on the plane together? I squint. There's something else about her face that's changed, too. Her cheeks are blotched and her eyelashes are all moist. Yep, no doubt about it. Legs has been crying. Which almost makes me feel a bit bad for her. Almost.

"Don't act so shocked to see me," she says. "I *was* here first, you know. Just like in line. Or have you forgotten about that already?"

I look away. "This key thing is broken or something." I shove the card in the slot and pull it out another three times. The light goes red. Red. And red. "See? It doesn't work."

She takes it from me. "Here. You have to put the key in slowly, wait for the light to turn green, and *then* take it out." She demonstrates it for me and then hands the key back. "It's no big deal. Lots of people have issues with it."

"I don't have issues," I say and push in past her. I plop my bag down on the second bed, the one that's not full of clothes, make-up, earphones, magazines, and about twenty tubes of lip gloss.

"Hey, make yourself at home," she says.

I don't say anything back, but she can't help herself. "It's not like you can switch rooms to be with George or Rio. So I guess I'm all there is, other than that tapper girl." She shudders. "Can you believe her? I bet she smiles in her sleep, too. Who'd want to room with that? Then again, I guess you could ask to stay with one of the parents or chaperones or whatever, if that's your thing."

"Thanks but no thanks."

"Right? Anyway, it'll give you a chance to pay me back for letting you cut in line. I totally knew you did that, by the way. Can you believe that was only yesterday? Man, it feels like a million years ago that we competed and met Camilla Sky and the judges. And Astrid looks so much older in person, don't you think?"

I blink. Whoa.

This girl just spouted off more words in the last fifteen seconds than I've said in forty-eight hours. Maybe it's because she's as nervous as I am. Or maybe it's because I just caught her, like, ten seconds post-cry about something I know nothing—and want to know nothing—about.

"So like I said, I'm about all you've got now that your little posse's ditched you for greener pastures or whatever."

"What?"

She waggles a finger at me. "You know what I'm talking about. Don't pretend that you don't."

I wish I could say that I didn't know what this girl was talking about, but I do. George and Rio. Our fight. Sure, there was a crowd around us when our argument began. Absolutely, the crowd grew as our argument turned to an all-out brawl. But I never saw Legs there. Then again, I wasn't looking for her.

Legs laughs again, but it sounds less evil than it did a minute ago. "You don't need to beat around the bush about it. Everyone knows. Pretty sure they caught the whole thing on tape. I mean, even the people who weren't there are going to know soon." She twists her hair into a messy bun on top her head and then drops it. "Your little backstage drama was just about all anyone could talk about on the plane."

"You guys were talking about it on the plane? Like, everyone?"

"Well okay, maybe not everyone. Most of us had our parents with us. Not like we were going to talk about it with them." Legs slaps one palm over her mouth. "Wait. Didn't you know that everyone knew?

"No." I slump down on the bed and fiddle with a loose thread on the beige blanket. It's no pillowcase piece, but it'll have to do. "I knew that the people who were backstage when it happened knew. But that wasn't everyone." I run my hands through my hair. "At least I didn't think it was everyone. And

I saw the cameras. But why would they air all that?"

"Because it's drama. Because it's TV."

I swallow, thinking of that TV store in Portland. I didn't see George or me up on that screen. But I guess I knew to walk away before I did. "Are you sure they all know? Even the judges?"

"Yeah, maybe. I heard something about one of the producer's assistants walking in on you guys mid-brawl. But maybe everyone's forgotten about it. Maybe they didn't put it on YouTube like Jacks said they did."

"Jacks said that? Shit. I'm in so much shit."

"Forget about it. He's kind of a douche, if you haven't noticed."

"Yeah. I've noticed. Okay." I breathe deep. "Yeah, okay. I'm sure it's not true."

"Right. Unless." Legs's face brightens. She scrambles to her bag and rummages around for her phone. "Let's see if it's up there now."

"Now?" I hear my voice rise a million octaves.

"Why not?" Legs shrugs. "Liquid said there's this whole YouTube channel just for *Live to Dance*."

My throat closes. My heart beats so fast I feel like it's going to burst. "When did he tell you that?" I think of that cigarette dangling from his lips. His hands gripping my arms. His shaking head, walking away all resigned like he's used to walking away like that. "The guy barely speaks!"

"Oh, he talks. Mostly it's all gibberish and riddles that I think is supposed to be poetic or something. People say he's really smart. Personally, I think he's spent too much time with his BFF, Smack McSmackerson, if you get my drift. He's pretty hard to understand. But I did understand what he said about this." She taps a few buttons on her phone. "Here it is!"

She scoots next to me so we can both watch the screen. It's absolute torture. Scrolling through video after video of auditions and interviews with Camilla and some of the other dancers warming up and cooling down. But then Legs really does find it. The video itself is called *Friends Fornever*. I think I'm going to be sick.

She hits play and I hold my breath. It's all there: George, me, Rio, our fight. My hands on George's chest. My arms pinned back by Liquid, who never says a thing through it. I watch Rio grab at my tissue, use it to dab George's blood, throw it away. It's like I'm reliving every second of it and it doesn't hurt any less the second time around.

"Turn it off," I tell her. "I don't want to see anymore."

She watches for another second, but then she does close the screen and tosses her phone on the bed.

I bury my face in my hands, the tears behind my eyes stinging.

Legs puts one hand on my shoulder. "Hey, don't worry about it. You remember what happened during Season Five, right? There was that whole thing going on between that hot ballroom dancer, Dom, and one of the old female judges. The cougar one. Tina Gallati. Remember her? One of the other contestants caught them getting their groove on in the dressing room and ratted them out. I thought he was going to be kicked off the show for good." Legs laughs. "As it turns out, the producers love that kind of stuff."

"Was there a YouTube clip for that, too?"

"I don't think so." She picks at a rough patch of skin near her ankle. "I think it was before they started posting all this stuff. But I heard the producers *were* totally pissed that the cameramen missed it all and wanted to air it when the dancer was eliminated. I heard they tried to pay Dom and Tina to recreate the whole scene all over again, but in front of the cameras."

My head shoots up. "Do you think they're going to make me and George do that?"

Legs shrugs. "Maybe."

I roll forward, my arm cradling my gut. A low moan escapes me.

"It could be good for your rep."

"It's definitely not good for my rep."

"Why?" Legs squeals. "You're totally my hero! You ragged on him pretty good and it was nothing short of awesome. Mothers across America will love you for giving their daughters a role model who doesn't take shit from shitty boys. The producers will love you because you'll help spike ratings. I bet there's going to be, like, this whole Team Magnolia versus Team George thing going on before you know it."

"Right. Who'd ever choose my team over George's?"

"Everyone! Did you know people are already making bets about who gets kicked off first, you or him? Everyone thinks he will. Except for Hayden, that is. And of course Rio." Legs laughs. "They're just about the two most annoying people on the planet. You, on the other hand, have got that whole poor-sweet-Magnolia-with-the-scumbag-best-friend thing going on." She brightens. "Did you know they're calling you Mad

Mags now? Jacks made it up, I think. But it's good."

"Are you serious?" I close my eyes.

"Check it out." She picks up her phone again and clicks a few buttons until she finds the *Live to Dance* website. Sure enough, all of our photos are there. Underneath mine, it says the words *AKA Mad Mags*.

"I've got to stop this." I push the phone away. "I've got to stop this all before it's too late."

"Why?" She studies the site, lingering on her own picture.

"Because. This isn't the same as making out with some stupid judge. They could kick me off for fighting."

Legs scoots closer to me. "They won't kick you off for that." She pauses. "At least I don't think they will."

I groan.

"You know, I saw what George did out there and I'll vouch for you if the judges try to say anything about it. He was kind of ridiculous. Can you believe they didn't even notice?" Legs's face brightens. "Wait. Maybe they *do* know what he did. Maybe they just let him on to add to the drama."

"No. They let him on because he's good."

"But, seriously. I mean, come on. Those sobs were too much." Legs rubs her eyes and pretends to bawl, I guess, in imitation of George's best performance to date. Then she sticks her finger down her throat and fake gags. "I almost lost my lunch watching him melt into that pool of patheticness."

"Mad Mags." I shut my eyes. "I can't believe this."

"I kind of like it. It's catchy. It gives you an edge."

An edge. Right.

Yesterday, I had no idea that what I was going to need to get anywhere in this competition, in this life, was an edge.

Had no idea that my only two allies would turn into my enemies and that the seemingly bitchiest girl on the planet would turn into my one and only cheerleader.

I get up and walk toward the window. The curtains are still partly closed so I pull one away from the other, revealing the California scenery in all its glory: skinny palm trees with ballooning fronds and coconuts sprouting from each one, kidney-shaped swimming pool equipped with a swim-up bar, scores of white chaise lounges with neat little orange towels rolled up like Tootsie Rolls, each one waiting for some hard, tanned, Californian body to occupy them.

Bright, bright sunshine.

Blue, blue sky.

And then my gaze travels further, beyond the hotel grounds, to the beach, and to the ocean.

But the sand and sea are nothing like the ones I know and love and breathe back in Summerland. Here, the water is actually blue. Sky blue, not black-blue like the water in Oregon. And the beach. It's not peppered with weeds and brush, but with people. Board-shorted and bikinied people, running, jumping, splashing in water that must be a hell of a lot warmer than my water because they don't seem to mind the waves as they smack against their bare hips and stomachs.

It's all there, exactly how I imagined it. And it isn't. I mean, something's missing. Something that I just can't put my finger on. If only Rose could be here to see it with me. She'd know what's missing. She'd find every difference between this place and the place we know.

I know what Legs said about my new little nickname giving me an edge, but it's the not the kind of edge I'm thinking of now. Sure, this beach is pretty, but I know what it's missing. Shovels, with sharp edges. Guns that make suction so fast you can't believe it. There isn't any of that here. No people digging their brains out, hopeful that one little razor clam edge will stick itself out of the sand and into their world.

Rose would never hang out on this kind of beach. She would look too white in comparison to these tanned people. Too big. Too composed in this mess of chaos. No. She belongs with Summerland and clamming and all the things that we've always known and been part of, even when we're not.

And if Rose were here with me, there wouldn't be any Mad Mags. I wouldn't need an edge because I'd have my sister and my sister is so much sharper, tougher, better than any kind of edge could be.

"Hello?" Legs says, breaking my train of thought. "Did you hear anything I just said?"

"Sorry. It's been a long day."

"Yeah. For you and me both. I asked you two questions." She points to my sad little backpack, still wilting on the bedspread, unopened. "One, is this all you brought? And two, do you even know my name?" She wrinkles her nose and doesn't wait for an answer. "If you need to borrow some stuff like a new T-shirt or a hairbrush or whatever, you can." She flips open her own ginormous suitcase and pulls out a long, black, very expensive-looking silk-or-something dress. "Or if you find yourself in the mood for something like this, it's all yours."

I think back to the plane, her mom and her coming down the aisle. Why would she purposely fight with her mom about bringing one nice dress when she had brought a dress all along? It doesn't make sense.

Legs shakes the dress in my face.

I shield my eyes. "I don't think I'll need anything like that on this trip, but thanks."

"But in case you *do* find yourself on your way to a red carpet event with nothing to wear"—she balls her dress up with both hands and whips it onto my bed, fast, the way one might a baseball—"I've got you covered."

I know I should at least *attempt* to figure out what the heck is going on with this girl, but I'm no mood for her dress drama, which seems minute in comparison with what I'm dealing with. *Mad Mags.* It isn't exactly what I had in mind when I decided to change my reputation. I move her dress to the foot of the bed and set my own backpack down. "Thanks, but I brought the things I need—"

"Olivia. From Arizona. Scottsdale, actually."

I blink.

She sighs super hard. "I brought the things I need, *Olivia.* My name. I knew you didn't know it."

"I did know it! I just forgot it when you said that. About me borrowing your brush. You shouldn't let people do that, you know. You could get lice."

"I wouldn't have actually let you use it. I was just trying to be nice."

Olivia walks over to the mini fridge. She taps a few keys and the fridge door opens.

"So, remind me how this works again?"

"The minibar? The stuff all costs a fortune, but the trick is to just replace whatever you eat before the maid comes in the next day. It sucks. They took out all the mini bottles of booze because we're minors. Like, who couldn't use a Jack and Coke right about now, right? But whatever, there's still peanut M&Ms. They'll have to do." She grabs the yellow bag, tears it open with her teeth, and pours half the contents down her throat.

"No. I mean the show. I haven't seen it in a while."

"Are you crazy? What else were you watching that was better than *Live to Dance?*" She tosses her hair back. "We never miss an episode. We save every single one so that we can play them back later and critique all the stuff that everyone screwed up. That's how we learn what not to do."

"Who's we?"

Olivia turns her back to me and rummages through the minibar fridge again, this time coming back with a Snickers, which she tosses to me. She doesn't answer my question.

I take a bite of the Snickers. "We used to watch it. My mom and I did. We'd even shut all the blinds and lock the doors, unplug the phone just so that people wouldn't bother us when it was on. It was the one thing we did, just the two of us." I inhale. "Until they took our TV away."

Olivia stands up, sets the M&Ms wrapper on the desk, and wipes her rainbow-smudged hands on the front of her sweatpants, leaving these little yellow and blue streaks. "Well, now you don't have to worry about not watching the show. I can't wait to draw dance styles." She removes a piece of candy shell from her teeth. "I can't believe we actually get to pick them out of Camilla's hat."

"We pull them out of the fedora? How do you know that?"

"Everyone knows. They've been doing it the last couple of seasons. They say the hat's got magical powers or something."

She bites her lip. "I hope I get contemporary or classical my first round. With one week to learn and perfect each routine and then perform it live, I don't want to go in there with something totally foreign like hip-hop or salsa or—"

"*Live* live? Like, no practice rounds or anything?"

Olivia rolls her eyes. "You're sure you've seen it?"

"I said it's been a while."

"One wrong step and you're off the show." Olivia drags one finger across her throat. "Do or die. That's the only real part of reality TV."

My gaze plummets to my bag, still slumped on the bed. I rub my arms to keep them from shaking, the reality of Olivia's words and my situation sinking in. In one week, I'll either make them proud that I'm from Summerland, or I'll embarrass myself so badly I'll make them all wish Rose and I were never even born.

But then Chloe's words cut through these thoughts, clean, like a blade. *What do you think of you?* I know what she's saying, and deep down I even know she's right. But the thing is, she's not the one who has to go back there and live under their microscopes.

Olivia slips off the bed and floats to the other side of the room. She talks about how it's crazy to think about going home, but by the end of next week we will all definitely be thinking about it. She tells me that's how it works. Fridays, we find out our style for the next week. We have three days to practice, and then on Tuesdays we perform a new routine. Thursdays, two are voted off. And we'll be each doing six new styles in six weeks. They've never made the contestants learn so much, so quickly. She talks about the ballroom couple who, she says, will have to split up and dance separately eventually. She talks about Jacks and Hayden and Zyera and Liquid and a bunch of other people whom I don't even remember though obviously she does, and well. She tells me what each of them can do and what each of them can't, and I wonder if she knows that information about me, too.

I listen to her fast voice go through it all. Telling me how tough it's going to be, how important it is we stay focused and stay on, because if we don't, the cameras will catch us when we're weak, when we're down. And I try to listen. I really do. But I all I can think of is George and what he'd think if he heard my nickname. *Mad Mags*. Or maybe he already has.

Then I think of what *they're* going to say when they hear it. Not just Rose, who's always cheered for me through school and dance and everything I've ever wanted in life. And not just Mrs. Moutsous, who's loved me through lying and through this.

But them. Summerland. The only other people I've known for as long as I can remember. I can almost hear their voices, passing through Main Street. *Mad Mags*. At the Pic 'N' Pay. *She's crazy*. At Xanadu Mini Golf. *Both of them are crazy. Just like her mother.*

"At this point, all of it seems like a long shot. Don't you think, *Mad Mags*?" Olivia shoots me a look. She knows I've tuned her out.

I close my eyes. Not because of Jacks's sucky nickname or because I could be on my way home, away from these palm trees and women whose boobs don't move, away from Crayola-colored oceans and chatty roommates who seem to like me for some strange reason. But because in six weeks—

six weeks max—I'll either be famous, the best thing that's ever happened to Summerland, or I'll be the same as I was before. Except without George by my side. Without Rose by my side, either. *Mad Mags.*

Without a reason to go back home at all.

TWENTY-FOUR

Backstage.

Black wooden floor.

Camilla's tapping foot.

Fedora, upside down, in her hand.

Pursed lips.

I see it all in pieces, like flashes in a movie. One I've been wrongly cast in. The other ten contestants are already here and murmuring to each other, but we're late and rude and bursting in all sweating and heaving because Olivia *just had to* apply thirty layers of mascara before she could leave our room. She told me to go without her if I didn't want to wait, but in the end I stayed. Olivia's all I've got at the moment and having something is better than having nothing, so they say.

I apologize like crazy as we scramble for spots on the floor—as far from George and Rio as we can get—but Olivia doesn't. Which doesn't really surprise me.

The cameras are on, so Camilla's got that smile plastered on her face. When we're settled she says, "Aren't you all so excited to work with our choreographers? I know that every one of you will benefit so much from their instruction."

Olivia jabs me in the ribs and whispers, "Yeah. She knows everything about everything. And nothing about dance."

I stare at her, incredulously. For one, I have no idea what she's talking about. And for two, I really wish she wouldn't loud-whisper like that when we're supposed to be quiet and supposed to be listening. Doesn't she see the cameras behind us and above us? While I'm sure she sees them, she doesn't know how it feels to have the second-lowest moment of your life blasted on YouTube for the world to see.

On the other side of the circle, Rio and George ignore us, but Liquid, who's sitting on the other side of George, glares at Olivia with the slittiest of eyes and Jacks makes a gun with his finger and thumb and pretends to shoot Olivia in the head with it. Olivia doesn't seem to notice any of it. Or if she does, she doesn't seem to care. "Did you hear she's never taken a dance class in her life?"

Since I know about Google and I know about tabloids, I don't ask her where she's heard it. More than anything, I'm sort of surprised Olivia's bothered to research Camilla Sky at all. It's not like she's one of the contestants. Or the judges. Not like she's anyone we need to impress to get through this. I squint in Camilla's direction. Then again, Olivia knows way more about this show than I do. So maybe she also knows something important about the impenetrable Camilla Sky that I don't, too.

I lean over to Olivia. "Are you sure? She really can't dance at all?"

"Not one single tendu. Look at her. She's like a giraffe." Olivia licks her lips and tosses her hair in what's actually a pretty impressive Camilla Sky imitation. "A girl just knows that kind of thing," she says, which cracks me up and causes the real Camilla Sky to send us both beady-eyed glances.

Olivia whispers, "If you ask me, she probably boned Elliot Townsend to get this gig to begin with. Everyone knows the quickest way to any guy's heart and wallet is through his pants."

I almost laugh again. But then my mind flashes to Rose and her "extra income" from Urban Outfitters. To Mom, somehow always managing to scrape by. And then I see that cop's face and the cameras, pointed at me and *my* face, and all the joy I felt a second ago with Olivia plus Camilla the giraffe is sucked back to the place from which it came. Camilla's legs are long, and toned, and beautiful. I don't blame her for using them to get her where she needs to be if where she needed to be was here. It's no laughing matter.

"Okay," Camilla says and the cameras swoop down close to her face. "The crew wants to get you kids on film—*only* you kids on film—for this next part. That means I need all parents, guardians, groupies, whatever, to go wait outside." She points to a row of television sets on both sides of the auditorium. "You can watch your kids live from those TVs over there. Got it?"

Instantly, Olivia's gaze shoots toward her mom. And I'm almost positive I see her mom glare back at Olivia.

But she gets up along with all the other moms and dads and non-contestants and follows them out of the room, leaving us alone backstage. Just us. The contestants. The judges. And Camilla.

The cameras zero in on Elliot's face. He perks up, but it's not the same as when Camilla does it. "Okay, who would like to choose their dance style first?"

Olivia shoots her hand up as fast as she can. Too bad for her, because Rio is quicker, which makes Olivia sink into her seat on the floor, heavy and fast, like quicksand.

"You're up, Ms. Bonnet," Elliot says, putting emphasis on her last name.

Rio's face darkens, but then she reaches into the hat, sifts around in the sea of folded up papers, and pulls her hand out. She unfolds her piece of paper and hollers "Hip-hop!" Her eyes get all glowy and she smiles this wry little smile—one I didn't know she was capable of when I met her back in Portland.

Next to me, Olivia whispers, "It's probably rigged. They're giving her special privileges because of who she is. Everyone here knows she's awesome at hip-hop, too."

I stare at her but I don't say what I'm thinking. Which is, *yeah, everyone. Everyone but me.*

Elliot tells Rio to pick the person to go next. And of course, she chooses George. George steps forward. Olivia doesn't protest. I hold my breath while his hand brushes past the brim of Camilla's fedora. The cameras get closer to his steady hand. He pauses and pauses while they circle him, zooming in, zooming out. He must be loving this.

But then he finally does pull out a paper and opens it, his face spreading into that wide grin that makes me think of Wick Beach, of Summerland, of home. "Jazz!" he shouts. "It says jazz!"

I lean back on my hands. Of *course* George got jazz. Along with our thousand hours in ballet and contemporary training at Katina's, we're also pretty solid in jazz, since jazz dance has some of its roots in ballet. Of course he got it. No *way* he'd bomb out and pull something horrible, like the fox trot, the pasodoble, or tap. That kind of thing's always been my luck, not the luck of He Who Was Born With Horseshoes Up His Ass.

Hayden chooses next. Elliot makes her wait until the cameras are ready and rolling, but it's not like it matters. Hayden's ear-to-ear grin is there and on whether there're cameras around her or not. Her hand quickly digs into the hat. She pulls out her paper. Her smile never droops, but her face sort of pales, draining of all that shininess she had a second ago. "Classical ballet," she whispers and then covers her eyes with the backs of her hands for six whole seconds. But then she lets her hands drop down to her sides and her color is back and her perkiness is back and I wonder what she hides behind her hands, behind her smile.

After Hayden, Liquid chooses Broadway, and the cameras shake because the cameramen are laughing, struggling to film Liquid while he pools around the floor as if he's paint. I think of what Olivia told me about Liquid and drugs. I wonder if it's the drugs that make Liquid like this, like *actual* liquid instead of human, or he's always been this way and if he's like this—more worm than warrior—even on the street.

Jacks picks next. He thrusts his fist into the hat and pulls out krumping, which makes him leap in the air and pump his fist around like a maniac for several seconds before he realizes that only *one* of the cameras is even on him. Nobody even cheers for him because he is a douche, and it seems that Olivia and I aren't the only ones who've noticed. Elliot's jaw gets tight and a few of the other dancers roll their eyes. Jacks stops jumping. He sits back down, his fists shoved under his chin.

Next, Zyera picks Bollywood and the ballroom couple choose a pas de deux. Lawrence gets breaking; Juliette, clogging. I relax a little. Whatever I get, it can't be worse than clogging. Finally, Elliot calls Olivia's name. She steps up, eyelashes fluttering, looking exactly like the Olivia me and George and Rio met outside the Heritage Building. Composed. Polished. No M&Ms stains anywhere in sight. Her hand searches inside the hat and then settles on one crumpled paper. We lock eyes. I give her a thumbs-up. She pulls the paper out, unfurls it, studies the word. "Contemporary!" she shouts. "I got contemporary!" Olivia leaps off the floor and spins around and around in front of the cameras, waving her triumphant paper in front of the lenses, just as her mom bursts through the door.

"Are you sure? Let me see that thing. We need to be absolutely sure. I can't read it from those pathetic little TV screens you guys have out there."

"I got it, Mom." Olivia holds the piece of paper out and her mom grabs it. "I did it!" Her voice is shaking.

Olivia's mom takes her by the elbow and whooshes her to the far corner of the room, which is not at all out of earshot. "You better not screw this up," she says. Olivia's face is crumbling, her mom's claws digging into Olivia's forearm. I've never seen a mom like hers before. The only ones I really know are my own mom and Mrs. Moutsous. Neither one of them wanted things for me bad enough to dig them into my skin.

When I peer back at the group, Elliot Townsend's totally staring at me. He adjusts his jacket, purses his lips. I wait for him to say the words I've been dreading hearing him say since the second we got backstage and I saw him here amongst us:

We know who you are, Magnolia. We know what your mom did. You aren't fooling anyone.

But he doesn't. Instead he tells me it's my turn and then shoos Olivia's mom out of the room so Olivia can reclaim her space next to me. He nods to the cameras. They zoom in on my face. Olivia told me to put foundation on, at least powder or blush or something, but I didn't. Suddenly I'm very aware of my visible pores and shiny nose.

"We're waiting," Elliot says.

My hand lingers over the hat. Hovering above it. Not touching it.

I can feel about a gazillion eyes swarming me. My fingers won't do what my brain tells it to. *Grab a paper, Magnolia. Just grab one.*

Someone coughs. Rio. The cameras turn to film her. Liquid scoots away from her.

Someone else sighs, real loud. Loud enough to make sure I know they're all waiting for me. George. My face gets hot. It's not just the cameras. Or maybe it is. This will all be online and on those millions of TVs in Portland and maybe even the TVs in Summerland.

"How long can she stand there before they kick her off for holding us up," Jacks says.

"It's not like it's hard. Pick one," Hayden says.

And they're right, it's not that hard. Or at least, it shouldn't be. George doesn't seem all broken up over that YouTube video, and I bet he's seen it. I stare down at the papers. Maybe they're the reason I'm sweating bullets. Most of the good styles have already been taken, which leaves only three left in Camilla's hat: African. Lyrical. And tap. Two that are possibly okay. One that is very, very bad.

"Ms. Woodson," Elliot says, and the sound of my name makes my hand plummet inside the hat. My fingers settle on one paper that calls my name.

I uncurl my hand. No. *No*. This can't be happening.

"What does it say?" Olivia's voice.

"Read it!" Jacks's voice.

"Tap." My voice comes out small, more like a whimper, a whisper than a real voice.

"What?" someone says. "What did she say?" Liquid. I heard him loud and clear.

"I can't hear her." Jacks. "Her voice is like a squeaky little rat's."

"We didn't catch that either," one of the cameramen says.

"Tap." I say it louder and I hear it reverberate off these floors. Out of all the styles I could have pulled, two very doable and one inconceivable, tap is not what I wanted. A death sentence for me. I take a deep breath. It'll never be enough air. "I got tap. With Thomas Scandalli."

"Okay, everyone!" Elliot shoos us away with a wave of his hand. "Go find your choreographers. You've got seven days to learn and perfect your routines. This is the most time you'll have during the competition. I suggest you use your time wisely."

Everyone cheers and then splits up into little groups and then the cameramen follow each contestant. I hang back. There's no point rushing off to meet super-tapper Thomas Scandalli, known in the nineties for his work on Broadway and in another hundred-plus movies that all involved outrageously skillful tap routines. It doesn't matter that he's some kind of tapping miracle worker. Not even a miracle can save me now. I bend down and fiddle with the laces on my left shoe. Tying. Untying. Tying. It doesn't untie my thoughts. Any way I think about it, there's just no way I can do this. And worse, I know I'm going to disappoint Thomas Scandalli with what I don't know about tap, which is everything. I know I'll only get to dance the first week, because once America sees me tap, I'll be sent home, and that's a fact.

In front of me, someone clears his throat. My head snaps up.

It's George. Staring at me. "I know you." His eyes shoot left. Right. A camera's coming toward us, but Elliot waves it away. "You can't tap. And you're scared to death to try."

I stare at my shoes. "You don't know a thing about me."

"Yes, I do. I know you don't know a good thing even when it slaps you across the face. I know you don't know what you've lost by acting like this. And what you're about to lose permanently if you keep this up." His face softens. "Come on, Mags. Why can't we just forget the whole thing?"

I stand up straight so that we're eye level. "And what about you?"

"What about me?"

"You think you know me. But I've never known you."

"How can you say that? You've *always* known me. Right from that first day on the beach. With our moms."

"You betrayed me. You betrayed me then and you've betrayed me now."

"I have no idea what you're—"

"I thought you were gay, George. All this time you let me believe that you didn't like girls and that included me and now"—I shake my head—"now I don't know what you are."

George flinches. "I didn't *let* you believe anything. You're the one who decided I was gay. Not me."

"I saw you. I saw you that day at the beach with Sammy Baker. And what about Liquid? What about all that stuff with him?"

George studies his feet. His eyebrows are furrowed together and the rest of his face is all muddled, which isn't a look I've seen on him often. "I guess I'm just not like you. Not into labels the way you are."

"I'm not into labels."

"Yes you are. In your world, people are either good or bad, nice or evil. You're way more concerned about what people think than actually forgiving yourself. At least I'm true to myself."

I snort. "Yeah, right. You can't even say what you are out loud." I shake my head. "I just don't get you." A second cameraman comes toward us. Elliot's nowhere in sight to make it back off so he stands between us, equipment on his shoulder. The camera's red light blinks at me. It's like a warning. A warning George doesn't heed.

"You've got it all wrong," he says. "You're more like me than you'll ever admit. We all have our shadows. We all have things we run from. You've got your sad little reputation. And I—"

"Have your glowing one."

George's jaw tenses. "If you already made up your mind that I was gay a long time ago, what else about me is there to get?"

The cameraman waves over another. "Sexuality issues," he says to the new guy with a camera on his shoulder. "This is great stuff. Start rolling."

George glares at the guy with so much hate, and I don't know if I've ever seen George that mad, especially in front of a camera.

I glance at the cameraman to make sure he's watching. Why should I be the one with the tragic story? Why should I be the one with the mortifying nickname while George gets nothing but glory? I raise my voice. "No. I only *thought* I was right about you being gay. One minute you were all hot for those lifeguards and the next you're calling that freshman girl"—I cringe, remembering that brief (albeit painful) second at Deelish—"hot. And what about that call from Mary?" My voice gets quieter. "You were so weird and giggly when she called. Like you were in love or something."

George's head snaps up. "Who's Mary? I don't know any Mary."

"I saw it. I saw her name on your phone."

George opens his mouth to presumably deny his obsession over anyone with that name, but then he bursts out laughing. Which seriously catches me off guard.

"The name on my phone that you saw? Not Mary. *Mark.*"

"What? No way. I saw the letters, George."

"Uh-huh." George whips his phone out of his pocket and scrolls through his calls until he finds what he's looking for. He flips the phone around and shows me his screen. "M. A. R. K. With a K on the end, not a Y." He grins at me. "Pretty easy to mix the two up when you're spying upside down, I guess."

"Wait. So then who's this Mark guy? Are you guys a couple?"

"No, you idiot. It's *Mark.* Mark from Katina's. You know, Mark-the-Pan-Part-Stealer? At least that's what I prefer to call him."

I blink, my mind flipping to the day George lost the lead to Mark and swore he'd sooner quit dance than dance with Mark again. Of course, George was only being his usual dramatic self, but Mark took it kind of hard and slipped out of Katina's studio, mumbling something about George being there long before he ever was. Even though I did manage to convince George to cool off and come to his senses, I still had to take six sampler tubs of Deelish's best ice cream to Mark's house that night to talk him into accepting his Pan role after all. I knew George felt bad about making Mark feel like he had no right to be there. I also knew George wouldn't apologize because, as George put it, sometimes apologies were implied. So if George wouldn't face Mark and face the music, I would, on George's behalf.

"That's who your giggly call was from? The same Mark you almost pummeled three years back?"

George grins. "That's the one."

"I thought you loathed Mark."

"Loathe is a pretty strong word."

"I thought you guys weren't on speaking terms."

"We weren't. But now we are." George grins.

"I didn't know Mark was gay."

"He's not gay." George scratches his head. "At least I think he's not. But that call was about *you*, Mags. You're so blind sometimes."

Next to me, one of the cameramen whispers words to the other, but I hear it loud and clear. *Love triangle.* I glare at him, too. That's not what this is.

But then I let it sink in. The way he was at dance and on the beach and outside Deelish. The way he was always staring. I thought it was bad staring. Maybe it wasn't. I try to go back farther, but all my memories are the same. Mark was nice. Mark *is* nice. There isn't anything more than that. But then suddenly I do remember something else about that ice cream delivery day.

I had wanted to just drop it off and go. Set the six miniature tubs of perfection down at his door and jet without another word about it. But Mark caught me off guard before I had the chance to put down the ice cream and bolt.

"Magnolia?" he had said, stepping out on to his front porch. "What are you doing here?" I turned around and suddenly felt all tongue-tied in his presence. His lean torso, propped against his doorframe. His wavy hair, so thick it almost didn't look real. His skin. Like ceramic. Or steel. I didn't know why I was noticing these things about Mark when I'd known him so long. Maybe it was because I was at his house. Maybe it was because there wasn't anyone else around to distract me.

"I just came to bring you these." I held out the tray of ice creams and pointed to my favorite double-churned flavor-of-the-month, Smooth Operator. "This one's really good."

He took the tray, his fingertips grazing mine. "You came all the way here to bring me these?"

I shrugged and turned to go, but Mark opened the door a little wider and stepped aside so I could see inside his warm, well-loved home. "Wait. Do you want to come in for a bit? Just for a minute. I promise I won't keep you longer than that."

So I did. I went in. Mark had always been sweet to me, always the perfect gentleman, so really, there was no reason not to go in. Saying no to him at that moment would have felt like treason or something. We hung out in his living room for a bit. Flipped through a couple of back issues of *Dance Magazine*. He pointed out all his favorite dancers, steps he was dying to try, places he wanted to go to study dance under mentors I'd only heard about.

After a few minutes, I said I had to go. Rose was expecting me home and it sort of felt like Mark and I had talked about all there was to talk about. He had so many big dreams. I didn't have any.

He walked me to his foyer. Waited, hands shoved into the front pockets of his jeans, while I slipped into my old boots. He leaned over me and opened the door. Which is when his arm bumped mine and his chest came close to mine. We stayed like that for a second or minute or I don't even know. Our eyes were locked on each other. I didn't know what it meant—if it meant anything. But then the moment ended, and he said good-bye, and he never said a word to me at school the next day. Everything was normal. He was with Abby and Quinn and the rest of them and I was with George. I had imagined it all. Or, at least, I thought I had.

I turn to George. "Wait. Mark likes me?"

"No. Mark *loves* you. He has for years, or that's what he told me, anyway. He loves you so much he's even willing to talk to *me* to get to *you*, and we both know he's not my biggest fan. Loathe, no. Have a general disdain for anyone who actually thinks he's better than me? Maybe." George sighs. "It's been pretty obvious how into you he is. But I guess you've been too busy wallowing in your own self-pity to even notice it."

"I don't get it. Why didn't you tell me this earlier? You definitely should have. No, he should have told me if that's how he felt."

"He wanted to. He was going to come to your house and declare it to you before we left Summerland until I stopped him. I told him to wait until this was all over. That you just weren't ready yet. That you needed to do this first."

"You have no business telling him what I'm ready for!" I shout and feel the cameras get closer to my face. "As if you'd even know."

"I was trying to help you. Help him help you. I was trying to—"

"Just stop, okay? I need to think." I tap my forehead, the picture of Mark's eyes when he told me what dance meant to him. I thought that, despite all his congeniality in my general direction, what he was really saying was that he saw me. He saw me the same as everyone else in Summerland did. And then I think of his phone call with George. "Wait. I don't understand. I heard you call him 'babe.'"

George shrugs. "The guy's hot. Who could help himself? Anyway, I wasn't flirting with him. I was just happy. And I actually like him. I'd like anyone who loves you the way he does."

I close my eyes, letting the weight of George's words wind through me. *Mark loves me?* How could I have missed it? I thought everyone there hated me. How could I have been so wrong?

"The dude's been texting me like crazy to find out which schools you're applying to next year. He's going for some fancy one right here in California. One that focuses on the 'art of dance' instead of competition or some crap like that."

I hold up one hand. "Wait. So you are gay or not?"

"That's what you're worried about? In this entire situation? After everything I've just told you? Who *cares* what I am?"

"I care. You told me under the bridge. You kissed me because you wanted to find out. So tell me, George. What did kissing me make you realize?"

He slings his bag over his shoulder and sneers, all in one fluid motion. "You'll never change, Magnolia. You've always felt this profound need to classify things—stuff people into these pretty little boxes that fit your ideals of who and what they should be. But maybe I don't fit into any of your boxes. Maybe I don't want to. Or maybe I just can't. Not anymore."

"This isn't a trick question, George. You either like girls, or guys. You don't get to have it all, you know. No one does. Not in this world."

George raises his head to look at me with those bright eyes. Two days ago, it would have floored me. "Why? Who says I can't have it all?"

"Forget it. I'm done playing your little guessing games. 'Cause that's all you're about. So forget about me. Forget I even exist, okay?"

"No problem. It's not like it'll be hard to forget about you. Because after this week, you'll be back there. Back in Summerland. Small-town Magnolia. Clamming with the rest of them. Exactly where you belong."

A fire ignites from inside of me. I turn my face to the cameras. Say it loud so they don't miss it. "No, G. Unlike you, I *belong* here."

"Why?" he says. He's talking to the cameras, too. "Because you made it on the show? So did eleven other people, in case you've forgotten."

"Yeah, and ten of them here didn't slip in tryouts and then lie about it afterward."

George's mouth drops open and his eyes get wide. Huge. His cheeks redden and he glances between the cameras and the men behind them who are kind of glancing at each and other, their cameras rolling.

For a second, I get this scared kind of feeling like he's going to slap me or spit on me or something. So I take a small step back. But he doesn't. Instead, he turns around, putting his back to me for what feels like the millionth time in the last two days, and walks toward the door. Toward Liquid, who's been standing there watching the whole time, that damn cigarette dangling from his damn lips. Liquid reaches out to touch George, his hand limp and wanting or needing or maybe both or neither. He stares at George, but for the first time since I saw Liquid outside the Heritage Building, I notice that Liquid's eyes are kind of gray and dull and devoid of any kind of emotion at all. Unlike George's, whose are always, always full of spark. But instead of stopping when he reaches Liquid, George turns around to make sure the cameras are still on and following him, which they are. Then he slaps Liquid on the ass and sails right on past him.

To Rio.

Who's waiting for him too, just outside the door. He glances over his shoulder a second time. Our eyes meet. Then he turns back to Rio and wraps his arms around her tiny waist and kisses her. Hard. Deliberately. And on the lips.

Twenty-five

After hours upon hours of rehearsal, during which time I've fumbled more steps than I ever thought was humanly possible, paired with serious bruising to my knees and calves from these metal taps, Thomas Scandalli places both hands on my shoulders and says, "You're going to be great." He holds his head high and erect. "Just do it how we rehearsed and you'll be perfect." With his thumb and forefinger, he straightens the bottom of my costume, making sure all the feathers that trail from my skirt are straight and unobtrusive.

I swallow. My words come out in spurts, like I'm choking on them. "I know. It'll be fine."

Thomas reaches into his pocket to retrieve a small pair of tailor's scissors. He snips off a rogue thread from my hemline, then tucks it into his pocket. "You look amazing. Like a bird. A bird of paradise."

Bird of paradise flowers don't grow in Summerland, that much I know. But I think of that word, paradise. How it's funny the way people talk about it sometimes. Like it's this real place, somewhere you can go to relax or feel warm, like Hawaii or Fiji. A place people can fly to or drive to or sail to where their stresses won't matter, where their dreams will.

But when I think of paradise, I always imagine it more like a state of mind than a place. Like the highest form of happiness. The perfect impossible. Heaven. Bliss.

Like Rose and Summerland and Grandma and Mrs. Moutsous and the old George and the good Mom and clamming. And others too. Other people from Summerland on all sides of us, but happy. Happy that we're there, next to them. That would be my paradise.

I smooth out the top part of my costume with my palms. My eyes dart left and right as a few of the cameramen come closer to me and Thomas. I see them zoom in on my hands, my legs, my left eye, then my right one. It's been a week, and by now I know I should be used to living in this kind of fishbowl where everything is seen and watched and observed. I don't think I'll ever get used to it.

"I want to go over that last part again. Just one more time."

Thomas shakes his head, looking at the cameras.

"Please," I say. "Just the bombershay. Just once."

"You've got this. You don't need to go over it again."

My shoulders sag. When we started rehearsing this routine, I sucked. Like, really, *really* sucked, right from the moment he started showing me all those darn clicking steps that seemed so weird, so freaking freakish. And even though Thomas didn't say outright how frustrated he must have felt with me and my non-tapping abilities, I could feel it from his heart. Feel his soul sink a little lower with every single bombershay I tried, every triple buffalo I screwed up. In all honesty, I gained a little respect for Hayden and what she does. It actually made me wonder if that smile of hers is so frozen and always there because it's a method of coping with her near-impossible style of dance.

Now, four days later, I watch Hayden practice with Collette Vertefeuille, her choreographer, rehearsing each precise step of her first classical ballet routine ever. Hayden notices the cameras capturing every mistake she makes and stops what she's doing. She covers her face with her hands. Collette wraps one lithe arm around Hayden's shoulders and then kneels in front of her. She holds each supporting leg taut while Hayden points her toes on her left foot, then right, curved and hard, going over series after series of basic tendus—ones I learned to do when I was five.

I look to the other side of the room to where Jacks is, Liquid is, Rio is. I let my gaze linger on Rio. She's with her choreographers, too—that legendary husband and wife hip-hop duo that Rio called "soul mates" when George and I first met her in Portland.

I watch Rio rehearse a series of fast squats, abdominal rolls, and shoulder pop-and-locks. I guess Rio can feel my eyes on her because she stops practicing, looks right up at me, and smiles what looks like a real, genuine, non-smirking smile.

I turn away from her and there's a camera in front of me. Watching me watch Rio. I can only imagine what the TVs will say. *Oregon nobody seethes with jealousy over Bonnet legacy.* I look away from both of them.

Thomas takes a long drink from his water bottle and then nudges my shoulder with his bottle. "Stay focused, Magnolia." He nods to the cameras. "Forget about them."

"I can't."

"You can. They want to get under your skin. It's their job. It's your job to get in the zone. Do that and you'll be perfect."

I take a series of deep breaths, my hands resting on my shaking knees. I don't want to let him down. I don't want to let any of them down, but if they see me like this, I will.

"I think if we just ran through the whole thing one more time."

"We don't need to do it again, and definitely not in front of them." He shakes his head and the cameras back off. I doubt they'd do that for any of the other choreographers, but this is Thomas Scandalli.

"You've been breathing this thing for days," he says. "You've got it down pat." He removes my hands from my bodysuit and places them down at my sides. But he doesn't let go of me. Instead, he squeezes my hands hard enough so that I can feel his heart pumping through my fingertips. "You can do this, Magnolia. You can."

"Okay."

"Just do it exactly how we rehearsed it."

"Okay."

Thomas cups the sides of my face in his palms, forcing my gaze to meet his deep brown eyes that mirror my own—and not the cameras, not at the eyes and faces of the other dancers around me. My competition.

Hayden. Jacks. Olivia. Liquid. Rio. And the others: Zyera. Juliette. Lawrence. The ballroom couple. And George.

They're all around me. All with their choreographers. Some of them, like Jacks, are bouncing up and down. Some of them, like Rio, are going through the one-two-three-four counts of their own routines. Some of them, like Liquid, have their headphones on and are counting out beats to music. And some of them are staring back at me.

But we're all here together. Waiting for Camilla Sky's voice to catapult us toward our destiny. Toward our paradise.

And then we hear her.

"Welcome, ladies and gentlemen, to *Live to Dance*, Season Six! We have an amazing group for you this year!"

I hear the audience go wild and then I hear Camilla say some other things about who we are, who we were before we started this journey. I hear her introduce the judges, much like she did for us eight days ago back in Portland. I hear the voices of the audience hush and her voice silence as well. And even though my gaze is still one with Thomas's, somewhere in my periphery, I see the lights from upstage dim, which means they're showing the video—the one from our auditions last week—the one I saw part of in Portland. The one I've been dreading this whole time.

I can only imagine what my own face looks like on that big screen. I wonder if the people watching me feel any of the anger, the sorrow I felt as George sobbed in front of them, my story shooting from his lips like some kind of ammunition.

When I open my eyes I hear more cheering. The video's over. The show is starting.

I finger the braid that weaves across my forehead. Then my hand drops down to my bra strap. My fingertips search for my pillowcase piece, but when all they feel is my skin, dewy and empty, they pull away.

There's a full-length mirror to the left of me. My eyes flicker toward it, traveling up and down my reflection. I wonder if anyone from home will recognize me with this sea-foam-green and peacock-blue makeup that fans away from my eyes and trails down my cheeks into swirls and slashes.

The makeup artists say it makes me look whimsical. I think it makes me look wrecked.

I wonder if anyone from home will think about how far I've come—me—surrounded by these important and glamorous people, looking like I belong. Like I'm one of them. I wonder if they'll want me to come back there, to be one of *them*, instead.

"Magnolia."

They'll say my name: Mrs. Miller. Mrs. Moutsous. Mayor Chamberlain. The freshman. Their voices are warm and familiar but different, too. One of them touches my shoulder, lightly. The hand is soft. Their touch tells me all I need to know: they've forgiven me.

They say the words again.

"Magnolia Woodson. You're up."

Thomas puts both hands on my arms and gives me a little shake. His eyes are huge as he searches my face. "Magnolia. Are you all right?"

"I—I don't know." I hold my stomach, my body trembling with a shake I can't stop.

Thomas wipes under both my eyes. His palms are wet. Whether the moisture is from his skin or mine, I'm not sure.

"You can't do this." He squeezes my arms. A camera turns on us and zooms in on his hands, my arms, my face, my eyes. I'm shaking. "You can't do this to yourself. I won't let you. You've got to go. You're on right now."

I scurry toward the stage but I hear him say it, as if he's read my heart and my mind. "Magnolia. Don't let me down."

Twenty-six

The music starts and I spin around to face the judges, audience, cameras.

Only the blackness stares back at me.

I slide my right foot out, and then tap.

Thomas taught me how do this, this smooth gliding motion with my toe, then heel, then toe, my taps grazing the vinyl floor. My mind repeats the name of each step. My body obeys.

Black essence. Triple buffalo. *Tap, goddammit. Tap.*

The music helps my feet, giving them direction with each beat, each syllable of Coltrane's song, his sax crooning through my limbs like fuel.

"You want me to dance to a classic?" I had said to Thomas, his fingertips pressing play on the stereo fifteen minutes after he met me for the first time outside the studio. Fifteen minutes after George locked lips with Rio, and meant it.

"Yes," Thomas said. "Because you're a classic."

I leaned against the wall and listened, knowing I had heard that song before.

Mrs. Moutsous kept a huge crate of records in the garage next to her good set of silverware that she only took out at Christmas and Thanksgiving. Occasionally, she let us borrow one or two, making us promise to return them to their sleeves the second we were finished.

On rainy nights, George and I would stretch out across his floor, my head to his heels, our skin absorbing the sultry notes. The music always seemed more sacred coming from that old player than it ever did belting from people's iPods and phones. But I never knew if it was the hearty quality of the records themselves, or if it was just me and George, locked in the single magic minute we shared, that made it seem that way.

"I want to dance to stuff like this," George said, seconds after the first time we heard this song. He lifted the needle and set it back down, replaying it. He stared into my eyes. "I want it to mean something."

His words filled me up, made me whole. "I want that, too."

He scooted his butt closer to mine. Rested his hand on my leg. I closed my eyes, feeling his heart beat in time with mine. Feeling his breath on my lips.

When I opened my eyes, George wasn't next to me. Wasn't touching me, wasn't caressing my thigh. Wasn't kissing me. He was still where he always was, lying on his back, his head resting against the wood frame of his bed, eyes closed, head moving in slow, tapping time to that sax. None of it had happened at all.

Now, my legs are bent, my knees shaking from the burn. Buck single time step. Bombershay, toe-clip. *Tap, goddammit. Tap.*

My mind shifts from George's room to Deelish, the shop I know is filled with wide-eyed people watching the TV that hangs in the back. Watching me do this. Tapping, of all things, *tapping.*

I know my feet will not betray my soul as they hammer out every ball change that scuffs the floor, every stomp, stamp, brush, spank, hop, click, and roll that I've rehearsed, over and over and over, but never got exactly right. Until now.

Their faces are happy, hopeful, proud. I'm doing it. Showing them that I can do something for Summerland. It makes me happy, hopeful, proud. Until they see the word rolling across their screen. *Murderer*. Their faces fall. They turn away, their eyes lowered. *She's still the daughter of a murderer, no matter how well she dances.*

Irish flap. Pendulum shuffle. *Tap, goddammit. Tap.*

I picture the first time I saw Gene Kelly tap on some old TV show in black-and-white. It seemed so hard yet so cool and smooth, like gloss. I imagine that I am him. Imagine that I'm part of his body, his fluency in this soft, dripping language. Dolores's words skim over me. *I'd never let my flower girl be out here all alone.* And then Chloe's words, too. *How do you feel about you?* Their faces glide through me every time my feet graze the floor. *How do you feel about you?*

My feet tap, fast. My arms fan out at my side in circles, propelling my feet faster, faster, until my legs, knees, torso separate. Until everything feels clear.

After what seems like forever, my music stops. I face the audience, smiling. Because I didn't fall or slip or make some complete tapping mess of myself like George and all of Summerland thought I would.

I bow my head, slightly, in *reverence*. Then I step forward to accept the judges' critique.

"You were stunning, Magnolia. They loved you."

Those are Thomas's words when I scurry backstage, my first-ever tap routine over and done. A camera follows me back and Thomas wraps his arms around me and I hug him too, my face resting on his shoulder. We stay like that, frozen in my moment. I don't care that they'll air this later. I don't care because it's nice to be held like this even if Thomas is only doing it because they're filming. And his hug doesn't feel like that. It feels like how I imagine a dad doing it. Warm and real and protective and something else. Proud. That's what this feels like. It feels like he's proud of me.

I hear someone shout my name. It's Rio, running across the room. Jacks laughs at her and he nudges Liquid in the ribs even though I thought they hated each other. Liquid scoots away and replaces his headphones over his ears.

Rio reaches me and gives me this giant hug. Unlike Thomas's embrace, her touch feels so awkward and wrong because we're not friends. Never had the chance to be friends.

"You were amazing," she says. "I didn't even know you could tap. Especially when George said all that about you not being able to." She glances left and right, presumably for *him*, and then takes a big breath. "Listen," she says, her voice hushed. "I need to talk to you. About something important."

"Rio. There you are." A stage manager comes up behind her and smacks her over the head with a piece of paper. "You gotta go, girl. You're on now." Then he mumbles into his little walkie-talkie thing, "I've got her. She'll be there in two."

"Find me later, okay?" Rio says, the guy pulling her toward the stage. She grabs my hand. "Promise me you'll come and find me after this is done." She releases me, but holds my gaze. I watch her go, her eyes pleading.

I don't hate the girl or anything. But I don't want to talk to her about the rise of her and George's coupledom either, especially not now. I mean, what would be the point? I have to let it go. I know that now.

I turn away from her, toward Thomas's bright face, smiling at me like I'm his lucky penny. He takes hold of my elbow and leads me to the flat-screen at the back of the room. Camilla's on, introducing Rio. I knew this screen was back here, but when I was dancing, I didn't think about how everyone back here would be watching me on it, too.

"No one could take their eyes off you," Thomas says, studying my face. "Even Hayden was blown away, and she's been tapping since she was six. She even said she didn't believe it was your first time, that the producers were lying about it so it'd make your performance look better." He smirks. "She was just about to query them on it when I set her straight."

"You told her that I couldn't tap?"

"Nope. I wasn't going to lie to her. I told her that you were capable of anything." He sighs like he's the happiest man in the world. "You're a wonderful tapper. So wonderful, in fact, you absolutely terrified that poor girl." He motions to George, whose miserable face is now looking everywhere but at me. "Even *he* was glued to the monitor." For a second, I say nothing. Just kind of stand there watching George visually dissecting a piece of fluff in the far corner of the room.

I hold my head high, let the words out in one swift breath. "He was probably just putting on a show. Making nice for the cameras. He couldn't care less if I did well or not."

While I give the pads of my feet a little squeeze, Thomas wipes the back of my neck with a cool cloth. "I somehow doubt that. You're pretty impossible to 'care less' about." He bends down to whisper in my ear. "And if he really didn't care about you, then why did *she* go stomping off five seconds after your routine started?"

"Why would she do that?"

"Because. He couldn't keep his eyes off you."

So that's what Rio wanted to talk to me about? To tell me to stay well away from her (ugh) boyfriend? At first I feel my teeth kind of gritting together. He was *my* guy before he was ever hers. I knew him and loved him way before she even existed in our world.

My thoughts dissipate, suddenly replaced by my tap routine and how, somehow, through my clicking feet, came my revelation. The people of Summerland will never accept me, will never welcome me back with open arms and want me there, because Colleen will still be dead. No matter what I do to dance my best for them, it won't bring her back. I can't undo what's already done.

And George.

George doesn't love me, doesn't want to kiss me. Doesn't yearn for his hands around my waist or his mouth on mine. No matter how much I try to be the person he wants, I can't be.

Those were my dreams. Not theirs. Not his.

A jolt of pain runs up through my ankle and then down through my toes on my left foot. I bend down and take off my shoe. Glance up to see if any of the cameras are pointed at me and filming. None are. I rub my foot a few times and the pain lifts. "You've got it wrong about George and Rio."

"See for yourself." Thomas tilts his head at the TV. "She's a bit rattled up there, don't you think? If you ask me, she's nothing like the Aimee Bonnet I knew."

My head snaps up toward the monitor. I inspect the last twenty seconds of her routine. She hits every motion. Every hip-thrust and arm-pump, punching each motion out hard and clean.

But Thomas is right.

Something *is* missing. She hasn't tripped or forgotten the routine, but still, I see what he's talking about. I scan Rio's lean body, ending at her heart-shaped face. It's all there. All in the eyes.

"They don't have the passion you do," Thomas says. A camera turns in his direction, getting closer to hear his every word because everything Thomas says means something. "Like she doesn't even care about what she's doing up there. Her motions are hollow. Good to the untrained eye but immature to those that know. She dances like a child. I danced with her grandmother when I was still up and coming. She never danced so mechanically. Aimee Bonnet was all heart."

Watching her, I can only imagine what the rest of the dancers saw as they watched me from this screen: a junkie's daughter. A murderer. And the audience, too. Now that they know where I came from, there's no taking it back.

Rio finishes her routine and the cameras swoop down and the audience cheers and the judges give her a standing ovation just like they did for me after my tap routine.

Astrid Scott grabs the microphone. She makes some comment about Rio living up to her family name. Gia Gianni's eyes are all sparkles because she's just seen what she calls "a great technician in action." They seem to have missed everything that Thomas was talking about. Seem to have forgotten what it means to dance like you need it to live.

Elliot's face flashes on the screen. Thomas nudges me. "Look there. He sees it. He knows that a dancer's only as good as the fire in her heart."

I squint, trying my best to see what it is that Thomas sees. And then I *do* see it. Thomas is right. Elliot's smile never reaches his eyes. Because Rio isn't who he thought she was, either.

I peek at George, hoping he's noticed it, too. I wonder what the hell happened between the two of them and just how long it's going to take before he comes to her rescue and makes it all better, all over again. Saves her, like he used to save me.

But George isn't even watching Rio as she takes her final bow and glisses off stage. Instead, he's still focused on that dirty piece of fluff on the floor in the corner of the room, collecting dust.

I wonder what he's thinking. If he's missing home the way I am or if it's me he's longing for. Not Magnolia, the girl who wishes that kiss wasn't once, and only once. But Magnolia, the girl he swore he'd never let out of his sight.

TWENTY-SEVEN

Game day.

The one we've all been waiting for and *not* waiting for, because today's the day where they tell us our fates, proclaim us either winners of this round and on to the next, or losers. Losers.

Olivia picks a piece of purple nail polish from her thumb with her teeth.

Her eyes are puffy, like she hasn't slept in about a month. I doubt I look much better. My stomach gurgles with this unsettling feeling that I can't quite place. Like I'm going in for a root canal. But more like ten root canals. Plus a lobotomy.

"It doesn't look good," Olivia says in low voice. "For me at least."

I glance up from one of her magazines I've been pretending to flip through, sprawled out on my bed. Anything to keep my mind off the fact that tonight is our first results show. "What doesn't?"

"The reports. You know, what they say about us."

I throw down the mag and then hop up on the hotel room desk facing the mirror, cross my legs, and then smooth a glob of Olivia's "calming cream" all over my face and neck. It's pudding-smooth and rich, like the kind they sell in those department stores where the women are pretty and polished and stare at you because you're not. I inhale it. It smells like George's house, too. I screw the lid back on.

Olivia hands me a purple sheet of paper. "Here. See for yourself. I printed this out downstairs. It predicts who's staying and who's going home tonight. Poor Jacks," she says. "It's almost never wrong."

I take the paper from her and read it over and over. Up and down. The words are all there, in black and white. It says that Jacks is going home tonight. I don't know why Olivia feels bad for him when he doesn't feel bad for anyone, ever. "This is awful."

"What are you worried about? You're ranked as the second favorite to win."

"Yeah. Second favorite. Not the same as favorite."

"So what? Team George has way less votes than Team Magnolia. See for yourself." She taps the part of the page where it says, literally, "Team Magnolia has obtained more popularity than Team George." I swallow. I have no idea how this has all happened in one week. How these people—the audience or reviewers or Internet gods—know anything about us at all.

Olivia peers over my shoulder. "You should be grateful that they think you'll beat him."

I shrug. Hop off the desk and pick up the mag from my bed.

"No way," Olivia says, one hand in front of her. "Don't tell me that after everything that's happened, you're still all soft and mushy over that guy."

"It's not that."

"Then what?"

"Second place isn't what I came here for."

Olivia studies the printout, a frown creasing her forehead. "She might not win, you know. This thing doesn't know everything."

"You just said it did." I point to the top of the page that says Rio's the favorite to win. Not just this round, but the whole thing. "Maybe she'll get disqualified for using supplements or maybe she'll fall asleep and miss her performance. Or better yet, maybe she'll sprain her ankle and won't perform at all." I pick up the page and read it over again. Then another thought dawns on me. "How can it predict the results when we've only just started this?"

"Not *it*, you idiot. *Them*. The judges. Astrid and Gia and Elliot. And Camilla Sky, too. Especially Camilla Sky. The bloggers from that site poll them to see who they think will be the first ones to kick it. The audience is influenced by the pros and vote accordingly." She flips her head over and douses her hair with hair spray. "It's a fine science," she mumbles. "I'm going to die."

"Give me a break, Liv." My eyebrows furrow, thinking about the latest YouTube video she played for me. This one was called *Magnolia Questions George Like She's in the CIA*. Naturally, it was filled with tons of *are you gay or not* talk that made me seem small-town and ignorant, when it's never been about that. Not for us. "There have been no YouTube videos about you at all."

"You think that's a good thing? It's publicity. I need that publicity."

"You're a great dancer. It speaks for itself."

"Did you read this thing? I obviously didn't wow anyone on Tuesday, even in my own style, which is pretty pathetic considering I've been dancing since I was, like, six." She waves it in my face. "Look. Even those ballroom guys beat me. And Juliette too. They were *mediocre*." She taps the page. "It says I'm in danger. I might even be going home tonight."

I go over all the motions from this week's performance, two days ago. We watched Rio come offstage, her face calm and pretty much pleased with her performance, despite what Thomas thought about her soul, or lack thereof. We watched George perform his jazz routine, and it seemed flawless this time—no play for the cameras—just perfect, shining-light George. We watched Liquid perform Broadway and we listened as Astrid and Gia and even Elliot congratulated him on attempting a dance style so far from his own, which everyone knows is code for *you blew it*, and we watched him slither off stage after, like he didn't even care. We watched Hayden execute her classical ballet routine—same smile plastered on her face like it always is—totally flowing and graceful, like it was nothing at all for her. We watched the ballroom couple glide through their pas de deux, Zyera burn through Bollywood, Juliette's feet click through the toughest (and possibly only) Irish step routine I've ever seen. We watched Jacks krump, every motion brewing from somewhere deep inside of him, every pop full of strength and anger and power.

And we watched Olivia soar through her contemporary routine as easily and as flawlessly as if she had been doing those steps in that one single routine for her entire life.

"So what if you don't win?" I say.

She gapes at me with huge eyes.

"I mean, you'll probably still have an amazing career in dance, even if you do go home tonight. Some choreographer will snatch you up as their assistant." I turn back to the mirror and search my face for the cream's results. "If I were you, I wouldn't care if I went home tonight or not."

Olivia's reflection in the mirror glares at me. "Are you serious? You actually think I'd be okay with that? You think that would be enough for me? For my—"

"Your mom? Is *that* who you're worried about? That your mom will be disappointed if you don't win? Big deal. So she's a tiger mom. She'll get over it. That's what moms do. But it's different for me. You know my story." I stare at myself in the mirror. Stupid cream. Doesn't look like it's doing a thing. "Everyone does, because of him."

Olivia sneers. "Get your head out of your ass, Magnolia."

"Am I wrong? You'll go back to your perfect life. Things will be okay for you. But I still have to go back there. Everyone will still hate me." I swallow. "Even if I win, it won't change things."

"You're just like him, you know that?"

I hop off the desk. "What did you just say?"

"You heard me. Jacks's routine was awesome. He was perfect out there and everyone knows it. It says he's going home. And what about me? It says I'm in danger of elimination too. You don't get to have a monopoly on heartache."

"I never said I did."

"You're pissed because he's used this, used you, to get here. But you're doing the exact same thing. You think you're the only one who needs this?"

I stare down at my hands. "I know I'm not. But where you're from isn't like where I am. Nobody treats you the way they treat me."

"Is that right? Who are you talking about, anyway? Who are these people that hate you so much?"

"People." My eyes avoid hers. "Just people from my town."

"From where, Summerville?"

"Summer*land*."

"Exactly," she says. "Who cares about some dinky people from some dinky town no one's even heard of? Everyone who knows you loves you, Magnolia. That's all that matters."

When I shut my eyes, the faces of my loved ones are there, like always. Rose. George. Mrs. Moutsous. *None* of them are here with me. Olivia's mom might be tough, but none of my people even care that I'm here, doing this thing. If they really loved me, wouldn't they be here to show me? And my mom. If she really loved me and Rose, would she have left us in the first place? "At least you have your mom."

"My mom who's given me an ultimatum," Olivia says. "Either I win this contest, or I'm out of the house, out of her life." Her shoulders slump and her head dips. "My mom says I don't have it in me, that I'm a loser. Always been a loser." Olivia shuts her eyes, too. The tears break through and stream down her cheeks.

My voice is quiet. "I had no idea. I knew she was difficult. But I didn't know that she was awful."

"Of course you didn't. You've been so wrapped up in what *they* think and what *he* did, you haven't even seen what's been all around you the whole time." She slaps her chest. "We all need this. Don't you see? We all have our reasons."

Olivia crumples the page in a ball and shoots it across the room. Then she ducks into the bathroom. I hear the door lock, water run, glass door of the shower close, hard.

For a second I sit very still, listening to the other noises around me, other contestants getting ready in rooms nearby, echoing through the walls of this one. Maybe everyone does need this just as bad as I do. Maybe some of them even need it more.

I slump down on the bed and untangle my braid, run my brush through my hair, making the up-down-pull motions of my hand over and over and over until it's smooth.

Olivia's words run through me.

Tonight. Tonight, I might be boarding my second-ever flight, heading home to Summerland. I reach across her bed to her cell phone still lying on her pillow. She won't mind if I use it. I won't be on it long.

I flip it over, punch in the numbers. It rings twice. And then she answers. "Magnolia? Is that you?" The sound of her voice crushes me. I picture her in our house, our kitchen, sitting at the fold-up kitchen chairs. She sounds so alone. She sounds almost as alone as I feel right now. I hit the end button because I can't talk to her here. Not from this hotel room that's clean and smells so good and is everything that where she is isn't.

But a friendly voice would be good. I try to remember his number, though I haven't called him in so long and never for something that wasn't about rehearsal times or changes in one of our dances. It rings six times and I think it's going to go to voice mail. Then he answers. His voice sounds like salve, running over my wounds.

"Mark?"

"Yeah?"

"It's Magnolia."

There's a huge pause on his end. At first I think he's hung up or maybe we've been disconnected, but then I hear him breathing and he clears his throat and says, "I can't believe you're calling. I've been watching you."

"Oh."

He laughs and it sounds nervous. It sounds like him. "Not *watching* you, watching you. I mean like on the show. You've been incredible up there."

"I don't know why I'm calling." But as the words slip out, I do know why. I don't want to go back there. Back to Summerland where things are cold, where things never change. Not now. Not yet. But hearing someone's voice. Someone who's known me for so long and maybe even *loves* me feels good, too. Like I want to be there. Not now but someday. Maybe even someday soon. "How are things on the home front?"

"You know," he says.

I ask him for details and he gives me a rundown of Miller's new sign and the new lifeguard tower at the south end of the beach. I know he's trying his hardest to think of things to tell me. It's Summerland. There isn't much.

"Mags?" he says when he's done.

"Yeah?"

"I'm cheering for you. You can do this. I know you can. You're special. On that stage and on TV. Everyone knows it. Okay?"

I don't say anything else. Like that day with the ice creams, Mark and I have always had this thing where words are said, but aren't really necessary. We aren't good at small talk. I've never really noticed that we're the same like that, but now I do. The silence between us is there, but comfortable. I can hear his breath. I know he can hear mine.

From the bathroom, I hear Olivia shut the water off and slide the door across the tub. "I've got to go," I say. He says thanks for calling and that he'll still be watching, and I say thanks, too. I go to hang up but before I do, I say, "Hey. And thanks for being my friend."

And he says, "Always."

I toss the phone back on Olivia's pillow and lie on my own bed, letting my truth seep through me. Summerland is inside of me. Its people are inside of me. But here is where I want to be. And I know the other contestants want it bad, but Olivia's wrong. She knows where her mom is and that's more than I've got. And Mark's wrong, too. Even if he says I'm special out there, I don't have my town's love the way they do, no matter what happens here tonight.

No. No way. It's not the same for people like her, for people like him. It's just not the same. Any way you slice it.

TWENTY-EIGHT

Olivia slaps my hand away from my mouth. "You know, if you'd stop fiddling with that hair of yours, it might actually be pretty."

I quickly hide both my hands behind my back. "I know. I can't help it." Really, I can't. Ever since I lost—no—was *robbed* of my pillowcase piece, the end of my braid has taken a serious beating. I keep my hands at my side until I'm sure Olivia's regained focus on the shouting people, swooping cameras, and flashing lights all around us. Then my hands shove the two-inch tip of hair into the corner of my mouth.

But the girl's got some serious peripheral skills. She yanks my hand away from my hair. "You better help it. No one wants to see a hair sucker on national television. They'll show it for the playback moments. They'll use it to get more people over to Team George. You better knock it off. It's now or never."

I watch as the cameras pivot between me and Olivia and the other ten of us, standing shoulder to shoulder on stage. I hope my hair is right and my makeup's right and I hope they haven't caught that hair-in-mouth thing but I bet they have. I wonder if, somewhere out there, my mom will see me doing it and I think of how I used to do it when I was little and she'd come home and find me sitting under the kitchen table, hair in mouth. Mom never minded because she said it reminded her of herself somehow and, back then, I thought that was a good thing. I think about Mrs. Perkins and how she'd caught me doing it once, inside her shop, and slapped my hand away just like Olivia did.

I glance at Olivia. How is it that she seems totally put together, her long-legged body wickedly composed, while I feel like I'm going to melt into a pool of drizzle right here on center stage? Then again, like George, she always knows when the eyes are watching and the ears are listening. Except that I can't decide if that's who she is, or who her mom tells her she has to be.

I think of the printout she showed me when we were in our room just two hours ago. The one that said I was going to come in second place in the finale show. The one that also said Olivia wouldn't make it past Week Two, at best. Yet somehow, after she came out of the bathroom, Olivia pulled her shit together like it was her patriotic duty to do so. She painted her nails Bahama Mama pink and then she shaved her legs and then she said nothing while she applied four different products to her hair while I applied none and thought about how many cameras would focus on the fact that Olivia's hair is like ribbons while mine's like sandpaper.

And while Olivia did these things, I stared out the window, into the LA abyss, my thoughts landing in Summerland. I know she thinks my town is nothing because no one's ever heard of it—or hadn't, until George and I made it on the show. But it doesn't matter what she thinks. Not when my nothing is the only nothing I've ever known.

Five minutes later, one of the producer's lackeys called up to our room and told us we had "five minutes to get our skinny butts downstairs" to wardrobe and makeup, or we'd be off the show. As if they'd do that.

Now the lights dim and the *Live to Dance* theme song blares.

"Here we go," I mutter under my breath.

Olivia squeezes my hand. She hisses at me through clamped teeth. "Smile for God's sake, will you?"

I nod, but of course, my mouth can't really do that on command.

So instead, I scan the gazillion people that make up the live studio audience. But because we're in the light and they're in the dark, I can't really make out any of the faces. They're just sort of blurred together in these dull gray swirls that remind me of the mid-morning sky in Summerland. But then a pair of eyes stand out to me and hold my gaze. I blink and then turn my head to look at George and Rio but they're way down the line, holding up the opposite end to me. When I look back into the crowd and try to find those eyes again, I can't. They're gone. Dissolved into the collective haze of eyes around them. My gaze focuses, instead, on a new face.

This face is smiling with these glossy lips—shined and red like an eighties Corvette. Glimmering in the dark, like glow sticks. I know those lips. They're exact replicas of the snot-bag-turned-sort-of-new-best-friend standing next to me. I peek at Olivia, who's looking everywhere but at her mom. Maybe it's because she's not ready to go eye-to-eye with the woman that told her, point blank, that she's a loser. I can't believe her own mother said that to her. When I first saw her, I definitely thought she was the quintessential Martha Stewart mom—one who does needlepoint by day and drinks pretty pink cocktails with pretty names by night. I thought she was nice. Like Mrs. Moutsous. Like the kind of cookie-baking mom anyone in my shoes would kiss earth to share a last name with. I didn't think she was the kind of mom to make her daughter feel bad just because she could.

The overhead announcer shouts, "Welcome to Season Six, *Live to Dance!*" On cue, Camilla Sky saunters to the front of the stage in the shortest of minidresses and the highest of heels. She grabs her microphone. The cameras swarm her. "It's the moment you've all been waiting for, ladies and gentlemen! Tonight we're concluding Week One, which brings us one step closer to finding out which dancers will be in our finale in only five weeks' time!" The crowd blows up. Camilla waves her hand in front of her. "Unfortunately, it also means we're closer to sending home two unlucky contestants who will *not* be going on to compete next week."

Camilla pauses while the audience boos. Next to me, Olivia grabs my left hand again. On her other side, Hayden grabs her left one. And on down the line, the other dancers have joined hands too, all of us connected like one giant string of paper dolls. The audience oohs and aahs and claps their heads off, because this is what they want. For us to love each other. So it'll be really good entertainment when they snip some of us off and send them home. Crumpled and disposed.

Camilla takes an envelope from her assistant. "Okay, we're going to get right to it. After we hear a few words from our judges."

The spotlight brightens on the wooden table where all three judges sit. They've pulled their faces into these tight smiles, too, which makes me think of Hayden. Even when the cameras aren't around us, Hayden keeps her smile on and ready and I wish I had those kind of skills right about now.

"Let's start with the lovely Astrid Scott. Astrid, you've seen the blogs. You know what everyone's saying about our dancers. Do you think the predictions are pretty accurate?"

Astrid laughs, as if this question has never occurred to her. When, according to Olivia, she's one of the biggest sources for most of the bloggers. "Loose Lips Scott"—that's what Olivia called her.

Astrid leans forward, making sure that her signature bazookas smile for the cameras that love them. "If we lived in a perfect world, we'd never listen to the things people say about us. But we don't, so I think it'd be impossible to ignore the rumors about what's going to happen in this show. However, I think it's equally important to remember that it's *America* that votes. Not just the bloggers."

Camilla raises one shaped eyebrow. "So what you're trying to say is that anything can happen at this point?"

"Exactly, Camilla. You might as well expect the unexpected." She zeroes in on Jacks. The cameras swoop from Astrid to focus on Jacks's face. She's talking about him. We all know she's talking about him because of those blogs and even though she says that the blogs don't matter as much as we think they do, it's obvious they do. Jacks isn't looking at the cameras at all. Instead, he's staring at his feet and biting his lip and if I didn't know better, I'd say that Jacks is worried. Or sad. Or maybe even both. But then he lifts his head and winks for the cameras and smiles that crooked, broken smile of his and I know how wrong I've been.

"Very sage words from someone who's been in this business a long time." Camilla thanks Astrid and then takes a few steps to the left of her. "And now to the legendary Gia Gianni. You haven't seen the names that are in this envelope. Am I correct in assuming that?"

Gia leans back in her chair, one hand to her chest, her face splattered with a horrified expression. "Camilla, are you asking if I peeked at the results?"

"I know you'd never do that," Camilla says. "But what I think America really wants to know is if you can predict who's going home tonight by how well they competed on Tuesday?"

Gia leans in closer to the microphone. "Camilla, darling, I didn't get where I am in this business by chance. I know who the winners are. And that means I know who the losers are, too."

A chorus of *oohs* sweep through the crowd.

Camilla runs her hands through her mane. She lets a piece fall in front of her eyes, which makes her look sultry and mysterious. Which, I guess, is the point.

"A woman who doesn't mince her words," Camilla purrs. "I like that." She takes three steps to her left, her eyes gleaming when they meet the piercing gaze of the third judge. "Last, but certainly not least, Sir Elliot Townsend. The king of *Live to Dance*. I'm sure our audience, as well as our viewers at home, would like to hear from you about what's going to happen after two dancers are sent home tonight. Where will they go from here?"

Elliot slowly scans the line.

My heart thuds with the strength of a hundred clam guns. I want him to tell me. Tell me with his eyes that I'm not going home tonight. Not going home until I've done what I came here to do.

Elliot passes over me without stopping. "Well, that depends."

Camilla taps her foot. "On?"

"On the dancers. This competition isn't a one-time shot. Yes, the dancer who wins will take the prize money and the title, but it's so much more than that. This is a journey. A chance to grow. Even dancers who leave here tonight can leave with something. They can go armed with what they've learned here and use it to get better, or they can go home and live the life they had before any of this started."

Camilla nods and spins around to us. She waggles one finger at us. "Listen up, little lambs. This is good advice for you all." She smoothes the bottom of her dress and laughs for her cameras. "Now, ladies and gentlemen. The moment we've all been waiting for. Without further ado, can we dim the lights, please!"

I bow my head and close my eyes. I feel the cameras on me but I know they're not on me, they're on everyone. It doesn't help. It's all happening, right now.

Next to me, Olivia squeezes my hand, hard. I look at her and then over her to Hayden. And then to Jacks. Liquid. Rio. George. And the others. Their eyes are shut tight, making little creases in the corners.

My heart booms so loud. So I break my hand free from Olivia's and place it over my chest. She gawks at me with eyes as wide and round as UFOs. She grabs my hand in hers again.

The lights darken. Camilla waves her envelope across the air. "The futures of these dancers are in the palm of my hand." She tears one corner of the envelope open with her nails.

Smiles. Nods. Smiles again. Pauses.

My heart pounds. Boom. Boom. Boom.

"The first dancer to go on to the next round of *Live to Dance* is—"

Pause. Pause. Pause.

Boom. Boom. Boom.

"Rio Bonnet."

Rio breaks free from our chain and jumps up and down, her curls bouncing all over the place like tiny little springs. The cameras follow her up and down the stage and I watch as one cameraman smiles behind his lens. She's gorgeous. And she's a Bonnet. The cameras must love her. I knew Rio would make it. I knew she would no matter what Thomas thought. Of course the audience loved her. Even when I met her my only thought about Rio is how loveable she truly was. Is.

Camilla shimmies back to the microphone. "The second dancer to go on to round two is—" Pause. Pause. Pause.

Please. Please say it.

"Olivia Palmetto!"

I give Olivia's hand a two-beat squeeze while the audience goes berserk at the sound of her name and the cameras zoom in close to her face and flash her profile on the screen behind us. She bounces on the balls of her feet and waves to the cameras, because she's never been afraid of them the way I was. Am. Then again, she has no reason to be. She peers straight into the blackened audience and gives a solid thumbs-up.

I'm happy for her—I really am. If anyone deserves this, Olivia does, so of course I'm happy for her. But the thing is, it means that report was wrong. It also means there's one less spot for me.

I take a deep breath. Hold it in. There are only nine spots left. One has to be for me. It just has to.

Camilla clears her throat. Waits for the audience to quiet. "The third dancer going on to Week Two," she says, "is Jackson Wiles!"

Jacks spins around with his eyes so wide and runs down our line, high-fiving us all. He jumps up and down all around the stage and the cameras are loving it, moving all around his feet and following him as he uses the whole stage to do back handsprings from one side to the other. A few of the audience members are booing, because he's Bad Jacks and everyone knows it, but mostly people are cheering for Jacks and his happy dance which, I have to admit, is pretty darn happy. The screen blasts behind us, replaying his back handsprings over and over because it's exactly the kind of thing that people at home will want to see. The reports weren't just wrong, they were *really* wrong. Next to me, Olivia's giggling, so I guess everyone really does love an underdog. But then Jacks turns to the rest us still standing here, begging for the universe to call our names next, and mouths the word *suckers*. He slides up center stage on his knees.

He's such an ass.

I squeeze my hands into fists inside Olivia's. Please. I'll do anything. Anything.

Camilla raises her hand. "The fourth person who will go on to compete is—"

I shut my eyes and hear my own name run through my mind, hear Camilla's voice saying it. *Magnolia Woodson.* It has to be me. *Magnolia Woodson.* It sounds so right.

"Juliette Mancini!" The crowd goes wild for her, too, but Camilla reins them in faster than the other two. And the fifth person to go on to Week Two of *Live to Dance* is the incredible, unstoppable—"

I hold my breath.

"Hayden Pettiwater!"

I bow my head and close my eyes, while a few inches away from me Hayden shakes but is still sort of not moving, like her feet are bound to the stage by superglue. Her shoulders are trembling.

Camilla touches Hayden's arms. She waves a couple of the cameras over. "You made it, Miss Pettiwater! You made it to round two! Aren't you excited?"

Hayden nods her head. The screen behind us shows her grinning face, but then cuts quickly to Camilla's face, which looks much more comfortable on that huge screen.

Camilla clears her throat. I stand up a little straighter. There's still a chance. There's still a possibility for me. "Ladies and gentlemen, the sixth person to proceed to Week Two of the show is Zyera Jones!"

I feel my knees get weak. It can't be me now. There are too many good dancers left. It just can't be.

"Okay, ladies and gentlemen," Camilla says. "Our seventh and eighth competitors who will go on to round two are the ballroom couple from New Mexico, Thaiss Morgen and Gabriel de los Suenos!"

My heart falls into my chest. Now I know it's true. I didn't win. Because the last two spots have to be for Liquid and—"

"George Moutsous!"

He made it! He really really made it! Without thinking, I bend forward and my eyes search for his. He leaps around the stage, accepting his rounds of cheers and whoops. The cameras swoop over him and around him and he's facing them and jumping up and down and the crowd is going wild because he's George. But then, and only for a second, he peeks over his shoulder and our eyes meet. Hold each other. I inhale. I feel him inhale, too. And then he turns away.

When the audience's noise dies down, Camilla walks down our line, surveying the rest of us.. But as she walks past me, I notice her stare travels over me, my face, my body, quicker than everyone else. I look toward the cameras and they're not even on me at all, just panning across the other contestants. Something's wrong. She must know that they've already eliminated me. I don't understand. I thought I did my best. I thought I did okay. She turns to face the cameras.

"And the last person to make it on to next round of *Live to Dance* is—"

My heart crackles. The silence fills my chest like helium. And lead. How can this be the moment where they tell me I'm going home? I've gone through it a million times in my head. It never looked like this.

I shut my eyes. All the noise drains from my ears. I am deaf. I am blind. I am floating somewhere above myself, looking down on the crowd. The stage. And then I see me. Standing there, knowing that I haven't made it.

Knowing that I've lost everything.

"Magnolia Woodson."

What?

I open my eyes.

"Magnolia Woodson!" she repeats, this time screaming my name.

It's me!

I jump up in the air with my arms and fists raised to the ceiling. The cameras zoom in and for the first time since I got here and they've been all over me, I don't even care. The audience is out of their seats. They're whooping and dancing and cheering because I did it I did it I did it. Me. Magnolia. Me. No-good Woodson girl.

Olivia grabs me and throws me into this kind of bear hug and then, still tangled in embrace, we're dancing around and laughing and everyone else is dancing all around us too while the cameras catch every single second of it on film.

For that glorious forty-five seconds, we are the chosen ones.

Me. Olivia. Hayden. Jacks. Rio. George. The ballroom couple. Zyera. Juliette.

And then, all it once, it hits me who it is that's going home. Lawrence, the West Coast Swing guy from New Jersey who was supposed to place third overall and made the judges cry both times they saw him dance. And Liquid from God knows which street corner in New York. Liquid, who held me back from creaming George because, somehow, he knew I shouldn't. Liquid, who barely speaks with his mouth or his eyes.

Lawrence is braving the cameras, his grin wide. The screen behind us flashes with his face. He talks about how lucky he was to be here for this opportunity and he says he wouldn't trade it for anything. Liquid's staring at the cameras, too. The screen changes to show his face but he doesn't tell his story the way Lawrence did. He nods and accepts his defeat, but it's not the same. There's something different about him, but there's always been something different about him. And then it hits me. I know.

Liquid isn't vapid, devoid of any emotion the way Jacks is because he's tough and mean and hurtful for the sake of hurting. Liquid is defeated. I don't know if it's the streets that made him this way or if it's something else. The only things I've seen from him—touching me and touching George and maybe wanting someone to touch him back—I thought were the same things he came here for. Dancing and getting laid. But I bet he has no problem achieving either of those things in New York. He wanted something different. That's why he came here.

My heart sinks for both them, but I think Lawrence will be okay. He's standing with Liquid and talking to Liquid and maybe even trying to exchange private moments of pain with Liquid. But Liquid's not even moving. Not saying a thing. Like he was already gone, long before he came to this show.

I feel a stab of regret, a stab of pain. Not for me, but for them. Even if Liquid can't show it. Even if he can't feel it. He's got to know he did everything he could to be here and it wasn't enough.

But I can't worry about him now. As the cameras swivel from them to me and the other winners, I know I can't worry about George or how he doesn't seem to notice Liquid's hunched shoulders, shielding hair, dead eyes.

I straighten my back and hold my own head high. Behind me, I know it's my face they're showing because now the whole audience is shouting, "Mad Mags! Mad Mags!" It's me

I came here for—not them—not any of them. It's me who's going on to the next round, and the five after that. It's me who's going to win this whole darn thing.

TWENTY-NINE

Two weeks later, we're walking through the white-washed pathway to the hotel's pool and bar area, happy to finally have an afternoon off. We've only got three hours before our next dance styles are posted, but it's three hours where the cameras have strict orders to leave us alone, and that's more than we've had since we came to LA. It's also three hours to try to mesh in with this swanky LA scene, which isn't easy for a group of mostly small-town kids who have been locked up in sunlight-deprived dance studios for three weeks. I mean, physically we all fit in thanks to the fact that, as a rule, most dancers are fit. But still, on a metaphysical level, most of us have little to no knowledge of Brazilian bikini bottoms and manscaping.

I skim the deck for a couple of empty lounge chairs. Behind Olivia and me, Jacks shouts, "Would you look at the bods around here? Welcome to Hump Town USA!" which makes me cringe and wish I didn't have to walk anywhere with him.

I glance at Olivia, but she's not cringing. Only when his feet catch the back of her flip-flops does she roll her eyes in my direction. "What an idiot."

"I was so hoping he would leave last night, not Juliette," I say. "And definitely not Zyera."

"I know. They were cool." Olivia shudders. "He's a cretin. It almost makes me miss those ballroom guys. Hell, I'd even take Liquid back at this point."

I glance back over my shoulder at George. I wonder if he wishes Liquid were still here, but I doubt it, considering he barely even blinked when Liquid was eliminated.

George's face reveals nothing. But then he lifts his head and his eyes meet mine and hold them. He misses me. He has to miss me, because not missing me would mean that he never valued our friendship the way I did. Do. But he's the first one to break his eyes away from mine, letting his gaze fall to his feet like he can't bear to see me for another second.

I mean, after the Tuesday performance show where I danced a Broadway routine and George took on a tap number, both of us earning glowing cheers from the audience, George never looked my way once. And in the Thursday results show that followed, where the ballroom couple was eliminated for their "lack of chemistry," before they even had to dance solo, all I could think about was the way George and I used to exude natural chemistry. Like, all the time. I stared at him, hoping he was feeling the same thing as me, but he never looked in my direction. Not for a second. And last night, when Zyera and Juliette were both let go, which was so shocking and sad but exciting, too, because it left me and George both safe going into Week Four, George ignored me like I didn't even exist.

It's been three weeks since we had our fight. Three weeks since the universe turned our world upside down and made the sky no longer up and the sea no longer down and our friendship no longer the most important thing either of us have ever had. It's the longest we've gone without talking. It's the longest we've gone without finding every single reason to be around each other. I know they say that time heals all wounds, but I'm not sure that that's true. At least, I'm not sure that it's true for George and me.

"Where do you guys want to sit?" Hayden says. Her voice is so high and tinny. Sometimes it's all I can do not to tune her out. But part of me feels bad for her, too. It's obvious no one really likes her because she never stops smiling and always-smiling means fake, but then I wonder what they say about me behind my back, too. I'm afraid to ask Olivia. If I did, I know she'd tell me the truth.

"There's a bunch of chairs over there by the bar, and a few over there by the sand," Hayden says. "What do you guys think? Beach or booze?"

"Booze, definitely booze." Jacks cups his left hand around the top of his mouth and waves his right one in front of him which, I guess, is supposed to seem tough. Then he raps—literally *raps*. "Bring me booze, bring it fast, if you don't I'll slap your—"

"Okay, we get it." Olivia puts one hand out to intercept Jacks. "Booze it is." She sticks her tongue out at him. That girl cracks me up.

She spots a set of double chaise lounges with rolled-up orange towels near the DJ and pulls us toward them while the others dump their stuff a few chairs over. I plunk my bag down, watching the DJ guy bob his head while holding a massive pair of earphones up to his right ear. He's spinning house music. The kind that's overlaid with some beautiful woman's voice, singing about music and wine and summer love.

This kind of music all sounds the same. All chi-chi and pretentious. Soulless.

Or at least, that's what George used to say. Among other things that I've always known, and could never forget. Like about him wanting dance to mean something, us to mean something. About music transcending him and giving him the strength to be who he really was. Is. *Was*.

Although I still have no idea who that is. Was.

I plop myself in my chaise and lean way back. Then I adjust my sunglasses—Olivia's sunglasses, ones that she lent me the day I appeared in her room, a million years ago. I'm not kidding when I say that LA must be the sunniest place on the planet. Luckily for me, Olivia was also nice enough to lend me one of her oodles of bikinis that she brought "just in case."

She tosses me a magazine to read, but I leave it closed next to my leg. My gaze bounces between the DJ and Olivia, Hayden, Jacks, and George, who have already stripped off their shorts and tees.

"Hey, you guys. Who's swimming?" Jacks says. When nobody answers him, he catapults himself, cannonball-style, into the pool. "This place is awesome!" he shouts, splashing everyone around him.

"See? What did I tell you? He's polluting the atmosphere," Olivia mumbles. She watches him do laps from one end of the pool to the other.

On the other side of Jacks's vacant chair, George sits up and pulls his SUMMERLAND OR BUST T-shirt over his head. I have an identical T-shirt—same color, same size, everything—hanging in my closet at home, freebies from the summer we turned thirteen, the night the Hood to Coast race after-party was held on our beach. That party lasted three glorious days, all filled with me and George eating corn dogs and riding around the flat sand on our bikes, barefoot. Our toes and heels got so calloused from those pedals. And the T-shirts. They got so smelly because we didn't stop to change them for the three whole days. Not that either of us noticed.

And when Monday rolled around, which was my and Rose's usual day at the Laundromat, I sniffed that shirt long and hard before tossing it into the machine. I remember how my nose filled with the smell that made me feel more whole than anything else on the planet: salt and seawater. George and bliss.

Now, George tosses his inside out T-shirt to the end of the chaise. He smoothes his perfect chest with some kind of boutique sunscreen. One I can't imagine any place in Summerland selling.

I inhale deeply. But not because of the sunscreen.

I've seen George in his swimsuit a million times. But seeing the V shape that frames his hips, peeking up from both sides of his board shorts, doesn't get old, ever, though I wish it did. I don't know what rattles me more: seeing George with his body more toned than ever after these weeks dancing, or seeing the shirt. Just lying there. Discarded.

I've never felt so far away from George as I do now. This is the farthest. And I've never known him to look so different to me as he does now. This is the newest.

Olivia pokes my side. "Stare much?"

"What?" My head snaps up.

"I can tell that you're totally checking him out, you know." She leans over and taps the lens of my glasses. "I can still see your eyes through these."

"I wasn't looking at anyone."

"Do you want me to ask him?"

I put my index finger to my lips and make my eyes go as wide and scary as humanly possible. Because I know what question she's referring to and there's no way I want her to ask him that. "No. Just shut up, okay?"

I look toward George and, no doubt about it, there's a space next to him that's empty. Not literally empty—Jacks is out of the pool now and is dripping his chlorinated self all over the corner of George's towel, while the chair on the other side of George is occupied by an overweight balding man talking way too loud on a cell phone encrusted with fake diamonds.

But that's not who *should* be there next to him.

I've seen him and Rio together again, off in some corner, whispering to each other like no one else on the planet exists. So I guess their little lover's spat is over and she's forgiven him for watching me dance. Which is good, I guess. Except she isn't here now.

"Don't say anything, okay? He'll know the question's actually coming from me. And then he'll think that I care where she is and why she isn't with him, when I definitely don't."

Olivia shrugs, but she doesn't say a thing. Because she doesn't have to.

A second later, Jacks sits up and nudges George in the ribs. He waves a driver's license in George's face. "Come on, let's get cocktails."

"No, you go ahead. I'm staying here." George leans back in his chair.

"What for?" Jacks says. "To wait for your chick? Dude. Snap out of it. Have you looked around you? It's like one big naked party around here."

"I guess. Whatever."

"I can't believe you hooked up with someone from the show. Seriously. LA is babe central, so why you'd waste your time with a girlfriend like that, I'll never know."

"She's not my girlfriend." George pops his earphones in his ears and rolls over so that his back is to Jacks.

Whoa. This is definitely something new.

George seems cranky—no, downright pissed. But why? Because Jacks called Rio his girlfriend? Or because he said George was wasting his time when he could be doing it with California girls? I blink a couple times, trying to make sense of it, but nope. It's no use. I'm more confused than ever about George, his suddenly pissy mood and—let's just say it here— whether he prefers male or female genitalia.

Jacks, on the other hand, is relentless.

"What's your deal, man? You sort of suck as a roommate, you know that? You've been moping around here for days and after that funk you sunk into after Liquid went home, I can't take another round of this from you." Jacks puffs out his chest. "Look around you. We're in LA. Life is great. You don't see me feeling sorry for those losers. Especially that Liquid guy." He mutters, "What a tool."

George glares at Jacks. I guess because, to George at least, Jacks is the tool, not Liquid. But it's weird to see George pining over someone that was only in his life for like a minute, and even then it didn't really seem like George cared about Liquid at all. I think of Liquid when we first saw him back in Portland, the morning of tryouts. I can still picture his sunken eyes staring at George like he had seen him before.

Like he knew him. Then I think of the way Liquid was when he was eliminated. He looked so empty. George looked like he didn't even care. But maybe there was more between them than I knew. Maybe it wasn't just attraction, a way to use each other for sex or, in George's case, for revenge. Not like I'd know. George used to tell me things about his life. Until he didn't.

"I feel bad every time someone has to leave the show," George says, lifting the left side of his headphones off. He glances at me again. "I'm not heartless, you know."

I watch him pick up his SUMMERLAND OR BUST tee and pick an imaginary piece of fluff off the "B." His eyes are glassy, and he must know that I've noticed, because he grabs his aviator shades from his pack and slides them on.

Jacks shrugs. "Who cares who goes home? Gets us closer to the prize. You won't catch me all broken up when any of you guys are eliminated."

George tosses his headphones back on the chaise. "Right." His left eyebrow rises over his sunglasses. "We'll see about that."

Jacks shoots him a look. "Hey, where is your hot piece of ass anyway?"

"Front desk," George says. "She had a message waiting for her."

Under my glasses, I close my eyes. Instantly, I get this flash inside my head, this picture. Rio with a broken leg. Rio off the show for good. I shake it off because I know it's mean and not the kind of person I've ever been. And then I wonder if George has pictured *me* like that—broken and off the show—the way I just did to Rio.

"Save my seat, okay, you guys?" Hayden says. "I have to go back to the lobby, too."

"For what?" Olivia says.

"My cell's dead. I forgot to call my parents." She fiddles with her ponytail. "I won't be long. Like five minutes, okay?"

"I just saw you on the phone ten minutes ago, crying like a baby," Jacks says. "Wasn't that them you were talking to? What are you, twelve?"

I can't imagine Hayden doing anything but grinning 24/7. She swallows hard. It looks like it hurts. "I wasn't crying. I had to call them once before we came out here. I have to call them now because I just got this feeling that—" She takes a gulping breath of air. "You'd call them too if you—"

"Cared? Because if you don't call them a million times a day, the earth will spontaneously combust?" Jacks laughs. It sounds so mean.

I look away, look at George and Olivia who, I notice, are looking away too. Jacks has always been an ass. But he's taking it too far.

"That's not why I call," Hayden says super slowly. I lift my glasses to get an unshaded view of her face. And for the first time ever—that I've seen at least—Hayden's smile totally, completely falls. Her bottom lip quivers. She bites on both sides of her cheeks. "That's not why I need to phone them. Oh whatever." Her eyes brim with tears. "What the hell do you know about my life anyway?" She chucks one of Jacks's empty plastic cups at him and pulls her knees up tight to her chest. Then she blinks, letting two little drops dribble from her eyes, down her cheeks, and onto her knees.

But Jacks doesn't care. He lets the cup bounce off his chest and then tosses his hat to the ground. "Who'd *want* to know anything about your life anyway, Little Miss Sunshine?" He motions around to the rest of us. "Not me. Not anyone around here."

"Fuck you, Jacks," Hayden yells. She turns to me and Olivia and even George, too. "And fuck the rest of you too." Hayden's face is getting redder and her hands are balled in fists. Olivia's eyes are huge and so are George's. Pretty much all three of us are frozen stiff. Hayden's never even *frowned* for a second in our company, let alone yelled at anyone. Using some pretty serious profanities. In the pool area of a fancy LA hotel.

Jacks jumps out of his chair. "You better watch your language."

"Hey, come on now," George says. "Cool it, you guys, okay?"

Jacks sticks one finger in between Hayden's eyes, not quite touching her but almost. "You don't know who you're messing with. People don't call me shit and get away with—"

"It's my brother," Hayden says. "I call them to make sure he's alive, okay?" Her head drops low. Her voice cracks, so much that it's barely in one piece at all. "He's only four years old. He's got this thing in his brain that makes him have seizures, like, all the time. He was born with it. At first we thought he'd get better but now my mom and dad can't ever leave his side. Not both at once."

"So he might die?" Olivia says.

Hayden shrugs. "Yeah. I don't know. Maybe. They've been saying that pretty much every month of his life. He hasn't died yet though." Then she inhales and wipes under both eyes.

Inside my chest, I feel my heart turn over. Is *that* why? My mind swirls with all the times I've cringed watching her, that perma-smile spread across her face.

"That's awful." Olivia leans over and touches Hayden's shoulder.

Hayden stands up. Takes one small step back. "But they did leave him. Because I got mad. I told them I'm sick and tired of them living every single day of their life for *him*, when *I'm* important too. My life is worth something too." She shakes her head back and forth. "I said it all, just to make them feel bad. And it worked. This time, they did leave him with my grandma to come here and support me. It's the only time they've ever done that."

Hayden tilts her head up to the sky, just kind of staring into it without blinking or anything. The rest of us stay totally still. "But then my grandma called and said he was really sick again. So they had to go."

"Is he—" My breath catches. I can't get the words out. I can't imagine life without Rose. It settles inside my gut. She might not be dying, but she won't want me in her life after this is all over.

"He's not dead." Hayden wipes her eyes with the back of her hands. "No flipping way. I'm not doing this here. Not in front of you guys. You already talk so much crap behind my back."

"Well can you blame us for talking shit?" Jacks says. "You're like a weird clown with that stupid frozen grin of yours all the time. Seriously. I was beginning to think you were mentally handicapped or something."

I close my eyes. I cannot believe he said that. I mean, I *so cannot believe* he said that. Everyone else must be stunned by it too because we all sit there, silent and awkward, until Olivia jumps up and slaps Jacks clear across the face. Hard. Super-duper hard.

Jacks looks totally stunned. He cups his cheek and then stares up at Olivia, who looks a little stunned, too. At first I think he's going to rip her head off. But then I see that he's looking at her like she's some kind of goddess.

Hayden bursts out laughing. Not one of her ear-to-ear plastic laughs, but a true one. A holding-her-gut one. She points to Jacks. "She totally got you. Look at your face. You're going to look like shit on TV." She punches him, lightly, in the shoulder. "I wouldn't want to go on national television looking like that." She motions around to the rest of us. "Pretty sure no one around here would either."

I can't help but crack up because she's right. He *is* going to look like shit on TV. And to the left and right of me, Olivia and George are laughing too. Even Jacks's face looks less hard. I study him as Olivia sits down next to him and takes his beverage and holds it up to his cheek. She doesn't say sorry, but it's close. He doesn't rip her head off, but I guess he wouldn't have anyway. In fact, it's almost like he's smiling. Almost like he's *happy*, which is weird, because I think we all would have slapped him ages ago if we'd known that this was what it took to make him act like a normal human being. He rubs the strawberry mark on his cheek. "Yeah," he says, patting Olivia's ankle. "I guess I am."

THIRTY

Olivia's face is a shade of pink I've never seen on her before. Not even on one of her twenty-plus bikinis or from one of her two zillion tubes of gloss. She stares down at Jacks's hand, still resting on her ankle even though it's been a good eight minutes since he put it there. She covers his hand with her own until she spots Hayden sprinting toward us.

Hayden stops herself in front of our chairs and places one hand against her heaving chest. "You guys won't believe this."

"You look like your head's going to pop off," Olivia says. Then she sits up straight, claps one hand over her mouth. "I'm sorry. Is your brother okay?"

"He's fine. It's nothing about that. But this is big." Her mouth is still smiling—even after everything that's happened—but her eyes. There's something in her eyes that wasn't there before. Relief, maybe. "It's huge actually. I mean, I can't even believe it."

"What is it?" Olivia says. "Are our next dance styles posted already? They said the list wouldn't be up till noon. I almost wish we still drew them from the hat." Olivia grabs my arm. "Want to walk back to the lobby with me and see if it's up?"

Hayden shakes her head. "No, that's not it. I mean, they were just about to post it but they've had to change everything now."

Olivia wrinkles her nose. "Change what?"

"That's what I'm trying to tell you. After I called home, I stopped by the lobby gift shop to grab a bottle of water. And that's when I saw Rio."

George, who up until this point has remained very quiet and totally un-George, lifts his sunglasses and rests them on his head. He stares up at Hayden, which wouldn't be that weird except that there's something in his expression that I just can't place. Something that makes my heart beat just a little bit faster.

Jacks groans. "Who cares if you saw George's booty call there?"

"No, you guys," Hayden says. "She was with the producers of the show. And Elliot Townsend was there and everything. And she was crying."

I bite my lip. Shit shit shit. I swear that when I wished for her to break something, I didn't mean it. But it's too late. I can't suck those words back in now, no matter how bad I want to. "Why?"

"Because they've just disqualified her, *that's* why."

Olivia bolts upright. "Are you serious?"

"I saw it all for myself," Hayden says. "But go on inside if you don't believe me."

My heart sinks into my gut. Okay, so she's not injured. But disqualified? I didn't wish for that to happen. At least, I don't think I did.

"Man," Jacks says. "Why do you think they disqualified her? She had serious chops."

"I know why," Hayden says. "They kicked her off because Rio turned sixteen last month."

Olivia grabs the metal of her chair to steady herself. "You're not serious."

"How is that even possible?" I say. "They checked our IDs when we tried out."

Jacks waves his cocktail in my face. "Um, hello? Fake IDs?" He slides his card over. "Says here I'm a twenty-five-year-old marine."

Olivia swats his hand away from me. Jacks scoops her off her chair and dangles her over the pool like he's going to throw her in while George keeps his eyes closed. It's like his mind has gone someplace else. Someplace very far away. I wish I knew where he went so I could go there, too.

"Wait," Hayden says. "I haven't even told you the best part."

Olivia slaps Jacks's arm until he sets her down.

"They chose Rio to dance in her own style for Week Four."

No way. Rio's style is contemporary. Now that she's out—

"Contemporary will probably be up for grabs! There's no way the judges will have *no one* dance it, since Gia's a contemporary choreographer and influences pretty much everything on the show. We're so close to the end. They have to give it to someone, and someone who's good at it." She nods toward me and Olivia and then to George. "I guess that means one of you guys is going to get it."

"Yes!" Olivia screeches, pumping her arm. Only I don't really know why, because Olivia's already had contemporary *and* classical ballet, so the chances the producers are going to let her have it again are minimal. But me. Though I've done styles close to my own, I haven't had contemporary. Yet.

I stand up and search for a way to get off this pool deck and fast. I pull Olivia aside and tell her that if Hayden knew that

Rio was supposed to dance contemporary, maybe the dance styles are up after all. While Jacks sips his cocktail and George and Hayden soak up some sun, Olivia and I slink out of there before they notice.

Hayden's so right. They'll want to give the most popular of all the styles to someone, and that someone's got to be me. There's only three weeks left in this whole competition. Three measly weeks. Which means I have three weeks to show them that I deserve to win this whole thing. Maybe even more than anyone else. And with Rio out and contemporary back on the table, I've got a better chance than ever of making everything I've ever wished for come true.

Olivia and I burst through the lobby door, running at full tilt until we reach the bulletin board outside the gift shop. Olivia stops and breathes when she sees two cameramen coming our way. She smoothes her hair and pushes her shoulders back just as the red lights from their cameras go on. "Is it up? Where is it?" She searches around, above the board and below it. She whips out her phone and frowns when she sees she's got like twelve missed calls, which are all probably from her mom. Then she stares at the clock. She shakes her phone in front of my face. "It's 12:02. It should be here by now. Why isn't it up yet?"

"Because it's right here," a voice behind us says. Olivia and I turn to see Elliot Townsend standing behind us. "There've been some complications. You'll see the official announcement during a segue shot." He reads the page in front of him.

Shakes his head, almost regretfully. He glances at the cameras and shoos them away. "Tomorrow when the show airs, you'll see it all."

Olivia and I exchange glances while Elliot squeezes in past us and tacks up the single white page to the board. I read the first name listed. "Oh my God," a voice says. It takes me a second to realize that it's my voice that said it.

"It's you," Olivia whispers. Her voice gets louder and louder until it's pretty much shrieking. "You got it, Magnolia!" She grabs a hold of my arms and shakes me a little. "George didn't get it. *You* did."

I stumble backward. The single most beautiful word I think I've ever seen is next to my name. It glows bright, like a sunset fading from the sea in Summerland. *Contemporary.* Now I'm sure of it. I'm going to show them what I can do for Summerland. Show them that I'm not her, have never been anything like her. In two days, I'll be dancing in my own style. And I'm going to rock their worlds doing it.

Elliot's face breaks into this broad smile that's so warm and real. He touches my arm. "You got it. After four weeks of doing every style but your own, you've earned this. Congratulations."

"Thank you." My words are slow and I don't even know if they come out right, the way I mean them to. "Thank you so much." In my head they're all muddled and choppy, like one of those badly dubbed Chinese films you see on late-night TV. Unlike most of the characters in those films, I'm sure as hell no samurai soldier, though I sure as hell *feel* like one right now.

But then I remember that I wished for Rio to be gone. The night of the first results show, I wished she were off the show.

Elliot smiles at Olivia and then at me. His eyes hold mine for what seems like forever. Like he's proud of me the way a father would be. Proud of his daughter who's done something really, really good. Which makes me feel really, really bad.

And then he walks off. Whistling the tune to some old-fashioned song I've never heard.

Olivia squeezes my hand and bounces up and down. "You're finally dancing contemporary."

"I know. But I shouldn't be."

Olivia stops bouncing. "If anyone deserves it, you do. If it was classical ballet, they probably would have given it to me again. But it's *contemporary*. Everyone knows you're the best at that."

"Being the best at something doesn't make you deserve it."

I think of the days that followed Colleen's death. I was so mad at Mom. Not only for what happened to Colleen, but I was mad at her for us. For Rose and me. I knew our lives would always be different, and it was the kind of different that would be hard—no, impossible—to fix. I wished my mom would go. I wished she'd leave us alone and never come back. I wished it so hard and then, one day, my wish came true. This isn't any different. I'm the one making the things happen. Even if Rio and I weren't exactly friends, I still wished for her to be off the show. "I wanted her gone," I say. "You heard me. Now I have the style she was supposed to dance."

"We all wished she was gone," Olivia says. "The same way we all wished you were gone, too. And George. And Jacks. And everyone else who stands a chance in this whole thing. It's a *competition*, Magnolia. Hoping for the best and silently praying the others will be knocked out. It's all part of it." She places one hand on my shoulder. "You didn't mean what you said about Rio. I know you didn't. You aren't any different from the rest of us. All you've done every day since this started is show up and dance your heart out." She shrugs. "You've probably worked harder than anyone else here."

I look at the list where Rio's name used to be. Where her name still is, now crossed out by one very permanent marker. Rio Bonnet. Crossed out. Contemporary. Crossed out. Thick black marker. Bulldozing over her name. Over and over.

"Hey, check it out," Olivia says. She elbows me in the ribs and then nods to the far side of the room. There, huddled up in a corner by the complimentary coffee station, is Rio. She's got her head down between her knees and her arms up, like she's doing her best to hide from the world.

"What's she still doing here?" Olivia says. "I thought they were supposed to send her home like right away." She grabs my arm and takes a couple of steps toward Rio's crumpled frame. "Come on. We're going over there."

"What? No. I'm sure she wants to be alone."

"She might have lied about her age," Olivia says. "She might have been our competition, but she's still one of us. She danced hard, too. She never complained when things got tough. She supported everyone and she stood up for people when she thought they were right." Olivia shrugs. "She's one of us."

I know what she's talking about. But Rio didn't stand up for people, she stood up for one person. *My* person. George. It feels like it was years ago since my fight with George happened. Looking at Rio now, so small and so very sad, it's hard to believe she could stand up to anyone. But Olivia's right. Rio might not be the bestie I'd pegged her for when we first met, but she's still one of us. Struggling, fighting, reaching for our dreams that seem so far from reach sometimes, and yet other times feel so close.

"You're right. I need to go talk to her."

"Oh, now you want to go talk to her. I thought you hated her," Olivia says.

"I never said I hated her."

"You did. I heard you. Twice."

My eyes bug out.

"You were in the bathroom." Olivia shrugs. "The walls are thin." She reaches over and gives my hand a little squeeze. "I'll stay here." She sits down on the faux leather chair, opens up a magazine, and flips through it. Which is when I realize that it's a *Men's Health* magazine. And that it's upside down.

Right away, I can tell there's something different about Rio. When I get close, I realize it's that she's crying. Hayden had just told us that Rio was crying, but seeing her slight frame, crippled by shaking shoulders, just seems so off. I guess it's because the Rio I've secretly watched for three weeks has always seemed so full of confidence. Which makes me wonder if I've ever known her. Which also makes me wonder how the others here see *me*. I mean, we've been here, doing this thing together for what seems like forever. But how much time have we really spent getting to know who we are?

Rio wipes her eyes and then peers behind me at a cameraman trailing close. She frowns. "What do you want?"

I sit down on the floor next to her. But I don't put my arm around her or tell her not to cry or that it'll be okay because I know that she can't and that it won't. "I don't know."

"You must be thrilled to finally have me out of here."

"No, I'm not."

It sounds strange, but it's true. Yes, I was practically stabbing Rio with voodoo pins up until a few hours ago. But now, I *don't* want Rio out of here. Not this way, I don't. I want her to dance next to me in the semifinal. I want to kick her ass fair and square.

"I know it was hard for you because of your grandma."

"Dead grandma." She flicks her head to the camera. "You're just saying all that because of *them*."

I shift in my seat. I'm not going to lie; I'm getting more used to them than I ever thought I could. Sometimes I don't even notice them anymore, and I don't check YouTube for videos either. But this isn't like that. "Why didn't you tell me you were underage?"

"I couldn't. You were my *competition*." She sticks her hands in her hair and rubs. I think about Olivia's words. How she said we all felt—feel—that way about each other because we're meant to. How she said that she's wished I'd go home before, too, though I know she never meant it. I stare at Rio and try to figure out if I meant it about her or not. The answer comes quickly. No. I didn't mean I wanted her gone this way. I was just mad. Mad that she didn't turn out like I thought she would. Mad at myself for letting this get to me. And mostly, mad at George for choosing her over me.

"I tried to tell you, once," Rio says. "Not when we first met but later. When you finished that tap routine in Week One. I told you I needed to talk to you but then that guy pulled me away and after that, I don't know, you seemed like you were trying so hard to avoid me all the time. I thought you hated me."

I take a big breath. "I never hated you."

"Really?"

"Well, I guess I *thought* I did for a while. I was mad. And madness makes people do crazy things." I take a deep breath. "I thought you were going to tell me to stay away from George."

"Why would I do that? You guys have been friends forever."

"I thought you were jealous that he was watching me or something. Thomas said—" I stop short. It sounds so stupid. All of it. Why would Rio want me to stay away from George? She knew there was nothing between us. She knew it, even before there was something between *them*.

"I wanted to tell you."

"Don't say anything you don't want aired."

"It doesn't matter anymore. I'd already told George how old I was. Man, he was so pissed. He wanted me to go to the judges and tell them and beg for mercy so they'd let me stay but I just couldn't." Rio stares into her lap. "It all felt so wrong. I couldn't picture myself begging for something I earned. We've been fighting about it ever since." She sighs and then presses her fists into her temples. "I didn't know what to do. I told him I was going to ask *you* for advice, which is when he flipped out. He said that if I couldn't find it in me to do the right thing, he still could."

"He was going to rat you out?"

She shakes her head, her curls bouncing around her face. "The weird thing is, I don't think he was. I mean, he could have, two weeks ago, but he didn't. Anyway, it didn't seem like that's what he was talking about. He just kept saying he needed to make things right. It was all so strange." Rio exhales, huge, and wipes her nose with the back of her hand. "But the judges found out about my age on their own, and made this big scene about it all, with the cameras rolling and everything." She glares at the cameras and then turns to me, wide-eyed. "Did you know they had people that do that kind of stuff for them? Like, dig for information?"

I smile, just a little. "Yeah, that's what I heard."

"I don't get why they didn't do that *before* I came all the way out here and made it through three weeks of this crap." She flips the camera off. "Only to look like a total fool on national television."

"For ratings, I guess. They've got to amp the drama when things get slow, right? I bet they planned this one all along. Let Aimee Bonnet's granddaughter on the show so everyone sees how great she is, then kick her off right when the going gets good. Think about it. I bet this is all going to be *really* good for their ratings." The cameraman behind us rolls his eyes, but he knows we're right. I elbow Rio, which makes her kind of smile.

"Yeah. That's one thing I did right, I guess."

"You did a lot right." I stand up. "You were good, you know. Really good. That's why you made it through every round. Don't ever let anyone tell you differently. Especially no dead grandmothers."

Rio smiles. It's not a thank you, but it's enough.

I turn around and take a few steps back toward Olivia.

"Hey, Mags," Rio calls.

"Yeah?"

"Break a leg out there tomorrow. I heard you got contemporary. There's no stopping you now."

When I reach Olivia, she lets the magazine fall into her lap. "So?"

I shrug. "Done and dusted."

She gives me a little smile. "Aren't you even going to ask me what style I got?"

My mouth drops open. It makes her laugh.

"You're not the only one on this show that has things to worry about, Magnolia Woodson."

"I know I'm not. I never thought—"

Olivia holds up one hand. I shut my mouth and don't tell her how sorry I am that I've been so wrapped up in my own drama with George and Rio and my mom and everything, *everything*, but her. I don't tell her, because I know I don't need to. Since the day I walked into Olivia's room and saw her for who she really is—sweatpants, M&Ms, chipping nails, and all—I've known that Olivia isn't the kind of girl that values sorries, but she does value friendship. The kind that takes the good with the bad because only good friendships come with both good and bad.

I pull her off her butt and toward the board, never letting go of her hand. I scan the page for her name. And, admittedly, for his. "Jacks got Bollywood," I say. "Hayden got hip-hop. George got tap. Again." I turn to her. "You got jazz!"

Olivia shrugs. "It's no contemporary, but I'm happy. To tell you the truth, I don't even care that much. I'm glad to still be here at all."

"Say what?" I nudge her side. "What about this competition being a life-or-death situation and all that?"

Olivia waves one hand in front of her, like she's clearing the air. "Oh that. Yeah, well. I told my alpha mom to leave me alone. And for once, she actually listened. Said she's going to stay with her sister in Oregon for a while. Should be on her way there by now." She chuckles. "To Salem. With the other witches."

"I thought it was so important that she knew you weren't a nobody."

"Not anymore it's not." Olivia reaches into her back pocket and uncrumples a piece of paper. She hands it to me. "I told her that I'm not my father—not the deadbeat loser he was—and no matter what she says to me, no matter how she drags his name through the dirt, I'll never be like him." She points to the paper. "It's from Julliard. I guess them telling me I'm not a nobody turned out to be just as good as my mom saying it herself. I'm in, next year, on a full scholarship. Julliard's a whole coast away, you know."

I can't believe it. A few weeks ago, I thought Olivia had the perfect life, the kind no one would ever want to run away from.

She reaches up and touches the names on the board, one last time. "When I told her I'd rather be like him than the heartless woman she is, she actually left." She shakes her head. At first I think it's because she can't believe it herself, until I realize she's shaking the tears free from her eyes. Free, at last. "She can't stop me now. She can't stop my life from being great. Not anymore."

I grab both Olivia's hands and squeeze. Because really, what else can you say to that?

"So do you want to go back to the pool and give the others their news?" Olivia says. "I don't know about you, but I can't wait to see the look on Jacks's face when we tell him that he's dancing Bollywood." She laughs. "He's gonna be so pissed. I sure as hell don't want to miss it."

I follow behind her. But it's not Jacks's face I'm dying to see.

It's George's.

THIRTY-ONE

Gia Gianni cups her hands around her mouth and shouts, "One more time from the top." She claps her hands together as if that will make the brutal choreography I've had four days to learn and master any easier. "I want to see it all again, but this time I want you to dance from the inside out." She curls her palms around my cheeks. Her hands are warm. The lights from the cameras are warm. My skin feels like it's burning.

"Close your eyes," she says. "Just forget about the steps. Listen to your heartbeat, and your body will follow."

"Okay."

"Magnolia, are you listening to me? Feel the music."

"I'm listening. I said okay."

I poise myself in my starting position. Head bent. Arms bent around my body, my left hand cupping my right shoulder, my right hand wrapping my waist.

"You're the raven, bound by chains. A shell encases your wings. Think of your cage. Think of your armor. Think of breaking free from it all so you can fly."

I nod, breathless. "Chains. Wings. I'm ready."

Gia grabs my arm and spins me around. She holds my hand in hers and presses it to my chest. "Even if you go through these motions a thousand times, it won't be enough. It will never be enough, until you feel it pulse through your veins.

Until you need it to live. More than water. More than air."

"I'm trying, okay? I do need this to live," I say. Because I am. And I do. I know all about chains and wanting to break through them. I know all about my cage. This should be easy for me, but Gia's not feeling it. I know she's not because like six counts into my music, she throws her hands up in the air and slaps the stop button on the stereo and then walks around the room in circles, head thrown back, fists tapping her eyelids like the sight of my movement has made her blind.

"Magnolia," she says, her voice tight. "The time is now. You have to feel it. What does this song mean to you?"

I cover my face with my hands. "I don't know. It's some kind of love song, right? About a breakup or something?"

"Look underneath that. Listen to the words and then look deeper within yourself." She thuds her own chest with her hand, still curled up in a fist. "Dig deeper."

I want so hard to see what she sees and hear what she hears when the song starts. I'd never heard it till she played it for me last Friday, but now I've heard it a billion times. In the last few days, I've breathed and sweated over every impossible step she's thrown my way, moves that defy gravity and make my body bend in ways I never knew it could. The melody is slow and building, sending sparks through my body.

"I need to see it in your face. Show me everything you're feeling in your heart. Let it flow through your eyes." Gia grimaces. "No, Magnolia. I said let it *flow* through your eyes." She smacks my shoulder. "No scrunching. You're going to ruin your makeup before you even get on stage."

Makeup isn't what I'd call it.

Though my whole face is covered in a thick black charcoal paint, this time I'm no beautiful peacock adorned in blue-green feathers. Now, my hair is slicked and I'm dressed in my own black leotard, the one I've had for three years with the growing hole just above my breastbone. Faded so that it's barely black, like ashes. Hushed black, like Summerland's sky after dusk, right before the quiet of night settles in.

"I look awful," I said to my stylist, when he spun me around to face the mirror.

"You look perfect," he said. "Raw. Wearing your own sores."

The song picks up speed. Across the room, I see myself on the monitor. I see how everyone at home will see me. Like me. Like nothing like me.

I try not to think about the motions and this time, she lets me run through the whole thing until the song's done and I'm done, too. I crouch over. Rest my hands on my knees. "I did it," I breathe. I smile at her. But my smile fades the second I see her face.

"You're still wearing that shell," Gia says. "It's just not going to happen for you if you can't break free from it. Do you understand what I'm saying?"

"I want to. I want to so bad."

She points to the stage. "They're almost done with the clips."

I turn to the TV and to the others huddled around it. Gia hangs back.

At the beginning of each performance show on Tuesdays, they always play a recap from the last week to remind the viewing audience of what happened. But that isn't what's on the monitor now. It's some sort "behind the scenes" clip. Rio's on it, crying, as Elliot and Astrid and Gia tell her that she's been disqualified. The screen switches to show the audience gasp and then get silent. It changes back to Rio, begging and pleading with the judges to give her the second chance she deserves. The judges' faces are blank, even when the audience boos. They tell her how disappointed they are in her for lying to them after everything they've given her. Not one of them says a darn thing about how they knew she was underage, right from the get-go.

The screen changes again and then it's me this time that's with Rio. Sitting in the lobby of the hotel, our backs to the wall. Rio's laughing and I'm laughing and the audience smiles because they think she'll be okay, when I doubt she'll ever get over this.

But that's how the cameras are, I guess. They're filming all the time but not everything makes it to the screen, and even what does doesn't convey what really happened. I think of that first YouTube video with George. The cameras caught our fight all right, but they didn't capture our friendship, beaten, bruised, torn, wrecked, destroyed. There's no way they could have caught any of that.

The clip finishes and suddenly Gia's shaking my arm. I guess she didn't need to see Rio's pain on the screen because she was there, in person, doing her part to ruin Rio's career in dance.

"Magnolia," she says. Her voice is cold but her eyes are hot. "Remember who you need to be to get this done." She pulls me toward her. Takes hold of my shoulders and stares into me, igniting me. "You can do this. Do it for yourself."

Camilla's voice rings out, welcoming everyone to the Week Four performance episode of *Live to Dance*. And then I hear her say, "Please welcome Magnolia Woodson to the stage."

Gia pushes me forward.

I glide on stage, and the music starts.

Inside of me, a small earth grew.

Kissed by the moon, it grew. Lit by the sun, it smiled.

The lyrics pour out. Gia's words bleed in. *Dig deeper, Magnolia.* I let them flow through my ears and into my lungs, my liver, my heart. *Dig deep.* I close my eyes but the only image that comes, the only one that beats through my soul and pumps through my veins, is the same one I've seen since I left Summerland. Mom and Rose on our beach. Digging deep. For razor clams.

Mom thrusts her shovel into the sand when the bubbles pop up. In her eyes, love glows.

"Dig!" she says to us. "Dig deep!"

I whirl, I curve. The music feeds me.

I think about home. I think about clamming and Mom's shovel and that damn gun. I think about Deelish and Urban Outfitters and Rose's damn boss.

The music picks up speed.

But you tore at it with fingertips until it was no more.

You cast out my heart. You cast out my breath.

I stretch and I leap and I bend, and bend again. I think about Colleen. How she must have looked, lying lifeless in my living room, no one helping her.

I live in your darkness.

I think about Mayor Chamberlain, his house. Dark. Desolate.

I dream in your shadow. But your shadow, I won't be.

I spin and I point my toes so damn hard. I think about Mom's face, the second to last time I saw her. The day before she left us. We got up that morning early to clam, the sky unusually clear, sunny almost. Mom was in good spirits. Her daily therapy sessions were working, she had said. She was feeling better, she had said.

"Looks ripe for razors." She pointed to the horizon, flanked by bits of pink and gold.

"Yeah." I rubbed my arms because they were cold, even though I had two sweaters on. Mom took off her jacket, torn under both armpits. Draped it over my shoulders.

"You should keep that on," Rose said. "You're so thin. You need the warmth."

Mom shrugged, her face light and happy, like the air. "I don't feel anything."

We clammed a bit, pulling three or four moderate-sized ones. Tossed them into the bucket, proud each time we heard the gentle thud of the shell touching metal. None of us talked much, but it was okay because things were getting better, just like Mom's group therapist said it would. And I could feel it, too. Or at least, I thought I could.

"What are you three doing out here?"

I was the first to turn toward the voice. Mom froze, her face motionless, staring out to sea. Next to her, Rose stopped sifting.

"It's only been a couple of weeks," Mrs. Perkins said. Her face was pinched, puckered by too many cold mornings clamming all alone. She had never been all that friendly to us in the past and we knew to avoid her. For the most part, she avoided us too. Until recently. "You should be ashamed of yourselves for being out here, in public. His family is still wrought with grief. You have no right to do this to him. To us."

We'd heard the whispers before, but nothing until that morning had been so clear. No one, until that moment, had said it outright.

Mom grabbed the sleeve of my coat so hard, the hole under the right pit tore bigger. She seized Rose's elbow too, pushed us both toward the house, not stopping, until we were inside with the door locked.

Rose went straight to her room and slammed the door. I stood in the hall not knowing what to do. Even from there, I could hear Mom's soft cries that started on the beach, growing louder and louder and louder with every passing second. Rose turned her music on and up. I left, went to George's, and stayed there until my shift at Deelish began.

When I came home that night, she was still there, in her room on her bed, still crying. Making that huge wet spot all over her pillowcase.

The beat drops.

I listen for your voice, but only hear the rain.

I call for you, but the water is our wall.

I throw my head back and beat my chest and think about George.

I fall back, but you don't catch me.

I will beat in your heart once again.

How much I loved him. Will always love him.

I hear your songs,

But you never hear mine.

I think about the people of Summerland. Mrs. Perkins. Mrs. Miller. The freshman. The others. I can't picture any of their faces anymore. It's like they're gone. It's like they never were.

I rise. I fall. I twist. I fly. I spin the sky.

The release. My release.

I spin the sky.

I am the darkness. I am the night. I am the raven. Black and smooth. Poised and perched. Wings spread. Ready to soar, high, against the muted sky.

I will ascend. Because in my eyes, love glows.

Now there is dawn and with it, light.

I do everything Gia told me to.

Stretch my arms and legs to the ceiling, crawl along the floor and cover every inch of it with my body. I do it perfectly because I have no choice other than to do this, to break free, to fly, to be the raven. I do it all. Because I have to.

I'm in your shadow, but your shadow, I won't be.

I leap, my last leap of the routine, and finish with my C jump. I do it perfectly. Head back, arms back, legs bent behind my body. And then I land.

But I don't hear the soft, collapsing whoosh my feet should make against the polished floor. Instead, I hear a loud noise. Crashing metal, *no*. Cracking glass, *no*. Screaming. Screaming.

But it takes my brain a second to figure out that the screaming is coming from inside of me. Knives shoot up from every bone in my left foot, up, up, all the way into my throat. My chest, my armor, my legs, my foot, my bleeding, broken heart.

I'm in your shadow, but your shadow I won't be.

"Help her! Christ. Help her."

"Get her up! Someone get her up. She needs a medic."

"Where's her family?"

"She's here alone." Something smashes. A camera being pushed out the way. Booming footsteps. "I'm staying with her. She doesn't have anyone else here." A boy's voice. Quiet, soft, almost unrecognizable. Jacks.

Voices echo all around me. Backstage. Front stage. Camilla Sky. Hayden. "Someone call for help! She can't move!"

Olivia.

More footsteps. Feet scuffling, screeching against the floor. "Get this out of her face!" Floor that feels so different than the floor at Katina's studio.

"I need to see her. I need to make sure she's okay." A different girl's voice. Pleading. *Rose?* Pleading. *No. It can't be.* Pleading. *She never came.*

"Let us through," a woman says. Mrs. Moutsous. "We're with her."

"You can't be up here," a man's voice says.

"She's my sister," the girl says. "Stop! Get away! Leave her alone!" She puts her face to mine. "Magnolia. Please get up. Please help her up!"

Your shadow, I won't be.

I feel something—someone—on top of me, wrapping their body around mine, shielding me, encasing me, protecting me like the outer shell of a razor clam. "Get those cameras out of here, *now!*"

"George, help her. Please," Rose whimpers.

The same arms that shield my limp body lift me off the ground. My right arm wraps around his strong neck. My head rests against his chest. His heart pounds into my cheek.

"Leave her alone. Get away from us." His voice quiets. "Mom. Stay here and make sure none of these people follow us out of here. Rosie, let's go through the back and call for an ambulance."

I hear them with me, feel him with me, but it doesn't matter. Because it's over now. It's over.

This shadow, I've become.

"You can't go," Camilla says to George. "Let the sister take her. Our staff will call an ambulance. But you stay here. You're up next."

I feel his body immobilize. Against my skin, his heart races. "I'm going with her to the hospital." He growls at someone else, "Don't you dare try to follow us."

Camilla comes closer. I smell her breath—her poison spreading between us. "They need to film this. If you leave now, you'll be disqualified, too."

George strokes my hair and for a brief second, my eyes open and look into his. They're so damn blue, his eyes. Fresh and real, like our ocean in Summerland. Not aquamarine. Not like the sea here in LA. Black-blue and endless. I picture myself swimming away in them—in those eyes—for eternity. I let my own fall closed again.

"I don't care," George says. "I don't care about this. I'm getting her out of here." He rests his chin on my head and whispers, "I'll get you out of here."

"It's okay, George," Mrs. M. says. "Go with her. I'll take care of the rest."

George nods and whisks me and Rose offstage. "It's going to be okay, Mags," he breathes into my chest. "I'm here now."

Next to him, Rose's hand squeezes mine.

"You came," I say.

"Shh," she whispers into my hair. "Of course I came. You were so beautiful, baby sister. You made us all so proud."

But my brain barely registers his words or her words that would have changed everything fifteen minutes ago. Now, it doesn't matter. It's over for me here. After days and weeks of doing everything I could. It's over it's over it's over.

I'm going home. I'm going back to Summerland.

THIRTY-TWO

When a stone-faced nurse shoves a third rock-hard pillow under my head, I wake up with a jolt. "You can't sleep your life away," she says. "You need to sit up for a bit. It'll do you good."

"I don't want to." I swat the pillows out from under me and hide my face with my elbows.

Rose hurries into the room in time to see me pull the covers over my head. "Mags! You're awake!" She shoves a flimsy paper cup filled with ice chips and tap water toward my mouth. "Here. Drink some of this. You must be thirsty."

I push it away. I'm not thirsty. I'm not anything. I shut my eyes and think of Rio, disqualified. Karma is a bitch.

No matter how much I don't want to, I think of last night. George carrying me in his arms. George saving me from Camilla and those cameras and those people. I never want to see any of them again. Now I'll never have to. The only person I want to see George, and he isn't here.

Rose sits on the edge of my bed and waits for the nurse to leave, her rubber clogs clonking across the hollow floor. When she's gone, Rose peers over her shoulder and then back at me, her eyes sparkling. "There's someone here to see you."

I try to sit up, but the pain holds me down. "George? Where is he?"

"Someone else," she says.

I turn my head. "I don't want to see anyone else."

Rose hops off my bed and skips to the door. She flings it open and in walks Mark, looking more sheepish than I think I've ever seen him.

"What are you doing here?" I say, and he smiles.

"I watched every show on TV. And tonight, I saw you on stage. You were amazing."

My heart beats unsteadily.

He seems sad, dark circles under each one of his eyes. But the rest of him looks so good, like always. I search for the right words like I always do when he's anywhere near me. I know it won't matter. He's never judged what I say or don't say. What I do or don't do. I can't believe he came here for me.

He points to the foot of my bed. "Can I sit?" I nod and he holds a paper bag out to me. "I bet you can't guess what's in here."

"More coffee for your mom?"

He laughs, but shakes his head. Inches himself closer to me and dangles the open bag under my nose. Behind him, I spot Rose backing out of my room. She closes the door behind her, quietly. I reach for the bag. Mark snatches it away, with this mischievous look that I don't think I've seen on him before.

Even through the paper, the smell of pure heaven hits my nostrils like nothing else. "That's not what I think it is in there, is it?"

"I knew that would get you," he says. "You can take the girl out of Summerland, but you can't take Summerland out of the girl." He sets the bag on my lap. "See for yourself."

I stick my nose through the top. Razor clam fritters, wrapped in newspaper just the way they're supposed to be to maintain optimal freshness. He didn't just come here to see me. He came here to bring me a piece of home.

He grabs an envelope from his back pocket and hands it to me. "This is for you, too."

I take it from him and open it, carefully. It's a card. On the front is a really good hand-drawn picture of a dancer *en pointe*. But instead of arms, the dancer has big, sprawling gray wings. Like Odette in *Swan Lake*.

"She's beautiful," I whisper.

"She's you," Mark says.

I flip it open and read the words scrawled in blue pen.

Your heart is what you are. And what you are is everything.

"Did you draw this? And write this? For me?"

He frowns. "It could have been better, I know. There's so much I wanted to say. I wrote about twenty lines and then started over and ended with this one."

I flip it over. I didn't even know he could sketch like that, with so much talent and heart I could cry. I know what George said about him loving me, but I didn't feel it then. And our phone call. I could tell that he cared about me and I know I cared about him but that wasn't anything new. We've always been friends. And friends care about each other. But everything feels different now. Everything feels like maybe I haven't felt anything the way I should. Until now.

"Why me?" I whisper.

He inches closer. Closer. So close I can almost hear his heartbeat, like I did that day in his house. "This is how I see you. Strong. Powerful. More determined than anyone I know. The girl who won't let life get her down because she can rise above it all. You don't just dance." He shakes his head, his eyes watery. "You're not like anyone else. You don't ever just dance. You fly."

"I didn't fly on stage. I—" My voice breaks. "I fell."

"Your body gave out. It's not your fault." He twines his pinky finger in mine.

"Is it online? The clip of my dance? I want to see it."

Mark bites his lip. He shakes his head, which is how I know that I shouldn't see it, wouldn't like what I saw if I did. "The show's not everything." He takes my hand and places it over his heart. "You're so much more inside of dance than this. You always have been."

I nod. Can't speak. Because if I do, I won't be able to stop my tears from coming. But he must sense it. Sense the crumbling inside of me, so near the surface. He pulls me closer. I lay my head against his chest. My whole body fills with warmth. I want him. I do. I don't know why I haven't known I did until now.

He smoothes my hair. "They've offered me a place in the company at the California Ballet School, in San Diego. I went there to check it out. It's a great school. A great opportunity."

My chest aches. He can't go. Not now. Not when it's just beginning. "I'm happy for you."

"Magnolia," Mark says. "That's not what I meant. I mean, would you consider coming with me?"

I pull away. "You don't need to do this. I'll be fine. You don't need to make me feel better."

Mark takes a deep breath. "I want you to come with me. I already know they want you."

I pull away. Shake my head. I want to be with him. But it can't be like this. "I can't leave Summerland. Not like this."

"I know you think you can't," he says. He gathers both my hands in his. "But you can. The question you should be asking yourself is, do you want to?"

My mind swirls, my head hurts. A school in California that wants me. A boy that wants me, too. I let my eyes close and think about what it would be like. To be in the warmth of this place all the time, dancing at school and deserving to be there. To be with a boy who thinks I'm everything. With a boy who makes me *feel* like I am everything.

I hold Mark's hands. I should know better than to turn my back on him, on any of what he's offering me. But I came here for a reason. I came here to win the show and change things and now it's over.

I open my mouth to tell him that no matter how he feels about me and makes me feel, I can't have him. Not like this. Not when I have to go home now and everything will be the same as when I left.

But before I can get any of those thoughts out, Mark leans in toward me and kisses me so softly and warmly and it makes me know that things have changed. I have changed. I might be going back to that same place with those same people, but the girl who came from Summerland isn't the same girl as the one who left.

Rose strolls in and sits next to Mark at the foot of the bed. I feel so tired. So worn. So hungry that I don't even care that the only place in town that sells fritters like these, packaged like these, is Miller's Bakery. I tear through the paper, rip off a corner of one of the fritters, and shove it into my mouth. The taste is total liquid gold. There's just no other way to describe it.

"Thanks," I tell them both, my mouth still full of fritter. "For coming to see me." I turn to Rose. "I didn't think you would."

"I wasn't sure if I would either." Rose takes a deep breath. "When I saw you on the show, I wanted to come so bad, right away. But I had to work. There was no one to cover my shifts and I had to wait until I could get the time off. And the money—" She takes a deep breath. "Flights to LA aren't cheap. Mrs. M. was kind enough to call me every night with updates. I was grateful, but it wasn't enough." She grabs my left hand while Mark holds on to my right. "I couldn't stay away. I would have been here the whole time if I could have." She shoulder-bumps Mark. "And when I got to the airport, I ran into him. Seems like we both were thinking the same thing."

"You sounded so sad over the phone," Mark says. "It's all I could think about."

"We had to see you," Rose says. "There's no way we could have stayed away."

Mark lets go of my hand, but gently, like he never wants to let it go. He excuses himself to make a phone call. To his mom, he says. Let her know he's okay, he says. And that I'm going to be okay, too.

I peer out the window adjacent to my bed. For the last half hour with Mark here and Rose here, I've almost been able to forget about what's happened to me. Now, it crashes on top of me like the whole world's crushed me with its weight. Rose must see my shoulders shake, my back breathing with everything I can't let go of.

"I wish this hadn't happened to you." Rose's voice is quiet. "I know you wanted it so bad."

"Yeah, but you didn't. Probably for the best. Like you said."

"I wanted this for you. I really did. I just wanted *you* to want it. Not because you wanted to convince Summerland that we're not these awful people you think we are, but because you were ready to do this. For you."

"It doesn't matter why I wanted it."

"It matters. When you told me about the competition, I was so excited about what it could mean for you and for what I thought it meant for *us*." She rubs her eyes and pulls her hair back with her hands and then lets the whole mess of it fall to her face, exactly the same way I do it. She places one hand over my good foot, kind of like she's checking to make sure it's still there—still in one piece instead of broken in twelve different places like my other one. "I thought it meant that you had finally let go of what happened to Colleen. I thought it could be our fresh start." Rose gets up. Goes to the window. "If there's one thing we've ever done that's been worthwhile, it's making sure you danced."

"So then maybe there's still a chance."

"There will always be another chance for you in dance. Not on the show, but—"

"No." I shake my head. "Maybe what I did up there was enough. Maybe they'll forgive us for what she did and we can go back there and live a good life."

Rose's eyebrows push together. "Who is it, exactly, that you need to forgive us?"

"The people. Everyone."

"Who, Mags?"

I feel my bottom lip quiver as my mind rolls through the names, the voices, the whispers. "Mrs. Perkins," I say. "Mrs. Miller. The kids from school. That family on the beach who said we had no right to be there. Everyone."

"After all this," Rose says, "who are those people to you now? What do they mean to your life?" She waves her hands around the room. "Look who you've met, what you've done. Why do you still care what they think of you when so many others think the opposite?"

"You don't understand."

"There's always going to be people who want to push you down. You have to learn to stand tall against them. Mom couldn't. Mom wouldn't."

"What about you?"

"What about me?"

"You and your pipe. Your boss. You call that standing tall against them?"

Rose shakes her head. "You're wrong. I've never used that pipe. I just kept it. I don't know why." She fiddles with a piece of her hair. "I guess to remind me of her. Like you and that piece of cloth you always kept with you."

I had no idea Rose knew about my piece of pillowcase. No clue she knew I was hanging on to more than just changing our town's minds.

"You're wrong about my boss, too. He's my boyfriend." She looks sheepish. "Joey. We met at my interview. I wanted to tell you. I tried to tell you before you left. You wouldn't hear me. We've been together almost a year."

"Your boyfriend? But he's so *old.*"

Rose laughs. "He's thirty. And I've lived a lifetime to make up for the years between us. Joey wanted me to tell you about us when we first started seeing each other, but I couldn't. I didn't want you to think I was leaving you for him, the way she left us, for—" Now it's her turn to break. She swallows. "The truth is, she just couldn't be with us anymore," Rose says. "Or maybe she just didn't want to."

"Don't say that."

Rose sits on my bed, holds the sides of my arms. "You need to hear this," she says. "Mom didn't want us, Magnolia. She didn't know how to take care of us. And she didn't want to try anymore. That morning on the beach with Mrs. Perkins . . . she was looking for a way out long before that."

"You don't know anything about her. You made her leave in the first place. She knew you blamed her for what happened to Colleen. It's your fault she left."

Rose's lips part, but no words come out.

"You made her leave us. If you would have forgiven her then maybe the town would have too."

"I did forgive her, and so did they. Except for the ones who couldn't, or wouldn't. But those people never mattered. Those people weren't in her life, loving her through it. We were. Us, and Mrs. Moutsous. They didn't make her leave." Her voice gets small and soft. "She left because she wanted to."

"She had to leave," I say the words for what feels like the millionth time, although this time, they sound different coming from my mouth. Like I'm saying them, but not believing them. "No." I push Rose away from me. "I hate you. I hate her, too. I hope she's dead and bleeding and alone and dead." I dig my fists into my eyes. "I wish I was dead."

"Stop," Rose whispers. "Don't ever say that." She holds my face. Makes me look into her eyes. "Colleen was my friend but she was our *mom*. I forgave her. I loved her." Rose cradles my head against her chest. Her heart beats into my temple. "I loved her like you do."

But I can't hear the things she says. It's just too much, these words, making my head hurt, making it hard for me to hear, see, think, breathe. Breathe. Breathe.

Tears drop, slowly at first, but then faster and bigger and heavier. Mocking me with everything I should have known all along. The town didn't hate her, didn't hate us for what happened. Sure, a few of them did, but who were they, really? Summerland losers. People who had nothing going on in their own lives.

And then I'm not crying. I'm sobbing.

Letting it all out. Letting it go.

I cry for George who jumped up on stage, shielding my body with his while the cameras swooped over and in for close-ups of my cries and of my foot.

I cry for Olivia, who I watched, from the TV in this room, stand tall and try so hard not to let the world see her break as Camilla Sky announced that I would not be returning to Season Six, *Live to Dance*.

I cry for Mrs. Moutsous, who was always there for us. Who loved me and Rose and loved Mom even though Mom gave her every reason not to.

I cry for Rose. Who sits here looking sorry.

I cry for me.

Me, who begged Elliot Townsend as someone carried me somewhere, into some car or ambulance or something before it all went black to please, please let me try again when my foot's all healed, maybe next season or the one after, let me try out and compete again so that this time I'll be better on camera and this time they'll see me win.

I cry for me.

Me, who only wanted them to see that I'm not bad, not a no-good Woodson girl. That I'm not my Mom and have never *been* my mom. Because if I were, I would have let that cop slide his hand up my thigh, further, further, further. Because if I were, my body would be my curse and not my freedom.

I cry for me.

Because Elliot shook his head while I begged him and said, "No, Magnolia. I'm sorry. You can't be on the show again. We only let people on once. That was your shot. I'm sorry you didn't win."

And I cry for me.

Because now I know for sure that I never, ever will.

THIRTY-THREE

The phone next to my bed rings, waking me out of one of those dreams where everything seems so clear and right. When I open my eyes, I remember it all. Mark is gone. I told him I wasn't going with him even though a huge part of me wanted to. Wants to.

The phone rings a fifth time and I pick it up. "Hello?"

"Magnolia?"

"Yeah."

On the other end I hear Olivia's voice exhale. "Are you okay?"

"I think so. My foot will be okay. They said I'll be able to dance again. It'll take a long time to heal but I'll dance again."

"Man, I was so worried about you."

"I know. Thanks for helping me and for, you know, everything."

"You would have won," she says all hurried. Like if she doesn't say it fast, she might change her mind.

"Nah. You've got your name all over that winning title. So, results show tomorrow, huh?"

"No," Olivia says. "Didn't you hear? No one gets eliminated this week."

"Really?"

"Yeah. Since Rio's out and now you are too." Silence on her end. "Magnolia, I'm so sorry."

"I know."

Olivia exhales and then I hear a muffled shuffling noise and her voice saying something to someone else that must be with her. "Hey, hold on a sec, okay? Someone wants to talk to you." Then there's more shuffling and then a guy comes on and says a gruff hello.

"You gonna live or what?" Jacks says. I close my eyes and think about his words as I lay on stage, crumpled, broken. He didn't sound like him. Or I guess he did. A different version of him.

"Yeah. I guess so."

"You did good. Just like at tryouts. You were really good then. And last night too. Before you totally blew it, that is."

"Thanks," I say. But I'm kind of laughing.

"No prob."

Neither of us says anything else. It's kind of like neither of us needs to.

Olivia comes back on the phone, her voice all giddy and happy. I guess that's how it is when you finally let go of all the things you thought you couldn't. There's nothing left to feel but goodness.

"So. You and Jacks, huh?"

"Oh, I don't know," she says. "Maybe. He's not so bad. Friends for now. And then who knows?" Olivia's voice shakes. "So, will you look me up sometime? After this is over, I mean?"

I nod my head, although I know Olivia can't see me and can't see me smile. "Of course. Isn't that what friends do?"

The next time I open my eyes, Mrs. Moutsous is here.

She's sitting on the foot of my bed, just kind of watching me and Rose sleep, our heads resting against one shared pillow.

I lift my head and rub my eyes. Rose opens hers too.

"What are we going to do now?" I whisper. Not to Rose or to Mrs. M. Not even to myself. Just to put the question out there. Out in the open, once and for all.

Rose wipes under her eyes with the back of her hand. "Exactly what we've always done. We don't have to live under the weight of their words, you know. We get to choose. Either let them in. Or don't."

"I thought I'd still be in the competition right now. I wonder if those polls are saying Olivia's the new favorite to win. I didn't even ask her when she called. And George." I sit upright, turn to Mrs. M. "Why aren't you with George right now?"

"I needed to know you're okay," she says. "And the only way I could get George out of here was if I promised him I'd stay." She laughs. "He loves fame. But he loves you more."

"He's not off the show for good, is he?"

"No. They never had any intention of kicking him off. Even when he confessed to slipping back in Portland. They certainly weren't going to kick him off for helping you." Mrs. Moutsous inches herself toward us. "You girls are the amazing ones. I promise you. This will get easier with time."

"The people at home," Rose says. "The ones who said those things to us. They'll move on to something else in time, *some-*

one else."

I imagine Rose and me "back to normal." Back in our house. The one that's been in our family for years and that's held our Woodson name together even when it felt like the walls were crumbling all around us. Gram's house. Mom's house.

It's the only thing we've ever owned. It's the only thing we've ever had, other than each other. And yet, being out of it—away from it—I know it's what's stopped us from being something other than we've always been. Something other than a Woodson.

I raise my head so that my eyes meet Rose's.

Rose's eyes, still so full of tears and truth. Like a life preserver, they're keeping me afloat. How could I ever have thought Rio's eyes looked anything like Rose's when no one's could ever come close?

"We can't go back to the way things were," I say.

Rose furrows her eyebrows. "What do you mean? I told you already. Most of the people in town don't hold us responsible for what happened to Colleen. Not directly, anyway." She swallows. "Only the assholes do. We won't listen to them. We never should have to begin with."

I inhale, letting my chest fill with the heavy air around us. "When we get back there, we need a fresh start. I think I want to leave Summerland."

Rose shakes her head. "We can't run away. It won't fix anything."

"Not run away. Just get ourselves some breathing room. See how things look when we're not looking at them from Summerland. A fresh perspective." I grab her hand. "We need this."

Rose leans her head against the pillow. But her face isn't all shocked the way I expected and even felt myself as the words flew from my mouth, so unprecedented. Instead, Rose's mouth is open and, for the first time in so very long, her eyes are full of hope. Not just toughness or wisdom, but hope. Real, genuine excitement for a bright future and future filled with possibility. And although I can't see them, I can tell by Mrs. Moutsous's own proud expression that mine must look that way, too.

Rose goes downstairs to the cafeteria for a cup of "real coffee," while Mrs. Moutsous and I talk about everything but the obvious. That when we get back to Summerland, Rose and I are leaving. Maybe even for forever.

She undoes my long braid and brushes my hair out for me. We flip through the magazines she's bought in the gift shop, skipping over the pictures of me and the other *Live to Dance* contestants. We pick out the outfits and hairstyles we like best. We laugh when she suggests going through the magazines a second time and picking out the best boob jobs, too.

But when this thick, inevitable silence passes over us both, Mrs. Moutsous says, "If you're waiting for my blessing, you've got it." She gets up and sticks one of the pillows I've shoved to the floor under my bum leg. "As much as it's going to kill me when you and Rose are gone, I know that it's time for you both to spread your wings." She plops herself back on the bed, closer to me this time. We sit there for a couple seconds, not saying anything. No one says "please don't go." No one says that doors won't be closed and lives will be changed when we leave, either. Because those are the kinds of words that families don't need to say. Those are the kinds of things that, between families, are just known.

I stare at the mirror across from my bed. I bring my hair forward, one half of it on each side. It trails past my belly button. Mrs. M. watches me, her eyes smiling. "You look so much like her," she says. "Sometimes it's hard. Sometimes I get a little sad because I miss her, too. But I'm proud to know you."

"Mrs. M.? Will you do something for me?"

"You know I'd do anything for you."

I lean over my armrest and press the nurse call button. Within seconds, the same huffy nurse returns and starts checking my cast for leakage and my blood pressure for, I guess, spikeage. I wave her away. "No. I'm fine. I was just wondering if you could bring me a pair of scissors."

The nurse glances between me and Mrs. M. She crosses her meaty arms and squints.

"Don't even think about taking it off. It needs to stay on for at least eight weeks."

"I'm not going to cut the cast off."

"We're cutting out photos. From the magazines." Mrs. M. holds one up to show the nurse. It's one of us. All of the finalists from *Live to Dance* standing with our arms around each other, taken right after Liquid was eliminated. I remember the cameras flashing all around us. I remember being blinded and wanting it to end and never wanting it to end. I remember feeling like a star. Like I could do anything. Mrs. M. winks at me. "We're not used to this kind of glamour where we're from."

The nurse purses her lips and then leaves the room. A couple of minutes later, she comes back with a pair of small surgical scissors. "If anyone asks, you didn't get them from me. We're not supposed to give these to patients." She holds them out to me, hesitates, and then hands them over to Mrs. Moutsous instead. "Especially teenage ones." The nurse leaves and Mrs. M. and I listen to her clogs squeak all the way down the hall.

"Thanks," I say.

"You're welcome." She pauses for a moment, and then holds up the scissors and smiles at me. "So. How short do you want it?"

When Rose gets back from the cafeteria, she takes one look at me and almost spills the coffee she brought for Mrs. M. all over my bed.

"Magnolia! What are you doing?"

I laugh. "I'm not doing anything. Mrs. M. is."

Mrs. Moutsous grins at Rose, snips another piece of my hair off, and sets it on the table next to her.

"You've never wanted to cut your hair before," Rose says.

I shrug. "New life, new look."

Mrs. M. fingers another chunk of hair between her thumb and forefinger. "When I was young, everyone had long hair. Back then it was almost taboo for women to cut it short." She clips another strand. Rose's and my eyes follow it as it falls to the ground. "When I met your mom, she had the most stylish short haircut. Do you remember that?"

"I don't think so," I say. "I always remember it being kind of long."

"I remember it short," Rose says.

Mrs. M. nods. "She was always changing her hair. Always dying it blonde and cutting it short. Growing it long and then coloring it red. Her hair changed with the seasons. Changed with her moods."

The images come seconds later. Not clear—not exactly. But glimmers of them.

Her hands, running a towel through her freshly washed, short, newly caramel-colored strands.

Her hand, stroking my hair.

There. Now I look more like you.

"Wait. I remember that." I scrunch my nose. "At least, I think I do."

Mrs. M. snips off another large chunk of hair from the back. "When I met your mom, I had never cut my hair before."

"Never? Like, never *ever*?"

"Nope. Mr. Moutsous always liked it long and before that my mother would never let me cut it. But when I met your mom, I was ready for a change."

Mrs. M. musses the remaining hair on my head with her fingertips. She stands back and gives it a long look before snipping a little more off the sides. "It's not an easy thing to come by in a place like Summerland. Change, I mean. Of course, people come and go, but for the most part things stay the same. And then when change *does* happen, people resent it."

"Yeah," Rose says. "Sometimes it can make you feel a bit like a rat in a cage. But when that cage is gone, you kind of just want it back."

Mrs. Moutsous nods, thoughtful. "One day, I asked your mom to cut off my hair." She touches the back of her own head and smiles. "She did a fabulous job. She used to be a stylist in the city before she came back to Summerland to live in your grandmother's house. Her styles even won a few awards in hair shows."

Rose brushes a few rogue locks of my hair off the bed. "I remember Grandma telling me that once. It seems so hard to believe." She turns to me. "Doesn't it?"

I don't answer. Because, for one, I had no idea that Mom used to do hair in some other lifetime that didn't include Summerland. And two, I didn't know that Mom used to be anything, anyone before Rose and I existed. I guess I've been spending my whole life hoping that Mom would just stay good for one more day, one more week, one more month, that I never really had time to figure out who she was, when she was somebody else.

"I want to tell you girls something. Something I should have told you a long time ago." Mrs. M. stops talking and Rose and I are silent, too, as the snipping sound of Mrs. M.'s scissors fills the spaces between us. "It wasn't your fault. What happened to Colleen. It had nothing to do with either of you."

I feel my whole body stiffen. Next to me, Rose is staring at her lap. "Okay," I say.

"Magnolia, look at me." Still holding the scissors, she walks around the opposite side of my bed so that we're face to face. "You couldn't have stopped it from happening. Neither of you could have. Your mom made her own choices and so did Colleen. Nobody is responsible for what happened, except for the two of them."

"But we're the ones who had to clean up her mess," Rose says, her voice curt. "Mags walked into it that night. I had to deal with the fact that Colleen was my friend. If it wasn't our fault, why did it have everything to do with us?"

Mrs. M. sets her scissors on the countertop behind her. She reaches across the bed to grab Rose's hand, and then she grabs mine too. "I don't know, honey. I wish so badly I *did* know why your mom had to drag the two of you into her pit of ugliness. I've spent days and weeks and months wondering why she couldn't get better and give you the lives you deserve. There were always these moments where I thought maybe she had. Like the time where she showed up all washed and pretty for your and George's end-of-the-year recital. Do you remember? She wore that lime green dress."

"I remember it." I close my eyes and feel the smooth, satiny material between my fingertips, like I'm touching it. Feel her warmth on me, her words saying she'd put it on for my special night. "It made her look nice. Healthy even."

"That was a great night," Rose says. "But then the next day she turned around and sold our television because she needed her fix." Rose looks down at her empty palms.

I stare at Rose. "She didn't sell the television. It wasn't for drugs."

Rose and Mrs. M. exchange glances. "I couldn't believe it, either, when Rose told me," Mrs. M. says. "You girls barely had anything as it was."

"She said they took it," I say. "She said it was to help cover the bills and to stop them from taking our whole house away."

Mrs. M. shakes her head in the saddest way I've ever seen. "No, honey. Your house is all paid off, has been for a long, long time. Your grandmother left it to you and to Rose in her will when she passed on."

"But Mom said—" My voice cracks. "I heard her say it."

"I know what she probably told you," Mrs. M. says. "What she felt like she *needed* to tell you to make it all okay inside her head. At the time, I couldn't imagine anyone doing anything more selfish than that. But when Colleen died, I realized that it was who she was. Who she had become. Selfish." Mrs. M. purses her lips. "Trust me, I've blamed everyone for what your mom became. I've blamed Summerland and the people who live there. I even blamed your grandma for leaving this world so early. For not sticking around to take care of her and to take care of you girls, when you needed her. But the only truth there is is that your mom was sick. She had a disease and she spread that disease to Colleen, too. It was something no one could cure them of but themselves."

"I don't understand that," Rose says. "Colleen had everything. Mayor Chamberlain was good to her, and her mom was, too." Rose's voice gets quiet and small. "She had everything."

Mrs. M. shrugs. "We might not ever understand the choices people make. But we can't let it own us. We can't let it become a part of who we are." She draws Rose in close to her and then leans my head against her chest too so that the three of us are locked in this hug that's so real and full. Being held by a mother should feel like this.

My eyes meet Rose's eyes. They're wet and tired, maybe from the pain of getting old. Too soon. Too fast.

Mrs. M. rubs our backs. "It's time to let it go. Let Colleen go and the words go and your mom go, too."

Like I have so often since I met her, I think of Chloe. I think of her bridge. "Someone once told me that you can't make people do or feel or think what you want them to. You have to let them come around, on their own time. Or you have to let them go. I know that now. But even when we're gone, I won't stop loving Summerland. I won't stop loving her, either."

Mrs. M. strokes Rose's long head of hair, and my short one. "Summerland will always be what's inside of you. Just don't let it become *who* you are." She smiles, sadly. "Or it'll eat you alive."

Rose nods and I nod and together, we take the deepest, longest breaths I've ever known. Mrs. M. is right. Our lives don't belong to Summerland, or the people in it. Our live are *ours*. Ours to do what we want with.

Finally.

THIRTY-FOUR

The first thing Rose notices when we step outside the airport is the air. Portland's literally like twenty degrees colder than LA was, and the air here's heavy, not from smog or pollution, but there's this thickness here that actually makes it hard to swallow. But the first thing I notice is that there aren't cameras anywhere. We're just in Oregon. It's not LA. I'm not on show for anyone here. Not anymore.

Rose hails a taxi and we climb on in. "Summerland," she tells the driver.

He peers back at us. "That'll be at least fifty bucks. You girls got that kind of cash?"

I open my wallet and hand her my thirty bucks. The show paid for everything.

I'm coming home with everything I left here with. Rose waves me away and digs to the bottom of her purse. She pulls out a small stack of crisp twenties.

I stare at the bills in her palm. "Where did you get that kind of money? Did your boyfriend—" I stop. Take a deep breath and try again. "I mean, does Joey—"

"He doesn't support our life. Even though he'd like it if I'd let him every now and then. He doesn't take care of us. We take care of us." She shrugs. "I've been saving. Just because your foot's broken, doesn't mean our dreams have to be, too."

The sight of her bills is enough for the driver. He pulls out of the airport and onto the highway, heading toward the coast.

Exactly an hour and a half later, we pull into Summerland. We pass the Pic 'N' Pay and Summerland Liquors. We pass Xanadu Mini Golf and the disco bowl. We pass Miller's Bakery and we pass Deelish and Mr. Moutsous's car, there, in front of it.

Everything's exactly the same as when I left. Why shouldn't it? It's not like I've been gone long. But as I stare at this town— my town—the only town I've ever known and lived in since I was born, I notice how everything looks so different, too.

Smaller. Older. Sadder.

"Look!" Rose squeals as we pass Katina's studio. Hanging above the door is a gigantic banner. White, with red and black block letters, professionally done, not hand drawn. GOOD LUCK, GEORGE AND MAGNOLIA! WE DIG YOU! it says.

"Katina must have had Old Lady Miller do it with her printer." Rose laughs. "I wonder how much she charged her to have it done."

I smile, thinking of Katina going to bat for me against Mrs. Miller, one of the ones who couldn't—*wouldn't*—let it go. I wonder how much of the show she watched, if any of it. I wonder how much of the show the rest of them watched. I know it doesn't matter. Not when I was the one living it.

As we pass the sign, I stare under the words, at the picture of me and George, our faces smooshed together so that they're more like one head than two.

I remember that picture.

Someone from the *Summerland Sun* took it on the first day of Season, the summer before George and I started high school. I remember that day, because that was when I decided that George was gay and could never be my boyfriend. That afternoon, George napped next to Sammy Baker, just feet away from the tide's end. He played with Sammy's hair while Sam dozed. And when he finally woke up, George rolled over and kissed Sammy. Softly, on the lips, like the two of them were the only two beings on the whole entire planet. While I sat on my own towel and watched, from several feet behind them.

But this picture. This picture was taken before all that happened. When I still hung on to the memory of that *other* day, under the pier, when we were twelve. George and I were hanging out down there, talking about the kinds of things that twelve-year-olds talk about. Teachers and school assignments and the new clothes that so-and-so's parents bought them in Portland. And then suddenly, without warning or reason, George leaned over and kissed *me*. On the lips. My heart stopped. Time stood still.

I can't remember who pulled away first on that glorious June afternoon, nearly six years ago, but I do know two things: One, I had been hoping and dreaming that George would kiss me like that for an entire twelve months before he actually did. And two, although I thought our kiss was warm and perfect and everything, George never kissed me again. Even though I knew and accepted Sammy Baker and the lifeguards and all the other people George wanted to kiss—and maybe even had—I held on to *our* kiss for so long. It's what made me believe that anything was possible, even the things that feel like they weren't. I knew then that no matter what happened between me and George, we'd always have that kiss. And maybe it's more than most people get. Maybe it's even enough.

But now, staring up at that banner, that photo of the two of us, it kind of hits me that most of the time, dreams don't come true. Or at least, not in the way you thought they would. Sometimes they shift—change—into the kinds of dreams you didn't even know you wanted, instead.

The cab turns the corner, and a second later we pull up in front of our house. Rose tosses the driver his cash and helps me out of the cab on the opposite side. Standing with our shoulders touching, we stare at our weathered house for a long, long time.

Rose nudges my side. "It doesn't really feel like ours anymore, does it?"

"Maybe that's a good thing." I link my arm through Rose's and together we hobble up the three steps toward our front door. "Maybe good-byes aren't supposed to be hard. Maybe that's why you say them. Not because you have to, but because it's time."

THIRTY-FIVE

The next ten days are so crazy busy I feel like my head is going to explode. Even though Rose's boyfriend, Joey, stops by to bring us a new TV, I barely have time to think straight, let alone watch the show that felt so much a part of me less than two weeks ago. In fact, when I do sit down the Thursday after we get back to watch it, I almost forget that it's the *results* show I'm watching, not the *performance* one, it being Thursday and all. So it makes it even harder to watch when Hayden and Jacks get eliminated, when I haven't even been there to witness why—from the bits of their performances they play on the screen, both of them looked amazing and solid and exactly how they should have. And it's harder still to watch Olivia crumble to her knees at the sound of their names being announced, not just because it leaves her and George going into Week Six—the final episode—but because I know her tears are partly for her friends who won't be going with her.

When Rose and I actually start our big "clean up and get out" initiative the next day, I feel more ready to do this than ever.

I limp to the kitchen with a photo album, periwinkle blue with little white polka dots on it. I open the cover and flip through it. Rose looks like she's about eight in most of the photos and my face only makes an appearance a handful of times. But this album is one of the only ones Mom ever put together, so it's coming with us. Rose doesn't even glance over my shoulder as I finger through the yellowing pages, but when I close it, she plucks it from my hands and puts it in her gigantic box.

"Tell me again. Tell me about the palm trees we're going to nap under. Tell me about all those beautiful bodies."

I laugh. "That was Los Angeles. I don't know if San Diego will be like that." But inside, I know it will. Know it will be sun-filled and warm. Know that it won't have the perma-chill thing that Summerland has, even in the summer. The kind that's good for preserving heartaches and not much else.

"I didn't get the chance to see either one. I spent my only time there in that hospital." She puts her finger to her lips. "Hey, I wonder if my new store will only carry summer clothes all year 'round?"

I want to ask her about him, but I hesitate. Not because she's still hiding her relationship with Joey from me, but because I'm afraid of her answer. Afraid that saying it out loud might make her change her mind. "Aren't you worried the distance will change things between you?"

Rose shrugs. "It's like Mrs. Moutsous said. We need to think about us for change. We need to be who we want to be."

I hand Rose a vase to wrap but I don't say anything else. I know what Rose and Mrs. Moutsous are saying is true. But I also know I won't ever stop thinking about my mom. I don't think I'll ever stop wondering where she is, what she's doing, who she's with, or if she's with anyone at all. The anger I felt toward her in the hospital feels different now. Kind of like the show, actually. Something I did for a while. Something I did to learn who I was and grow and figure things out and now it's over. While I know my anger was justified, it doesn't feel right to take it with me. I guess that's what Chloe was trying to tell me all along. That I had to let it go in order to be the person I'm really meant to be. And if I'm able to let this house go, this town go, this childhood that wasn't always good and wasn't always bad go, I think I can say good-bye to the anger, too. While we'll always be Mom's daughters and talk like her or have her love of the beach and clamming, the fact is we're *not* her. Other than her name, we really don't share anything with our mom at all.

But I'd be lying if I said a part of me won't always hope she comes back here one day. Not a different mom altogether, but one who's no longer sick. And if that day happens, I know Mrs. Moutsous will be here to tell her where we are and how we've been waiting for her for a long, long time. That's the kind of thing I don't think I'll ever stop dreaming about. Because if we don't have our dreams, we don't have much at all.

Rose hands me another stack of newspapers and then saunters off, whistling. She does this comical little arabesque and tosses a few more fake plants and household knickknacks into her box. And even though she doesn't say it, I have the feeling that she and Joey will work out. She seems too happy about him for it not to.

When she first asked him for the transfer, he was totally supportive. He said he was sad to see her go, but he also said he knew she was better than this. I don't know if he meant this life or this place or this state of mind or what, but part of me wonders if he didn't actually mean all three.

When I called the California Ballet School in San Diego and asked them if I could audition for their program, they signed me up right then and there. Because they saw me on the show and knew my name. My name. Magnolia Grace Woodson. Fan favorite from Season Six, *Live to Dance*.

"Come on. Let's finish this up." Rose waves her watch in the air. "It's seven thirty already. We can get the rest done later. You don't want to miss the final show, do you?"

I wrap my last ceramic mug in newspaper and then plop down next to our La-Z-Boy recliner. "No way. I wouldn't miss it for the world."

THIRTY-SIX

Olivia and George stand together on stage, their bodies two inches apart.

They hold hands. Their faces are blank. Or at least, I'm sure they appear blank to those who don't know a darn thing about just how freaked out they must be right now.

But I know the difference—know both of them and know the fear that they must feel, pulsing through their veins. Know it so much that my own muscles tighten at the sight of them. As though I'm up there on that stage, too.

Rose passes me the bowl of popcorn, sprinkled with the razor clam seasoning we bought, special, for this occasion. The show cuts to commercial and I dig my hand in and shove a handful of the popcorn into my mouth. It's good. So unbelievably good. The spice is just the right amount and the butter is just the right amount and it slides down my throat and tastes like Summerland and happiness.

I wonder if Rose is thinking it, too. She's chewing away, but the sight of her reminds me that there's something I love even more than this seasoning—being here with Rose. I grab a handful of popcorn and flick it in Rose's face. She looks totally shocked for a second, but then she reaches into the bowl and chucks an even bigger handful at me. Pretty soon we're all over the living room, me dragging my cast around, her hopping over boxes and ducking behind the TV, both of us shrieking and tossing what's left of the popcorn at each other and in the air, trying to catch it in our mouths.

We don't have many moments like this, me and Rose. Most of the time she's big sister and I'm little and that's how it'll always be between us—how it's always been. Which is kind of what makes these moments between us mean so much. When they happen, I know she's feeling it and I'm feeling it and there's nothing better than when two sisters feel the exact same thing at the exact same time because you know that there's no one else on the planet who does.

A few seconds later, we hear the theme song for *Live to Dance*, so we fill up a new bowl of popcorn and lie on the floor, our backs heaving, out of breath, our shoulders touching.

"Wow," Rose says. She stares at the screen, at Olivia wearing the dress her mother made her bring to LA. The one she said she'd never ever wear. "Olivia really is stunning."

"Always. The cameras love her. George looks great, too."

Rose snorts. "Yeah, great. And kind of like he's about to piss himself."

I smile at her, so happy to have things back to normal, even if it's a different version of normal. I watch as Camilla Sky trots on stage wearing a petal-pink Oscars-esque gown that reaches her toes. Her hair is swept off her face and her eyes are done up all smoky and dramatic. Which is so perfect for her.

"What was it like being so close to her?" Rose says.

"When you first see her, you can't help but feel overwhelmed. She's tall and modelly and yeah, she's really glamorous. But when you spend a bit of time with her, you see that she's just a normal person." I think of how she was with the cameras and how she was so different when they weren't on her at all. "She's probably got her own stuff to deal with."

"You know, when you got hurt, I glanced back at her. She was actually kind of smiling. Like she *knew* you were going to get hurt. Or maybe she hoped it was going to happen." Rose looks down, like she wishes she could suck those words back in. "I wish things would have gone differently. I wish you were up there right now."

I inch my butt closer to Rose's and rest my head on her shoulder. "I don't. This is exactly where I'm meant to be. For today, at least."

Camilla waits for the audience to stop cheering and whistling before she addresses the judges, who have so much to say about the season as a whole and how it compared to previous seasons. They talk about the drama of the auditions. They talk about which state they're going to choose for next season. They talk about Rio's scandal.

"But what surprised you most about this season?" Camilla asks.

Elliot pauses for a whole three seconds before he speaks. The screen flashes to his face, enlarged by a million. I miss seeing him. I didn't really get the chance to know him, but I know he was different from the other judges. It was always in his eyes.

"Things aren't always what they seem," he says. "And don't always turn out the way you expect them to. It's true for our show. It's true for life."

"Can you be more specific?" Camilla says.

Elliot waves a hand in front of him. "If you would have asked me three weeks ago who would win the *Best Dancer, USA* title, I wouldn't have thought twice about it. Not for a second."

Camilla's eyes widen. "And now? Has your opinion changed?"

"Well, Cam. I don't want to take anything away from the big night these dancers up here have ahead of them." He studies George and Olivia and smiles. "But yes, it has."

Camilla taps her foot. "If you're speaking of someone specific, I'm sure our viewers would love to hear it."

"I'm not naming names, if that's what you're getting at." Elliot adjusts the collar of his leather jacket. "But I will tell you this. The contestant I would have picked danced with conviction. When her routines started, I always inhaled. And I never let my breath out until she was done. That's called passion. And passion beats perfection any day of the week."

I choke on a bit of popcorn and then Rose slams her hand on my back, and then hands me her water bottle. "He's talking about you," she says.

"It could be anyone. Zyera. Juliette. Rio was really amazing. They all are. Even when the cameras aren't rolling."

On screen, Camilla crosses her arms. "This dancing goddess of yours, it wouldn't be a certain someone out there with a sore foot, would it?"

Elliot grins with his mouth and eyes. "Like I said, whoever wins tonight undoubtedly deserves it. But my dancing goddess moved like she was dancing for her life. Every single time."

I suck in a big breath. Rose is right. I would have won the whole darn show. I would have won, if my fate allowed it. But maybe that kind of knowledge—just knowing that I stood a chance—is just as good.

Camilla shrugs. "Well, there you have it, folks. The last word from Elliot Townsend. And now, without further ado, I present you with your Season Six top two finalists!"

Olivia and George exchange looks and bounce up and down on their hard-worked toes. I look down at my own foot, still aching in most places but definitely healing in others. I stick my finger inside the cast to give it a little scratch. A little rub for good luck.

As if I need it.

Camilla turns to stage left. "May I have the envelope, please."

Rose grips my arm. "Here it comes!"

I nod at her but I can't take my eyes off the screen. I'm so scared for whoever is—and isn't—the winner up there. I mean, it's George and Olivia. They both deserve their place in the sun. And even though this huge part of me wants it to be Olivia, there's this other part of me that wants George to win.

Camilla tears the envelope open with her silver manicured nails. In my chest, my heart beats so heavy and fast.

"The winner of *Live to Dance* is—"

My heart pounds as though trying to free itself from my chest.

"George Moutsous!"

Forgetting about my foot, I jump off the floor and cheer. The pain sends me to the ground, immediately. Rose takes hold of my arms to steady me. Together, we laugh, cry, shout,

"He did it! He really did it!"

From the TV screen, the crowd's going totally crazy and cheering while producers whisk Olivia offstage with her runner-up bouquet. The first two rows of the audience rush the stage to lift George up on their shoulders. George pumps his fists and leans back, letting the cameras swarm him and the magic of the moment consume him.

And maybe I'm not there to help lift him to the sky, the way he did for me. Maybe I'm not there to hug Mrs. M. while she cries and cries because her baby is everything, either. But I am here. And I am watching. And maybe—just maybe—that's enough, too.

Rose doesn't ask me to use the gun once.

In fact, we haven't even bothered to bring it out here. It's still there, in the hall closet, one of the only things that isn't coming with us.

"There's one!" Rose shouts after completing her routine of stomping out three perfect figure eights. "Dig!"

I thrust Mom's old shovel into the ground and pull up a mound of mud. Then I throw the shovel in again and again, until at last I spot one fantastically huge razor clam. Rose pushes me and my cast out of her way and drops down to her knees. After a second or two of some serious grunt-and-pull maneuvering, she draws it out.

"It's huge!" She jumps up and down on the balls of her feet, shakes her booty all around. "We still got it! The biggest one of the season! Mrs. Perkins, eat your heart out!"

She grabs my arm and helps me to the water's edge to rinse our catch in the lapping waves. We won't stick around to fill our quota today, or any day. We have our biggie. Our own supersized trophy. Laughing our heads off, we jump around and whoop because it's so awesome to be out here, bundled up in the cold, cold air, touching the cold, cold sea, celebrating a slimy piece of fish.

Rose's face gets all serious. "Looks like you got yourself one last clam to crack."

"No way. We can't do better than this baby today."

"Look."

She points to the dry sand part of our beach. The part right in front of our old house. And then at the figure there carrying some kind of paper bag and walking toward us, bundled up, shivering, and very, very tanned.

Rose nudges me with her elbow. "Remember what you said about good-byes."

I squeeze her hand and mouth the word "thanks." She smiles and walks away from me, toward George. Their shoulders almost touch as they pass each other. George nods to Rose. Rose sticks her tongue out at him before running, full tilt, away from the two of us.

I stand still until George reaches me. He motions to my clam. "Looks like you girls lucked out."

"I saw you on TV. I saw you luck out, too."

"Aw, Mags. You know as well as I do, luck ain't got nothing to do with it."

George and I laugh. And then, because neither of us knows how we're supposed to do this, to say our so-longs, we go silent.

After a couple of seconds he says, "You're really leaving Summerland?"

"Your mom told you?"

"Yeah, she told me. But I saw the Sold sign on my way home from the airport. You really got, like, half a million bucks for that dump?"

I laugh. "Something like that. Let's just say it was worth way more than I thought it was."

George peers over his shoulder, back at our house, just kind of staring at it for what seems like forever.

I think of the day after we got back to Summerland. Rose looked up the phone number for Jude Benson, local Summerland realtor/go-getter, who was all too excited to list our little beach-front shack. Rose said it was because of my newfound semicelebrity status from being on "that dancing show." But I think it's because women like Jude can smell cash in their pockets a mile away.

A day later, Jude, equipped with two muscly men, came and posted For Sale signs outside both our front and back doors.

"How much do you think we'll get for this place?" I'd asked Jude. My eyes darted from her immaculate manicure and tailored suit to our house, complete with cracked floorboards, chipping paint, and one very leaky kitchen sink.

"Prime property like yours," Jude said, running her hands through her hair, "it'll go fast. Tourists around here are hungry for a piece of the good life."

I laughed. "Yeah. The good life."

Jude raised one eyebrow and passed me a stack of spec sheets to hand out to prospective buyers if any came knocking on our doors, which, she said, they most definitely would.

She looked from Rose to me. "You two are doing the right thing, you know. Your grandma was smart to put the house in your name. I bet you could do a lot of things with the money you'll make."

When she excused herself to make a phone call a few minutes later, I whispered to Rose, "Don't you think it's weird that she's so confident about this place? I mean, has she even looked around?"

"It's not weird, Mags. Not for her." Rose smiled at me, but in a sad sort of way. "You and I are the only ones who can see the ghosts that live here."

Now, I look George in the eyes. "George. I wanted to say thank you. For getting me off that stage. I know you put yourself on the line by doing that."

George shrugs, his grin never drooping. "Not like I could have just left you there. How would that have made me look?"

I smile and shake my head. "Not like the George I know, that's for sure."

He stares at the beach for a second or two before his eyes meet mine. "So. San Diego, huh?"

"Yep. Apparently there's this fancy ballet school there that might be worth checking into for next year."

"I've heard of it. Wouldn't have anything to do with the fact that Mark's going there, would it?"

I shrug, but I can't help but smile. Mark didn't leave me when I told him I couldn't go with him. He simply waited for me to come back here to change my mind. Waited for me, like he always had. And it hadn't taken me long to see that while I wanted to leave Summerland, I didn't want to leave him. Or rather, I didn't want him to leave me.

"Maybe, maybe not," I say. "Wouldn't *you* like to know?"

"I already do know. When it comes to you, Magnolia Woodson, I've always known."

"You've got to admit, the guy's got way better abs than you."

"Not even close," George says, with a deep inhale of his chest. "But he's okay. Perfect for you, actually." Then he makes these stupid kissing sounds on the back of his hand while muttering Mark's name and my name so I push him over until he lands his butt down in the sand with a thud. I squat down next to him, letting my sore foot stretch to my side. "Are you ever going to grow up?"

"What fun would that be?"

"Well, you better. You've got to get your ass in gear before you head back to LA and your adoring audience. I heard you accepted a job as a junior choreographer for the next season of *Live to Dance*. You must be totally amped to get out of here again."

George punches me, playfully, on my arm. In a mock-Magnolia voice he says, "Not really. Why would anyone want to leave Summerland?"

"You never know what the future holds." I punch his arm back. "The possibilities are endless."

George raises one eyebrow. "Wow. Brand-new Mags, right? Decided to give up your life of eternal pessimism?"

"It wasn't really working for me. We both know that." I scoot closer to him. "George."

"Mags," he says at the exact same time. But then neither of us says anything else. Our gazes hold each other. He hands me the paper bag he's clutching. "I told them, you know. I told the judges I slipped."

I kick the sand below my toes. "You didn't have to."

"Yeah, I did."

I squeeze his hand. My own way of letting him know that I'm proud of him. Not for just winning the whole damn show, but for doing it the way he should have done it in the first place. I go to open the bag he's given me but he places one hand over mine. "Not right now. Wait, okay? Wait until you're alone. Wait until you miss me and you can't picture my face."

"This isn't over for good. Not between you and me, it isn't. Rose and I need to get away from this place. Shed the skeletons. Start new." I look beyond George's head at my house. Still my house, for one more day. "But you and me. This doesn't have to be the end of us."

"Are you kidding me? I'd never let that happen. Just like I told Dolores." George digs one toe into the sand and then does the same with his other foot. "I'd search the globe, day and night, if you tried to leave me for good. I can do that, you know."

"I know. Is there anything that George Moutsous can't do?"

"Hey. I was just going to say the exact same thing about you."

The two of us laugh, but then George bites his lip. His face gets all serious and thoughtful and so I wait. Wait, while he gathers the strength and courage to say it. Say everything I need him to. "I'm not sad to be out of this place, you know."

His words should hurt because I'm part of this place, part of everything he knows here. But they don't hurt now. Now, I understand them more than I ever have.

"It's not that I don't love it here," he says. "It's home. But being popular isn't always easy, either. People say they love you. Even act like they love you." He shakes his head. "It doesn't mean they know a damn thing about who you are on the inside." He kicks at the sand. "It's stupid. It doesn't make sense."

I nudge my foot with his. "It's not stupid." I should have said this so long ago. If I was the kind of friend to George I always thought I was, I wouldn't need to say it to him now. But the fact is, I do. "What I did to you. The way I judged you and tried to label you as gay or straight--"

"Mags, it doesn't matter."

"It matters. It wasn't right. Whether you're good or bad or smart or stupid or gay or straight or neither or both. It's all judgment, no matter which way that pendulum swings."

He stares at me. Smiles with all his teeth and it looks so good. "You know, maybe I'll look you up the next time I'm in LA. I mean, it's only like a two-hour drive. We could meet halfway or something. See if the beaches down the California coast compare to Summerland's in the clamming world. I could even check out your fancy-pants school sometime, too. Who knows?"

"Yeah." I repeat his words. His words that really do say it all. "Who knows?"

Then, out of the blue, George leans over and gives me this super-quick hug, and then scrambles to his feet, turns around, and walks away from me, down our beach. Leaving me sitting there alone, just holding his paper bag. My heart aches as I watch his strong back get smaller and smaller with every step he takes away from me. I meant what I said. It doesn't have to be good-bye between us. Not for forever. But still, the hurt inside of me is there, growing, manifesting, with every second he's away from me.

I wait for him to look over his shoulder, just look at me one last time, but he doesn't. And even though I may never get inside his head, probably will *never* fully know just who he is and what makes him tick, whom he loves and whom he doesn't, I still know him well enough to know that, in all likelihood, George is crying right now.

For everything that was. For everything that never will be.

I can't help myself. I open his bag, just a bit, and peer inside. And what I see makes my heart stop. I nuzzle my face in it. Breathe in the scent of our life. It brings me to my feet.

"George!" I call. "Wait!"

He stops. Turns. His eyes, which I've spent most of my life dying to be a part of, bore into me. And then I know the truth.

I just don't know why it's taken me so long to figure it out.

I run toward him.

Well, not actually *run* because of my foot, but do my best to skip, dragging my cast behind me. And then he's running to me, too. And two seconds later, our chests are together and we're in each other's arms.

Not kissing.

Of *course* not kissing, because that's not who George and I are. That's not who we've ever been. Not in fourteen years. Not even the day his lips touched mine for one brief second. But we're touching and hugging and laughing. And then suddenly, our Summerland sky opens up and it's thundering and lightning and then pissing down this rain that's cold and so darn miserable, just like everything about this place. Like nothing about this place.

"You really want me to have these?"

I hold up George's bag, filled with his gum boots, the red fire truck ones with the little wheels on the toes and heels that he was wearing the day we met on this beach.

"Yeah. But if I ask for them back one day." His face flushes. "Well, you'll understand."

I nod, but neither of us says another word. Instead, we just stand there, our arms locked together, holding on like we'll never let go. And then I know. Everything I've ever needed to know about the two of us.

That we're a part of each other. Like two halves of a razor clam shell.

Sometimes we're open. Sometimes we're closed.

But always, we're connected.

ACKNOWLEDGMENTS

They say it takes a village.

And I know that when they say it they're usually talking about raising babies, but I happen to think that it applies to writing books, too. Or, at least, it did for me with this book. Luckily for me, there were so many people in my village. So it's like a big village; a town, really. I wish I could name all the people in my town. To anyone I've missed here, my sincerest apologies. Please know that you are loved and that I appreciated every single way you contributed to my journey with this story.

First and foremost, I'd like to thank my super-agent, Victoria Marini. I seriously doubt there is any agent on the planet more patient, encouraging, steadfast, or cool than you. Thank you for always bringing me back down to earth. I know it's no easy feat.

Thank you to Julie Matysik for loving and acquiring this little story to begin with. And for handing it to my super-editor-extraordinaire, Adrienne Szpyrka, who continued to love it and worked on it, tirelessly, to make it what it is today. I know how lucky I am to have fallen into your hands, Adrienne. You are a magic worker. And I am grateful.

Thank you to Georgia Morrissey for creating the kind of cover that truly represents Magnolia's story, and to Joshua

Barnaby for putting it out into the world as the beautiful finished product it is. Thank you to Katherine Kiger for being the most careful copy editor out there. And to Kylie Brien for coming in toward the end and loving it like you had been there all along. I feel so lucky to have you as my editor partie trois. I guess everything really does happen for a reason, and I'm happy that it did.

Thank you to everyone from SCBWI Florida. There are so many people here I want to mention—probably like a hundred of you guys, actually. Forgive me for not naming you all, but know that I am grateful that you came into my life. You are an incredible organization that helped make my dreams come true.

Kerry O'Malley Cerra, I have thought long and hard about how to thank you here. When I first arrived in Florida, you took me under your wing. You taught me about craft when I really had no idea. You introduced me to the people I needed to know and you never let me quit when I thought I'd quit a thousand times over. And the crazy thing is, you still do all of that today, ten years later. Without you, none of this would even be possible. Thank you, Kerry. I am so grateful for you.

Thank you to Joyce Sweeney and Marjetta Geerling for being two of my earliest, wisest teachers. I will always look up to your work, your words, and hear your advice in my head even when I don't see you for so long. Thank you for sharing your knowledge with me, and for being really great friends.

Thank you to my L2W peeps. Kristina Miranda and Michelle Delisle. I'll never forget when I walked into Panera and saw you guys. I knew I'd always know you. The moment is etched into my mind forever. Meredith McCardle, thank you for sharing with me your incredible smarts. And Nicole Cabrera, your sweetness. I've learned so much from you all. I love being part of you guys. I hope it never ends.

Thank you to Steven Dos Santos for being one of my earliest readers of this book, who muddled through my first draft and pointed me in the right direction with where to take it. You were gentle with your advice and kind with your critique, even though you had every reason not to be.

Thank you to Jonathan Rosen, Mindy Weiss, Stacie Ramey, Faran Fagan, Laen Ghiloni, David Case, Cathy Castelli, Nicole Lataif, and Lorin Oberwerger. You have all helped me along the way—some with your brilliant writing and helpful suggestions, others with your wise words and friendship. I am lucky, and I am grateful to know you all.

To my entire MFA program at the University of British Columbia, thank you. Specifically, thank you to my buds, Danielle Daniel and Sarah Richards. You two are the best, not only because you're both writers I admire, but because you always keep it real.

Thank you to Sarah Glenn Marsh, Cara Chow, Kathryn Holmes, Liz Coley, Beth Neal, and Liz Czukas for reading the almost finished version of this. Your kind words mean so much to me because I look up to you all.

Thank you to my writing bestie, the girl I call early in the morning or late at night with a new idea. The girl I send crazy amounts of pages to, saying, "Hey, can you have this back to me by noon?" and she always does. The girl who taught me how to write love scenes and really, really mean them. Ty Shiver, I feel so comforted knowing that we will travel this dusty road side by side for many, many years to come.

And thank you to my "civvie" friends. You listened to me talk (shout, sob, grumble) about writing when you really had no idea what I was talking about and I'm sure I probably bored you to tears with this stuff. Amie Thomas, Eden Scanlon, Brigette Barker, Amanda Furia. And the others—there are others I'm surely forgetting here. Thank you for your support and your friendship. I love you guys.

To the real people of real Summerland. You know who you are. Thank you for letting me borrow you and bend you for this story. I hope to meet you again one day.

And to my family. My mom, my dad, Jody and Darryl. Thank you for knowing that in order to get me back, you had to first let me go. I know you thought I was doing the impossible when I started this whole thing, but I'm grateful that you stepped back and let me do it anyway. Only you guys could know everything about me and love me anyway. This is a work of *fiction*. Please tell yourselves that over and over when you read this thing. I know it's hard, but you have to know it's true. I love you guys.

Thank you to the loves of my life: my Alice and my Lila. You are everything to me. I hope you forever spin your own skies.

And finally, thank you to my husband, Gus, for giving me the single most important thing I needed to write this book: time. Truly, you are the most patient and tolerant man I've ever known. I am lucky to be your wife.

About the Author

Jill Mackenzie spent a good part of her youth reading books that she wasn't supposed to while wandering beaches in Hawaii, Australia, and Oregon. Though Jill danced for most of her life, the most important thing she learned from dancing was how good it feels to dance herself clean on a regular basis. Jill has an MFA in Creative Writing with a focus on Children's Literature from the University of British Columbia. Jill lives in Florida with her non-dancing husband, two beach-loving daughters, and two cats who (Jill swears) dance whenever the music is on.